Prince of Darkness

C. H. Rowand

Cover Design: Juniper Hartmann of The Red Fox Creative

Editing: Black Fern Edits

Formatting by Tellicoee Publishing

For Kim,
Because without you, this story would still be languishing in draft hell.

Trigger Warnings

Potential triggers include: past sexual abuse of a side character (implied), mildly graphic violence including maiming, on-page death of a side character, lots of swearing, child endangerment and murder (not shown on the page), mercy killings, depiction of third-degree burns, and the use of shapeshifting for dubious sexual consent (implied).

Please be kind to yourself and keep these potential triggers in mind when choosing to read. <3

Playlist

"**Walk on Water**" - Thirty Seconds To Mars
"**Valkyrie**" - Battle Tapes
"**Me and the Devil**" - Soap&Skin
"**I Will Follow You into the Dark**" - Death Cab for Cutie
"**Dying in LA**" - Panic! At The Disco
"**The One You Trusted**" - Glum Aleks
"**Dancing With The Devil**" - Demi Lovato
"**Daylight**" - David Kushner
"**Heartwork**" - The Used
"**Sanctuary**" - Allie X
"**Mercy**" - Brett Young
"**Sinners and Saints**" - Andrea Wasse
"**Kiss With A Fist**" - Florence + The Machine
"**Rescue Me**" - Thirty Seconds To Mars
"**Back To December**" - Taylor Swift
"**Fly Away**" - G-Eazy ft. Ugochi
"**Someone You Loved**" - Lewis Capaldi
"**Lucifer**" - JAY-Z
"**The Wicked**" - Andrea Wasse
"**I'll Be Good**" - Jaymes Young

"Used to the Darkness" - Des Rocs
"Living in the Shadows" - Matthew Perryman Jones

Chapter One

A cool wind whistled through stone halls, carrying a mingled scent of smoke and damp as it hurtled toward a dimly glowing chamber. The warm light, cast by a rotating ring of slender black candles suspended in midair, flickered over the stone slab beneath but left the edges of the room in shadow. Various objects were illuminated in turn—dark puddles of some sticky liquid, a mortar and pestle coated in white residue, small bones and a raggedly drawn pentagram.

A man stood at the cluttered counter, his features skewed by the shifting glow, dark brows furrowed in concentration as his lips rapidly formed unintelligible sounds. The wind swept in and swirled fast around him, ruffling his thick hair and tugging at his clothes, whipping papers and scattered powders from the counter into a miniature cyclone.

The man hissed and snagged a fluttering sheet of parchment as it drifted past his ear, pressing it impatiently to the stone with a manicured hand laden with rings. His muttering grew louder, low voice dragging out the guttural syllables of an incomprehensible language, and the wind swirled faster as if in answer.

The candles flared then guttered out, sending the room deeper into gloom as the man broke off his chanting with a sharp exclamation. "How many tablespoons, would you say, are in a quarter of a cup?"

Here, in the bowels of the earth, the Devil was asking the spirits for baking advice. The wind abruptly died, dropping various items wherever they happened to land in a chorus of clatters and thumps. The skull of a small rodent rolled off into the void. A new sound echoed; a feminine clearing of the throat. Light flooded the space and The Devil winced.

The features of the room were revealed: gleaming chrome appliances, a beautiful mosaic backsplash in ocean tones, the full sprawl of the black granite island, now in shambles, cake batter half-mixed in the center of it all. And most importantly, a voluptuous brunette woman leaning against the doorframe, reclaimed skull in one hand and the other perched on her hip.

"Alas, poor Yorick," she murmured dramatically. "I knew him, and his atrocious baking skills."

"Ah yes, very funny Mags." The man frowned, then sighed. "I assume you come bearing good news?"

"Not in the least." She smiled, tossing him the skull and giggling when he fumbled to catch it and set it back down. "Well, unless you count me sparing anyone your patisserie failings as good news. Think of the mockery you'd endure otherwise."

"Always a treasure, your rapier wit." He licked his fingers absently, clearing away the remnants of chocolate batter. The lingering unease that had spurred him into his kitchen fluttered in his chest. "I think this one was going to be delicious."

"Luce, my darling," she said, eyes dancing with mirth as she flashed him a smile. "You always think that, and you are always the only one who does. You'd probably have better results if you followed *recipes* instead of asking the spirits."

"Hush, you." He flapped his hand dismissively but gave her his full attention at last. Mags only interrupted his antics when she had pressing news. "What was so urgent that you had to barge in on me?"

"Best that you see for yourself, I think."

She spoke lightly, but Lucifer couldn't help the cold shiver that slid down his spine at the way she avoided his gaze. His dreams had been plagued with dark omens for weeks now, and Mags was being unusually cagey. He had the sense that his life was about to become as messy as his kitchen.

Contrary to popular belief and mortal propaganda, Lucifer felt that Hell was quite homey. This could possibly have been due to the fact it had been his home for the past several millennia, but he liked to think it was due to the realm's inherent charm and ambience.

He trailed his fingers along the polished slate that made up the interior walls of his estate as they walked through the long hallways, a perfect match to the freckled marble that clicked by under his expensive loafers. Was he due for another renovation? No. He'd just redone the place during the Renaissance, he could wait at least another century.

They reached the end of the hall, and Luce gripped the handle of the door that led outside. Mags touched the gleaming, ornately carved snake, stroking its emerald eyes where they peeked out from under Luce's palm. "You love your irony, don't you?"

"I will have you know the serpent is a magnificent omen. Immortality, rebirth, healing—*these* are the traditional meanings of the snake. It was my brother who chose to make my symbol into something wicked."

"Yeah." She sucked her teeth. "He does tend to slander you a bit."

Lucifer scoffed. "That's being generous. The man tried to paint me as a reprobate in the eyes of our followers."

"Oh Luce," Mags stroked his cheek with a soft hand, then pinched hard. "You're literally a criminal, convicted of heresy and attempted mutiny. You're the very definition of a reprobate."

"Most of those claims are unfounded, for the record, and the rest are *alleged*. Luckily humans tend to be stubborn, and I have a healthy contingent who see my side of things." He yanked the door open and ushered her out. "After you, darling."

They stepped out into the central courtyard and Luce subconsciously lifted his chin to soak in the sunlight streaming down. It was artificial, unfortunately, but it was close enough to make him long for the real thing. He had been too occupied with his duties to take any trips to the mortal realm lately, and he missed it dearly. He missed more than just true sunlight, if he were being honest with himself, but it had been years. If he went back now, if he saw him, what would he even say?

His thoughts derailed as a small, winged demon blew quickly past, fluttering between them at a speed that whipped Mags's hair like a windstorm. It was roughly the size of a shoebox, pale blue and heavily feathered, and clutching a small parcel in its sharply taloned feet.

"No, that's fine!" Mags called indignantly after the demon. "Just the King of Hell and his best friend, no need to apologize for almost running us over!"

The creature spun back around, narrowly missing a collision with a sycamore tree, its three bright red eyes wide with what might have been shock. It waved long, spindly arms in a frantic gesture while it squeaked and babbled in its own language, before abruptly turning and zipping away again. Mags made an irritated sound, throwing up her hands. Luce chuckled. He loved when Mags let out her inner spitfire, even if it meant she was feeling stressed or upset. She was normally so soft and quiet that people forgot she was one half of an incredible power couple.

"You know Lidae demons never have time to chat," he chided, but couldn't keep himself from smiling at her put-out expression while she fixed her tousled hair. "Balthazar keeps them on their toes."

Mags harrumphed, casting a sidelong gaze at him. "Ah yes, glorified carrier pigeons with manners to match. How ignorant of me to insult such hardworking creatures."

"What's that expression again? Neither rain nor sleet nor burning hellfire?"

Her disgruntled expression melted into delight, and she laughed. "Oh, absolutely."

"I knew it." His grin widened. "I'm never wrong, you know."

She snorted and pantomimed opening an envelope. "The lie detector determined that was utter bullshit."

He gripped his chest in mock horror. "Madam, you wound me."

"I would never," she sang sweetly.

"How *does* Christos put up with you?"

"*He* has the good sense to treat me like the goddess I clearly am,"

Mags sniffed haughtily. "Showers me with gifts and undying affection."

"A very wise man." Luce nodded sagely and made a show of offering her his arm, which she accepted. He walked with Mags along her preferred route to her chambers—directly through the Evergarden in the courtyard of his estate.

It was one of Luce's favorite places as well. The sprawling garden was lovingly curated and tended with as much care and attention to detail as he'd used the first time around. Towering fruit trees ringed the perimeter, casting delicious pools of shade over the nocturnal blooms. Flowers that craved light were arranged in careful spirals toward the center, where a fountain boasted a statue of a terrifying and glorious angel that poured water from its crying eyes.

It was a tender and emotional rendering of the Archangel Michael, who had once been very dear to Lucifer's heart. Normally it brought him peace; some small comfort that he at least had good memories of what he had lost. He averted his gaze tonight, as if the anxiety building within him might spill over if he looked too closely at the long-lost face.

Mags paused, considering the statue. "You've made him truly larger than life."

Luce smiled fondly. "Because he is. Few people have seen him this way—resplendent with fury and Divine purpose. I could hardly put him in *this* of all places and not accurately represent the scene."

She blinked slowly. "It always amazes me how you can speak so gently of one of the worst moments of your life."

"Who says it was the worst?" He mused with a smirk. "I still say he did me a favor."

They continued through the Evergarden, both so lost in thought that all the beauty and serenity they normally enjoyed went unappreciated. Luce plucked an apple off a tree as they passed, handing it absently to Mags and taking another for himself. She looked at it briefly, then arched a dark brow wordlessly, her expression clearly saying 'Really?'

"Oh, come on," he protested.

"Can you blame me? The devil just offered some fruit to a naïve maiden in *this* of all gardens."

He huffed. "Firstly, this garden is a *loose replica,* and barely half the size. Secondly, you are neither naïve *nor* a maiden, Mary Magdalene."

"And isn't that the honest truth." She laughed, a touch bitterly perhaps, and bit into her apple with a decisive *crunch.* Luce grimaced at her intentionally exaggerated chewing.

"Yet still so classy," he teased. "Besides, the Tree of Knowledge was a fig tree."

"Wasn't it an apple?"

"Oh, *I'm* sorry, were you there? Now, enough stalling," Luce declared. "I'm practically dying of anticipation."

"Well, you're certainly in the right place to do so." After a moment, she tentatively began, "Though, the rumors—"

"No." Luce cut her off sharply. "I've been tired of those stupid rumors since I first heard them. Whoever started them is supremely uncreative; you of all people should know that's not my style." At her meek protest, he held up a firm hand. "Enough, Mary. What is so urgently weighing on you? You only get pushy about my past when you're deflecting."

Mags gripped his sleeve with gentle fingers before slipping down to take his hand. "It really is better to show you."

Mags had been gifted since her Rising with the abilities of a lesser Divine, akin to a demigod's, but she also had a uniquely powerful gift of foresight. It typically manifested at random, but she had taught herself to pull energy from within herself as well as from other sources to share her visions with others. It was a skill that had proven invaluable to Luce on more than one occasion. Luce could feel the slight tremor in her grip, and concern overtook the brief flare of annoyance.

* * *

He had gifted Mags an unused cottage on the border of his estate long ago, and she had managed to make her secluded corner of the land just a touch cozier than the rest of his realm.

The cobbled walk led to a cushioned swing on her veranda, bedecked in colorful throw pillows, overlooking a small vegetable garden. A thriving fishpond bubbled happily beneath a willow tree and fairy lights twined through the branches above. Colors seemed more vibrant here. Her space felt warmer and more alive than the subdued vibe of Hell as a whole.

But this small shift in atmosphere could never prepare one for what they would find beyond her door. Luce saw Mags as a little sister and treated her like one, so any delusions of her as mature and mysterious had long since washed away. She was eclectic, to put it kindly, and had the unfortunate habit of renovating and redecorating her space on a whim. Every time he entered, he found something more outlandish and alarming.

On this occasion, Luce felt as if he had stepped into a sixteen-year-old girl's fever dream of a princess's bedroom. An opulent queen-sized bed topped with a mountain of pillows and throws stood hidden behind a canopy of pink gossamer and silk. Plush footstools and rugs cluttered the lounge space, arranged around a massive chocolate fountain that was situated on the glass coffee table.

A vanity dominated one wall, overflowing with makeup in a variety of tubes, jars, palettes, and compacts, interspersed with assorted bottles of perfumes and scattered pieces of jewelry. The same wall was adorned with several framed paintings. At first they appeared to be random splatters of pastel, but the longer he looked, the more he could infer the vague suggestion of flowers. He wondered briefly if Mags had done those herself, or if perhaps Sachi had helped.

The closest seat was an overstuffed burgundy abomination that was a mix of beanbag and armchair. Luce eyed it dubiously before deciding to take the risk, gently perching on the edge and immediately slipping into the chair's gaping maw.

"Mags! Your chair is eating me!" He flailed a bit in an attempt to escape but only succeeded in sinking further into it.

Mags eyed him with a mixture of pity, amusement, and disdain.

"Behold!" She intoned dramatically, adopting a mockery of Luce's deeper voice. "Lucifer of the Morning Star, mighty Seraphim Eterna, Lord of Hell and highly worshipped Divine being," she paused for effect, then switched back to her own gently mocking deadpan, "lain low by a poufy lounge chair."

She leaned over him with a wicked grin and gave the chair a hard shove to tip him out of it. "How the masses will quake to hear the tale."

Lucifer gave an undignified shriek and jabbed a black-lacquered nail in her general direction. "Don't you dare!"

"Oh hush," she waved a hand dismissively as she set about arranging her scrying basin on her vanity. "Who would I tell?"

"Christos," he said immediately.

Mags paused mid-pour of her rose-scented holy water and nodded enthusiastically. "Yeah, you're right. I am *definitely* telling Christos."

Lucifer grumbled but made no real complaint. After the horrors she had been through, he could hardly begrudge her finding someone she could be completely happy and open with. And of all people to know Luce's every embarrassing moment, his nephew at least wouldn't be *too* gleeful in his teasing.

He gave up on anything resembling a chair and just tucked his long legs under him on the floor to watch as Mags set up for her spell. She opened a cabinet set against the wall, pulling out several wooden boxes of varying sizes. Placing them on her assortment of footstools—which Luce eyed with distrust after his encounter with the chair—she then pulled out crystals and candles in an assortment of colors and arranged them around the pearlescent seashell basin.

Luce arched a brow. "You need this many amplifiers?"

She sighed, lighting her candles with a long match. "Unfortunately, this vision is particularly...difficult. I hope it doesn't affect you too strongly."

"Please Mags, don't insult me."

"I'm not." She snapped her fingers and the candle flames shot high, the heat and the water creating a mist in the air. With a spin of her finger, it deepened and spread until it rolled like smoke across the room. "You want to see so badly? I hope you're ready for what I'm going to show you."

That chill crept down his spine again and dragged the smile off his face. Something was clearly under her skin in a way he hadn't seen in a long time. A part of him began to be very afraid. Maybe he wasn't as prepared as he had thought. Luce reminded himself sternly that he was the Lord of Hell and really, what could it be that he wasn't powerful enough to endure? Then a chaotic scene began to flicker into focus over the mist, as if cast by a projector.

There was a cloudy quality to this vision, like trying to view a scene through a fogged windowpane. Even with her amplifying elements, it was obvious this vision had been a twisting, awful nightmare of scattered glimpses and vague hints. A shadowy form resolved itself into a human shape, and Luce realized it was his son Foster, walking in an empty alleyway.

After all his eons, there were still things that could catch him off guard.

The scene shifted, becoming more abstract. Angela, his departed wife, but just a close-cropped view of her beautiful face, smiling serenely. The image faded out and came back as a glaring golden light. There was the sound of ruffling feathers, a sensation of cold so intense it nearly burned.

Light flashed in the corners of his vision, like cracks of lightning across dark skies. There was a splash of blood, and someone dragging long, tanned fingers through it to paint a messy sigil. A smell like rotting garbage pervaded. He caught a glimpse of pale skin, the sickly pallor of fading life. The images spun and dipped wildly around him, never lingering long enough for a proper look. The clang of metal against metal, accompanied by an enraged shout and a flash of dark hair. Smoke swirling over a building, the crackle of fire? He couldn't be sure. A book splayed on a table, worn pages inked with dark symbols and scrawls that looked like Aramaic. A white-hot pain in his chest.

A hand touched his shoulder gently, but he couldn't be sure if it was Mags or a part of the vision. Luce's head throbbed, a rush of vertigo swelling as the images and sensations flickered past at lightning speed.

A cold laugh, silver eyes like clouded moonlight, a little girl coughing violently, a leather jacket smoldering in embers.

The flash of a blade sweeping forward as if to cut his throat.

Luce gasped, leaning instinctively away from the phantom threat, and felt his world tip sideways as the visions spun away. The room vanished in a spill of sudden, blessed darkness.

The darkness was not empty. He could feel another presence. Luce blinked slowly, looking around curiously, but nothing was apparent.

"Hello?" He called out, his voice echoing away into the distance.

"Hello," a voice called back, clear and mellifluous. It was utterly androgynous and devoid of inflection. He knew it wasn't his own echo but couldn't identify it beyond that. Luce frowned, taking an experimental step towards the voice.

There was nothing to step onto. He found himself falling, but not the drastic plummet of a freefall. This was a much more controlled descent, like coming in for a landing after a flight. His scarred shoulder blades ached with the phantom memory; muscles built over centuries twitched with the desire to fulfill their invalidated function. The darkness lightened and his feet touched down on a solid floor of rough oak.

A dim amber glow rose around him, and he could see the shadow of figures in the distance. He stepped cautiously forward, relieved at the click of his own footstep against the wood. As he approached the figures, he recognized Mags, Gloriana, Raguel—all his friends, in fact. They were clustered around a large bed piled high with blankets and pillows, where a woman in a blue silk robe lay, exhausted, in the center.

"See them," the foreign voice reappeared, close at his ear. The same lack of inflection but somehow conveying a sense of urgency. "See him."

Luce started with a jolt—*him*. This was the day Foster was born. He approached cautiously, as if expecting someone to turn and tell him he was intruding. But no one noticed him; he was seeing a memory, not truly returned to this moment when everyone had gathered at his panicked summons.

Angela had been much more composed than he had, despite the clear pain written on her face. She'd been the one to comfort *him* through his panic, all while laying down towels and fresh sheets on their large bed and directing several Lidae demons on where to place pitchers of water and spare towels. Her sheer willpower was astonishing to watch, though Luce had always known he had been blessed with a strong, determined wife.

The labor dragged on for hours, with Gloriana and Camiel attentively catering to the exhausted mother and guiding her through the birth. They couldn't risk a hospital – not when they couldn't be sure exactly how their son would come into the world. Coming from his mixed origins, there was the possibility he could come out with horns, or possibly even wings, as unlikely as it was.

A small part of Luce hoped his son might inherit wings, if only to experience the joy that was flight. But Foster had turned out to be perfectly human in appearance, pink-skinned and so *small*, though he wailed loudly from the moment he drew his first breath.

"As dramatic as his father," Angela had teased affectionately, sinking back into her pillows with a relieved sigh. A swell of warmth burst in Luce's chest as he watched his past self stroke her flushed cheek gently, brushing her honey-brown hair off her sweaty brow.

"You did so beautifully," he leaned down to press a kiss to her hairline, and Luce didn't need to hear the words to remember what he had whispered against her skin. "I am so proud of you, my love."

And he loved her deeply, even now. Even after she had been gone for years, Angela was a constant presence in his heart and mind. Everyone Luce loved managed to worm their way into his soul so completely that he would never be rid of them even if he wanted to. His desires were so rarely considered by fate, though it had done him a kindness this day.

He had never expected to be a father, yet there he was, humbled and awed by the new, tiny life that his wife placed into his trembling hands. His memory self rocked the infant gently as their friends crowded around to see the baby. Luce walked closer, a part of him aching to experience this moment again. It had been—and still was— the happiest moment of his life.

But why was he here? What was he meant to see?

"Your heir," the foreign, phantom voice returned with a tingling sensation, as if the speaker was whispering at the nape of his neck.

His heir, Luce mused. Foster was meant to be here with him and was not. He had consented to Angela's request to raise the boy among mortals—to show him the world and instill a humanity that she found lacking in most immortals. Luce had been present in his son's life, between his visits to the mortal realm and Angela's returns to his kingdom, not to mention all the gifts he sent to the boy. But why not show him his son in the present? What was specific about this day?

He watched himself bounce his infant, until he'd given in to the incessant nudging at his ribs and offered the baby for Mags to hold. She reached out eagerly, grinning. She had barely touched him or looked at him before the vision struck. *Oh.* Luce realized why he was here with a sudden, heart-wrenching ache.

A particularly strong or nasty vision could make her spasm or render her motionless as she was lost to it. This one ripped through her with violent intensity. She shuddered, shoving the baby back into his father's arms, as she would surely have dropped him. Her body shook and trembled, her eyes glazing over milky white instead of their normal dark ochre as tears poured freely down her bronze cheeks. Her breath choked off with a strangled sob. It lasted only a few minutes, but Luce had felt as if it dragged on for hours.

The Fallen watched with concern, but they all knew better than to try and interrupt the vision. Gloriana wrung her hands anxiously, and Camiel fell against her husband Sachiel for support. Remi looked like she wanted to punch the something but settled for pacing laps around the smaller woman instead.

As she returned to herself, Mags's expression fell somewhere between shock and horror, and she seemed unable to even form words. She refused to look at Foster, refused to be within a few feet of him. Angela reached for her, as if to console the smaller woman, but Mags bolted from the room. She fled Luce's domain, returning to Heaven without a word of goodbye.

"Understand," the voice returned, finally conveying some emotion through an anxious tone as it echoed from directly in front of him "Understand, Fallen One, and correct your mistakes."

An intense pressure bore down on Luce and coalesced at his shoulders, accompanied by the strong scent of ammonia. The vision before him scattered like ashes, giving way to blackness as he was shoved backwards once more into the void.

Luce faded back into the present moment, the old memories clinging to him like the smelling salts Mags wafted under his nose. Her bedroom ceiling arched above him, strings of origami figures dangling down from the rafters. He must have collapsed when the visions overwhelmed him.

"Yes," she said simply, seeing the pure grief on his face now. "The time has come, Lucifer. Your son is turning down the path."

"No," he murmured insistently, pushing himself back to a sitting position. "There is a way to prevent this, there must be. We took so many precautions after you had that vision."

Mags sighed, chewing her lip. "We knew there was the possibility it wouldn't matter. And... this feels like a vision that is bearing down on us quickly. I think things may already be in motion."

Disappointment crashed over him, destroying any fledgling hope Luce had been building. "If Foster has gone down this path...I won't be strong enough to stop him. Emotionally *or* literally, not since... well, you were there. You know I'm not the Devil I used to be."

"Actually," she brightened, if only marginally, "I think I might have an idea. But I'll need access to your archive."

Chapter Two

Lucifer was very, very close to breaking something—or baking something. He took a moment to mourn the ruined cake he'd been crafting before Mags had arrived and dropped a bomb all over his good mood.

Said woman was currently tearing apart his private library. She was a force of nature, pulling countless manuscripts, tomes and scrolls from his densely packed shelves, rifling quickly through them, and then tossing them aside when she deemed them lacking. Luce had tried to help, but when she struggled to articulate exactly what she was looking for, he had been relegated to rescuing the discarded books from her careless hands.

He arranged them neatly on his desk at first, maintaining the ordering system he used on the shelves, but he had to settle for laying them carefully on any flat surface he could find as Mags increased her pace.

She began to yank the books down with not only her hands, but her power, giving them a quick skim and then flinging them away with an agitated shake of her head. It was all he could do to keep them off the parquet floor. It helped to have a task, even if he wasn't entirely sure what she was looking for. Anything to avoid thinking about his hopeless position.

That familiar itch to create something was taking over again, as it often did when he was overwhelmed or stressed. It was the urge that had resulted in the pile of scrapped paintings half-finished in a closet somewhere, or the many discarded manuscripts in progress, or the scarves and blankets he'd attempted to knit. Again, he thought of the mortal realm and his other unfinished business there. A sick feeling wound through his gut, and Luce frowned.

Several books suspended in midair dropped sharply to the ground before he could grab them. Mags spun around, exclaiming in triumph and derailing his train of thought—probably for the best, if his short-lived obsession with sewing his own clothing was any indication. "I found it!"

"Mhm," Luce nodded, eyebrows lifted in expectation. "Care to enlighten the rest of us?"

"A long time ago," she began excitedly, "when I was first Risen, Christos could see how scared and confused I was. He said something that stuck with me, and I thought it was only a figure of speech. Just something to make me feel better, like a fairy tale. I should've known nothing is ever truly a myth in our world."

She laughed, a small bitter thing not like her normal giggle, as if chastising herself for being naive. Luce bit his tongue hard to avoid interrupting, though he desperately wished she would get to the point.

"But it's *not*," she waved the book, a thick volume bound in worn sheepskin leather. "It's right here, Luce."

"What is?"

"The Armor of God."

Luce's heart sank. He wanted to revel in that gleam in her warm eyes, to feel the hope she clearly did. But he knew what she did not.

"Oh, Mary, no," he spoke softly, as if afraid to hurt her by speaking too harshly. "That's not a viable option."

"It is," Mags insisted, shoving aside a crystal paperweight in the shape of an apple to make space for the book. Opening it to the first page, she trailed a pink lacquered nail down a long list of names. "This is an index of weapons of old; of ancient artifacts and their purpose.

And right here, between the James Ossuary and the Coat of Dreams
—"

"Yes, I know," Luce broke in, keeping his voice soft and soothing.
"But did you read the pages attributed to the Armor?"

"No," she admitted. "I didn't get that far."

Luce took the book from her, flipping to the corresponding
section of the compendium, and began to read aloud.

*"Therefore, take up the whole armor of the Gods, that you may be able to
withstand true evil. Stand with assurance, having fastened on the belt of
truth and having put on the breastplate of righteousness. In all circumstances, take up the shield of faith, with which you can extinguish all the
flaming darts of the evil one. Take the helmet of salvation and the sword of
the Spirit. Do all this with supplication to the holiest of holies, and you will
attain the readiness of the Gospel of Peace."*

"Why are you insisting this isn't an option for us?" Mags
demanded. "It sounds like you just have to put on the armor and pray
to someone, right? And you'll have the power to overcome any evil."

Luce closed the book with a snap. "Nothing is ever that simple,
Mary. You think this armor is just sitting in a closet somewhere,
waiting to be picked up and used?"

"Well, that would make sense," she said, crossing her arms.
"Though I'm sure you're about to tell me otherwise."

"Firstly, not just anyone can wear the armor. You need to be of the
highest divine ranks—"

"Which you are," she pointed out. "Seraphim Eterna or an
Archangel, right?"

"Secondly," Luce continued as if she hadn't spoken, "you must earn
each piece of the armor, one by one, with the proper supplication and
tithing to craft it."

"Seems reasonable enough," Mags said, jutting out her chin
stubbornly.

"And lastly," Luce glared at her constant interruptions, "the
instructions for how to attain each piece of armor are contained in
the Gospel of Peace—which no one can access."

"And why not?"

"Because, dearest, my brother keeps it locked away in his Vault."

"What? Why?"

Luce snorted, running a hand through his hair. "Because he's an arrogant prick with control issues? He claims the armor is 'too powerful' to be left for 'just anyone' to access."

"'Just anyone'?" She scoffed, frowning. "There are barely any Divine left who rank highly enough to use it."

"I'm aware," Luce said, mouth twisting in a grimace. "He keeps it locked away so that *I* cannot access it. Despite that it is the armor of *the Gods*, he calls it the armor *of God* and claims it's his by right of being King."

"That's absurd."

"Have you met my brother?" Luce laughed grimly. "No, this is not an option for us. He'll never allow it."

"He might," Mags said slowly, clearly coming up with an idea. "If the right person were to ask."

"Highly unlikely."

"Well, we have to try."

Luce groaned. "I'm sure my darling brother will be overjoyed to help us."

"Probably not," she smiled and grabbed her bag from a nearby chair. "But you know Christos will be."

"So, all our hopes depend on my brother listening to his son and lending me one of the most powerful artifacts in his collection. Great."

Mags patted his cheek fondly. "I'll be back with good news, I promise."

She was gone before he could respond, hurrying out of his study with a hopeful spring in her light steps.

Luce picked up the index, turning back to the page they had been studying. The hand-painted image of the golden armor glinted with shimmering pigment, twinkling at him in a way that seemed almost taunting. He traced the shape of the painted helmet, trailed his fingers over the breastplate and down the length of the sword's blade. Once upon a time, Luce had crafted a single piece of this armor, before Jehovah had revoked access to the Gospel, and it had been a true work of art.

He hated being at his brother's mercy more than anything in the world. He threw down the tome; it *thumped* loudly against the floor, missing the table, and he kicked it in a flare of rage like a petulant child. Flopping into his wingback chair, Luce dragged his hands over his face and groaned.

"What am I going to *do?*" He demanded of the room, slumping forward to rest his throbbing head on his desk.

"You could try talking about your problems for a change," a sickly-sweet voice chirped back at him. Luce could hear the smirk.

"Remiel," he muttered dryly, not even bothering to lift his head. "Sure, I don't need any alone time, no, of course you can come harass me. Can the Devil have no peace?"

A small hand patted him gently on the back of the head.

"Hi Luci," she trilled, then twisted her fingers quickly into his hair and yanked his head up, voice dropping several octaves back to her normal tone. "It's rude not to look at someone when you greet them."

He narrowed his eyes at her too-large grin, the little sadist. Her normally spiked hair was disheveled and hanging into her face, small beads of water dripping off the ends and onto his desk.

"You're wet," he spoke slowly, as if Remiel needed extra care to comprehend. "And you're dripping on the Scrolls of Mammon."

"Yeah?" She lifted her brows in mock surprise and shook her head like a dog, scattering thick droplets across his desk and the other books and manuscripts. Luce flicked his fingers sharply, and the falling droplets froze in midair. He sent the books floating back to their respective shelves with another careless gesture, glowering.

Remi's grin widened to reveal her sharp canines. "I hadn't noticed! Maybe it's because you're brooding *in here*, so it's pouring *out there!*"

"What?" The frozen droplets dropped abruptly to the desktop as his concentration broke, some shattering on impact while others rolled across the wood like marbles.

"You heard me," she snapped, tightening her grip and leaning right into his face. "Storm clouds darker than my soul. Thunder like a giant is humping a mountain. Fucking *downpour.*"

"Okay, I get it," Luce waved a hand between them. "Can you let go of my hair now, you crazy bitch?"

"Only because you asked so nicely," her voice slipped back into those honeyed tones, and she brought his face down hard onto the desk before releasing him. His nose snapped with a crunch, and thick golden blood poured onto the wood and squirted down his shirtfront.

"Whad da vuck, Rebi!" He hissed, his hand shooting out on instinct to grip her by her slender throat, partly out of shock and partly to keep her from making any more moves to assault him.

"That's for calling me a bitch." She leaned into his grip, the little masochist, before she pulled away to hop up and perch on the edge of his desk. She gave him a feral grin, smearing his blood with her combat boots as she rested one against the desk and pressed the other to his groin. "Sometimes, when you love someone, you have to kick 'em in the ass for their own good."

Luce blinked in astonishment. "Whad da FUCK."

"Shut up," Remi pressed her foot down slightly, "or I will crush your tiny balls."

Lucifer narrowed his eyes, his nose gave an awful throb, and he hissed again. With a flick of his wrist and a brief flash of white light, his nose righted itself, and he gave the imperious little terror the full force of his glower.

"Tell me, Remiel, why I shouldn't beat the fear of the Devil into the flesh of your hide for this insolent behavior?" Everything in him was screaming to dig his fingers in harder, to choke the life out of the little brat. But Remiel wasn't just one of his seven generals, or the vessel of his wrath—she was his *friend*, and that designation had him reigning in his fury.

"Because I have the upper hand here?" She didn't cower from his glare, instead giving him one of her own right back and pressing the toe of her boot into his crotch harder. "Or, the upper foot, rather?"

Lucifer growled, golden light creeping into his irises as he gripped Remi's ankle and yanked it to the side with godly strength, sending her sprawling to the floor. "I may allow you many freedoms, Remiel, but do not *test* me today."

She scrambled up from the floor, expression just as fierce as his, markings spilling over her pale skin like bloody warpaint as her eyes took on a crimson glow. "Finally, we haven't sparred in ages."

"We will not be starting now," he snapped, golden light wreathing his palms as he faced her down. "This is a punishment."

"You can try," she taunted. Crimson energy bled from her palms, coalescing into a pair of daggers matching the gleam of her eyes.

"Enough!" Luce thrust one palm towards the slender woman and a bolt of white-golden light slammed into her chest. Remi flew back several feet into the nearest wall, slamming against a shelf laden with books that rattled under the impact. Scrolls and tomes spilled from the shelf, including one that landed directly on her head.

"Ow!" The red glow faded away, along with her manifested weapons and warpaint.

"I warned you, Remiel," Luce admonished, stalking towards her and gripping her tightly above the elbow. "Today is *not* the day."

"Between this and the storm, it's gotta be something pretty bad happening," she huffed, tugging uselessly against his hold as Luce hauled her to her feet. "I haven't seen you this worked up since the day Foster was born."

He was almost impressed by her perception. On the other hand, he was tempted to ignore her and banish her from the study. The fewer people who got dragged into this, the less chance there was of anyone he cared about getting hurt. And he did care about this little brat, even if she broke his nose and ruined his priceless documents.

Remiel had been the first to follow him into exile, snubbing her nose at Jehovah and crashing through his plans like an angry whirlwind. Luce had been content to wallow in his misery for several centuries, but Remi had stomped into his home one day and yanked him out by his hair.

"I sometimes wish you'd left me alone in the desert," he muttered absently, and Remi looked at him in disbelief.

"I don't give a *fuck* about that Luci, that was millennia ago. Talk to me about what's going on *now*."

"Nothing serious," he quipped irritably, towing her towards the entrance of the study. "Just Armageddon, if I don't find a way to stop it."

"Armageddon?" A single arched brow. "Is that all?"

"Oh, yeah. Just another day, you know." Luce raked a hand through his hair, massaging the sore spot Remi had given him.

"So, that's why you're this upset. It *is* related to the vision Mags had on Foster's birthday, isn't it?"

He sighed deeply, coming to a halt just inside the doorway. "She had another vision this morning..."

"And what did Foster say about it?"

The silence stretched awkwardly as they lingered at the room's threshold.

Remi narrowed her eyes. "You did talk to him, *right?*"

Luce blinked at her, before averting his gaze.

"Oh, for Hell's sake, Luci!" She massaged her temples with one hand, glaring at him.

"I've been a bit preoccupied!" He tried not to acknowledge how weak the defense sounded, even to him. Remi's glare sharpened.

"And," he continued, avoiding her gaze, "we're not exactly speaking right now."

"And why is that?" She leaned back against the doorway, eyebrows raised in expectation of an answer that wouldn't make her want to throttle him.

Another drawn-out pause while the Devil squirmed. "Well...we haven't ever since...Angela."

"What? Luci, that was fifteen years ago."

He winced, avoiding her fierce glare by inspecting the doorframe for damage he knew wasn't there. "Correct."

"You haven't spoken to your own son for fifteen years?!"

"It sounds so much worse when you say it like that," Luce grumbled, picking at a tiny crack in the wood until it started to widen.

"You know it's fucked up," Remi snapped, "because you *lied* to us! You said you were visiting him, Luce! That he just wasn't ready to come back to Hell!"

Luce groaned and abandoned his picking to scrub at his face with both hands—mostly to hide from Remi's now piercing glare. "He disowned me, Remi! I was trying to give him space to calm down!"

"Maybe they were right to call you the Prince of Lies," she snapped. "You didn't want to deal with the emotions and the mess, so you've been pretending everything was just fine! Fuck, Luce, how did you think this was the right thing to do?"

"I—" He sighed. "I couldn't bear to see him looking at me the way he did, Remiel. So much pain, so much anger..."

Remi scoffed. "So now you're playing the martyred father who had no choice but to back away. Reminds me of someone else we knew."

"Stop it." Luce glared back, temper flaring at her insinuation. "I am *not* my brother."

"Well, ignoring your problems until they blow up in your face sure seems to be a family trait!"

"Enough!" He shoved her backwards into the doorframe, slamming his palms down on either side of her face and leaning in close. "That is *enough*, Remiel! If you weren't one of my oldest friends, you'd be severely punished for this kind of insolence."

She didn't flinch, didn't even blink. "Not exactly contradicting my point with that one, Luci."

His glower was short lived, dissolving into a grimace at the comparison to his brother and the fact that it might be truer than he'd like. This was the difference, however, and it was the one he assured himself mattered most—Lucifer knew when to stop.

"I didn't know how to face him," he finally said, forcing out the words and dropping his arms back to his sides. "I still don't."

"I can't believe you haven't even seen him." Remi frowned. "When you forbid us from reaching out to him we respected that, because we thought you wanted space to bond. To fix whatever had broken."

Luce winced. "It's what I should have been doing."

"Instead, you left a heartbroken *child* to fend for himself."

"I had Balthazar's Eyes on him," he protested weakly. "Cwall, more often than not."

Remi scoffed. "That idiot is no substitute for his *father*, and you know it!"

"Cwall is highly capable."

"But he's not *you*. He's not even human!"

"Neither are we," Luce countered.

"Don't you start with semantics." She crossed her arms over her chest. "Not when you're hiding down here while you should be halfway through a Rift right now."

"I'm not hiding."

"You are," she interrupted his indignant rebuttal in her matter-of-fact manner, and he found it difficult to argue. "It's okay. But you can't get stuck wallowing for too long or it'll be another couple decades before we see you again."

He took a breath and held it until he felt a tiny bit more composed. "You're right."

"I'm always right." She uncrossed her arms to loop one around Luce's, tugging him by the elbow into the hallway. "I can't even remember a time I was wrong about something."

"I can."

"No—" her grip tightened on his arm until it twinged with the threat of violence, "—you can't. And anyway, I'm *absolutely* right about this. You're way overdue to apologize to your son after you've been neglecting your son for *fifteen years.*"

"I wasn't neglecting him," Luce grumbled under his breath. "He's a grown man and he knows where I live. He chose not to come home."

Remiel pointedly ignored him.

"What we're gonna do is this," she spoke loudly to drown his continued muttering. "I'm going to personally march you down to the Rift, since you apparently cannot be trusted to do it on your own, and you're going to go visit your fucking son. Try begging his forgiveness and hope he's willing to listen."

"The Devil doesn't *beg,*" Luce scowled. "This is a terrible idea."

"Well," Remi snapped, "maybe if you had talked to him years ago, we wouldn't be down to our worst options. It's time for you to eat some fucking crow, Lucifer, and hope it's enough."

The truth of that statement hit him like a brick. This was a disaster in motion, and the burden of it fell squarely on his shoulders. The nagging voice in his mind taunted him, an echo from the distant past.

You hold a darkness within that taints all that you touch.

Despite the warring emotions within, he allowed Remi to lead the way with no further protest.

Chapter Three

Peter stared down his long nose at Mags, the horn-rimmed spectacles that balanced precariously on the bridge partially obscuring his stern brown eyes. He sighed heavily, drumming his fingers against the edge of the marble lectern that was set before him. "Lady Mary."

"Saint Peter," she said, hands folded demurely in front of her, fingers laced. She rocked back on her heels, casting a casual glance at the massive golden gates that loomed mere inches behind him. Standing before them always managed to make her feel so impossibly small.

"Why do you insist on trying to sneak inside the border? You know your name is on the list." He gestured at the scroll stretched out on the lectern's top, which Mags knew was enchanted to contain the names of every soul permitted to pass through the Gates.

She smiled. "Well, you know the line is just *so* long. This gets me an escort straight to the front."

"And do you think that's fair to them?" Peter arched a brow, prompting Mags to turn and acknowledge the line of newly arrived souls, winding along the sandy path to a glimmering Rift some yards away.

As they watched, a petite blonde Reaper practically bounced

through the Rift with an eager grin, a terrified young man trembling beside her. There was a sound like a chiming bell, and the Rift flashed from its normal icy blue to a bold ruby red. The Reaper gasped, turning in alarm toward her charge, and muttered something they were too far to hear before dragging him roughly back the way they had come.

Peter sighed. "These new Reapers are nothing like their predecessors. Do you know how often that happens? At least twice a week. Unbelievable."

"Everyone takes time to adapt to their new responsibilities, yes?" Mags asked slyly.

They eyed each other warily, a long pause and much unspoken lying between them. Then Peter grinned and stepped down onto the cobbled path. "Stop acting like such a brat and come give us a hug, Mags."

"You only had to ask," she said sweetly, stepping into his outstretched arms and winding hers around his waist. "How is gate duty treating you?"

"Long, boring shifts," he sighed. "But better than what Bartholomew is tasked with."

"Oh?" The other Apostle was known for his mischief, and Mags wondered what trouble he had gotten into now.

"The Almighty is...displeased, with him," Peter smirked. "He's mucking stables for the King's horses."

Mags mock gasped. "Not the stables!"

"They're made of *sunbeams*, Mary. Can you imagine the burns?"

"The horror," she intoned dramatically, but her eyes were still sparkling with mirth.

"Mock me if you must—" he pointed sternly at her, "—but please stop trying to sneak through the wall. You're setting a bad example."

"Am I?" Mags turned to the nearest soul, a timid looking woman with mousy brown hair, who had apparently died on her way to the bathtub if her fluffy pink robe was any indication. "Excuse me, do you think that I'm a bad influence?"

The woman blinked, looking confused. *"Je vous connais?"*

"Ah," Mags said, flushing. *"Non, excusez-moi."*

"Miss?" The middle-aged man behind the French woman waved her over, smiling slightly. "Have you...you've been inside before?"

"I have," she said. "Many times."

"So..." He cleared his throat, looking hesitant. "We'll...be allowed to come and go?"

"Oh honey," she softened. "No, I'm afraid."

"Oh..." the man seemed to shrink a bit, his hopeful expression turning into something like grief. "Why?"

Mags felt her heart break for him. She knew firsthand how it felt to go through this—to suddenly find yourself removed from the world, from everything and everyone you knew.

"Well honey, there isn't anywhere else *to* go." She laid a small hand on his shoulder, carefully avoiding what looked like a piece of iron that had been jabbed through his collarbone. It was a miracle indeed that passing through the Gates would remove all traces of their death, because some of the ways a soul could pass on were...quite gruesome.

"Why can you leave?"

"Because I still have a body." Mags cupped his pudgy cheek gently. "I'm a goddess, not a departed soul."

The man squinted in disbelief, then blinked as realization dawned. "Wait...I know you."

She smiled. "You must be quite the dedicated theist if you recognize little ol' me."

"The bride of Jesus," the man continued, eyes bright, clearly enthused by his discovery. "Mary Magdalene."

Mags flushed. "We're not actually *married;* that's just an expression...um..."

"Richard," the man supplied eagerly.

"Right." Mags patted his shoulder once more and stepped away. "Well, don't let me hold up the line any longer, I'll just be going then."

Peter cast her a sidelong glance. "The *bride* of Jesus, is it?"

"Shut up," she smacked his elbow, the highest point she could reach now that he was back on his podium. "I will pluck your wings, Peter, I swear it."

He laughed, tossing his sandy head back. Mags yanked a single silver-grey feather from his wing as she swept past him between the

Gates, giggling at his startled yelp as she hurried up the path towards the palace.

* * *

Fast, upbeat music spilled beneath a dark wooden door, echoing faintly down the hallways of the palace. Passing angels looked curiously toward the noise, either smiling or shaking their heads when they identified the source, while the mortal souls working in the palace were more prone to open boggling.

Within the room, its occupant—pleasantly oblivious to the opinions being formed about his latest hobby—moved in awkward, hesitant steps to the Latin music. He was deeply tanned and tall, broad shouldered and finely muscled, none of which was helping him properly orient his feet to the rhythm of the song.

His dark, curling hair brushed his shoulders and fell into his eyes, and he swept it back with an irritated brush of his hand, regretting that he hadn't thought to tie it back. His dark brows furrowed intently as he counted the beats of the song in his head. The prophet formerly known as Jesus was learning some new dance moves.

To be fair, several people still called him Jesus, his parents included. Others referred to him by many different names, including but not limited to: Messiah, Savior, Light of the World, Logos, and Emmanuel. But he was going through another of what Mags called his "rebranding phases", and went by Christos these days.

Christos hummed along with the song, shimmying his hips and twisting, trying to move his feet in the right patterns. He stumbled, caught himself on his work bench, and sighed. This dance would be a lot easier with a partner to balance against—bachata was a sensual pairs dance. Tango's sexier cousin, by all accounts.

A soft knock at the door interrupted his thoughts, almost inaudible under the pulsing beat of the music that continued playing without him. But he heard her, as he always would. Her very presence reached out to him, like a warm breeze on a summer day, and Christos found himself turning to the door before he had consciously decided to move. His foot struck a haphazardly discarded chisel and made him pause. Amber eyes swept the room, taking in the mess.

A small pile of woodchips had accumulated beneath his lathe, which was otherwise tucked neatly in the alcove to the side of his room. Discarded shirts and pants from when he was choosing an outfit this morning littered his unmade king bed. There were several bowls and plates laid on every flat surface—evidence of the many meals he elected to take in his rooms instead of joining his parents.

Christos winced at the state of the room, then folded his hands as if in prayer. A faint wind stirred, sweeping the woodchips into the trash bin, carrying the clothes to the closet, and stacking the dishes into a neat pile before they were deposited in a dumbwaiter that descended to the kitchen with a hushed *whirr*.

The knock sounded again, and this time the door swung inward. Mags slipped inside with a knowing grin. "Are you done cleaning up your mess?"

Christos feigned indignation. "You wound me."

"Mhm." Mags smirked and bent to retrieve the chisel from the floor. "Missed a spot."

"Caught me." He laughed. "You know me too well."

She smiled, setting the tool on his nightstand as she pressed herself into his chest. A brief flare of guilt over the diversion tugged at her, but Mags pushed it aside for now. Time was of the essence, but in a world of chaos, this man was her anchor, and she needed this moment to collect herself. Christos wound his arms around her waist, settling his palms to the curve of her spine.

"This music is nice," she murmured, leaning her head against his collarbone. "You got bored of salsa?"

"I like variety." He began to rock gently from side to side, guiding her hips with his to the beat of the song. "Though you ruined the surprise."

He stepped to the left, leading her along with him as he began to work in the movements of the dance. Another step left, then two steps to the right, and the same cycle again. Mags giggled as he began to guide her backwards, then stepped back himself and pulled her along after him.

"This is still nice, surprise or no." She brought her hand up to cup his cheek as he twisted them to the side and led them into a turn.

"Mmm, speaking of surprises, I made you something."

"You did?" She pulled sharply back to gaze up at him in delight, throwing them off balance as Christos attempted to turn them again. They staggered together, Christos carefully tucking her to his chest as they fell sideways in a heap on his bed.

"Yes," he answered casually, as if his face wasn't half pressed into the sheets.

Mags laughed and rolled onto her back, looking up at his ceiling. They had painted it some decades ago; a parody of the Sistine Chapel with the cherubs all bearing the faces of their friends. Instead of Jehovah and Adam, Christos had insisted they insert themselves, reaching across the space to brush fingertips.

The longing in their painted expressions sent a warm pang of affection through her, tightening her throat and lungs. She turned back to lay facing him, head pillowed on her folded arms. "You're the sweetest."

"Only the sweetest?" He pouted. "Not the funniest, or smartest, or most handsome?"

"All that and more," she acquiesced, tapping his nose with the tip of her finger. "Now where is my gift?"

He smiled and reached over her to his nightstand, rummaging briefly in the drawer. Mags breathed in his cologne, a fresh and earthy mix of sage, mint, and smoked cedar. To be here with him, wrapped in his arms and his scent... It felt like comfort and home.

"Here it is," he muttered triumphantly, and pulled back to present her with a finely carved wooden lily. It was delicate and beautiful; its stem painted a deep green, the gently curling petals painted white with a deep red center spreading upwards. "I know you've always been fond of lilies."

"White lilies symbolize purity," she murmured, heart pounding in her chest and tears threatening to spill. "And red symbolizes romantic love."

"I know." Christos smiled at her, and it made Mags smile back reflexively.

The way he looked at her, like she was the most precious thing in the world... it was equal parts gratification and torture.

"You shouldn't have made this for me."

"I would do anything for you, my flower." He brought his hand up to stroke her cheek gently. "You need only say the word and I'm yours to command."

"And who is a whore to command the Prince of Heaven?" Mags sighed, and her smile faded away as she pulled away from him and rolled onto her back.

"This same sadness," Christos watched her with sad eyes and spoke with a soft and soothing tone. "Your past doesn't define you, Mags. You're more than the names you're called by cowards and ignorant fools."

"You've been telling me the same thing for centuries." She swallowed hard. "You're right, as usual. You'll have to forgive my mood, it's been...a difficult day."

"Tell me what's troubling you," he urged, reaching to pull her in with arms made strong by physical labor, folding her snugly against his chest. Her head tucked neatly under his chin, and she giggled when his close-cropped beard tickled her face. "Sorry."

"No, it's fine," she brushed off his apology. "It's nice to feel normal right now. It's helping."

"What happened? You know you can tell me anything."

So, she told him; about the terrible, disjointed vision that had wrenched her from a deep sleep and left her retching into her trash bin for hours, about Luce's naked grief, her memory of Christos's words to her so long ago, and about their desperate hope Jehovah would choose to help.

"Okay," Christos said carefully when she had finished, wiping fresh tears from her cheeks with gentle, calloused fingers. "When I said *anything*, I wasn't expecting that. I was hoping it was more along the lines of a broken scrying basin—I could fix that much more easily."

She made a muffled noise into his shirt but said nothing.

"Mags," he said, scratching at his beard—a sign of his anxiety, she knew. "You know he'll never agree with this."

"I know."

"What you're suggesting..."

"I *know*." She was regaining her composure now, and with it her resolve. She saw Luce's pained and broken expression whenever she closed her eyes. "But I have to try."

"You'll have more success if you can sway Gabriel to your side." He spoke with the air of someone who knows he's wasting his time.

He was right. "No," she said flatly.

"My father highly values his opinion."

Mags scrunched up her nose. "I'd rather claw my scars open than go crawling to *that slime* for help."

"Come on, he's not so bad."

"Christos, I say this with love, but you and your father are the only ones blindly loving enough to feel that way."

She couldn't stand Gabriel, and she wasn't alone in that feeling. He was the epitome of a whiny, snooty suck-up. His unparalleled bootlicking had made him the butt of many jokes, while his barbed responses had made him many disgruntled, reluctant acquaintances and few friends.

"Blind love is better than blind hate," Christos took up their familiar argument.

"And both are blind," she supplied her line easily, then switched tactics. "Besides, Gabriel isn't the only favored advisor your father has."

"Michael."

"He's always been *my* favorite. Much more honorable—and tolerable—than Gabriel."

"You're very biased," Christos pointed out mildly, but with no real conviction. He also considered Michael an ideal standard to compare other Seraphim to. The man was intense as he was reserved, but he had a wise mind, kind eyes, and open heart. It would be difficult to find a better friend or ally.

Mags grinned. "Indeed I am. I saw Michael entering the chapel on my way here, so I'll have to occupy myself for some time. Kiss me awhile before I go to save the world?"

He grinned like a little boy receiving a brand-new toy. "Didn't I already tell you your wish is my command?"

As he tilted her chin to claim her lips, another knock sounded at his door. Christos frowned as Mags sat up, looking curiously toward the sound.

"Jesu?" A woman's voice called, soft and lilting even as she raised it to be heard over the music. "Jesu, I'd like a word, if you have a moment?"

Christos sat up now too, silencing his stereo with a lazy wave. "Come inside, mother."

Mags quickly arranged her skirt, smoothing wrinkles and tucking the fabric neatly around her legs, which she crossed at the ankle. She kept her hands folded demurely in her lap, gently cradling her gift.

The door opened to reveal a tall, stately woman who bore a striking resemblance to her son. Thick, dark hair cascaded down her back, bound in golden cord to keep it neatly tucked away from her beautiful face. Her features were striking, with proud cheekbones and full lips arranged in perfect proportion beneath the same wide, brilliant amber eyes she had passed on to her son. A finely crafted silk dress wrapped her slender figure in a vision of champagne and cream that was more a work of art than garment.

Mags fought back the familiar burn of inadequacy that always threatened to choke her when she saw the Queen. How could she ever hope to compare to such regal elegance, such perfection? She would never be Christos's equal the way Queen Mary was so finely matched to her husband, Jehovah.

"Forgive me." The Queen hesitated in the doorway as her eyes landed on Mags, her expression unreadable. "I didn't mean to interrupt; I was unaware you had company."

Mags gripped her carved lily tight enough that the edges of the wood dug into her palms. She knew how it must look to find them here, on the bed in his room, with sensual music playing in the background. Though she knew that they were well within their rights to behave however they chose, it didn't make her feel any less violated as she considered all the torrid scenes the Queen could be imagining.

"You needed to speak with me?" Christos kept a tight rein on his tone, aiming for light and indifferent, but Mags could discern the subtle undercurrent of embarrassment there. Despite all his posturing with her, Christos was quite shy.

"It is a matter of no consequence," the Queen deferred. "I can return later, if I'm interrupting your time together."

"I was just leaving," Mags interjected, rising quickly from her tense perch on the edge of the mattress. "I have plans to meet with Michael and only stopped here on my way."

Queen Mary eyed her curiously, a small smile gracing her full lips. "I would be pleased to escort you, Lady Mary. We see each other so rarely these days, it would be a wonderful chance to catch up."

"But I thought -" Christos began, and his mother shushed him.

"We will speak later, Jesu. I'm much more interested in speaking with your lovely girlfriend."

Chapter Four

They traveled in silence down the cavernous halls of the palace for a time, the echo of their footsteps mimicking the hard pulse in Mags's wrists. She wished the queen would say something—she never knew what to say to the other woman. Even before they attained immortality, Mary had intimidated her. Didn't every girl seek the approval of her partner's mother? Joseph had been jovial, relaxed, and charming, but Mary had always had an air of distance, of having been touched by something *other* and left among the mundane.

"Tell me," the older woman finally interrupted Mags's racing thoughts. "How is my son?"

They both understood that she wasn't asking about Christos. "He's well. Misses you, of course."

"Of course." She smiled, but the shadow of grief had fallen over her beautiful face.

Mags's heart ached for her and the deeply sad truth of her loss. To lose a child was an awful thing, but to have your child removed from your life and know they lived just beyond your reach? It had to be agony.

"I wish that I could go to him."

"What stops you? Your *husband*?" The words slipped out before Mags could consider how impulsive they were. But a familiar frustration burned in her chest.

"Yes, my husband." Mary cut her eyes aside to Mags, and her gaze was as chastising as her tone—and perhaps a touch wounded. "You would do well to remember he rules this domain, Mary."

"What I *remember* is that he allowed my brother to die in agony so his son could make a spectacle of restoring him. He allowed *me* to die, not to mention your own sons. I am not so quick to forgive, and it amazes me that you are."

"You all returned to life."

"Of a sort." The words were bitter in her mouth, the smoldering anger in her chest coaxing her to uncharacteristically free speech. "And how well has it worked in your favor with your children?"

The Queen came to an abrupt halt, and Mags stumbled in her haste to do the same. She realized immediately that she had gone too far.

"I sat at the cross with you, Mary." Her tone was frigid and low. "I wept at the stone and tended a grave for three days without any certainty. Do not presume to question the manner in which I carry my grief."

The words cut her like knives, and Mags swallowed harshly. "I beg forgiveness, your majesty."

A long pause stretched, until Mary shook her head. "You need not. Sometimes I forget you are still so very young at heart."

"It was rude to question your feelings," Mags insisted. "Or your marriage."

"In a way, I admire your openness." She lifted a dainty hand and stroked her knuckles gently across Mags's cheek. "No one speaks to me like a person anymore. I've become a figurehead and an accessory. I remember a time when I too possessed such fire, though it feels like a distant dream now."

She resumed walking, Mags at her heels, and they soon approached the chapel. The hallway opened into an atrium that served as the grand foyer of the palace. The chapel doors were to their right, opposite the main entrance and nestled between two staircases sweeping up to the second floor. Across from them, another hallway led to the west wing of the ground floor.

They paused in the center of the atrium, and Queen Mary offered Mags a small smile. "For what's worth, my son is made better by your presence. He's always happiest with you at his side."

Mags flushed. "You flatter me."

"Well, I have always been quite fond of you." She looked over Mags's shoulder. "Though unfortunately I believe this brings an end to our time together."

Mags turned to see the doors of the chapel parting, swinging wide to allow Michael to step out of the shadowed sanctuary.

Queen Mary shooed her off. "Don't let me keep you, but do come by more often, darling. It gets so lonely sometimes."

"I will," Mags promised. She caught the Queen's hand and squeezed gently before they parted ways.

Michael closed the doors with as much effort as she would employ to close the cover of a book, even though they soared nearly twelve feet to the arched ceiling and were made from thick, sturdy oak. He was a hard man to miss, even if Mags hadn't known where to find him. Tall even for a Seraph, he towered over seven feet, with flawless sun-kissed skin and a mop of unruly honey-colored curls like those painted on cherubs. In contrast, he sported a perpetually stern expression—as if he knew whoever fell under his steely gaze had done wrong, and he intended to reprimand them appropriately. And all of this was bordered by massive, tawny wings sprouting proudly from his broad shoulders.

He paused to touch the carved wing door handles almost reverently. Mags approached with purpose in her stride and steel in her own gaze. She was determined to win him to her cause, and while she hoped he would make it easy for her, she knew Michael could be...set in his ways. Especially when it came to matters involving Lucifer.

"Michael," she called out brightly, and he turned abruptly, somehow managing to make startled recognition annoyingly attractive.

"Mags!" He opened his arms for a hug, and she smiled warmly as she stepped into his embrace. "How have you been?"

"Not well, I'm afraid," she said, her smile dimming and taking his down a notch with it.

"Something is wrong." He swept his gaze over her face and quickly discerned the severity of the situation. "Tell me immediately."

"Do you have a scrying basin? It's better if I show you."

"Come with me."

They moved swiftly through the halls. Michael's step quickened by impatience to hear the news, but he made a conscious effort to slow enough that Mags wouldn't be dragged behind him. She did her best to enjoy the view through the massive stained-glass windows as they walked, the beautiful soft pinks and deep blues that offered tinted glimpses of a sunny beachside, but she found her own thoughts troubled by the news she had to deliver. She knew she was about to visit painful revelations on another dear friend.

Michael paused before a smaller door, yet still one far grander than Mags's petite form required. She wondered what it must be like, to have a stature so grand that the palace had been specially crafted to accommodate it. She found it annoying having to climb things to reach any sort of height, and she assumed the Seraphim probably found it just as frustrating having to duck through doorways. They, however, were likely less inclined to throw tantrums about it—a state Mags was often resigned to, much to Luce and Christos's amusement.

They passed into a space like a small theater. Several rows of stone benches padded with plush burgundy cushions descended in tiers, spiraling around the circular room. A squat marble pillar was situated in the center of the sunken floor, beneath a massive glass skylight that allowed clear midday light to spill into the otherwise shadowed room. The pillar was unusually shaped, and it took Mags a moment to realize it was not one solid piece of marble, but two halves joined, carved in the form of small children. A boy and a girl both stood facing each other, with arms uplifted to hold an ornate basin of wrought gold filigree and rosy-pink glass.

She blinked in wonder at the sight. "How have I never seen this place?"

"It is new," Michael informed her brusquely. He was a man of few words at the best of times, and it tended to be worse when he was stressed.

"It's beautiful," she murmured reverently, releasing his arm to approach the basin and running her hands ever so gently along the smooth, polished edges. The surface of the water within seemed to shiver with tension, and the shiver that rolled down her own spine was from more than the faint chill that pervaded the cavernous room. Power exuded from this artifact, indicating that it had been crafted with spells and components woven into its form. She wouldn't need to request any amplifiers, it seemed.

Michael frowned, gesturing with a sweep of his bell sleeve to the basin. "Please, no more delay."

Mags swallowed harshly around the sudden tightness in her throat, nodding sharply. No posturing with Michael—he had no patience for moods and idiosyncrasies, hers or anyone's. One more deep breath and Mags brought her palms together with a clap.

Immediately, she understood this scry basin was a much more powerful artifact than she had thought.

The heat from the fire ghosted over her face, embers kissed her skin. The tang of blood and hot metal assaulted her nose. She gasped and her hands flew to her lips as if to smother the sound before it could be heard. They were not only viewing her vision but standing *in* the nightmare from all those years ago, brought to life around them.

This room was not designed for simple showcasing, she realized with a mixture of horror and awe. It was meant for spectacle; for overwhelming people in sensation and visuals. She began to tremble despite herself. It was a vision, nothing more, but her senses were caving under the onslaught of stimulus. The sights, smells, sounds—it was beginning to feel horribly real.

A warm hand on her shoulder brought her back to herself, and she glanced up, instinctively leaning into the comforting grip. Michael squeezed reassuringly, steadying her with his presence. Mags took a deep, slow breath.

"Explain," he prompted gently, eyes soft with concern but mouth still tightly pinched with impatience.

She nodded, lifting a trembling hand to point at a figure in the distance. Mercifully, he was facing away from them. She wasn't sure she could handle the sight of his eager grin and laughing eyes right now. Michael paled at the sight of such wanton carnage, strong jaw clenching with anger.

"Foster," Mags nearly whispered, knowing he would still hear. "This is the vision I saw the day he was born. The one I would never show you."

Flinty grey eyes cut sharply to her, and disbelief was etched on his face. "No."

"Yes." Mags could feel tears welling anew as she found the will to lift her hands and freeze the scene in place. She spun it so they faced the terrible sight head on—Foster, tall and handsome, killing and maiming with a gleeful expression, long fingers like his father's dripping with thick red blood.

Michael's face crumpled with sorrow, anger, and fear. It was such a mirror to Luce's grief that she was taken aback for a moment.

She let the scene unfold, still as painful as the first time. Foster in a burning city of bloody rubble, grinning with cold wickedness as he slashed a massive broadsword at any figure that tried to strike him down. Gore splattered over his face, eyes alight at the carnage.

Then another figure entered the scene. Lucifer—grim-faced and looking more tired than Mags had ever seen him but radiating raw power as he approached his son.

As he did, Foster lunged. His sword glanced off Luce's shimmering obsidian armor, leaving a harsh gash along his neck. Lucifer roared and fell back, cupping his own throat as golden blood poured between his fingers. Foster advanced on him, determined and furious, lifting his sword to strike again before the vision halted, their fates uncertain.

Michael fell to his knees and struck the ground with his fist once, twice, three times. His eyes flared with cold fire when he finally lifted his head.

"How?" he demanded. "Why does this happen, and when?"

"Soon," she whispered sadly. "Within a year, I think. I had another vision this morning, but much more...vague."

Unable to show him a second vision while they were inside the first, she did her best to describe the one from this morning that she had shared with Luce. Michael grew more tense the longer she spoke. He squeezed his eyes shut, and Mags felt a small tinge of relief to have that burning gaze off her even though she had done nothing wrong.

"What could have led him to this?"

"There may be one thing," she began, hesitantly. "I'm not sure, but...I noticed something earlier."

She moved her hands as if tugging a rope and the world shifted around them until they stood in the shadow of the distant building. What would have been a fuzzy but recognizable image in her seashell basin was an interactive, high-definition model in this elaborate chamber.

Michael's gaze narrowed. "What is this, Mary?"

Mags swallowed hard. "There was a book in the vision I saw this morning. I only caught a glimpse, but... It was familiar to me, and it reminded me of something I saw here. With such a detailed scene, I think maybe I could check..."

She knelt slowly, testing the limits of the vision's reality—loose asphalt crunched beneath her knees, but somewhere underneath she could feel the carpeted floor of the dais in the arena. She reached for an object poking out from beneath a pile of broken bricks, and carefully pulled free a small, tattered black book. Her fingers tightened on the worn leather cover when her worst fears were confirmed.

"The Gospel of Lazarus," she informed Michael somberly. "We both know what happened to my brother, Michael. We both know what awaits the one who performs these rituals."

"We must stop this from coming to pass."

"Foster is Lucifer's blood. *We* do nothing, because we couldn't hope to hold a candle to his raw power—let alone whatever these rituals can give him."

"Why are you here then, Mary? Surely it wasn't just to show me this vision."

"It's not," she admitted. "I need you to help me speak with Jehovah."

"I don't understand."

Mags rose slowly, brushing dust from her knees even though she knew it was only part of the vision. The book faded from her hand, returning to its original position beneath the rubble.

"Christos once told me...about an artifact that could imbue its owner with unlimited strength. A suit of armor that could protect its wearer from any attack."

"You refer to the Armor of God."

"I do."

"It isn't meant to be wielded by any but Jehovah. And he would never relinquish the Gospel that would lead them to it."

"I understand it wouldn't be a simple request." She laid a hand on his arm. "I would appreciate your support when I ask Him."

"He will never accept this."

"I need you to help me convince Him."

Michael shook his head sadly. "I can't."

"You must!" She was beginning to feel that desperate fear again. If Michael wouldn't help them, who could she depend on?

"You of all people should understand my reservations," he retorted. "The last time I went to beseech Him for help, it resulted in an attempted coup and a betrayal I still atone for. I curry much less favor with my King than I once did. You waste your time asking me this."

"Michael, we have to try." She dropped her voice, wary even when they were alone of someone overhearing what she was about to say. "You know that Lucifer has been weakened, Michael. Without his wings, without the power he gifted to the Deadly Sins, you *know* he can't stand against someone imbued with the strength of this grimoire."

"Enough!" Michael spun on his heel and stalked back to the original point they had entered the vision. His robes fluttered as he paced in circles, eyes darting around the ruined landscape all the while. "You have to give up on this delusion, Mary. I won't stake my name against your impulsive ideas, especially for Lucifer's benefit."

She blinked back frustrated tears. Michael had never been so curt with her. But he had a point, as much as she hated to accept it. His motives would always be questioned where Lucifer was concerned, not to mention the complicated emotions that clearly still simmered between the two men. She thought of Luce's short temper whenever she would try and discuss Michael, or the day of the Fall.

Michael made a distressed sound when he paused his pacing and saw her expression. "I'm sorry. As much as I'm loath to admit it, you might have better luck taking your request to Gabriel."

Mags laughed, waving away the vision impatiently. She was discomfited to find that rather than dissolving into mist as she was used to, this one seemed to slide from the skin like oil. She rubbed her arms uncomfortably, shivering. "You have more faith in my acting skills than I do, if you expect me to pretend that I like that cockroach long enough to ask him for help."

"If you don't want to speak with Gabe, we can take a stroll down the beach instead." Michael gestured to the door, smiling despite the mild reprimand in his eyes. "Come. It's a beautiful day, and your visions are not set in stone. Perhaps our meddling would even be the catalyst of this disaster."

"Thank you, but I think I'll have to take a rain check." She smiled faintly. "You're right, of course. Just because I saw it doesn't mean it will come to pass. I think I'll just enjoy the library for a while to take my mind off things and visit Raphael. Maybe he knows of some books we could search for another option."

"Yes." He smiled warmly. "That's an excellent idea. Please, seek me out if you change your mind about the walk."

She nodded absently and they parted ways. Michael headed towards the sparring fields, and after a moment, Mags turned down the hall leading to the grandiose library that spanned an entire building to itself. The gentle nudge in her mind was telling her not to ignore this. Michael was right that sometimes her visions never came to pass, but this didn't feel like one of those *possible* futures.

Immersing herself in that chamber had only solidified the persistent suggestion that Armageddon was coming *fast*. Without Michael she had no hope of convincing Jehovah to hear her out, and Michael had proven himself nothing if not consistent over these long eons. If he didn't change his own mind, it would not be swayed.

Michael didn't believe in her vision. Luce didn't believe that they could obtain this resource. But Mags knew the key to averting this crisis waited at the end of this hallway, and it was time to take matters into her own hands.

* * *

Michael often lost himself in sparring, in the rhythm of his breathing, the steady *thunk* as he struck out at the targets and found a mark. It helped him focus his mind and recenter when the racing of his heart replaced the racing of his thoughts. But today, Michael knocked down target after target and did not reach the calm he sought.

Today there was only the rush of blood in his ears and the lingering discomfort over what he had seen; over what it would mean if he was wrong. He refused any attempts for someone to partner him, choosing instead to abuse the inanimate targets, to allow himself to lose control and use his full strength.

He had seen the look on Mags's face; there was genuine panic there. She knew her gift better than anyone, and she seemed utterly convinced that this future was not only certain, but coming quickly. Michael grunted as he put his fist clean through the leather bag. Finely ground sand poured out onto the packed dirt ground of the arena.

Yanking his hand free and whirling back towards the armory to find something more durable to vent his frustrations upon, Michael could feel the tension rising in him again. He forced himself to stop, to take several deep breaths, and to *not* take a swing at the new object in the arena—the angel stepping silently towards him.

As always, his immediate thought was of how good it would feel to punch Gabriel right in his smug, sculpted face, high cheekbones breaking easily under his knuckles.

"Gabriel," he greeted him curtly, trying to disguise the tremor of anger in his hands. "Rare to see you here."

"Concerned, Michael?" He arched a perfectly groomed black brow, smirking. "Don't worry, I'm not here to challenge you. Lord knows I'd hate to mar any of that *rippling* masculinity."

Michael didn't need to study the other angel's slight build to know he spent little to no time training. He practically lived in this arena, and this was the first time in weeks that Gabe had entered it. He rolled his eyes. "You and I both know it wouldn't be a fair fight."

"Would you like to test that theory?"

Michael scowled at him. "Is there some reason you're here to bother me? I have bigger things to worry about than amusing you."

Gabriel ceased his taunting, bored with his game for the moment. "You're worried about something? Maybe I can help."

As much as Michael did *not* want to accept help from Gabriel, who was an annoyance on a good day and a painful reminder on a bad one, he paused to consider. If anyone in Heaven held more sway with Jehovah than he did, it was the angel standing before him. Even if said angel looked more like a bored trust fund heir in his fitted slacks and cashmere sweater than an advisor to the Ancient of Days.

Still, Michael hesitated, something in him recoiling from the idea of telling Gabe about what Mags had shown him. *Don't be petty*, he chided himself. Mags had come and laid bare her fears. If he couldn't petition Jehovah, the least he could do would be to seek an outside opinion.

Michael described everything as briefly as he could, but he withheld some key details—such as the identity of the monstrous figure. If history had taught him anything, it was that Gabriel was even more biased in matters of Lucifer than Michael was.

Gabriel nodded along, silent while he followed the story. When the blond got to the armor-related part of Mags's plan, Gabe's dark brows shot into his hairline.

"Sorry, she said *what*?"

"I know," Michael groaned. "It's a crazy idea."

"Well yeah, that girl is insane as they come."

Michael scowled. "No, she isn't."

"She has free reign to waltz around up here and chooses to spend most of her time in Hell with... well. You know with who."

"I don't want to talk about him."

Something mischievous glinted in Gabriel's eyes, and Michael already knew he was going to be pissed off by whatever came out of his wicked mouth next.

"Are you *sure* you don't want to talk about him, Michael?"

"Extremely," he said curtly. "I've spent enough of my life on... that man."

"You always did have rose colored glasses for him." Gabriel sighed, then his expression shifted into a sweet grin. "Among other... predispositions."

Michael's blood had already been simmering with anxiety, and then annoyance at dealing with Gabriel. Now it spiked sky high. "Fuck you."

He shoved Gabe aside, storming past him. Stupid—so stupid to think he could seek Gabriel's perspective; to think it was possible to work with him toward a solution. Gabe had proven a long time ago that he didn't deserve Michael's trust.

Michael left through the nearest archway, sending a group of meandering angels scattering from his path with indignant noises as he blew down the corridor like a storm. His tawny wings fluttered restlessly, longing to take flight, fury blinding him to everything but the sliver of perfect daylight shining at the end of the hall.

Gabe sauntered to the doorway after him but made no effort to call the warrior back. There was no point—Michael would just ignore him, and he was done having his fun for now. The brute nearly bowled over a group of bystanders as he ran to the exit, those powerful wings flaring wide as soon as he cleared the doorframe. Sunlight glinted off golden curls as he dipped and then swooped up, soaring off toward the glittering waves in the distance.

Perfect form, perfect figure, perfect weather and perfect world. Gabe sighed dreamily at the classic imagery, affection swelling for the realm he inhabited. Heaven truly was paradise

With his source of entertainment gone, his thoughts turned to Christos's little girlfriend and all the fun he could have working *her* into a frustrated rage. It was too easy to get under people's skin—Gabe had always had a talent for it, and it certainly made life interesting, especially with eons of days to occupy. Heaven was beautiful, but it could also be so dreadfully boring.

The images Michael had described flashed in his mind, and Gabe frowned. Not boring for long, it seemed. He wondered if there might be any credibility to Mags's plan and then shook the idea sharply from his mind. No, it would be too catastrophic. Lucifer would be enough of a threat if he got his full powers back—the Armor could never fall into his possession. Gabe would make sure of it himself if he had to.

With a last lingering look down the hall, Gabe turned and strolled back the opposite direction. It might be prudent to take a trip to the library. Just to check on things.

Chapter Five

Michael's only thought had been to get away, to leave Gabriel's grating presence and the crowded palace behind. He had leapt from the launching point with no destination in mind and now found himself soaring aimlessly over the Kingdom. The line from the Gates stretched endlessly back to the Rift; the shimmering split in the air that admitted souls to what Jehovah called their "final gift".

Maybe it was heretical to think it, but Michael had trouble supporting the criteria that decided whose names were entered in Peter's ledger. Too often he had seen unscrupulous lives absolved by someone's deathbed confessions. While he tried to be hopeful that these souls had truly "seen the light" and wanted to do better, it left a slimy feeling on his conscience. He angled away from the Gates subconsciously. He would visit with Peter later, when Matthew took the other man's place at the entrance.

Michael swept over the sprawling lawns, smiling tightly when residents that recognized him lifted their hands to wave as he passed. Normally he would stop to interact with them, but today he didn't have the patience for socializing. He crossed over farms that produced the food the spirits ate purely for the sake of indulgence and normalcy, and passed the small towns nestled in the hills and arranged into little communities.

He dipped low to drag his fingers through the rivers and skimmed the tops of the trees in the forests that bordered the northern edge of the palace grounds. He circled aimlessly, oblivious to the world, following patterns and flight paths that he knew by muscle memory alone.

When the strain of flight began to beat a dull ache into his trapezius and the pounding of his pulse had slowed from near-panic to the normal levels of exertion, he tucked his wings for a dive. Circling down slowly, he landed lightly on the empty beach below.

Sparkling sand filtered through the gaps in his leather sandals and a salty breeze tugged gently at his windblown curls. The familiar burn in his shoulders was welcome and comforting. Michael settled back to soothe his sore muscles against the pale golden sand, warm from the sun's unyielding rays.

He wasn't sure what he was looking for as his eyes absently scanned the slowly darkening sky. The other beaches hosted souls enjoying the water and each other's company, but Michael had instinctively navigated to a secluded stretch. Well hidden within a calm, quiet grotto, the only person who would have known to seek him in this hidden inlet was long gone from this land.

The fading light as the day wound down reminded him of another sunset, as riddled with tumultuous emotions as this one.

Dazzling sunbeams streamed through an ornate stained-glass window. Ruby, amethyst, emerald and sapphire mingled in dappled shards on gilded ivory wallpaper, painting the sparsely furnished room like a rainbow with the sunset's help.

A tall, muscular figure paced the small space, clad in a simple white garment that was equal parts tunic and robe. His honey blond curls were tied back in a neat tail at the nape of his neck. He scowled in the direction of the window, yanking a pale sash across the glass to blot out the brightness and warmth. This was not a day for beauty.

The traitorous doubt roiling in his gut made him want to be sick, as if it was a living creature trying to claw its way out. He spun on his heel and bent over his washbasin, gripping the ceramic until his knuckles turned white and glaring at himself in the mirror. He choked the feeling down and buried it.

He couldn't allow his personal feelings to cloud his judgement. Facts were facts no matter how you cut them, and he couldn't change those facts just because he didn't want them to be the truth. He released the basin and grasped the hilt of his sword instead, familiar warmth flooding his palm as he drew his power up from deep within himself. He'd need every scrap of his strength for this task. Hopefully it would steady not only his blade, but his shaken will.

A knock sounded, and he straightened, turning slowly. Raphael stood in the open doorway, his expression grim and emerald eyes unusually dull. The younger angel's typically playful demeanor was conspicuously sobered on this day, and it only served to set the blond further on edge.

"Mikha'el, my friend," his soft voice was roughened and taut with emotion. "It is time."

"Yes," Michael sighed. Saying it aloud only filled him with more dread. He couldn't believe that Luce of all people could be guilty of the crimes they accused him of. His Lucifer, so idealistic, full of passion and divine purpose. But apparently not as pure of heart as Michael had believed.

Raphael met his gaze evenly. The steady back and forth motion as he brushed the dark tail of his braid over his palm was the only indication of his own apprehension. "For what it may be worth...I wish it had not come to this."

"What are wishes but dreams we cannot realize?" Michael mused bitterly, then scoffed at his own 'poetic' thoughts. "We are wasting time."

He strode to the door, using each steady step to hide his trembling. Today his King would bestow the heaviest burden Michael had yet to bear, but he would not shirk his responsibilities. Those proud shoulders would square up to hold the weight of the world if Jehovah would command it. Duty, honor, loyalty...all the things Michael held dear.

Not all the things, *his traitorous mind whispered, and Michael squashed the flutter of grief.* All the things that mattered now. *His ties to Lucifer, such as they were, would need to be severed before they bound him and dragged him down.*

"Mikha'el, Rafa'el," their names—their old, true names—boomed from the stern lips of the figure seated in the ornate ivory throne atop the dais. Jehovah

was in his finery for the occasion, resplendent in a flowing white robe trimmed with gold and crimson. A finely wrought golden crown rested on his unbound hair, the color of sun-bleached sand. He lifted a tanned hand laden with jeweled rings and beckoned them closer, eyes weary and expression dark. "You are late."

Michael bowed deeply. "I hope you might forgive us, Almighty. Today is a...trying day."

"While I understand," the King frowned, "I still find it distasteful to be late to this, a most important trial."

A harsh swallow, but no argument. He was right, of course, and shame burned in Michael's chest along with the guilt and grief. Soon there would be no room left for these swirling emotions, and he was certain his heart would burst.

Jehovah heaved a sigh. "This brings me no joy. I know your heart is equally burdened."

"Yes," Michael answered, some of the raw pain leaking unbidden into his voice. He choked it back down, mentally reciting Lucifer's list of transgressions to solidify his resolve.

"Let us not drag this out," Jehovah decreed. "Bring me Lus'ior of the Morning Star and let us try the traitor for his numerous trespasses."

A smaller set of doors on the opposing wall swung inward, and a double line of warriors entered, splitting apart to form an arc of armed muscle before their King. The two soldiers at the end of either row led a figure bound in irons between them—a figure that was not hunched or cowed but walking proudly, with his shoulders squared and chin lifted in defiance. Michael shoved down his swell of mingled love and agony with a hard, sharp inhale and forced himself not to look away.

Even bound and beaten, Lucifer was glorious. Sweat and grime plastered his long, dark hair to his face. His normally immaculate beard had grown out, unruly and matted with blood on one side. A short scuffle ensued when the guards holding him tried to shove Lucifer roughly to his knees, the Prince resisting only until Ezekiel struck him roughly across the face. Lucifer glowered at the white-haired angel. As a dark bruise rose, purpling and livid on his cheek, he pointedly shrugged off his holders to lower himself unassisted.

He was still the most beautiful thing Michael had ever seen. His heart skipped and stuttered in rebellion, sending a wave of anguish through him.

How cruel fate could be, to give him this gift and so quickly snatch it back. And not only to tear it away, but to hold its loss over his head like this; to place an unbearable burden where there had once been a current of affection that had buoyed and lifted him.

Lucifer met his stare, and his expression lit with a hope and fondness that sliced his heart anew. Michael swallowed hard and tore his gaze away. He couldn't do this. His resolve was going to break, and he would be disgraced alongside his lover by failing to uphold his vows to their King. To see him there, brought to his knees by soldiers they trusted and fought beside—soldiers that he had helped Lucifer to train—dug at the wounds deep within and salted them.

Raphael shifted closer, as if sensing the tension in the way Michael's jaw tightened, or how his shoulders went stiff. The younger man rested his finger-tips lightly against Michael's spine, and it was a gentle reminder of how he was not alone. He would not be alone, even when Lucifer was not with him.

"Lus'ior of the Morning Star, Angel of Light, First of the Seraphim, Serpent of Old and Prince of the Air," Jehovah stirred the room with his sonorous intonation, each invocation of Lucifer's many titles bringing a wince to Michael's face and pain to Luce's eyes. "You are brought here today to face trial and be charged for the crimes you have wrought on Earth. You have defied my orders and the Divine Laws of Heaven, and you have tainted the fledgling mortals beyond reparation. How do you plead?"

His eyes blazing with controlled fury, Lucifer did not speak. Did not even open his lips in an attempt to defend his actions.

Jehovah frowned, eyes narrowing. "Speak, you insolent heretic, and let it be the truth."

Lucifer lifted his chin and stared down the King. His rich voice rang out over the silent room, even roughened as it was by days without water or reprieve from torture. "Not guilty."

A whisper of shock swept the room; a gasp pulled from Michael's own mouth at the audacity.

"You were seen," Michael spat, fury boiling in his chest as his grip tightened reflexively on the hilt of his sword. "There were witnesses to your treason, yet you can so easily spread lies in this room? Have some dignity in this moment and atone, Lus'ior."

The room went deadly quiet. Raphael pressed more insistently on

Michael's back. He cut his eyes to the side to see Jehovah's glower focused on him.

"Are you so eager to proceed, Mikha'ael, that you forget your place?" Unfathomable depths swirled in that cobalt glare, like turbulent oceans preparing to drown him. "Stay your blade and your tongue to follow, my warrior, or perhaps you will kneel beside the Deceiver."

Lucifer cast an alarmed glance at Michael, who could not bear to meet his eye. He was already on unstable footing with his king. Of course, he had been the first suspected of conspiring with Lucifer's treason; Michael would have made the same assumption himself. Even though he had obediently brought Lucifer before Jehovah, despite the open agony he had carried over what he had witnessed in the Garden...

After several long days of pledging his loyalty to Heaven, to Jehovah, and to upholding the Divine Laws, he had at last been declared free of corruption. But to prove that loyalty, he had been given a task that threatened to destroy him.

The very one which he waited even now to complete.

Michael tamped down his grief and anger. "I apologize again, my lord."

Jehovah tipped his head slightly, the only acknowledgement he would likely bestow, and returned his focus to the accused. Lucifer still knelt in place, once again defiantly meeting the King's gaze head on. It was as if he had no shame, no regret for what he had done. Michael's stomach twisted with nausea. How could Luce, his Luce, have become so twisted and cold?

But there was no denying what had happened in the Garden. Summoned there by the accusations of Jophiel and the will of Jehovah, Michael had seen it with his own eyes. He still felt the hard stab of betrayal at the scene they had stumbled upon, unmistakable and horrible; still felt the sword blazing in his hand as he rushed Lucifer in a wounded rage. He gripped that same sword now as he watched his former lover stare down their King, not a trace of remorse in Lucifer's furious expression.

"Do you insist upon denying your crimes, Lus'ior?" Jehovah demanded. "Knowing you have broken the Laws, knowing there were multiple witnesses to your crime—you will deny your very nature and feign innocence?"

"I feign nothing." He spat, and the Seraph to his right took a half step away from the phlegm that splattered the stone floor. "Shall I apologize every time a fool makes an incorrect assumption? I have never accepted the blame or glory of another, and I will not start today."

"So, you spit in the face of your titles, as if they were bestowed on a whim? Gifts are earned. Has Michael not risen in ranks as he has proven himself?" Jehovah flicked his wrist toward the blond, his tone still calm and measured.

Lucifer's searching gaze when Michael's name was tossed out left him stripped to the core. As if Luce combed through him with each second that slipped by, weighing his soul and the contents of his heart. Despite better judgement, he hoped Luce could see love there. Love and regret and loss. Because Michael knew he would follow Jehovah's next command. He must follow it. It was the right thing to do, however difficult.

"As he will prove himself again today."

The King of Heaven was ready to end this spectacle. Lucifer would not repent, and so he would be punished. And Michael would be the one to do it, even if he wasn't under pressure to prove his loyalty to his King. For all the love in his heart, he could not forget what his eyes had seen in that Garden. What Lucifer had done was unforgiveable; the Laws had been put in place for a reason. And to see the once dignified man here, utterly unapologetic and making such heretical claims... it only solidified his guilt.

"Do not do this, brother." Lucifer's haunted face twisted in grief and streaked with salt trails, but his brown eyes gleamed with determination. "It will be your biggest regret. You will curse yourself for casting me out, and you will never have a moment's peace from your conscience."

"You threaten me, Lus'ior? Here, in my Kingdom, with my soldiers standing at your side. What could you do, in this moment?"

"Oh, Jeho," Lucifer smirked bitterly. "You understand so little. You understand nothing."

"Mikha'el," Jehovah summoned with a commanding wave. "I have need of you once again, my loyal servant."

Michael hesitated, the briefest indication of his doubt as his feet refused to move. First the King would strip Lucifer's titles, and then... Raphael propelled him forward with a gentle shove, and the blond forced himself not to stare at the floor as he approached the center of the room.

"From this day forward, you are no longer the Prince of the Air or the Angel of Light," Jehovah decreed.

Lucifer's dark eyes tracked each agony-filled step with calm resolve. He knew what would come, and he was steeling himself just as Michael was.

"You are henceforth to be known as the Angel of the Bottomless Pit," intoned the King. "You are Lus'ior the Fallen Star, Son of Perdition. All Seraphim shall regard you as adversary, and any who choose to break bread with you will find their own angelic rights forfeit. You are banished from the Kingdom of Heaven and shall never again walk here so long as your days may be."

"Banish me if you like," Lucifer spat again. "I would sooner die an eternal death than see this place even once more. I have no need of a King of Lies."

"You have no King at all, Lus'ior." Jehovah's face hardened into a mask of rage, but he still spoke evenly as he declared, "Strip his wings and cast him out, Mikha'el. Prove your loyalty and rid us of this evil in one fell stroke."

"As you decree, my King," Michael forced his voice to stay steady, to not betray the riot of emotion within his heart. It left him sounding hollow, mechanical, but it was better than revealing the torrent roiling within him.

How could Lucifer say these dark things and accuse their King of such wickedness, when he himself had been plotting and working against the Kingdom of Heaven? Any affectionate feelings he harbored could not trump the disgust and disappointment that flooded him.

Michael drew his sword slowly and composed himself as he met Luce's waiting stare. "For the crimes you have committed and intended to commit, the Ancient of Days has sentenced you to banishment but mercifully spared your life. You forfeit your wings and your titles, and you will never walk among your kind again."

The guards surrounding Lucifer shifted away, as if reluctant to be anywhere close to the tension pouring between the two men. A lifetime passed in those short moments.

Michael's heartbeat thrummed in his chest, blood rushing hard in his ears. He could feel every eye in the room fixed on him. Remiel glared at him with an intensity so sharp, Michael was surprised it didn't cut a hole in him. Her husband Raguel held her bicep in a comforting but restraining gesture. Disappointment creased his face, which was arguably more painful than Remiel's glare.

Michael looked away and caught Gabriel's gleaming sapphire gaze. The dark-haired angel watched him with a mingled expression of pain and vindi-

cation. If anyone in this room understood Michael's turmoil, it would be Gabriel. Michael's eyes stung as he wrenched them away and forced himself to blink back the tears threatening to spill.

He couldn't do this.

He had to do this.

Lucifer nodded, regarding Michael with an indecipherable expression. "Alright then," he spoke low, his voice ragged and deep, for only Michael and the surrounding guards to hear. "If you choose his side, I'll grant you that. It's what I'm fighting for, after all. Choice."

"Silence, Deceiver," Michael snapped. He couldn't bear to hear that voice, the one he had spent long nights of private conversations savoring. The tone Luce used with him alone. "You hold a darkness within that taints all that you touch. Look at what you have wrought upon Eve, upon Adam! I will hear no more of your twisted rhetoric."

"Oh, that's very witty Mike, 'twisted rhetoric'. You always had a way with words." Michael began to tear up again but maintained his composure even in the face of Lucifer's judgement. "You will also come to regret this day. But I respect your right to make this choice."

Michael roared, "I said I will hear no more!"

He couldn't bear to.

"Do it then!" Lucifer shouted back, matching him even now. He spun so his back was to the furious warrior, goading him into action. "Do your worst, oh faithful lapdog!"

With a cry of rage, Michael raised his sword and brought it down swiftly. Lucifer's screams rent the air as the tempered steel sliced cleanly through muscle and cartilage, the magnificent golden wings dropping from proud shoulders like lead weights. Feathers scattered across the polished floor along with heavy drops of thick golden blood.

The Devil screamed until his throat was raw, until his voice gave out from the strain. Thick trails of gold slid down his back, pooling beneath him and soaking into his tattered trousers. His barren shoulders slumped, but he lifted his exhausted face to meet Michael's gaze and the fury smoldering there.

"Are you proud?" He whispered hoarsely, unable to manage more. "Is your conscience appeased? Jeho's favorite attack dog, restored to glory."

"It is what you deserve," Michael hissed, and spit on the ground before his

lover. How much of their relationship had been a farce? How much of it was crafted to deceive and blind him to the truth? "You are a traitor and a coward, and I am glad to be rid of you. I am glad to spare this Kingdom your wicked manipulations. It is my greatest joy."

"Is it?" Lucifer hissed, sucking in deep breaths to distract from the pain decimating his shoulders and back. "Well, for what it is worth, you were mine."

The admission seared Michael to the soul.

"Enough!" He raised his hand sharply and Lucifer's back was engulfed in blazing golden flame, the stumps of his wings burning away to dust and razing the blood and grime from his skin.

He was radiant even in the flames of judgement.

At a gesture from Jehovah, the twins Jophiel and Gloriana approached the fallen prince. Clasping hands, they closed their eyes and summoned forth a portal, a more temporary thing than the Rifts but good enough for quick passage between realms. A flickering gash of blue and white light, it cast shadows that deepened the lines of pain on the newly minted Devil's face. He was a shell of himself, pale and sweating and hunched over from the pain.

"Goodbye, Mikha'el," he murmured, shifting from his knees to rise unsteadily to his feet.

"Good riddance," Michael spat back at him, masking his pain with his rage.

Luce smiled grimly as he stepped backwards through the tear in the world, eyes hard and accusing and refusing to look away from Michael until the portal sealed between them. His resolve broke, and Michael forced himself to breathe evenly as he turned slowly to face his king. Dropping to one knee and bowing his head, hiding his storm cloud eyes behind unruly blond bangs, he curled a fist over his shattered heart.

"My faithful warrior," Jehovah declared proudly, voice laced with warmth and kindness. "The epitome of justice and devotion, who would cast out his own lover when he defiled the Divine Law. Your sacrifice and loyalty are proof of your inherent goodness, Mikha'el."

And yet, Michael didn't feel honorable or just in this moment. He felt sick and cold and furious at how he had been used and what he had been made to do. To strip an angel's wings, to cast them out...it was difficult under the best of circumstances. But to be forced to do it to someone you loved was almost unbearable. It could have been Uriel or Jophiel who performed the act, or Sachiel or Raphael. It didn't have to be him. Underneath it all was a simmering resentment that Jehovah had asked this of him.

He continued kneeling, eyes burning a hole into the polished stones as he let Jehovah's words wash numbly over him. The sounds, the room—everything faded away until there was only the dull throb of his heart in his chest, reminding him he was still alive. Eventually, he felt a gentle touch on his shoulder, followed by another on his other side. Raphael observed him quietly, a steady and constant presence, while Uriel seethed with turmoil and resolve.

"Rise, my friend," Raphael murmured. "Come away from here and compose yourself. Life must go on, and you cannot process this here."

He nodded dumbly, lifting his head to find his neck aching and the room emptied. How long had he knelt here, lost in his thoughts? He stood on sore and shaking legs and allowed himself to be led from the room, trying to feel anything but the sharp sense of loss and confusion.

When he slipped out of his memories and back into the present day, the sunset had dwindled to the purples and reds of old bruises. Stars twinkled blithely overhead, and Michael hated them for it. The perfect balance of this afterlife oasis was maintained with the careless thought of the omnipotent king, Jehovah. But Michael knew firsthand that the eternal sunshine could belie a darkness in this Kingdom, one that lived within him.

Protecting and serving had led to all of this. Swearing oaths and bonds to a man he believed in, blindly following and assuming that his path was the right one—the only one—had cost him dearly. Now, he wasn't so sure that he had made his choices correctly. He still regretted the horrible things he had said in that room. He lifted a trembling hand and touched his calloused fingertips to his lips. A spiteful tongue, and warrior's hands to back it.

Eons could pass and Michael would never forgive himself for his role in what happened that day. Lucifer had hoped his lover might speak in his defense. He could have done the honorable thing and heard Luce's explanations—honored the requests he had sent through Sachiel for Michael to come and visit him in the dungeons. If he had listened, maybe he would have been able to understand. A traitorous part of him wondered if he might even have agreed with Lucifer's beliefs.

But he knew, in the darkest corner of his heart, that it would not have mattered. The thorn that dug deepest into his wounds was that he had been too proud to hear Lucifer's side. He was bitter and vengeful on that day. Michael had heaped more blame and judgement upon the fallen Prince. He had believed what suited his pain, and now he was paying for it evermore.

Chapter Six

Foster Morningstar ducked out of his shower stall to avoid hitting his head on the curtain rod, grabbing a fluffy towel and wrapping it securely around his waist. He paused a moment to inspect his appearance, frowning at the inky circles that had been lingering under his eyes for the past few weeks.

His dreams were constantly disrupted by his tossing and turning, but when he did manage to slip into uneasy sleep, Piper's tired, sunken eyes regarded him with an understanding beyond her meager ten years. He saw the trust and desperate hope that gutted him over and over.

You're doing the right thing, Foster, Gabe's smooth, consoling voice drifted up from his memories. *She's suffering, and now her death can have a greater meaning. Don't you want to help her? A sacrifice like this all but guarantees her a favored place in Heaven.*

He closed his eyes tightly, trying to block out the words. Logic didn't help him sleep at night, the same way it hadn't made his actions any easier on that day. With a low growl, Foster turned away from his exhausted and angry reflection and yanked open the bathroom door.

Cool air swirled in, disrupting the warmth of the lingering steam and making him shiver as he stalked out and down the hall. Might as well start his coffee before getting dressed, with the day he had ahead of him.

Or not, he realized with a sigh, as he entered his kitchen and found a small, purple creature balanced on his counter, eating his coffee beans.

"Cwall, what the fuck?" Foster groaned. "Why do you always do this?"

The imp let out a loud belch and tossed down the decimated packet, leaning back against the checkered backsplash and picking his teeth with a long, yellowed fingernail. "Because ya got the real good Arabian shit." He shrugged his skinny shoulders.

"First of all, it's Arabica," Foster launched into the familiar tirade, knowing full well that Cwall *knew* all of this, but unable to resist proving his point, "and secondly, that specific bag is an Arabica and Robusta blend imported from Hawaii, and it costs me twenty bucks a pound so cough up, asshat."

"I'm good." The tiny demon grinned, flaring his batlike wings in a stretch as he rolled over to lounge on his elbows. "We both know ya can afford it, and I was hungry."

"And all you could find in my fully stocked kitchen was the last bag of my favorite coffee beans?"

"All I could find that I wanted ta eat." He shrugged again, and Foster lunged. Cwall yelped and scrambled backwards, but Foster was faster, snagging a scrawny ankle in his fist and tugging the imp toward him.

"Stop struggling, or next time I grab for the tail!" He snapped, dangling the flailing creature upside down and giving him a little shake.

"Not my tail!" Cwall wailed. "You know it's sensitive!"

"Why are you in my apartment, Cwall?"

"Ah, a guy can't just come ta visit?"

"You *never* come just to visit anymore," Foster deadpanned.

Cwall grumbled, "Not since ya started hangin' out with that slimy angel."

"Just because Gabe is an angel doesn't mean you need to hate him."

"I don't hate 'im for bein' an angel," Cwall protested. "I know lotsa angels, and I like them. Remi's great, Cami's fun, Glory's easy on the eyes. I hate Gabe for bein' a slimeball suckup, it's different."

"He's pretty much the only person who actually gives a damn about me," Foster snapped, "so forgive me if I'd prefer you respected him."

"And what am I, chopped liver?"

"You show up randomly, eat me out of house and home, and insult my friends before disappearing again," Foster said. "Not to mention you spy on me for my sperm donor, so fuck you for that."

"I do not spy," Cwall pouted. "I tell him you're alive and it keeps 'im off your back, so you're *welcome* ya lil shit, 'cause I know ya don't wanna see 'im."

"Yeah, yeah, do all his work for him, give him even more excuses."

"I just do my job." Cwall looked somewhere between dizzy and affronted. "Can ya put me down now?"

"Sure," Foster grinned and flung the imp towards the living room.

He flapped his wings frantically, righting himself just before hitting the far wall and hovering like an angry, oversized chicken. "Rude."

"Not my fault you picked a form that's easily tossed around." Foster rifled through his pantry for his backup coffee. He found the bag, an unfortunately lesser quality he'd been given as a gift and only kept for emergencies—like when he forgot to stop by the store, or when Cwall made his random appearances to mooch.

"I like the purple and the wings." Cwall settled on the back of the couch like an overgrown parrot. "But I don't like being manhandled."

He flared his wings then folded them, letting them melt into his back. His limbs stretched and swelled and rapidly lost color, elongating and turning to milky white. His three fingers and toes split into the standard five, and his ratlike face blurred and grew, morphing into a humanoid skull. Cwall groaned and rolled his joints, stretching his new skeletal form. Lidless eye sockets lit with acid green flame as he offered Foster a ghastly smirk.

"Better?"

Foster shrugged. "More badass at least. You're gonna need skin if you come outside with me though."

"Where ya goin'?"

"Library," Foster lied with a smile, knowing that answer was sure to get his Guardian Demon off his tail.

"Ew, no thanks." Cwall shuddered. "You Morningstar men sure love to fuckin' read."

Foster laughed bitterly. "Well, at least he gave me one good thing."

"More than one." Cwall flashed that hideous rictus grin again. "Ya got your pretty face from ol' Luci too."

"Get out of my house, Cwall."

"So testy," Cwall clicked his teeth together. "All this time with the humans has made ya so tempermetal, Fostie."

"Temperamental," Foster corrected, rolling his eyes. "And I've always been this way."

"No," Cwall lost a bit of his jovial tone and his eyes flickered briefly. "Ya really weren't like this before."

He blinked out of sight, presumably gone back to whatever limbo he hung around in when he wasn't bothering the Prince of Hell, and Foster relaxed a bit. Something in the way Cwall watched him made him anxious sometimes, as if the strange demon was reading him more deeply than his lackadaisical nature suggested. As if he was seeing parts of Foster that even the man himself didn't like to look at.

Foster sighed and turned his attention back to measuring the beans into his grinder. Coffee would help, even subpar coffee. He could analyze the motives of demons after he studied the next ritual. When his mother was returned to his side, he'd have all the time in the world to reflect on Cwall's cryptic judgements.

* * *

Foster closed the front door of his apartment building firmly behind him, jiggling the handle to make sure the latch caught the doorframe. The last thing they needed was another homeless man sleeping in the entryway—it made it almost impossible to get to the mailboxes. He straightened his jacket, raked his hands through his carefully tousled hair, and checked his pocket for the package he had almost forgotten to bring.

His fingers brushed the cloth wrapping and he stepped confidently off the cracked front stoop, crossing the yellowing front lawn in a few long strides. He patted the stone columns that capped the old iron fence as he slipped through the gap where the gate used to hang, and a piece of the crumbling brick broke off the left side.

"I should probably fix that," he muttered, tossing it into the grass and making a mental note to pick up some stone adhesive. Their lazy, absentee 'landlord' wasn't going to put in any effort. Jeff was a balding, overweight sleaze who would probably put his back out lifting anything heavier than a slice of pizza. Foster might have forgotten Jeff existed, if it weren't for the way he came hounding everyone once a month to mail his rent checks on time.

"Hey, Foster!" A stout older man bustled out the door, silver handlebar mustache perfectly groomed as always, wearing an outrageous Hawaiian print button down. "When you have time, could you maybe look at my window? It's jammed open and the rain keeps coming in."

Foster offered him a smile, keeping his groans internal. He didn't exactly love that repairs fell on his shoulders, but he couldn't let the residents suffer when he could do something to help. "No problem, Mr. Ryan."

"How many times have I said to call me Carter?"

"Fair enough. I'll take a look once I get home."

"You're a saint, Foster."

The younger man couldn't contain his laugh as he turned away. "Hardly."

Foster whistled to himself as he walked. Sure, he could've done the trip in a fraction of the time if he had made a portal, but some innately human part of him preferred these opportunities to people-watch.

One of his favorite things about where he lived was how little attention people paid to their surroundings. Teenagers moved in small clusters, eyes glued to their phones or chattering away. Young mothers pushed strollers while business professionals wove through with purposeful strides of their clicking heels. Children giggled and yelped as they chased each other across the asphalt, the autumn sun still strong enough that warmth from the pavement radiated through the soles of his converse.

Everyone was intent on getting from one place to another, scurrying around like frantic little mice. It made it so much easier to observe them without being noticed himself. It didn't hurt that he fit into the neighborhood. Secoroya was a city of a thousand cultures—the food, architecture, and languages were never from any one discernable place. Every corner was a new world of color and music and life.

Nobody looked twice in this part of town at a twenty-something brown-skinned man in tattered jeans and a leather jacket. He might as well be a part of the scenery, as much as the bodega he and his neighbors shopped at.

"Hey Mrs. Hem." He waved at the petite Cambodian woman as he passed the laundromat the apartment residents all patronized, and she lifted a hand in return. "How are the boys?"

"Six boys, Foster! And how many here to help mommy with the laundry?" She shook her head, her fists at her hips. "Yeah, none!"

"Tell them to help you bring it all home, or I won't fix the basketball hoop."

Mrs. Hem smiled. "You a good boy, Foster. Remember to come get *bok lahong* when I make it this weekend."

"Definitely; I love that shrimp paste you use." Foster grinned back at her before continuing on his way.

He glanced into shop windows as he passed the deli, the florist and the independent bookstore. He inhaled deeply when he passed the taco truck that was a permanent fixture on the curb. Foster drank in the vibrancy and bustle of the lively street.

Of course, there was another reason he lived in this neighborhood. It just so happened to be the quiet heart of Secoroya's metaphysical scene. That wasn't to say there were a plethora of tarot shops or palmistry and chakra massage parlors; those more commercial scenes were found in the city center, closer to the highway and the sports centers than to Foster's little neighborhood. And most of those—along with the charlatan mediums and "apothecaries"—were nothing but gimmicky money pits.

No, this was the more genuine, protected magical undercurrent in the city. All the major cities had them, some more well-hidden than others, and all with their quirks and differences. There were hints here and there; the florist sold bundles of sage and rosemary along with bouquets and the butcher was happy to offer slightly stranger cuts and organs if you knew how to ask. The small vintage boutique had a special display case of genuine crystals and gemstones sandwiched between racks of old dresses and cabinets of ceramics.

Subtle but definite giveaways for anyone who knew what to look for, even if they couldn't sense the current of magic itself. His destination was a bit more overt—the local Church of the Arcane.

Foster stopped on the sidewalk, surveying the old Gothic façade with a twinge of guilt. The hands that labored over this architecture, the love that went into maintaining the building and keeping the faith alive...and it was shit all over by the world at large.

Religion, as a general rule, was a tricky beast. Countless thousands of people believed in Hellenic Paganism or tithed to the Norse deities. There were pyramid temples to worship Egyptian gods, Muslim mosques, Jewish synagogues, and spiraling towers devoted to Buddhist teachings. And each one of them was considered the sole truth of the universe by its followers. Even Lucio-Arcanism was born of a rift between Christian followers—those who saw Lucifer as the supreme evil, and those who thought him a misunderstood victim.

Here he stood, mere feet from devout believers who worshipped his father, who by extension would worship *him*, and he had the power to prove them right. With a simple gesture he could reveal himself and make centuries of suffering and contempt worth something. He could give these people the proof and validation they had been seeking and praying for all these long eons.

Instead, Foster stuffed his hands back into his pockets and ascended the sweeping stone steps, head ducked against the soft breeze that ruffled his hair. He wasn't trying to be some savior. Anonymity was his friend here, where they all believed him to be just another follower of the faith, and he wasn't even sure he agreed with the teachings of the Church.

He averted his eyes as he passed the statue of his father, rendered with surprising accuracy and care. In a small fit of anger he flicked the statue's foot, sending a hairline crack up its leg. Especially here, his father haunted him. If he didn't have such an important meeting, he would turn and walk back out right now.

In an alcove further down the opposite wall, the statue of Gabriel gazed serenely back at him. He made his way across to it, resting his fingers lightly on the outstretched stone palm and smiling softly as it warmed in response. If there was judgement radiating from his father's icon, the figure of Gabriel only bolstered his sense of confidence and comfort. Gabe always looked out for him. No matter what anyone else thought, Gabe knew who he was and didn't flinch away. He was the only one willing to help Foster save his mother, despite the consequences, and the young prince would be eternally grateful for that.

Foster made his way through the entrance hall lined with the statues of all the faces of his childhood, footsteps echoing slightly on the dark marble floor. He smirked at Remiel's long, intricate braids, and remembered the day she had taken a knife to them in an act of what she proudly declared "rebellious self-actualization".

He remembered Glory shaking her head and leaning down to his level, the soft smell of flowers permeating his senses as she told him sternly, *"Do not listen to her, Foster. There is nothing wrong with a woman embracing softness and beautiful things."* He didn't agree with his father on most things, but the company he kept tended to be wise.

Foster had dutifully filed the information away, and he still believed it to this day. He had seen powerful women in all shapes, sizes, and manner of feminine expression (or lack thereof) and he knew each of them was uniquely strong. Remi herself had knocked him on his ass enough times during his combat training that he knew better than to underestimate a woman. But reminiscing wasn't the motivator for today's visit.

Leaving the entrance hall and stepping into the main room of the cathedral was always a bit of a shock to the system. From the dark exterior and the relatively cloistered entryway, it would reason that the rest of the building would be similarly dark and dim. Instead, visitors to the Church of the Arcane were treated to a surprise upon clearing the foyer: a massive stained glass window dominated the rear wall, soaring from the floor to the high arch of the ceiling lost in shadow above.

It was a beautiful rendering of the story of creation, focused specifically on the creation of Eden. The myriad colors caught and reflected the afternoon light to turn the room into a kaleidoscope of glittering rainbows while the air seemed to hum with energy and warmth, lending a sense of comfort and security to the conversely open space.

Ornately carved dark wenge wood pews arranged in neat double rows bordered an aisle that ran from the entryway to the raised dais on the far wall. Foster's footsteps became muffled as he stepped from the marble onto the long navy runner of the aisle. He retraced a time-worn path up the front, steps he had taken every Saturday night for as long as he could remember.

Stopping at the second pew on the left, he touched two fingers solemnly to his lips and then each of his closed eyelids, then pressed his palm firmly over his heart. Even with his conflicting feelings for his father, his body remembered the movements his mother had lovingly worked into his memory as a child. He could almost hear her voice, whispering the words as she had when she taught him—*speak truth, seek truth, be true.*

"Very convincing for a heretic," a husky voice broke into his reverie.

Foster opened his eyes to cast an annoyed glance down at the man in the pew. He was slender, well-muscled and arguably handsome, with thick black hair and a close-cropped mustache and goatee. His smooth, fawn skin was scandalously exposed by his shirt, unbuttoned halfway down his chest, and his casual suit almost made Foster self-conscious in his tattered jeans and boots.

"That's still up for debate," Foster admitted, and slid into the booth beside his best friend. "So go fuck yourself, Judas."

Judas threw his head back with a sharp guffaw that drew nearby eyes to shower them in chastising glowers. "I'm a pure, celibate angel, I'll have you know."

"You're literally none of those things." Foster rolled his eyes, pulling the hardbound book from the plastic holder attached to the back of the pew in front of them. "Do you know what tonight's lecture is about?"

"Sacrifice," Judas informed him drily. "Maybe I should lead tonight?"

"The Arcanum would choke on his own shock if you tried."

The other man laughed again, albeit more quietly. "Can't go around killing the elderly I suppose."

"You shouldn't really be killing anyone, to be fair."

"Well, we both know that it's not always up to us." There was a taut undertone to his words, and Foster knew better than to press on that bruise. Hell, it was a fact he was coming to terms with firsthand.

"Sometimes we need to define our own path." Foster sighed, unconsciously sliding his hand back into his pocket. Judas followed the movement, dark eyes narrowing as he frowned.

"Fos, come on, you aren't still thinking about—"

"No," Foster lied, returning to paging through the hymnal. "Just disappointed."

Judas examined his expression, which Foster kept carefully neutral as he pretended to be invested in 'Lucifer, Our Broken Sword'. The other man made a sound of derision but pulled out his own book of songs.

"If you say so." He thumbed through the thin pages carefully. "I think we're actually starting with 'Blessed are the Knowing', by the way."

Foster groaned. "Ugh, again?"

"I know."

* * *

The service had been long, as usual, but time seemed to crawl even more slowly with the package resting like a heavy weight against his hip. When the final notes of 'Make Us Like Him' faded away and the congregation began to shuffle slowly to their feet, Foster strained to keep himself from bolting out of the pew.

Old men collected their coats as their wives collected gossip, chattering about lunch plans in the aisle. Foster slipped from his pew and managed not to trip over the small children chasing each other around and under the steadily emptying benches.

"You hungry?" Judas bumped his shoulder lightly as they headed towards the foyer. "There's a new halal place that's supposed to be awesome, just a few blocks towards the college."

"Actually, I'm supposed to see Praeceptor Sceros." Foster frowned. "Rain check though; I've been craving a good gyro."

"Alright, your loss." Judas grinned. "The waitresses are all gorgeous, so it's probably better I don't have your stupidly pretty face to compete with."

Foster laughed. "Shut up, I'm rugged—you're the pretty boy."

"I am." Judas fluttered his thick lashes dramatically, and they both laughed. "Alright, catch you later, Fos."

They clasped hands briefly, fingers locking tightly around each other's forearms before they parted. Judas sauntered out the front doors with one hand in his pocket and the other raised in mock salute.

Foster breathed a sigh of relief when Judas vanished down the steps—he hated lying to his best friend more than anyone else, but it was unavoidable this time. Judas had made it *very* clear that he thought this plan was both reckless and wrong. But Foster couldn't let it go.

"Young Foster," a low, rasping baritone came at his shoulder, and he turned to face the praeceptor. He was still in his ceremonial robes —long layers of charcoal and crimson, threaded with gold embroidery —but he had already draped his stole and belt over his arm. "I believe we have a meeting tonight?"

"Yes, Praeceptor." Foster inclined his head respectfully, and the older man waved him off.

"So formal," he said, smiling. "Come, my boy."

He led the way around the edge of the sanctum, with Foster following dutifully, gripping the bundle of cloth in his pocket like a lifeline. When they stopped before a simple wooden door that flanked the dais, the holy man pulled a key from his robes to open it, then led the way into his office.

Foster closed the door behind them and sank into a wingback chair. The praeceptor carefully folded his stole, placing it neatly into a carved ebony box and laying his rolled belt on top. He slipped off his rings, ruby stones winking in the low light, and set them inside before closing the lid gently. He hummed to himself as he worked, setting the box onto a low shelf and turning to his mirror to begin wiping the black inked sigils from his forearms.

Foster felt like he might combust if he had to wait any longer. Just when the tension in his gut was coiling to snap, the praeceptor smiled benevolently at him and took a seat of his own behind the desk.

"So, tell me, my boy," he said, a bright gleam lit his eyes and brought a touch of youthful excitement to the weathered old face. "How might I serve the Prince of Darkness?"

Chapter Seven

After their walk to the Rift turned into a debate over how best to expedite the soul intake process, Remiel eventually realized Lucifer was stalling. She declared herself the winner and promised to get to work implementing the changes, then shoved Luce through the portal before he could respond.

She leaned against a nearby pillar to ensure he wouldn't turn right back around, then turned to inspect the line of newly arrived souls that was, admittedly, much longer than the lines into Heaven used to be. They *did* need to do something about this, but she had lied when she said it would be now. They had bigger priorities, the first of which included tracking down Mags to get a refresher about what the vision had been *exactly*.

After searching for the smaller woman in her little cabin, the town square, and practically every room in the palace Lucifer called an 'estate', Remi grumbled the entire way to the kitchen, the last place left to check. The room was empty.

Mags was not currently in this dimension.

Remi made her way to the kitchen island and slumped onto one of the stools there. The stone countertop was cool where she laid her head down, soothing the gentle pounding that always seemed to follow most interactions with Luce.

"He better make this shit right," she muttered, glaring at the salt-shaker because it was the closest object in her sightline.

"Did that saltshaker personally offend you, babe, or did Luce piss you off again?" A smooth voice broke the quiet calm of the kitchen, wrapping around her like velvet and making Remi lift her head wearily. She narrowed her eyes at the way he always seemed to read her mind, but maybe it was to be expected after literal centuries together.

The exhausted woman groaned. "If I have to be Luce's mother one more time, I'm gonna strangle him. Or scream."

"Or you could scream *while* you strangle him," the newcomer grinned, stroking his long beard thoughtfully as he leaned against the counter.

Remi eyed it with distaste. "I swear I'm gonna cut that in your sleep, Rag."

"You wouldn't." He looked horrified. His beard was a curly ginger mass that reached down to his collarbones, and it was his pride and joy.

"Wouldn't I?" She grinned wickedly, but it didn't reach her tired eyes.

Rag frowned. "Was it that bad this time?"

"He mentioned Armageddon," she informed him drily. "Oh! And *apparently*, he hasn't spoken to his son in *fifteen years*!"

His brows raised sharply. "I figured it would take him a while to talk to the kid, but I never realized he just...didn't. Can't tell if I'm appalled or impressed at the levels of negligence there."

"Appalled!" she snapped in disbelief. "We're appalled and angry, because that's *bad* parenting."

"To be fair," he mused, "that's probably why we never had kids. I'd be awful at it."

"You'd be great at it," Remi softened, like she only did for her husband. "But neither of us wants kids, and that's fine."

He reached across the counter and tucked a piece of her hair—a curly, frizzy mess now, after drying on its own—behind her ear. The curl popped free immediately. "You're more than enough work for me, babe."

She nuzzled her face into his palm and bit hard on the fleshy pad between his thumb and index finger.

"Rem!" he yelped, yanking his hand away and cradling it to his chest.

She grinned, and this time it was genuine.

"Crazy bitch." He grinned back.

"Crazy about you, baby," she crooned, laughing.

"You guys are so weird," a melodious voice drifted from the doorway, announcing Gloriana's arrival—along with the subtle scent of morning glories that hung around her like a delicate shroud.

Remi and Mags had quizzed her on it multiple times, only for the statuesque blonde to vehemently deny altering her natural scent in any way with perfumes or magic. They unanimously did *not* believe this but eventually stopped asking.

"Weird is better than boring," Rag quipped.

"Is it?" Gloriana wrinkled her nose. "If *my* lover ever bit me..."

"You'd need a lover first, Glory," Remi teased sweetly. "Stop leading all the boys on and find a nice girl to torment."

"Why should I give up one to settle for another?" Gloriana flashed that temptress smile as she sauntered across the room to join them, painted ruby lips pulling up in a slow, sexy smile. "When you have as many admirers as I do, it simply isn't fair to limit myself to a single gender."

"Wicked girl." Remi said with a smirk. "You have to break *all* the hearts?"

"Absolutely all of them," she confirmed, cheeks dimpling. "It's my civic duty."

"Literally," Rag interrupted in his slow drawl, "but we're getting a bit off topic now. Rem, what were you saying about Armageddon?"

Gloriana's face dropped, all the laughter draining away. "How do you know about that?"

Remi eyed her curiously. "Luce mentioned it just now. How do *you* know about it?"

Glory averted her gaze, seeming to shrink into herself a bit. "How could I ever have forgotten?"

Husband and wife exchanged a look, and Remi laid a hand gently on the blonde's hunched shoulder. "I think you better tell us what you know."

With a delicate shudder, Gloriana turned away. "You remember when Foster was born...and Mags had that terrible vision she wouldn't talk about? Well, she eventually did tell me. She *showed* me. And...it's haunted me ever since."

Between frequent pauses bustling around the kitchen digging into various cabinets, she eventually told them how Mags had run off to Heaven when a vision this morning seemed to signal the disaster was imminent.

"She should be returning soon," Gloriana finished, slim hands wrapped tightly around the mug she'd prepared to distract herself. The tea inside was barely touched. "Supposedly, there's something that might be done, but it hinges on Jehovah's approval."

"What could it possibly have to do with *Him*?" Remi snorted.

"Well," Gloriana paused. "To stand a chance, Luce would need more power."

"Surely that has to be a simple problem?" Remi arched a dark brow. "Can't he do any number of rituals to boost his power?"

"I once saw him power up to attempt an especially difficult yoga position," Rag confirmed.

"Those are minor, temporary boosts," Gloriana sighed, beautiful features tight with grim resignation. "The situation is becoming desperate. This isn't some far-off possibility anymore. It's starting now, and Mags thinks we have less than a year before..."

"Before nothing can be done at all," Rag finished glumly. Gloriana said nothing.

Remi fumed. "And what does Mags plan to do, ask Jehovah to loan Luci some power?"

"In a sense, yes."

The three immortals at the counter jumped, turning to the doorway where Mags now stood, looking harried but pleased with herself.

"I didn't speak with Jehovah after all," she continued, and Remi relaxed back into her seat until Mags went on, "I actually just stole the book we needed."

"You *what!*" Out of her seat and across the room in a flash, Remi gripped Mags by both shoulders. "Please, please tell me you're joking, and you didn't *really* steal from the library of the King of Heaven."

"I didn't steal from the library," Mags acquiesced. Remi took a calming breath. "I stole from the *vault*, which just happens to be *in* the library."

Remi dropped her forehead onto Mags's shoulder in defeat. "You are an idiot."

"No," Rag grinned, "she's a *badass*."

"Okay yes," Remi muttered with a sigh, and Mags patted her back gently. "But *also* a reckless idiot! I know you have a self-preservation instinct; you just *suck* at following it."

Mags steered her friend back onto her stool and joining them at the kitchen island. She reached into the bag on her shoulder and drew out an ancient book bound in pale, cracked leather. The title was worn away to a faded imprint, gold leaf having flaked off centuries ago. A metal band wrapped the center of the book, secured with a small but sturdy padlock.

"What is it?" Rag raised his brows, peering at the deceptively plain book. "A book of spells?"

"Essentially," Mags inclined her head, smiling. "Though personally I'd call it a recipe book."

"You really stole from Jehovah." Gloriana looked torn between awe and terror.

"I think it's better than the alternative." Mags frowned. "I am still wary; I'll need to talk to Luce about it. But...I think it's the best option."

"Why?" Remi demanded. "Surely there has to be something, *anything* else."

"Luce has been trying to find another way," the smaller woman agreed. "But I can feel it in my bones, Remi. This is the most powerful, definitive vision I've had in a long time. And without this artifact..."

"Luce won't be strong enough," Rag spoke slowly, realization and horror dawning on him. "Because he hasn't been the same since he gave us such a hefty portion of his power."

The sink faucet released a drip with an unnaturally loud plop.

"I'm sorry," Remi forced cheer into her tone, "are you saying it's *our* fault that Luce can't face this threat?"

"Technically," Mags sighed, seemingly ignorant of the glare Remi leveled at her while she stroked the cover of the grimoire absently. "Since you can't exactly return those powers now, I needed to find an alternative."

They glanced uncomfortably amongst themselves for a moment, all considering the potential for things to go horribly wrong with this plan.

Rag was the one to finally break the silence. "Fuck it," he declared. "If the world is going to shit anyway, we might as well piss off the King of Heaven. Can't get much worse than the end of all existence, right?"

* * *

"This cannot be the right address." Lucifer cringed at the sight of the building before him, slowly scanning from the filthy shingles and clogged gutter, down five stories to the chipped foundation and over-grown shrubbery that seemed torn between wilting into the dirt and consuming the stained brick façade. "It's like a fire hazard and a ruin had a very unfortunate baby."

He pulled the scrap of paper from his pocket and squinted doubt-fully at the lopsided scrawl. Cwall had been adamant this was the place, and he should know, since he was the primary guard assigned to watch the prince.

The paper read '6060 S. Gold Street Apt. E3'. The rusted iron numbers 6060 were affixed to the building door, even if one of the zeroes hung at an odd angle. Luce turned and arched his neck to confirm that the worn sign on the street corner did say Gold and sighed heavily when he saw that it did.

"Well great. That means I have to go *inside*." He shuddered, tucked the paper back into the pocket of his slacks, and reluctantly approached the apartment.

Frustrated, stressed and more than a little nervous, he paced the tiny hallway furiously. Why was he here? He should have called on a

Projector first. Luce almost turned and walked back out. Those little boxes were a wonder, using magic to display images across leagues as if you had no more than a window between viewer and subject. But he sincerely doubted Foster would answer any message from him, and then Luce would only be *more* anxious, wondering and overthinking.

No, it had to be in person. He knew his son deserved that much, even if it made him that much more of a coward to be looking for another option. It certainly didn't help that he was in a decidedly unwelcoming, surprisingly cold place. Luce cast a disparaging eye over the cracked plaster revealed by peeling, dingy wallpaper. The threadbare carpet gave the suggestion of having once been red but was now near black from years of dirty feet and slapdash cleaning. There was a bag of trash near the stairs next to—oh damned souls, was that the carcass of some sort of vermin?

He shuddered and his nose wrinkled, in distaste and in rejection of the faint odor of mildew mingled with heavy spices that intensified as he climbed stairs. He found it hard to believe that his son lived *here*. His son, who at one point refused to leave the house before his hair was carefully styled and his shoes were polished to a shine? Impossible. But if Cwall said this was Foster's home, Lucifer had no reason to doubt him.

He scanned the hallway again as he reached E level, which was at least cleaner than most of the floors he had passed. Maybe he was doubting Cwall just a little. *Enough.* Luce brought himself up short, spinning on his heel to face door E3 head on.

He had passed through a rift to the mortal plane, he had taken a *cab* because he couldn't portal somewhere he hadn't been before, and he had climbed four flights of stairs in designer Italian loafers that would now need to be deep cleaned. It wasn't as if he could simply turn back now. So instead, he took the last few steps and knocked sharply on the door.

A long, long moment stretched after his knock. Only a few minutes. Less than a blip on the timeline of an immortal, but long enough for Luce to reconsider his entire life and all the choices that led him to be here. A baby cried somewhere in the floors below, and Luce thought the child might not have the wrong idea. Standing in this abysmal, filthy hallway, waiting to see if his son would open the door for him, the King of Hell felt very small.

The door swung inward with little ceremony, and Luce was greeted by the sight of a bowed head of brunette waves.

"Finally! I'm starving," the unruly mop of hair rumbled, digging in a dark denim pocket. A wallet was unearthed and popped open, head lifting to lock identical brown eyes with the man at his door. There was a long pause, and Luce drank in his son's face, so familiar and yet so different to the face he remembered. Foster's face twisted in fury, closer to the last time Luce had seen him. "You aren't the pizza guy."

"No," Luce began, then had to clear his throat to regain control of his pitch. "No, I'm certainly not."

"Might as well be, for all I've seen you." A snort. "Actually, I see the pizza guy more."

Luce winced. "I deserved that."

"You deserve a lot more and a lot less, honestly." A disgusted shake of those dark waves. "Why am I wasting time talking to you?"

The door snapped closed.

"Well." Luce forced a smile. "That went well."

"Go away," Foster called through the door. "You're ruining my appetite."

Two could play at this game. Luce eyed the carpet with distaste but swallowed his pride and sunk down to lean against the battered door, long legs stretched across and almost touching the opposite wall. "Who's to say I'm not going to wait here and steal your pizza?"

"I'll order another one, you petty fuck."

"Maybe I'll cancel your credit cards."

"You really are clueless if you haven't noticed I'm not even using the old accounts anymore."

Luce blinked. He wasn't?

"Hard to believe, I'm sure, but not everyone needs you to get by in life," Foster said with a snort. "You're not that fuckin' special."

Okay, he deserved that too. Truthfully, Luce couldn't say he disagreed with his son. He had struggled to rebuild his self-confidence more than once in his long life, and he was currently at a rather low point. Especially with the ridiculousness currently going on. He was sitting on a filthy floor pleading for his own son's attention.

"I may not be special, but at least I'm here. Can we please talk without a door between us?"

"No. Get lost."

"Foster, please. I'm your *father!*"

"You never seemed to care about that before!" Foster pounded the door with his fist. "Where was that paternal instinct when I needed your love and support?"

"I have always loved you," Luce snapped defensively. "*Always*, even when you were rebellious and hateful and all you cared about was your mother, I loved you! I still love you now, even with what you're doing!"

A click and a rush of air and then suddenly the door was gone. Luce fell backwards, displeased to note that the ceiling was as dingy and stained as the carpet. His son's apartment so far wasn't much cleaner than the rest of the building. The smell of old sweat assaulted his nose and Luce hauled himself up, gagging.

"Do you never clean your carpets?"

Foster just stared at him, eyes hard and expression frozen in an aggravated snarl. Luce remembered the methodical way he'd acted in Mags's latest vision, contrasted with the outright evil of the first vision, and found himself subconsciously checking his son's rough hands for blood.

Luce cleared his throat awkwardly, still sprawled half across the threshold but somehow hesitant to rise to his feet without permission. Incredible! Permission, to get up off the floor! Yet he felt inside that maybe abiding this situation was the least he could do to begin to atone.

"What I'm doing," Foster repeated Luce's words in a slow drawl. "What exactly is it you think I'm *doing?*"

Luce said nothing, cursing himself for blundering into this conversation and unsure of how he could even begin to answer that without further enraging his son.

"Because," Foster continued, tone slowly heating with barely restrained anger, "it must be a pretty significant event to drag your sorry ass out of the dark to find me after all this time."

"I didn't need to find you," Luce murmured, sitting up and leaning into the doorframe. "I always had someone looking after you."

"Yeah? What, you mean Cwall?" Foster sneered. "Not quite the same as being here yourself, is it? Send someone to do your job for you, and you wash your hands of me?"

"Cwall understood that we both needed space; he was glad to do it."

"I didn't need *space!* I needed my *dad!*"

What was he even supposed to say to that? It was undeniable that he had neglected his son.

"Oh Foster," he murmured sadly, and let his head *thunk* back against the doorframe. "I have failed you."

His son's expression was murderous. "It took you a trip topside to realize that? I could've saved you the effort and told you years ago!"

"I am so sorry—"

"No! No, you don't get to ignore me for this fucking long, leave me alone when I needed someone most, and then just show up to have a pity party on my doorstep!" Foster panted, fists clenching and unclenching at his sides. "You don't just get to come here like nothing happened and expect to slide back into being my dad like it's some job you get to come and go from!"

"Foster, I—"

The unchecked fury and grief in Foster's expression ripped into Luce's chest and gripped his heart like a vice. "I was *grieving!* I never expected you to fucking disappear!"

His son was in so much pain, and Lucifer felt the burden of the guilt. *He* did this, not only by neglecting the boy, but by keeping pieces of the truth from him. There was so much Foster didn't know about what had happened back then, and Luce wasn't sure he knew how to broach that topic now. This moment felt like the worst time to try, but he couldn't be sure Foster would give him another chance.

"I never meant to hurt you," Luce's voice was hoarse and tight. "I've made such a mess of things between us. I will always regret how events unfolded that day."

"Regret?" Foster spat. "You were *glad* to be rid of her, and I was too much of a reminder of your mistakes. My pain was too uncomfortable for you, so you *ran away* instead of being there for me."

"Don't you dare pretend I didn't love your mother!" Luce snapped. "I couldn't give you what you were asking for—no matter how much we both wanted it—and I saw how angry it made you. I thought you needed space to come to terms with it; that you would come home when you were ready."

He had been waiting to have that difficult conversation with his son when Foster returned. When he hadn't, Luce had assumed he wasn't ready. Now he was seeing the error of his assumptions firsthand.

"Fifteen years, and not a single sign you ever even *thought* of me. Why the fuck would I think you wanted me at home?"

Luce felt like he'd been slapped. "Because—because you're my *son!* I thought it was a given that you were always welcome!"

"That's the problem, *Dad*," his tone made a mockery of the title. "*You* thought, *you* felt, but did you ever *talk to me*?! Everything is always about *your* perspective, your feelings and opinions. You don't ever *communicate!*"

The air seemed to ring in the abrupt silence after his outburst. Luce burned with shame at the truth in those words—he'd taken so much for granted, acted out of fear and frustration. He had failed so *badly* as a parent. But that didn't change the reason he was here. No one would be nominating Luce for Father of the Year, but Foster had made the choices he had with no input—for better or worse—from his father.

"You want to talk about communication?" Luce murmured darkly. "You can't throw this all on me, son of mine. I may have been distant, but communication is a two-way street."

"Don't be an idiot," Foster snarled.

"What? You can criticize me for not making an effort, but I'm supposed to be a mind reader? I could be. Would you like that? Shall I slip into your mind and see exactly what you want from me?"

His son's voice was as icy as his glare as he hissed, "I would never forgive you."

"Then make up your mind! You made it *very clear* that the last thing you wanted was my presence. What was it that you said? Ah yes, I believe the exact quote was, 'If you ever gave a shit, just do me one favor and stay the hell away from me. You left me with Mom, and you can leave me alone forever'. Yes?"

Lucifer slapped the carpet, then winced slightly at both the diminished effect and the oily feel of the fabric. "We can agree that I was distant. But can you really say we had a bond even before we fought that day? Your mother insisted on raising you among mortals, and as a result, I barely know my own son!"

He didn't even see Foster move. One moment he was sitting in the doorway, furious and sad and desperate to get through to his son, and the next, he was flat on his back in the hallway. His jaw throbbed, sparks popping before his eyes, and in a strange way he was almost proud of the clean, powerful strike. He started to sit up, dazed, but there was a heavy weight pressing into his chest.

Foster loomed above him, shaking out his fist and glaring down at his father with pure rage. His brown eyes seemed lit with hellfire, and for a moment Luce felt a tremor of something close to despair. This wasn't the boy he had loved and raised; this was the young man he had neglected. This wasn't his doing, but it was still his fault.

"You have some *fucking nerve*," Foster snarled, grinding the heel of his shoe into Luce's ribs. "All this time, and you show up here and decide the best thing to do is *lecture me* and then say it's *my fault* you're a shit father. Fucking brilliant! Now I remember why I never missed you!"

"Foster, I –" he started but broke off with a wheeze as the boot pressed harder.

"*No.*" Yes, that was hellfire in his son's eyes, the force of his rage bringing forth literal flames. "No, that's *enough*. I'm done listening to you, because you clearly don't understand what an apology is supposed to be, and it still wouldn't be enough to make up for everything you put me through. All the years, all the time—even if you fucking *groveled*, I wouldn't forgive you."

A stray ember drifted down to settle on Luce's cheek, and the sting was nothing compared to what he deserved.

"I don't blame you," he nearly whispered. More scattered embers, each one a burning kiss where they landed and sizzled on tanned skin. He realized with a jolt that these were *tears*. Foster was *crying*. Luce hadn't seen his son cry since...since Angela died.

"You're right, Foster. I was a coward, and as your father I shouldn't have let things get this bad. I should never have blamed you for this distance between us. But why does that have to mean that we can't make the effort now? Can't we admit our mistakes and start over?"

The entire building seemed to be holding its breath in anticipation of Foster's response. Even the baby had gone quiet at some point during their argument, or perhaps because of it. The silence stretched between them until Lucifer began to wonder if his son simply wouldn't reply. Foster's eyes burned, his hardened expression betraying nothing.

Finally, he scoffed. "You're an idiot."

Luce furrowed his brow in confusion. That was *a* reaction, at least, but it didn't bode well for making amends.

"Did you not hear me?" He laughed, a hollow dark sound that made Luce shiver. "What part of 'even if you groveled' was confusing?"

He lifted his foot and Luce sucked down a deep breath, muscles twinging against what was definitely a cracked rib. Foster stepped back into his doorway, shaking his head. "You're pathetic. I can't believe you're my father sometimes. Do us both a favor and go back to pretending I don't exist."

That stung. "Foster, please. We need to talk properly. There are things you need to know."

"No." His son shook his head, those glowing eyes the only thing Luce could focus on as Foster retreated into the gloom of his apartment. "No, I'm done talking to you. Whatever you came here for, whatever dragged you to my door, it can drag you right back out. Get lost, and if I never see you again, I don't care."

He closed the door with a snap that reverberated off the dingy plaster walls, which were suddenly making Luce feel claustrophobic. He scrambled to his feet and nearly ran headfirst into the pizza boy, barely more than sixteen, frozen on the stairs. They stared at each other for a moment, the teenager blinking owlishly at the shoe print on Luce's white shirt while the King of Hell dusted himself off and assessed how much the kid had seen.

Finally, the kid croaked, "Please tell me that wasn't E3?"

Luce smiled. "It was. How much is the pizza? I'll take care of it for you."

"Thirty-six dollars," the boy blurted, looking relieved, "and eighteen cents, technically."

Luce grinned, reaching into his billfold and pulling out a fifty-dollar bill. "Keep the change."

He pressed it into the kid's palm as he passed, going down the stairs, plucking both boxes from his hands. So that hadn't gone well at all. His son clearly hated him, and Luce couldn't blame him. He'd have to work harder to try and mend this relationship, and hopefully it would be enough to prevent Armageddon.

In the meantime, now he had pizza. Maybe it was petty, but it *did* make him feel better. He summoned up another Rift, vanishing without a trace before the pizza boy had even cleared the first landing behind him.

Chapter Eight

Inside his blessedly father-free apartment, Foster sank to the floor, resting his back against the door and his head in his palms. He could hear said father speaking to someone in the hallway and had a sneaking suspicion the bastard was making good on his threat to steal the pizzas.

*How damned childish...*He groaned, scrubbing his hands over his face. Why the hell was that ass turning up at his door, *now* of all times?

The voices had stopped, so it was probably safe to stand up without his dad trying to break the door down. Stupid pushy asshole with his stupid self-pitying *excuses*. He stomped down the hall, muttering under his breath, and kicked open the door to his bedroom so hard that it clattered against the wall.

The small act of aggression helped slightly, but it wasn't enough. A mix of emotions swirled in his chest, building to a breaking point, until his cool façade snapped. Foster screamed, bringing his fist against the wall over and over as the primal sound rose to a furious bellow. It rang through the room, shaking the walls and rippling out in a wave of pain and frustration, and continued until his throat was raw and his knuckles were a bloodied mess.

His breath came in sharp pants and his injured hand twitched as he stood, trembling, and tried to calm down. As the echoes of his rage faded away, he became aware of a panicked thumping under his feet and the muffled sound of agitated Spanish from the floor below.

"*¡...vas a destruir todo este lugar!*" Señora Delgado had little patience for nonsense, and Foster wasn't surprised in the slightest that she was bold enough to confront him. He had seen the five-foot-nothing grandmother chase down many a delivery driver with whichever package they had haphazardly tossed on her doorstep, just to ream them out for being lazy. She continued her tirade in a frustrated mutter, but his enhanced hearing picked up her ranting easily. "*Estúpido idiota sin vergüenza. No sé qué está pensando. Vamos a morir porque este mojón no se puede controlar...*"

"*¡Ay, bruja!*" he shouted back, stomping his foot after every whack from her trusty Swiffer. "*¡Calmase!*"

Her pounding ceased, but he could still hear her cursing him out as he slumped into his armchair with a heavy sigh. The old lady was testy and judgmental, but her *pastelitos* were worth the stink eye, even if she did call him *Diablito*. He wondered sometimes if she saw more than he realized. The more likely possibility was the simple fact that he wore eyeliner and a fair bit of leather. It probably didn't help that he was prone to burning unusual spell components and bellowing like an enraged warthog when he was upset.

He glanced at his battered knuckles and was pleased to see they were already knitting back together. A quick assessment of the wall revealed that it wasn't faring quite as well. He grumbled a bit but decided to put off fixing it until after his call. He dug in his pocket for his projector cube, tossing it onto his bedside table. It landed beside a worn, vintage photo in a silver frame.

The sepia-toned image couldn't show you the young woman's caramel skin or the bronzed gold of her braid. It didn't tell you that she was wearing her favorite dress in her favorite color, deep midnight blue. But it captured the demure tilt of her head, in clear contrast to her mischievous smile, and the relaxed, open stance as she leaned against a doorframe.

Foster frowned, feeling a twinge of guilt over his outburst, as if she was here reprimanding him for it. Clearing his throat, he made a complex movement with his hands and enunciated, "Cube—Connect to Gabriel."

A low humming sounded from the box, and a beam of light spread from the top to form a rough square. The dim light brightened as a man's head and shoulders moved into the cube's range of view.

"Foster," Gabe was smiling, but it didn't quite reach his sapphire eyes and there was something guarded in his tone. "I didn't expect to hear from you today. What a…coincidence."

"You're acting weird," Foster informed him bluntly. "Has your day been as shit as mine?"

"Oh, I suppose you could say that." Gabe snorted and took a drink from a crystal goblet of red wine. "I saw darling Auntie Maggie today, and *apparently*, you're plotting the end of the world, did you know? Can't believe you didn't tell me."

Foster ignored his sarcasm in favor of groaning into his palms. "Now it all makes sense."

"What makes sense?" Gabe sipped leisurely at his wine.

"My 'father' was at my door just now."

The image was lost in a spray of red liquid. Gabe coughed, sputtering in the background, and wiped his mouth on a pale handkerchief. "Sorry, *what*?"

"Oh yeah, I had a similar reaction."

"The nerve! To show up when it suits him after abandoning and neglecting you? I hope you punched him!"

"I did." Foster frowned. "I should've done it twice."

"Oh." Gabe paused, momentarily stunned into silence. "Well, good!"

Foster picked at his knuckles where they were scabbing and sealing back into smooth flesh. "Why does everyone think I've been plotting something evil? Do they know about—"

"We've discussed this, Foster," Gabe cut him off with a sigh. "The spell to bring your mother back isn't one that's considered acceptable. Whether they know about the child or not, they would not approve."

Foster swallowed roughly, picturing the gentle little girl who lived in A2. Piper, who had smiled when she saw him and took great pride in modeling all her headscarves for his approval. He remembered her mother's exhausted face and glazed eyes when he had approached her to ask how the latest oncology appointment had gone. The sound of her quiet sobs still haunted his dreams.

"But from a couple deaths to the end of the world?! That seems like a bit of a leap, even for my dad."

Gabe looked away, but not before Foster caught his pained expression. "Eden was supposed to be a paradise, a beautiful piece of Heaven for the mortals. But after Lucifer defiled everything, his brother became even stricter and harsher. Any piece of magic that was even the slightest bit controversial was outlawed. And this one requires *death* energy."

"So even though the killing might be merciful…"

"It's still illegal." Gabe finished, nodding somberly. "And for those who were burned by your father, well… It's just a slippery slope in their eyes before—"

"Before I do something even worse," the younger man finished glumly.

"I'm sorry, Foster," Gabe reached out, as if to put a consoling hand on his shoulder, then drew back when he remembered they were realms apart. "Maybe I should come to see you? We could grab a drink, talk about it?"

"No." Foster rose, anger and frustration making him restless. "I'm not some little boy anymore. I never had a father who gave a shit, and I know you've tried to be there for me, but you aren't my father either."

Gabe had looked poised to interrupt but deflated at Foster's words. "I'm sorry I couldn't be a father to you, Foster. I'm sorry you had the one you did."

Foster scoffed. "So am I. His actions have tainted me since I was born."

"You're your own man, Foster. His reputation might shadow you, but *your* actions will define you, not his."

"If I bring my mother back—no, *when* I bring my mother back, everyone will see that this magic can be used for good. They won't fear it anymore, and they'll see I'm nothing like that spineless coward."

"I have always believed in you, Foster," Gabe swore. "Have you been searching like I told you, for the next conduit? Have you found a suitable candidate?"

"It would be a lot easier if you'd be less vague about it," Foster grumbled. "All you've told me is that they need to be 'wise and experienced'. Experienced in *what?*"

"Well," Gabe shrugged, "it could be anything, I suppose."

"The first time you flat out told me a child was the only sensible choice, because we needed purity and light and blah blah blah. Now it's just 'someone wise', which is not helpful."

"You seem frustrated," Gabe mused, sipping from his freshly refilled goblet. "We can always stop the rituals, let things cool off, give you time to find a conduit. I'd completely understand."

"No." Foster steeled himself. "If they're concerned enough to send my dad to harass me, they'll only keep getting in the way. We have to keep moving forward, I'll figure it out."

"But if it's too much—"

"I need to do this." Foster pounded his palm with his fist. "My mother is the one person who loved me unconditionally. She was beautiful and kind and she loved the entire world. She immediately befriended anyone she met. If my father showing up here proved anything, it's that I will never have someone in my life love me the way my mother did."

Gabe hummed softly. "I can appreciate that…I met your mother only once, and she was kinder to me than anyone else I have ever known."

"She's a beautiful soul, and I will find a way to do whatever it takes to return her to where she belongs—with me. And I'll never let anyone take her from me again."

"You know, kid," Gabe said with a smile, "I really believe that."

"This is an unforgivable betrayal," Luce declared somberly, gripping the edge of the counter until his fingertips went white.

"*Unforgivable,*" Remi agreed vehemently, slamming a balled-up fist onto the black marble.

Mags chewed her lip, averting her gaze. "That's a little extreme. It's not like there's no coming back from this."

"You're all being ridiculous." Rag laughed, reaching into the pizza box and grabbing a slice. "It's just pineapple."

"But it's on *pizza*!" Remi wailed, both hands fisted in her short hair.

Luce closed the box decisively and reached for the second, only to freeze as soon as he lifted the lid. "Unbelievable."

"What?" Mags peeked over. "What's wrong with that one?"

Luce ripped his horrified stare away from the tainted pizza. "Mushrooms," he finally forced out in a dazed whisper, "and *anchovies...*"

Remi wailed again, and even Glory made a strangled sound, looking repulsed.

Rag laughed so hard he snorted. "Oh man, I'm sorry, but this is so damn funny for me."

"Because you're a living garbage disposal who will eat *anything*," Remi snarked. "But some of us have taste buds and *morals*."

"This is true," he conceded with a dip of his copper head, top knot bobbing. "I am an immoral trashcan."

Mags giggled, earning a betrayed look from Remi.

"Don't encourage him, Mags," she pleaded. "He's beyond hope, but we can't afford to lose you too."

"Beyond hope?" Rag grinned, reaching out to grab Remi by her slim hips and drag her onto his lap. "Baby, I've been hopeless since I laid eyes on you."

Glory made a gagging motion as Remi sank against her husband with a soft look, and Mags laughed again. Luce drank in the scene like a man dying of thirst. These were his people, his family, and there was a strong possibility that these moments of peace and normalcy would soon be few and far between. Everything was such a mess, his son hated him, all their lives were spiraling out of control, and it was all his fault. He sighed deeply, and Rag laid a hand on his forearm.

"You're going to break the counter again, Luce," he murmured, those deep grey eyes burning into his soul and making Luce long for another steel gaze. How long had it been since he had last been face to face with Michael? *Entirely too long,* a small voice inside him whispered. *And isn't this the perfect excuse to seek him out?*

He squashed the idea. Now was not the time to open *that* can of snakes. He released the counter he'd been unconsciously gripping tighter and tighter, and narrowed his eyes at the hairline fissure that now marred the surface.

"Now look what I've gone and done," he muttered, the tiny crevasse in the surface seeming to mock him and his utter failure to resolve this mess. "Another thing I've broken because I didn't pay attention."

Remi hopped from Rag's lap and jabbed a finger in his direction. "Oh no you don't!"

Luce looked at her blankly.

"You're not about to sink into a funk," she ordered, and Rag immediately reached for his wife to drag her back into his lap. Remi dodged him and advanced on Luce with a look that clearly threatened bodily harm.

He backed up until she had him trapped against the wall, and she stabbed his shoulder with her nail. "You are a moody, emotional brat. We all know you're prone to these sulky moments, where you lock yourself away and come out decades later with some new hobby and a new haircut and all is well."

He gaped, mouth opening and closing with no sound coming out, like some sort of startled fish. Remi continued, relentless and indifferent to his dismay.

"We do not have *time* for that, Luci. We don't have time to sit and wait for you to deal with your feelings, because this is no longer about you. Yes, you fucked up! You have a *lot* to make up for. But do it by being involved, *not* by shutting down like you always do."

Luce shoved her away so hard, Remi's back hit the counter. A look of shock flitted across her face, and Remiel hissed and prepared to rush back at him, angling to rake her nails down his face. She never even got close.

It took half a thought—barely a whisper of effort—and Luce sent her flying back again, up and over the counter, into the opposite wall. She thrashed and screamed at him for a moment, tugging against invisible ropes that pinned her to the plaster, and then went deadly still.

"You let me down *right now*, Lucifer," her voice was hard and cool, a shard of ice that pierced the sudden silence of the room. "You can't just—"

"Shut up." Luce didn't raise his voice, didn't need to. Pure power dripped from each word, from his slightly spread stance, from the soft golden glow in his dark eyes. A hush spread across the room to witness the display. It wasn't often that Luce lost his temper with any of them, and Remi was the only one hotheaded enough to provoke him to it.

"Luce," Mags placed a hand on his shoulder, only to be shrugged off.

"No," he commanded, "stay out of this, Mags."

She reluctantly obeyed, but exchanged a concerned glance with Rag, who just clenched his jaw and shook his head. The furious expression Remi wore promised no forgiveness for anyone who interfered.

Mags slumped back onto her barstool. These two stubborn idiots were going to destroy the kitchen again. "Please," she sighed, knowing full well that they were going to ignore her, "no permanent damage. I was planning on making a lasagna later."

"You feel like you're entitled to speak to me that way?" Luce advanced on Remi slowly, golden sparks trailing from his eyes, a dark aura faintly shimmering over his form. "Just because you're my friend, because I recognize your anger and allow your outbursts, you can kick me when I'm down and treat me like a child? I am *ancient*, Remiel. I was ancient before you existed. I have seen the making of worlds."

"Yeah, and you're real fun at parties," she sneered. "Tell me something I don't know. Just because you don't want to hear something doesn't mean I'm going to bite my tongue."

"It's about *respect*, Remiel!" A wave of power swept out, pressing her harder into the wall. "It's about tact and knowing when and where to speak on something."

She grit her teeth against the strain. "This doesn't feel like respect."

"Because it's not," he snapped. "If you don't give it, neither do I. You toed the line when you compared me to my brother earlier, and now you've jumped that line into a pot of boiling water. I am *not* like my brother, but I *am* equivalent in power."

He abruptly released her, and Remi dropped to a crouch, glowering at him.

"Yes, I know your power," she said, cold and calm. "I happen to have a portion of it, if you recall."

Her eyes grew bright, a ruby cast overtaking her dark irises. For the second time today, red markings spread across her pale skin like spilled ink—a thick band across her eyes and the bridge of her nose, rough streaks from temples to jaw. The war paint of Wrath.

Lucifer hissed, a golden glow coming to his palms as he moved into a defensive stance. "Again? You must be joking."

"I have no room for humor in this fury," she spoke low, her voice husky with rage. "I'm tired of your 'woe is me' bullshit. You are not the only one who has lost or suffered, and you will not be the last."

"Silence!" Lucifer roared, and he lunged.

Remiel dodged his reach, focusing on her anger and frustration, and using it to form a weapon. A glowing red light grew between her palms as she circled Lucifer, who kept his furious gaze trained on her and matched her step for step. The light spread, wrapping around her hands and taking the shape of a menacing pair of brass knuckles, spikes jutting from them as she clenched her fists.

"You plan to fight me, truly?"

Remi sneered. "You're overdue for an ass-kicking."

He laughed hollowly and echoed her words from that morning. "You can try."

Remi sprung forward without warning, bringing her fist up to catch Luce under the jaw while he was off his guard. He reeled back a step, then caught himself against the counter.

"I'll succeed," Remi said, eyes flashing.

"No," Luce growled. "You will not."

He brought his hands up, cupping her jaw like he might a lover, and his eyes and hands radiated golden light. He didn't squeeze or make any movement, but Remiel gasped, sucking in gulps of air like she was drowning. The war paint faded from her pale skin. Her glowing weapons vanished in a puff of smoke. Luce released her and let her sink to the floor, where she curled over herself and struggled to regain her breath.

To Remi's credit, she didn't tremble or cry or even speak a single word. Luce turned his back on her, closing his eyes tightly and forcing the power to drain away. The golden aura faded to a slight shimmer before vanishing entirely, and when he opened his eyes, they had returned to their normal brown.

"Why do you push me like this, Remiel?" he sounded almost as old as he was, and the air seemed to hang on his shoulders with a tangible weight.

"Because someone needs to," she said, surprisingly calm. Rag reached out a broad hand, and she slipped her smaller one into it, letting him lift her back onto her stool. "Someone has to be honest with you, and I can take the fallout, so I do."

"You have no right to challenge me whenever my moods displease you."

"Sometimes you need to face reality, Luci."

An emotion somewhere between rage and disappointment glinted in his eyes.

"I am well aware of reality, Remiel." He flexed his hands and curled them into fists, fighting the urge to lash out at something. "For this second infraction in a single day, *your* reality for the next month will be to take all of Camiel's shifts at soul reception, in addition to your own."

He spun on his heel and stormed out of the room without looking back, leaving a heavy silence in his wake.

Remi groaned, resting her head on the countertop. "I am so fucked."

"You're lucky that's your only punishment," Mags said, frowning at the cracks in the island. "He's not in the best mental state right now; he could have killed you."

"The Deadly Sins don't break so easily," Remi muttered darkly. "We earned that title for a reason, you know."

"We can't afford for him to go AWOL right now." Rag laid a hand on Remi's back, giving Mags a pleading look. "Surely you understand that."

"Try to look at it from his perspective," Mags countered, worrying her lip with her teeth. "He just learned that his son is trying to *end the world*. There's a possibility here that we won't be able to sway him from that path."

"And then we'll have to kill him," Rag surmised bluntly, expression falling.

"Rag!" Glory looked scandalized.

He shrugged. "It's the truth. We all need to wrap our minds around the possibility, because this isn't the little boy you sang to sleep, Glory. This isn't the kid who baked cookies with Mags."

"Shut up," Remi groaned again. "I hate that you're right; shut the hell up."

Glory wrapped her arms around herself, as if to ward off the idea. "No, he *is* right. We need to consider all the outcomes."

"I refuse," Mags said quietly, then pushed back her seat. "I will not accept *that* until we've exhausted all other options."

"The Armor," Glory sighed.

"Yes," Mags laid her hand on the ancient book, stroking the space where there had once been a title. "I'm going to talk to Luce about it."

"And hopefully drag him out of whatever hole he's crawled into," Remi muttered.

"Knock it off," Rag cuffed her on the ear. "You're just mad because you didn't get as many hits in this time."

"Whatever." She buried her head in her arms.

Mags smiled fondly. "Don't worry, I'll tell him you still love him."

"I do not love him," the muffled retort was weak at best.

"Sure sweetie," Glory patted her shoulder gently. "We all definitely believe you."

"Fuck off," Remi reached out without lifting her head, groping along the table to grasp the first item her fingers found—the salt-shaker, which she blindly chucked towards the blonde. It flew wide, missing by a mile and landing with a clatter in the corner.

"On that note..." Tucking the book into the cradle of her arms,

Mags swept out of the kitchen in the direction of Luce's suite, leaving the others bickering softly behind her.

* * *

The home Luce had given Mags was more than generous. She had a spacious, open plan bedroom and living space. The bathroom's sunken tub could fit three people at once. There was a full, state-of-the-art kitchen with a fully stocked pantry, and a lounge to entertain guests. She was more than happy there and would never have thought to complain about the space.

But Lucifer's wing of his estate made her cottage look like a broom cupboard. On her visits here through the years, Mags had discovered a private cinema, a bathroom with a tub the size of a small swimming pool, an art studio, a gaming lounge, his own private kitchen, a sauna, several closets stuffed with forgotten projects, endless rooms of discarded clothing from eras past, a *wine cellar*, and of course, his bedroom. It was to the bedroom that she headed now, knowing exactly where she could find Luce when he was in a mood like this.

She slipped through the doorway into the silent darkness, knocking lightly on the doorframe as she entered. Even with all the lights off, she knew the path to the massive bed, swathed in its canopies of burgundy velvet. Many hours had been spent in this room, baring their souls until their voices were hoarse from tears and talking.

There was a reason Luce was her closest friend, and it was because they knew all of each other's secrets. This chamber was for long, whispered conversations and drunken confessions; for comforting hugs and gentle murmurs of reassurance whenever their tattered hearts got too ragged and broken to bury the pain.

"Lucifer," she laid her hand on the vaguely devil-shaped pile of blankets as she sunk onto the edge of the plush mattress.

"No," the burrito nest answered, and she smiled fondly.

"Uncover your face, please."

"Also no."

She discarded the gospel on the bedside table so she could lay

96

down beside the bundle of fabric. "Well come here, then." She hugged him tightly to her and felt him relax just a bit. "Tell me what you're feeling."

"Horrified," he admitted.

"Okay," Mags ran a soothing hand up and down his spine. "I can understand that."

"We have no real choice here." Luce curled tighter into her side. "I couldn't turn up anything else that would restore my power, short of...severing them. I can't do that."

"I know," she sighed. "But I did get what we needed, when I went up..."

A pause, and then the rustle of blankets. Luce's suspiciously narrowed eyes appeared in the gap. "What are you trying to say, Mary?"

"I'm saying that when I went to Heaven...I collected the Gospel of Peace."

"And my brother just handed it over to you? He saw our side of things?" He sounded understandably dubious, and his eyes narrowed further when she hesitated over her answer. "I know you didn't risk your life like a fool over this, Mary. Regardless of my brother's wrath, the wards on the book—"

"Um...not exactly. The book wasn't as heavily guarded as you were led to believe." She swallowed around a lump forming in her throat. "It was stored in the Vault of Relics."

"Mags, no." He struggled out of her grip and tossed off his blankets, sitting up and looming over her. "Please tell me you didn't."

"Okay, I didn't." She looked pointedly at anything other than his face.

"Don't lie to me," he deadpanned.

"Well, I can't do both," she protested.

He groaned, falling onto his back dramatically, and cut his eyes to the side to stare judgmentally at her. "Why are you like this?"

She snorted. "It's not like you could go do it."

"This is fair."

They laid in companionable misery for a moment, contemplating the turn their lives had taken and the choices they had made—and the harder ones soon to come.

Luce broke the silence, reaching out a hand to enfold her smaller one. "Do you think I was wrong, to stay away from him?"

Her heart broke at the doubt and regret in his tone. "You did what you thought was best. That's all any of us can ever really do. Our best."

"But do you think I was right or wrong? Look at Eden, or what happened to my wife. Look what's happening to Foster. The common thread is my influence. Am I just inherently evil? Destined to destroy everything I try to build?"

"I have never thought that about you, even once."

The silence settled back over them, and Mags rubbed her thumb in reassuring circles on the back of his palm. Lucifer closed his eyes and carefully locked away the doubt and regret. He could muse on the past once the future was secured.

"How can we be considering this?"

"It's kind of our only viable option." The tremor in her tone betrayed the anxiety hiding behind her casual words.

"Considering I'm not likely to be ready anytime soon, we might as well get the ball rolling. Tomorrow, I suppose, since I'll have to recall Camiel and the boys from the field. Then we can all sit down and discuss it."

She squeezed his hand wordlessly.

"Besides," Luce said with a weak grin, "you've already committed treason; it would be a shame to make it all for nothing."

Chapter Nine

Christos strolled down the hall, hoping he was projecting a casual air. The last thing he needed right now was undue attention. He whistled softly to himself, hands tucked into his pockets and sandals clopping lightly on the marble, inconspicuously casting his gaze along each corridor he passed. He had a sinking feeling about the conversation he'd had with Mags the day before, a persistent nagging in the back of his mind that he needed to appease before it drove him mad.

His girlfriend was many things: sweet, strong, beautiful...but she was also clever and secretive. He loved Mags, and he could hardly begrudge her for how her past had shaped her. Becoming crafty and adaptive had helped her survive her horrible situation. Christos only wished at times like this that she didn't feel the need to use those skills on him.

He reached the end of the hall and laid a calloused hand on the ornate double doors, hesitating. The rich cherry wood was sturdy and warm-hued, carved with an intricate depiction of the Tree of Knowledge. His lip quirked up at the irony and Christos shook out his mane of curls, trying to clear his thoughts. A hard shove and the door swung inward to reveal the library. A high, arched ceiling with massive skylights sent warm sunbeams cascading down on countless rows of towering stacks packed with books.

The smell of old parchment wafted over him, and Christos couldn't help but breathe deeply, enjoying the calm that it brought. He'd spent many hours at a desk in this room, studying the ancient texts and preparing for his 'future' when he'd succeed his father. As if he could imagine fulfilling that role. It would require his father to relinquish the throne first, something Christos knew he would never do of his own will. His father would die before giving up his reign.

A sharp yipping greeted him as he slipped inside, and the Prince smiled at the gargoyle lounging on a cushion beside the door, wings spread behind him like a blanket and rough tongue lolling out. Gently shutting out the world at his back, Christos knelt down to pat the creature on its stony head. The little creatures were generally sweet-tempered, kept by many angels as pets for their companionship and usefulness, though some had been known to accompany their masters even into battle.

This gargoyle in particular was Raphael's pet, Titanus, and he prided himself on guarding the library—even if that simply meant greeting and therefore announcing everyone who entered, now that he was getting on in years. Christos snapped his fingers to conjure a treat for the gargoyle, patting him on the head once more to rise and make a beeline for his favorite librarian.

"Raphael," he announced his presence to avoid startling the distracted scholar, but it was as if he hadn't even spoken. Christos sighed and approached the desk carefully, stopping less than a foot from his former tutor.

"Raphael," he repeated calmly, and only then did that bowed head snap up, alarm clear in those wide green eyes.

"Christos!" His pen skittered across this page, leaving a dark streak over the meticulously penned notes. He brushed his bangs from his eyes, leaving a smudge of ink on his cheek.

Christos arched a brow. "Is everything alright?"

"Yes, yes, of course!" Raphael smiled, waving off the concern. "You have a bad habit of sneaking up on people."

"Not quite," the prince grinned. "Some of us are just more oblivious to the world."

"Oh, come now," Raphael chucked with a rueful grin. "You can't blame an old man for being a bit scattered."

"Old man!" Christos exclaimed. "You're barely four thousand!"

"Compared to a young thing like you, we're all just dirt walking around." Raphael closed his book and stood, coming around the desk to greet him with an embrace. "What brings you into my domain?"

"Only visiting," Christos said lightly. Raphael fixed him with a shrewd look.

"Is that all?" he mused. "You aren't here to look at the vault?"

It was Christos' turn to start. "How—"

Raphael chuckled. "We've had an increased interest in that old vault this week. You're the fourth person to come asking about it. One of the visitors was your own Mary Magdalene. It wasn't a hard conclusion to reach."

"You're quite clever." Christos smiled. "I don't suppose you know what everyone's so interested in?"

"Oh, that's not my business," Raphael demurred. "There are so many artifacts in the vault, who could speculate?"

Christos hummed noncommittally, shuffling some papers on the desk absently. "Well, I'll be heading that way then, if I might have the key?"

"Of course, Christos." The librarian produced the ornate iron key from beneath his robes, extending the chain to the younger man. "You hardly need to ask so formally."

"Politeness supersedes politics," Christos quoted his mother fondly, accepting the key and striding off toward the rear of the library. He skimmed his fingertips lightly along the shelves as he walked, his other hand caressing the swirls and ridges of the old metal key. The tactile sensations were a pleasant momentary diversion, and Christos made a note to find time to visit his workshop later. It was always better to be working when he was restless; some of his best pieces were made trying to soothe his anxieties.

His steps went from muffled to echoing as he stepped from the newer, carpeted area of the library and into the older portion. The shelves here were worn and warped with age, the stone floor cold beneath his feet. Christos amended his mental note to use his workshop time to build some new shelving for this section.

As he wound through the ancient stacks, the bound tomes gave way to scrolls, then to loose stacks of papers tied with twine. A dusty smell permeated the air and made his nose twitch. He lifted his hand to rub the itch and cringed slightly at the thick dust caked on his fingertips.

Wiping the dust off on his linen pants, Christos elected to keep his hands firmly in his pockets until he reached the large, gilded vault set into the library's rear wall. He eyed it critically for a moment, assessing the gaudy embossing and ostentatious gleam of the doors, then slipped the key into its slot and twisted. The inside was much plainer, and Christos wondered if it shouldn't be the other way around, to deter prying eyes, not entice them. Then again, his father loved showing off.

He shut the door, glancing around the entrance foyer, at the more delicate and especially rare manuscripts housed on shelves that were literally hewn from the rock wall of the cavern. It was cooler here, and Christos shivered at the chill.

Two branching hallways swept off to either side of an alcove that housed a lone statue. Christos winced and couldn't repress a second shudder at the sight of himself, suspended on a cross by iron nails. His scarred palms itched as he shifted from one foot to the other. His hair was longer then, his form sallow and more emaciated. But that was his delicately carved face tightened by pain, and the crimson paint represented *his* blood leaking down gashed ribs. There was a very good reason this relief was stashed away in here: it made him sick to look at it.

Wrenching himself away, he turned and headed down the leftward hall, putting the memories and the phantom pains behind him. He was here to appease his subconscious, not to torment it.

Priceless images hung in the hallway, painted sceneries and carved masks and delicate woodcuttings. Some of these had been done by Christos himself and relegated here for safekeeping. He paused at an emotional rendering of Mags and his mother, painted sitting side by side, hands folded together as they laughed at some shared joke. His father's work.

The man certainly had a sensitive side; it was a shame so few people could claim to have seen it. He wanted to pray that Mags hadn't done what he suspected, but that would be rather counterintuitive. At that point he might as well march into his father's throne room and announce it.

A noise behind him made him jump, and for a moment he panicked, wondering if he had somehow done exactly that. But when he turned it wasn't his father approaching. Christos relaxed at the sight of Michael's eternally steady expression. Clearly, he wasn't about to be dragged away for judgement.

"Michael," he greeted warmly, but the tightening of the warrior's jaw made his smile falter. Maybe this wasn't such a casual visit. It would be a bit too coincidental if it were, he supposed, but he could still try at nonchalance. "What brings you down into the vault?"

"I have a feeling you are well aware." Michael said with resignation, arching a brow in question and thoroughly derailing the flimsy façade.

Christos sighed. "You would be correct."

"You don't think she would…?"

"There's only one way to be sure, isn't there?" He gestured to the archway he had been about to pass through. "Care to join?"

They continued deeper into the vault and eventually reached another sealed door. This one would not be opened by a simple key, and Christos swore when he saw there was already a sigil smeared in blood above the handle. Michael's expression darkened, and he yanked a small knife from a sheath on his hip.

Using the tip to prick his thumb, he traced the existing sigil carefully and left a trail of fresh gold over the dimming silver. The doorway seemed to shiver with light, then the heavy stone swung soundlessly inward.

"After you." Michael tipped his head toward the dark space beyond, and Christos stepped wordlessly inside.

The air seemed to hum with power in this room, the books and scrolls contained within emitting a cacophony of various energies, and it made him pause to even out his breathing. His eyes skimmed the shelves, searching for the one book he desperately hoped to see sitting in its place. His heart sank the moment his eyes lit upon the empty space between the Dead Sea Scrolls and the codices of Thomas' Gospel.

"Oh no," he said softly.

A broad hand settled on his shoulder and squeezed—either in reassurance or to help Michael ground himself, Christos couldn't be sure. He felt a bit like his world had just flipped on its head and he wondered if this was how Michael had felt those long eons ago, when Lucifer—

He shook off the thought. "This is not good."

"No," Michael agreed, "it is not. But I wonder…"

"Yes?" Christos realized his hands were trembling, and he curled his fingers tightly to stop it.

"Anyone who knows this sigil can open this door."

"Right, of course." Christos turned to face the angel, curiosity turning to creeping realization as Michael continued.

"But the vault itself requires a key. And only three people possess a copy of that key. Myself…"

"My father," Christos continued, picking up the thread, "and…"

"Raphael."

Christos unclenched his fist, and they both stared down at the key laid innocently over his scar.

* * *

Raphael was carefully transposing his ruined notes to a new sheet of paper—bent over the page and fastidiously checking and double-checking the copy to avoid any mistakes—when a resounding boom echoed through the otherwise silent library.

He jumped in alarm, his arm jerking and leaving a fresh swath of dark ink across his new page. He sighed at the sight, but quickly shoved his notes to the side, rising to investigate the source of the noise as Titanus approached in a hobbling run, growling and snarling.

Raphael managed about two steps before Michael strode out from between the stacks looking furious, Christos hustling in his wake to keep pace with the towering angel. Raphael's heart gave a stutter, and his skin went slick with a sheen of sweat.

Michael seldom made *that* face, and when he did, it was never good for the target of his rage. Raphael was a trained soldier—by Michael himself, in fact—but he had always been more scholar than warrior, and he knew he stood no chance whatsoever against someone of Michael's caliber.

"M-Michael!" he stammered, backing up into his desk and knocking over the cup that held his pens. They scattered and rolled across the wood surface and tumbled to the floor as Michael kept advancing on him. Raphael's knees and nerves grew weaker with every bit of ground his friend gained.

The blond emanated a visible aura of power as he reached Raphael and grabbed him by the front of his robes, lifting him clean off his feet and pressing him to the wall with a low growl. Titanus answered with a growl of his own, until Michael shot him a look so domineering, the gargoyle yipped and fled back to his cushion.

"We have some questions," Christos declared, and Raphael whimpered.

"I'm sure I can answer them on the ground?" he suggested, only for Michael to narrow his eyes and press him harder into the stone. "Or not! I can answer them up here, as well."

"You mentioned Mags had been here recently," Christos continued, steadfastly ignoring the unusual nature of this conversation, "and that she had been inside the vault."

Raphael nodded. "Yesterday, around noon. I remember because I had just finished my hummus and—"

"Did she leave here with anything?" the young prince interrupted, not particularly interested in the angel's lunch. "Something from the vault, specifically."

Raphael tried to school his features into something resembling neutrality. "No." He shook his head, only for Michael to shake *him* in response.

"Do not lie to us, Rapha," he spoke quietly, calmly, but there was a threat slipped under that command. The librarian trembled.

"I didn't see her with anything when she left," he said sincerely, and it was the truth. Anything Mags might have taken with her had been safely stowed inside the bag she had carried on her shoulder, and he was hardly going to search a lady's bag. Especially the consort of the prince.

Michael squinted suspiciously as he dropped his friend unceremoniously to the floor. "Half-truths are lies of omission, Raphael."

The librarian said nothing as he picked himself up from the floor, dusted off his robes, then collected his writing instruments and replaced them in their holder.

"Perhaps," he spoke at last, not looking up from his hands as he worked, "there are sometimes occasions in which a lie of omission becomes a necessity."

The library swallowed his quiet words, taking them and tucking them away as if to make his heresy merely another tale on countless shelves.

"That is a very bold statement," Christos spoke just as softly, eyes flashing with something close to anger, "and a very presumptuous one."

"Who are you to decide such things, Rapha?" Michael asked in a low, dangerous tone.

"Who am I?" his tone was tight. "I'm the one who had to help Mary tear apart these shelves decades ago, looking for a way to save the newborn Prince of Hell, and the one who tried to find a way to save its Queen. I'm the one who labors over these books and tomes for hints and clues despite the risk it lays upon me."

Raphael turned away, pacing restlessly as the old wounds reopened deep inside. "I am the one—" he spun back to face Michael, "—who stayed by your side and grieved for both of us when one by one, our friends defected. The one who stuffed your reckless, obstinate mouth with food and ambrosia when you gave up and wanted only to rot."

The larger man recoiled, casting his gaze aside with shame at the dark memories Raphael dragged up.

"I am the one," Raphael said, tugging his braid where it hung over his shoulder, some of his anger giving way to sadness, "who is tired of burying friends, and seeing them suffer."

Michael looked stricken. "Why didn't you ever tell me how it weighed on you, all this time?"

Raphael softened. "What good would it have done, old friend? Except to add to your own burdens? No, you have your demons, and these are mine. I have *never* approved of what happened to Lucifer, or later to his Fallen."

Christos winced. "You are not alone in that regard."

Raph brushed the tail of his braid over his palm, closing his eyes to center himself as he said, simply, "I am not sorry for what I have done, even if it is treason."

His companions went very still, and Michael cast a quick look around them to ensure they were alone.

"I would be very careful of saying such things, Raphael," Christos said, looking suddenly very tired.

The angel fixed him with a hard stare. "As if I haven't had to be cautious all these eons?"

The Prince scowled, hands flexing into fists. "You don't want to experience what my father will do to those who betray this kingdom."

"You need not warn me, Christos, for I have seen it with my own eyes."

"And still, you condemn the love of my life to such a fate!" His calm composure broke, and Christos strode forward until he was toe to toe with the angel. "You know what happens, and you *helped her do it anyway!*"

Raphael fixed him with a wrecked look and rested his hands gently on Christos's shoulders. "She knew what she was doing. She knows it's the right thing to do."

The younger man trembled. "I will lose her, Raphael. Even if he doesn't kill her, he will never let me follow her into exile."

"I know," he said softly. Christos came apart, tears welling up and spilling over, his gentle sobs the only sound disrupting the otherwise absolute quiet of the library. Raphael enfolded him in a tight embrace, the threat of tears shining in his own eyes.

Michael had to look away, his own heart aching for the young prince. It took everything in him not to rampage through the room and topple the useless towers of books. All this wisdom, all these tales and accounts of history, and nothing for them to do but sit here and wait for the world to come crashing down.

It was a hopelessness he had felt only once before, had hoped never to feel again. Even now, his fingers twitched at the memory of closing over Gabriel's throat, the fury he had smothered at the angel's casual disregard and veiled threats.

He met Raphael's gaze over Christos's shoulder, seeing a similar resigned anger in those emerald eyes, and decided they were overdue for a chat.

* * *

Gabriel could see the desire to rattle the foundations of the room written clearly on Michael's face, and he breathed a sigh of relief when the furious warrior managed to reign himself in. If he hadn't, Gabriel would have come toppling down with the books from his perch on top of the shelf.

He was occasionally prone to sprawling up near the stained-glass ceiling when he wanted a little bit of peace and quiet. It was sheer luck that he had been lounging here, casually flipping through what the humans considered a "classic" tale, when the comfortable silence was so *rudely* disrupted by a soldier throwing a tantrum.

How could he resist listening in on whatever had managed to rile the perpetually stoic *Michael*, he of the Glorious Elite, precious darling of Jehovah? Anything that could ruffle those stone feathers had to be more interesting than *Macbeth*.

And lo and behold, they confirmed what he had long suspected. Raphael was a heretic, and Mary Magdalene was not to be trusted. Ever since The Lamb had granted her divinity, Gabriel had felt a sense of unease around the young woman. Her face and figure were surely lovely, but the company she kept boded ill for Heaven and, clearly, she had been corrupting the prince.

"We cannot speak of this again," Christos finally composed himself and spoke, confirming Gabriel's fears. "All we can hope for at this point is that we will be able to return the book to its rightful place before my father notices it's missing."

Gabriel frowned. Well, that was certainly *not* the right course of action. Apparently, he'd have to take this news to Jehovah himself, if anything was to be done to prevent the utter disaster unfolding as they spoke. How could Christos allow his little girlfriend to threaten everything they held dear? The repercussions alone could very well destroy everything, not to mention what Lucifer could do with his powers supplemented...

His 'brothers' in wings escorted the prince from the library, and Gabriel used the brief diversion to unfurl his ebony wings and kick off from the bookshelf, spiraling up through the skylight and winging rapidly towards the throne room. Maybe if he hurried, something could still be done.

Chapter Ten

The meeting room was one of the more archaic rooms in Lucifer's estate, both in décor and function. Once upon a time, they had used the room regularly, discussing everything from establishing functions in Hell to how to expand their doctrine, such as it was, among the humans. The large space bordered on cavernous, nearly as dark as a tomb.

This room had never been fitted for electricity, as Lucifer preferred the ambiance when discussing 'matters of import'. As a result, the deep shadows creeping down from the high ceilings were repelled only by the pillar candles situated on tall pedestals along the walls.

Mags came into the space quietly, her footfalls muffled by the deep blue carpet runner that led the way to the massive round table in the center of the room. Behind her, Remi, Rag, and Judas followed, fanning out towards their usual seats at the table.

"So, what's the latest calamity on the agenda?" Judas swung his feet up onto the oak table, leaning his chair back on two legs and folding his arms behind his head. "It's been a while since we've had a formal meeting."

"Put your feet down," Mags chastised, settling into her chair and smoothing her skirt. Judas ignored her.

"She said feet *down*, Judy," Remi snapped, kicking his chair as she passed behind him and sending the young man sprawling to the floor.

"Rude!" he yelled, scrambling up and righting his seat. Remi only flipped him off over her shoulder, sinking into her own chair and offering Mags a bright grin.

Mags gave a small smile in return despite herself, even while turning her chastising tone on Remi. "You didn't need to dump him on the floor."

"Oh, but it made me feel better." Remi's grin widened, only to melt sharply into a scowl when her own chair was pulled from under her. She hit the ground hard. "Hey!"

Judas laughed, reaching for a high five from Balthazar who gripped the chair with an innocent expression as he examined his nails.

"Dick," Remi hissed, jumping up and jabbing her finger into Bal's chest.

"What?" he purred, in a voice like dark honey. "It made me feel better."

"You're all behaving like children," Luce declared, striding into the room and giving them all a hard look. He waved his hand and a strong wind swept briskly through the space, pushing them all into their chairs and moving the chairs up to the table. "Please try to act your ages."

"But that's *boring*," Bal grumbled, his dark hair falling over his eyes in a tousled wave that he shoved back with a jangle of his many layered bracelets.

"Yes, well," Luce sank into his seat with a heavy sigh. "It's about to become decidedly *un*-boring around here, so enjoy it while you can."

"We're still missing a few," Rag pointed out, dragging Remi's hand off the table so he could hold it in his own. He'd learned a long time ago that it was a simple trick to keep her calmer, and he had a sneaking suspicion this meeting would require that.

"Not for long," a new voice called, and the door opened again to admit a statuesque beauty with flashing blue eyes and a high black ponytail that swung as she moved. She walked with an easy swagger, leading an even taller man with waves like honey falling in his face and brushing his shoulders.

"Camiel," Luce greeted warmly. "How fares the work in the Pit?"

The woman's full, ruby-painted lips parted to reveal a sharp smile. "Bloody and terrible, as they deserve."

"You're a beast, my darling," the blonde leaned down to nuzzle her neck.

"While I love your love, Sachiel," Lucifer said, and the fondness on his face confirmed his words, "I do have some important information to share, if you can be disgustingly sweet while sitting?"

"Of course." Sachiel released his wife, letting her lead him to his seat where he pulled her into his lap instead of her own chair. Remiel pretended to vomit, and Rag fixed her with a look that clearly called her a hypocrite.

"Gross," Judas made a face, but his longing tone didn't match his feigned disgust.

"Don't be bitter because you're single." Bal kicked his own feet up on the table, drawing a tired frown from Mags, but no argument. Judas gave her a betrayed look, and Remi narrowed her eyes but was restrained from dumping his chair by Rag.

"Did we call a meeting just to comment on everyone's love lives?" Glory was the last to enter, smiling apologetically as she slid gracefully into her seat.

"This meeting was called to discuss an impending cataclysm, actually," Luce said dryly. "If everyone could *focus* long enough to do so. Mags, if you wouldn't mind sharing your recent vision?"

She swallowed hard, wringing her hands, and Camiel reached over to place a soothing hand over top of them.

"Breathe, honey," she murmured, and Mags nodded, smiling gratefully.

"Well, I should start back at the beginning, I think?" She paused, chewing her lip. "You all remember, when Foster was born, I had that horrible vision—"

"Of him ending the world," Sachi supplied, earning a tired sigh from Luce and a pointed glare from his wife for interrupting. "Sorry."

"It's okay," Mags said. "Yes, that one. Unfortunately, it has become…more likely to pass."

"I just saw him yesterday." Judas frowned. "He's been a little tetchy lately, but he didn't seem particularly…world-endy."

"'World-endy'," Remi parroted slowly, as if it was the dumbest thing she'd ever heard.

Mags cleared her throat loudly, clearly becoming frustrated by the constant interruptions. "Yes, well, in my newest vision he was murdering a child, so I'd say he's definitely on the path to *'world-endy'*."

The silence was abrupt and heavy, the tension palpable. Balthazar stopped fiddling with his rings. Judas's fingers froze where he had been drumming them against the table, splayed in midair. Sachiel went pale, and Cami looked like she might vomit.

"You didn't tell me that part, Mags," Glory whispered, her sultry voice hoarse. "You said he was looking for the Gospel of Lazarus."

"Wait, wait, no." Judas leaned forward, splaying his hands on the table. "We talked about this. Fos mentioned the gospel, and I shut it down."

"You *knew* he was doing this?" Lucifer leaned in too, but his expression was much angrier than Judas's mix of confusion and anxiety. "You knew, and said *nothing*?"

"No!" Judas protested, fixing him with a glare. "He mentioned it, and I thought I talked him out of it. I thought it was handled! But reading a forbidden text has nothing to do with *killing children!*"

"It does if you know what's *in* the Gospel of Lazarus." Lucifer leaned back, rubbing his hands over his face. "It's basically a how-to guide to Necromancy, and all of the rituals require human sacrifice."

"*What?!*" Remi leapt up from her chair, snatching her hand away from Rag to slam her palms to the tabletop. "How could you keep something like that from us?"

"Why is it even still allowed to exist?" Sachi frowned. "Wouldn't destroying it be better?"

"No one believed the rituals would work," Mags said softly. "I lost my brother to madness in his pursuit of recreating Christos's miracle."

Luce laid a comforting hand on her shoulder. "I should have destroyed it for that reason alone."

"No." She shook her head, hair falling in a curtain over her face before she swept it over her shoulder. "In a way, it was a bittersweet memento, preserved as a warning not to dabble in the dark arts. We could never have known that hiding it wouldn't be enough."

"We need full transparency," Rag said, drumming his fingers on the table. "I understand why we didn't know before, but that can't continue."

Bal hummed in agreement. "You can hardly expect us to mount a successful opposition without all the details."

"Which is why I called this meeting," Luce leaned forward, planting his elbows on the table and steepling his fingers in front of him. "There are several 'rituals' in the Gospel of Lazarus; all various attempts to bring back the dead. Most are nonsense, but some, in the hands of a Divine being, have real power."

"The first ritual," Mags whispered, "is the death of a 'being of purity'. The most obvious candidate is a child, I suppose."

The outrage and disgust in the room was palpable. Glory had her hands clasped over her mouth in horror, while Balthazar looked murderous, gripping the table's edge so hard his knuckles strained pale against his tanned flesh. Remiel was equally furious and would have likely thrown her chair across the room by now if her husband didn't have her biceps in a death grip. Sachiel had taken on a greenish tinge as if he might be sick.

"No," Judas was the first to speak, looking conflicted. "He wouldn't. I know Foster, and he just wouldn't."

"It's an evil book," Mags countered, her expression pained. "It holds my brother's madness, his essence. It has a way of…influencing you."

"Not ta mention," a gravelly new voice broke in, "he's got other bad influences."

"Cwall," Luce blinked in surprise. "I wasn't expecting you."

The demon drifted toward the table, batlike wings carrying his skeletal form across the space. "I heard mutterin' about a meetin' and I thought ya needed ta hear my update."

"By all means," Luce gestured for him to continue.

"It's not good news," he said, trying to prepare them for the impact. "Fos… well, he killed a kid."

Remi scoffed. "I thought the Eyes were more reliable, we already know about Mags's vision."

Cwall turned his gaze away, flames smoldering in the empty pits of his skull. "Yeah, but the kid… she was buried last week."

Luce felt his blood run very cold. He had seen the dark circles under Foster's eyes, felt the tension that was seeded down to the young man's core, but he had thought it was the weight of his intentions wearing on him. It had in fact been guilt.

"Why didn't you bring this information to me sooner?" Balthazar shot up from his chair as if he would lunge over the table to throttle the imp.

"I didn't realize it was connected at first," Cwall shrank back from his boss, but didn't flee. "But I overheard him sayin' it was for a ritual, an' that he has ta do another one."

"We're too late," Camiel said, shaken, and gripped Mags's hand reflexively.

"No," Luce extended a hand to Mags. "The Gospel, please."

Judas recoiled. "You have it *here*?"

"The Gospel of *Peace*," Mags clarified, pulling the tome from her satchel and passing it into Luce's hands. "Our last and best hope, especially if this has already begun."

"This book contains essentially a step-by-step process on how to tithe for the fabled Armor of the Gods," Luce said, casting his steady gaze around the table, "and instructions on how to forge each piece."

Bal sank into his chair. "How is this going to fix everything?"

"And it better fix *everything*," Remi snapped from where she was pacing up and down the carpet after wriggling out of Rag's grip.

"Enough," Luce snapped back at her. "I've had quite enough of your backtalk, Remiel, and if you all would just *shut up*, I could give you the answers you seek."

They went silent, restless but willing to wait—or at least not wanting to piss Luce off any more than they had. Remi halted her pacing but glowered at the Devil, holding the back of her chair in a white-knuckled grip.

"Thank you." Lucifer fixed each of them with his glare in turn to ensure he had a captive audience. "There are five pieces that make up the Armor of the Gods, and once upon a time I began to forge them. Jehovah, in his ceaseless fear of being usurped, panicked after only one had been crafted and locked the book away in his Vault so the others would not be made."

"Which one—" Sachiel started to speak but was quick to bite his tongue as Luce and Camiel both turned to glare at him, the latter placing a dainty hand over his mouth.

"Sorry," she said sweetly, and Luce sighed.

"It doesn't matter," he said, waving a hand. "I know where it is, and I'm working on a plan to reclaim it. The hard part will be crafting the others, as it has never been done before."

He rifled through the pages of the book with one hand as he spoke, opening the book to display a glittering title: The Belt of Truth.

"Is that the first piece we're making?" Rag leaned closer to try and view the page.

"If by 'we' you mean 'me', then yes," Luce sighed. "Unfortunately, this is a task I have to undertake alone."

"Why?" Glory peered up through her lashes at him, concern written in the lines on her brow and the frown on her lips. "Can't we help somehow?"

Luce offered her a sad smile. "You're sweet for asking, but no. I need to be the one to do this."

"But—"

"If you want to help," Luce cut her off gently, "you can focus on keeping things running behind the scenes. Hell won't stop needing governance simply because I have other things to focus on."

"I heard you'll be taking over my shifts at soul intake." Camiel leaned forward, resting her elbow on the table and smirking at Remiel, who scowled back. "I'm looking forward to being able to focus more on the Pit."

"Don't make me regret that decision," Luce shot Cami a warning look. "I have enough on my plate without having to worry about this realm falling into chaos too."

"Of course not," Cami dialed up the sweetness to sarcastic levels, and Luce narrowed his eyes at her. She sobered at his expression. "Aw, come on Luci, I'm kidding. You can trust us."

The Devil had his doubts. But he forced a smile onto his face for the sake of morale, and nodded. "I know that, of course. With so much to be done, I think it best we should adjourn this meeting for now."

Rag rose from his seat and laid a hand on Luce's shoulder. "If we're going to get to work, we should start by having the delicious dinner I've made for us all."

Remi made a choking sound. "We need him to fix the world, we don't want to *poison* him!"

Mags looked alarmed. "Rag! Why were you cooking?! I *said* I was making a lasagna."

"I made mac and cheese!" Rag protested. "There's no way I messed up mac and cheese!"

The tiny woman seemed to radiate pure threat as she glared up at the ginger. "I swear if you ruined my cookware *again* Raguel—"

"Mac and cheese!" Rag repeated with a note of pleading in his tone. He looked at Remi as if she might take his side.

"Don't look at me." She placed her hands on her hips. "You cook about as well as Luce bakes."

"Hey!" Luce interrupted. "What is this, everybody harasses Lucifer day?"

"Isn't that every day?" Judas deadpanned.

"Unbelievable."

A laugh broke into their little squabble, and they all turned to see Glory giggling so hard she snorted, hands flying to cover her mouth and nose in surprise.

"Sorry, sorry," she fluttered her hands, still smiling wide. "I just love this ridiculous family. Even with such darkness looming, you're all a spot of brightness in my life."

Judas narrowed his eyes. "Are you drunk?"

"I may have had some wine," Glory flushed. "Do I have to be drunk to be affectionate?"

"With this crowd of ingrates? Yes," Bal said, arching a brow. "Drunk, high, or seriously delusional."

"Not all of us are as jaded as you," Sachiel protested.

"It's disgustingly sweet." Remi shuddered. "I definitely don't understand it; I keep trying to get *out* of this hellscape."

"You lie," Luce said flatly. "I know, because I have *tried* to get rid of you and you just won't go."

"Well, someone has to stick around to make sure you're actually running this place and not just hiding in a room making papier-mâché dicks—" Luce shrieked, which she ignored, continuing as if he hadn't spoken, "or letting your son start Armageddon, apparently!"

The tension they had forced out with their attempts at light-hearted banter swept back in like the tide. There was only so much dark humor could do to buoy them in the sea of despair.

"Good job, Rem," Balthazar scowled. "Now I'm thinking about dead kids again."

"Fuck off," she snapped.

Camiel stepped between them, a perfectly manicured hand pressed to either of their chests. "Knock it off, both of you. Has anyone stopped to consider that all of this deflecting is part of the problem?"

Sachiel stepped up behind his wife, resting his hands on her shoulders and coaxing her to drop her arms. "We can't help it, Cam. It's too heavy to carry without trying to lighten the load."

"We shouldn't be trying to *lighten* it," she protested, turning in his arms to cup her husband's face in both palms. "We need to figure out how to *stop* it, before we lose Foster forever."

"Well, there's no way we can stop it on an empty stomach," Rag reasoned. "Let's move this over to the kitchen!"

"Speaking of kitchens," a voice came from the doorway, and they all turned to see one of Bal's sentries looking concerned and vaguely disgusted. "Something is either burning or rotting in ours."

"My macaroni!" Rag's face became a mask of horror, and he bolted from the room. Mags and Remi exchanged a wary look, and Mags sighed again, shoulders slumping.

"Don't worry, I still have a lasagna."

"In the meantime, I'd better go supervise my toddler husband." Remi had the air of a woman who continuously expected nothing but was still disappointed as she followed Rag's path from the room.

* * *

Judas kicked at the pavement in the alley across from Foster's apartment, smoking a cigarette down to the filter as he debated if he was going to do this. Luce had dropped a bomb at tonight's meeting, and while the King hadn't *expressly* forbidden anyone from talking to Foster about it, Judas knew Luce wouldn't be happy he was here.

But wasn't it worth sacrificing their upper hand, to try and do something to stop this from going any further? Judas had been the only member of the Fallen to stay by Foster's side after Angela's death —that had to count for something. He had always assumed the others were visiting. He knew Luce wasn't, but that wasn't his business to meddle in. He had his own family drama, and that was more than enough.

Judas sighed, dropped the butt of his cigarette to the pavement, and crushed it under his heel. The street was quiet as the day started to wind down, the sun dipping ever lower toward the horizon. The few mortals passing by wouldn't be able to see him through his glamour, but he knew it would do nothing to deter Foster. Should he try to call first?

His fingers twitched toward his pocket for another cigarette, but movement in one of the upstairs windows caught his eye. Judas glanced up, focusing in on the curtain that had been pulled aside on the fourth floor and the little Hispanic woman who stared directly at him. Her judgmental expression had him reconsidering another smoke, and he lifted his hands in surrender.

She sniffed haughtily, nodded in approval, and let the curtain fall closed again. Judas shivered. He had never quite warmed up to Foster's neighbor the way the other man had; she seemed to know way too much, even for a witch.

Shaking off his hesitation, Judas sauntered across the street and through the hole where a gate should've hung in the rickety fence. This place was a total shithole, but it was what Foster could afford on the remnants of his mother's estate, since he refused to use Luce's money anymore. Judas had tried to convince him to move somewhere

119

less dilapidated, even offered Foster a loan, but the other man was as stubborn as his father.

Judas slid his spare key into the lock on the front door and headed up the stairs to Foster's apartment, knocking briefly on the front door before letting himself into the apartment. Foster was halfway to the door and scowled when he saw Judas hadn't waited to be welcomed in.

"The spare key is for emergencies, asshole," Foster grumbled, but there was no heat behind it. Judas, on the other hand, was struggling to maintain his cool now that his friend was before him.

Foster looked tired, sure, but he also looked so... *normal*. Judas couldn't wrap his mind around the idea of his best friend having not only killed a child, but to then be able to go on about his life as if nothing had happened.

"What's the matter man?" Foster arched a thick eyebrow, concern etched on his face. "You look like you're gonna be sick."

"How often have you lied to me, Foster?" Judas forced the words out before he could lose his nerve. Tension mounted in creeping waves as they stood facing each other in the living room of the apartment, the air between them going thin and taut.

"What the hell are you talking about, Judas?"

"Don't insult me by lying *more*," Judas snarled, a spark of rage ripping through him at the weak attempt. "The *Gospel*, Foster. The goddamned rituals."

Silence stretched, until Foster cleared his throat and turned away to head into the kitchen. "You want a drink?"

"Seriously?" Judas asked, incredulous.

"All I have is Corona, that cool?" Foster called back as he bent into the fridge and came back with two glass bottles of beer.

"I didn't come here to drink, Foster."

"Well, this is a conversation I want a drink for." Foster eyed him flatly. "You might as well have one too."

He carried the beers to the armchairs that faced his tv stand, sinking into one and gesturing to the other. Judas frowned but came to sit in the second chair. He took the beer Foster passed him and removed the cap with a spark of magic before he took a swig.

Finally, he turned to his friend, hoping the hurt he was feeling wasn't visible on his face as he asked quietly, "What the hell, man?"

Foster took his time opening his beer and taking a long sip, and it seemed like he was choosing his words carefully. After a moment, he scrubbed his face roughly with his free hand and sighed. "I don't even know, Judas. It's all gotten so damned messy."

"You told me you weren't going to go through with it," Judas frowned. "You looked me in my face and you *lied*."

"I know."

"You killed a damn *kid*, Fos!"

"It was a mercy killing," the other man muttered, but Judas could see guilt and shame in the deep brown pools of his eyes. God, he was going through hell over this.

"Foster, you can still stop," Judas said softly, setting his beer on the coffee table to focus his attention on his friend. "It's not too late to end this."

Foster's glare was biting as he looked up at him. "End this, huh? Just give up on my mother, like the rest of you?"

"She's *dead*, man," the Fallen tried to keep his tone compassionate, despite the frustration that welled up in him. "I know it's hard, but it's a part of being mortal."

"And yet, here you are," Foster snapped. "Why is that you, Christos, Mags—*you* all got to Rise, while my mother's soul is trapped in the Void so that I can't even visit her spirit!"

"I don't know," Judas shook his head. "Sometimes, when souls are too damaged, they end up in the Void. It's awful, but man, you can't dabble in black magic to try and undo fate."

"Fuck fate," Foster snarled, and his grip tightened so hard on his beer that the bottle shattered in a pop of liquid and glass. "And fuck you, Judas. You're supposed to be on my side."

"Nah," he frowned. "I'm your friend, and that means telling you when you're wrong. You're making a mistake, Foster."

Foster rose to his feet abruptly, shaking out his dripping hand to clear away the mess, and jerked his chin towards the door. "Time to go."

"Foster," he protested, and the demigod lunged forward to grip him roughly by the bicep.

"Get the fuck out," he said, low and dangerous, as he dragged Judas to his feet and started towards the door. "I'm so tired of people who were content to do nothing trying to interfere now when I *finally* have a chance to see her again."

Judas struggled against his iron grip, trying to buy more time to talk and attempt to get through to his friend. "Foster, you don't understand. The Gospel, it's *dangerous*. It's forbidden for a reason."

"Yeah, Gabe said you would say that," Foster muttered.

"Because it's true," Judas insisted. "Mags had a vision—"

"Was it of my mother returning to life?"

"No, it was of—"

"Then I don't care," Foster interrupted, yanking the apartment door open and trying to shove Judas through it. "Now get out and give me my damn key back."

Judas frowned, digging his heels in to stay inside the apartment. "Come on, Foster, this isn't like you. Don't you see how insane this is?"

Foster's eyes narrowed. "I'm done entertaining this bullshit, Judas, and I'd appreciate if you all would stop coming around just to patronize me."

"We're worried about you."

A laugh that was more like a bark spilled from the demigod's lips. "Right, and that's why you're the only one who ever bothered to come around. You know what?"

Judas tensed, but Foster planted his hand in the center of the Fallen's back and shoved hard, sending him stumbling over the threshold. Judas could feel the sting of the wards as he passed through, letting him know he was officially *persona non grata* in Foster's apartment.

"Don't bother coming back around, *Judas*." Foster spat the name like venom and Judas recoiled. "You or the other sycophants who follow my father around like puppies. None of you are welcome here."

Before Judas could try any more feeble arguments, the door slammed in his face. He could feel a wash of power as Foster redoubled the wards, and his chest ached with the rebuff.

"Well, it was worth a shot," he grumbled, and turned back to the stairwell. He walked slowly down the steps, half-hoping that Foster would come after him but knowing that he wouldn't. Morningstar men were stubborn and proud, the damn fools.

The moment he cleared the front door, he jammed a fresh cigarette between his lips, looking up at the melting twilight as he lit the tip with a flame from his fingertip. Letting his head fall back against the exterior of the building, Judas closed his eyes with a heavy sigh.

He smoked the cigarette down to the filter, desperately wishing the little poison sticks could do anything to settle his nerves, like tobacco used to when he had been a mortal man. Unfortunately, they were just a bad habit with none of the side benefits now. He discarded the butt in the dirt and ground it out before tucking his hands into his jacket pockets and walked back into the night.

He had hoped Foster would see reason, but it turned out their friendship carried little weight against whatever hold Gabriel had on the other man. All the Fallen could hope for now was that something Judas had said might get through to the troubled demigod, before they ended up with more bodies on their hands.

Chapter Eleven

Shrugging into his leather jacket, Foster pocketed his projector cube and his keys before stepping out into the hall and locking his door. Not that a lock would keep out any of the people he was worried about getting in—the wards he'd just refreshed inside would have to pick up the slack at that point. The lock deterred the mortal residents of his building. Eyeing the grimy carpet and the ever-growing pile of trash bags at the head of the stairs, Foster could admit he didn't live in the most reputable neighborhood.

But as he descended the stairs, he picked up the scent of sizzling bell peppers and a hint of cilantro. Some of the building's residents weren't as bad as the others. As if he had summoned her with his thoughts, the door to D3 popped open. Señora Delgado bustled out into the hall like a woman on a mission, all five feet of her wrapped up in a colorful, striped cardigan.

"¡*Diablito!*" she announced his nickname matter-of-factly and with a hint of reprimand, as if she'd been expecting him and he was late. Her accent was thick and always sounded a bit agitated, but he could tell when she was genuinely mad and when she was just rambling in her peculiar way, like right now. "I knew it was you, *Diablito*. I'm always hearing you stomp-stamping down these stairs in you big scary *botas*. Always the stamping, like you need to making a fuss or you will die, *dio mío*."

"*Sí, señora*." He grinned, winking at her. "I will absolutely die."

"You a bad boy," she chastised, but smiled wide enough to reveal a slight snaggletooth. "Come inside, I cooking *pastelito*, and you *tan flaco, Diablito*! You need to eat more! You a growing boy!"

"*¡Yo tengo trente años!*" Foster protested, and okay, that wasn't exactly true, but it was a close enough approximation for mortals. There was no real point to his argument anyway, because he knew age was all relative to Señora Delgado. Anyone younger than her was considered a child, which was pretty much everyone in the building.

"I no care." She waved a chubby hand dismissively, and Foster caught it in his larger one so he could brush a kiss over her knuckles. She snatched her hand back, blushing, and swatted his head. "*¡Ay! ¡Este maldita chico, sin vergüenza!*"

He laughed, shoving his hands in his pockets. "*Sí, sí,* no shame. And also very busy, *lo siento*. Save me a plate, *abuela?*"

"Maybe," she sniffed haughtily, arms folded over her chest. "Always running around at every hours, doing what?"

Foster smiled and dodged the question. "I'll see you later, *abuela*. Lock your door!"

"*Sí, sí,*" she waved him off with a fond smile. "Nobody bother Sra. Delgado except you, *Diablito*."

"Because they know I'll be angry!" he tossed over his shoulder as he continued down the stairs, listening for the snap and the click that let him know she was safely returned to her locked apartment. He made a mental note to refresh the wards around her apartment when he got back home, even though he knew she didn't need his input. Señora Delgado was a capable witch on her own.

But Foster was compelled to do what he could to care for the people in his building, and he paused in the hallway when he reached the ground floor. Dark eyes drifted across to A2, still silent and shut off from the world. No one in the building had seen Lydia or Aaron since Piper's funeral, and Foster was constantly torn between knocking on the door to check on them and leaving them to their grief. He couldn't forgive himself for his role in it, and that ultimately led him to choose the second option.

He settled for a snap of his fingers that left a wicker basket of pastries outside their front door. It was the same gift basket he sent Lydia every year on her birthday, but this time she would find a card with his condolences in the bottom, along with enough cash to reimburse the funeral expenses. It was the least he could do, since he knew for a fact that they hadn't cashed the check he'd written after the wake.

Turning up his collar against the early fall chill, Foster buried his guilt and stepped out of the suddenly claustrophobic apartment building. He made his way into the darkening night, hoping the biting wind might drag away the lingering sorrow and the persistent sense of regret. Fuck Judas for showing up and bringing all of it back to the surface.

He was beginning to wish he hadn't scared Cwall off yesterday, but the demon was prone to sulking when his human charge was rude to him, and wouldn't likely reveal himself for several days. Foster always felt like he was being watched when he was out and about, and while he recognized that most of the time it probably *was* Cwall watching him, it would help to have the imp by his side so that he could be certain they were friendly eyes.

While it was *possible* for mortals to develop extrasensory abilities, and some were even born with an edge up on the others, it was extremely rare for a mortal to reach a level where they could pick up on who—or *what*—he was. Rare, but possible, and that slight chance was enough to give him pause. He was the product of one such long-shot meeting, after all.

His mother had told the story infrequently, but fondly. It could be coerced from her on special occasions, usually after she had a few glasses of her favorite honeyed mead, and Foster could still recall the way her amber eyes would glow with delight as she shared the tale.

"He was so handsome, your father," she would say, smile mischievous and eyes glittering as she tickled young Foster's sides. "Just like you will be, my little Devil."

"Stop, Mama!" Foster could almost hear the echo of his own

laughter as he twisted his skinny body away from her teasing hands. "Tell the story!"

"Oh, of course, of course," Angela would grin. "Ah, and what a story."

Angela wandered leisurely through the market, one hand looped through the handle of her shopping basket while the other reached out, endlessly seeking and sorting and touching the countless wares on display. Plump fruits, dried herbs, woven fabrics—everything was fair game for her curious perusal. She lingered at a produce stall, lifting a juicy tomato for inspection, and froze as a shiver raced down her spine. Carefully, casually, Angela paid for the tomato and tucked it into her basket, smoothing down her deep blue skirts as she turned and cast a sweeping glance over the market.

Nothing. There was nothing unusual, but there was... something, at the same time. She could feel it like a breeze against her skin; there was a powerful being in this market with her. And not just any being, but... could it be? Someone with Godblood? A thrill rose in her, in direct contradiction to everything her mother had tried to instill in her. Gods were not to be trusted; her mother always insisted. Angela pushed the feeling down, tucking a curl of gold behind her ear and resuming her shopping. Que sera, sera, *she told herself. I will meet them if it is fated.*

"And you did!" Foster would interrupt her with a giggle, only to be swept up into his mother's arms.

"Of course I did, *mijo*," she would trace his features with her slender fingers until he was laughing and squirming in her hold. "Fate, has a sense of humor, you see."

"You seem lost," a deep, smooth voice came at her shoulder, and Angela turned abruptly. A man had snuck up on her, somehow, and for a moment her surprise at his presence distracted her from his looks. But only a moment.

He was beautiful, which was a word she didn't often equate to men, but it was true. His dark hair swept over his forehead in waves, curling around his ears and the nape of his neck. Deep brown eyes with a ring of gold were fixed on her, set in a deeply tanned and finely featured face. His smile was easy and kind, and Angela found herself flushing at both his closeness and his attention.

"Excuse me?" She took a step back to put some distance between them.

"Lost," he repeated, still smiling. "The way you were looking around, I thought you were lost."

"I am not, thank you," she began to turn away.

"Oh?" His voice dipped lower, conspiratorial. "So perhaps... looking for something?"

There was a heavy implication in the casual question, and Angela tensed.

"No," she repeated. "I must be going."

The strange man continued to watch her, his gaze lingering on her face, and Angela began to worry about his intentions. But then he nodded and gave her a small bow.

"My mistake. Please have a good day." He turned away before she did, disappearing into the crowd like a ghost.

Everything in Angela's body was taut and alert, as if urging her to pay attention. She knew what had just transpired; she had spoken directly to a God. Every warning her mother had passed on weighed on her like a shroud, but Angela shook them all off, following the stranger into the crowd. She had talked to a God, and he was beautiful, and she was going to do it again, consequences be damned.

"Daddy is lucky," Foster would interrupt her again, gazing up at her with adoring eyes that mirrored his father's.

"Is he?" Angela would raise her brows in a pantomime of surprise, and Foster would nod solemnly. He would cup her face in his small hands, to ensure she was paying attention.

"Yes," the little demigod insisted every time. "Because you picked him when you could have left instead."

"I would never presume to defy destiny, *mi amor*," Angela always insisted gravely.

. . .

She found him leaning against a pillar, tossing a woven ball up into the air before catching it again, and when she approached him, he looked up with that same warm smile. She got the sense he had been expecting her.

"Hello again," he said sweetly, tossing and catching the ball with a flick of his wrist. Toss, catch. Toss, catch. The rhythm was steady, almost entrancing.

"Hello," she echoed, with a hint of amusement. "You knew I would follow."

It wasn't a question, not really, but he nodded. "I suspected, yes."

"How?"

"You could see me."

She swept him from tousled head to polished shoes, arching a brow at the vibrant rose-hued shirt paired with his cream summer suit. "I think you are not easy to miss."

"Ah, but you saw me before I wanted to be seen, which is very rare a talent indeed." He caught the ball, and this time tucked it into a pocket, pushing off the pillar to step toward her. "You sensed me."

She opened her mouth to deny it, but he held up a hand.

"Don't insult either of us by trying to lie to me. I know the touch of another sensitive mind when I feel it."

Angela pursed her lips. "I wasn't trying to."

"I know. You have great power, but untrained as it is, you can't control it."

"Untrue," she sniffed haughtily. "I am well trained."

"You sought me intentionally?"

She hesitated. "Not at first, no."

He grinned. "Then you were slacking."

A hot flush stole across her cheeks. "I don't think I can be expected to be on guard at all times."

"But you must," he stepped closer, and this time she did not back away.

Angela held herself straight and tall, refusing to be cowed. "And why is that?"

"Who knows what could be lurking, little mortal?" He leaned in, bringing his lips so close to her ear, warm breath tickled her skin as he spoke. "You could be snatched away in moments, and all because you let down your guard."

She tensed but would not let him intimidate her. "You overestimate your ability."

"Do I?" He leaned back, somehow giving her the most negligible space he could.

"Oh yes," it was her turn to smile. "Even Gods have weaknesses, you see."

"You know what I am?" A delighted spark lit behind his eyes, and it gave him an air of lightness that she found entrancing.

"I do."

"Will you tell me what you are?"

"I will not."

"What *are* you, Mama?"

He asked her every time, but Angela never gave her son a straight answer. Every time, she would squeeze him tightly in a hug or ruffle his hair lovingly and plant a kiss on his forehead.

"It doesn't matter, Foster," she would say. "Everything I have ever been pales in comparison to the most important thing."

"What's that?"

"Silly boy." Angela would smile wide, twirling his hair around her finger. "The best thing I have ever been is your mother."

He pouted. "That's unfair."

"You are a God," she laughed shortly. "This entire encounter is weighted in your favor, and you speak of fairness?"

"I will have you know; I find equal footing to be an essential foundation of any relationship."

"We do not have a relationship," she admonished him. "How very forward of you to presume such, from a simple conversation."

"Even an acquaintance is a relationship," he argued, "and I hope we could possibly even become friends."

"I don't even know your name." And yet she was drawn to him, curiosity and attraction mingling in a heady combination.

"Yes, you do," he said softly, and a certain sadness snuck into the edges of his smile. "My name is Lucifer."

Angela blinked slowly. She did know him, if only through legend.

"The Morning Star," she said, almost numb. Of all the Gods, this one was the most infamous.

"Now you know who I am, and here I know only that you are a very beautiful and unusually powerful mortal."

"Perhaps I should maintain my brief moment of control," she found herself smiling, his easy manner outweighing the shock of his pedigree. Besides, she had never put much stock in the rumors of Lucifer's 'evil'. She owed him quite a debt for her own lineage, in fact.

His eyes went wide, pleading with mock desperation, "Have mercy!"

"Hmmm," Angela tapped her chin with a slim finger, as if weighing her options. "I suppose it would be unfair to withhold my name, especially with your proclamations for equal footing."

"Precisely," he nodded solemnly, but his grin was bright and eager.

"My name is Angela," she smiled back, and extended her hand to him. "Angela Ortiz."

He took it without hesitation, bringing the back of her hand to his lips for a courtly kiss. "As lovely a name as one so beautiful would be expected to bear."

She laughed. "Are all Gods such blatant flirts?"

"Only when the woman is exceptionally intriguing," he replied easily, and she felt her cheeks warming again.

"I hope I can live up to such high expectations," she said.

"Oh, I expect you'll exceed them." Lucifer replied easily, extending his arm for her to tuck her hand into. "I have a very good feeling about you, you see."

* * *

There must have been something to his intuition because they were married three years later. It had cost Angela her family—unsurprisingly, they had not been enthused that she wanted to be with a Divine being—but they had been blessed with a son. That son scowled now, struggling to rationalize his mother's constant adoration for his father with the burning outrage he fostered. He stopped short with a groan at his own unintentional pun, shaking his head.

"Stupid," he muttered, kicking a rock along the sidewalk and into

131

the gutter. "Dwelling on the past when there's the present to worry about."

He looked up, surprised to find he had reached his destination, navigating to the church on muscle memory while lost in thought. Foster went up the steps and through the entry hall, glancing around and noting a few scattered visitors in various states of worship despite the odd hour. It was a surprisingly good turnout for after sundown on a weekday, but there weren't so many people that someone would be likely to notice his impromptu visit.

He cursed Judas's name as he made his way through the building. After the praeceptor had hemmed and hawed about giving Foster access to the Gospel of Lazarus, Foster had tried to let it go. Gabe had a copy of his own, but he had always been reluctant to let Foster have it, and if the praeceptor wouldn't give him access...Well, he'd have to trust his mentor.

But then his friend had shown up telling him that it was *dangerous*, and Foster needed to see the damn thing for himself. If he could just read through it, he could put his mind at rest that it was nothing nefarious, and he could get everyone off his back once and for all.

The praeceptor's office was empty when he passed under the archway and peeked through the door, so he took a short flight of steps down to a lower level. It was cooler down here, making Foster glad he'd worn his leather jacket and not something lighter. The stairs let out into a pathway that looped around in a circuit of rooms, mostly storage or rooms used for meetings, prayer sessions, or the occasional party.

Foster went directly to a familiar door on the right marked 'Archives', and he gave the old knob a sharp twist and a firm yank to loosen the joint that always seemed to stick a bit. He stepped into the dim room beyond, conjuring a small flame on the tip of his finger and using it to find the switch. It took a moment for the weak incandescent bulbs to flicker to life, a few of them stubbornly refusing to conjure a spark in their old age.

Unsurprising. The archives were seldom traveled, so no one had really seen a need to update the lighting. It was enough to see by at least, especially when Foster was blessed with far better senses than any mortal. Unfortunately, that included his sense of smell, and his nose twitched violently in revulsion at the lingering scent of mildew. There must have been a leak during the last big storm.

He wound his way through the room, slowly navigating the rows of books packed onto ancient wooden shelves, trying to determine which shelf was the right one. Sliding his finger gently along the spines, he deciphered titles in Aramaic, Hebrew, Yiddish, Greek, and even Enochian. Nothing. *Nothing?* How could there be nothing? He turned back the way he came, looking again through every shelf. It had to be here. He *needed* it to be here.

But it wasn't. With a growl of frustration, Foster lashed out with his boot, kicking one of the shelves so hard it shuddered and threatened to topple. The damned old man was hiding it from him because of his stupid 'moral reservations'—he must be.

Foster stormed out of the archive so recklessly that he nearly upended several shelves. He dashed back down the hall and up the stairs, pushing out through the side exit door at inhuman speed. He forcibly slowed his pace as he walked the path from the church to the parish housing, just in case any humans were around, then banged mercilessly on the ornate wooden door.

"Praeceptor! It's Foster. I need a word," he shouted, caring much less about those wandering human eye now. When no answer came, he slammed his fists harder into the door. He barely felt the wood give under his assault, even with splintering shards digging into his flesh.

"I'm coming," he heard the old man's tired voice as lights turned on inside. "I'm coming, dear boy."

"'Dear boy'?" Foster echoed in a mocking tone with a scoff. "Don't gimme that bullshit!"

The door swung inward, revealing Praeceptor Sceros clad in a robe as usual, but in this case it was a fluffy green housecoat and matching slippers. His brown eyes were weary, blurred with sleep, and his silver hair was tousled where it usually laid slick back against his scalp. For a half second, Foster felt guilty. Why was he here, disrupting the old man's sleep, making a scene and—

"Is something the matter?" his soft, concerned tone made the younger man's agitation flare in response.

"Yeah, something is the matter," Foster snapped. "The Gospel of Lazarus isn't in the archives."

The old man tensed, then softened. "Foster, we spoke about this. I cannot—"

"Stop, just stop." He raked his hands through his hair, then balled them into fists to steady them. "I brought you those diary pages in exchange."

"Foster, I told you, the Gospel is forbidden. Your donation was very generous, but—"

"It wasn't a donation!" His fist shot out and pounded into the doorframe as he loomed over the older man. "I was bringing those stupid diary pages for two reasons. To get another reminder of my damned father out of my house, and to help grease your greedy palms into slipping me the Gospel."

"I take objection to your tone, young man." The praeceptor straightened, gathering up some of his usual confidence to give the angry demigod a glower. "And to your insinuations that I am anything less than upstanding."

"Yeah, well," Foster scoffed, but deflated slightly. "You still reneged on the deal. What do you call that?"

"An unfortunate necessity."

"Explain."

The older man sighed. "You should come inside, son."

Foster stared down into the ceramic mug the holy man had pressed into his twitching palms, grateful for something to occupy his hands but tempted to smash the mug anyway. His hands clenched in tandem with his jaw.

"I'd appreciate it if you simply drank the tea and didn't break one of my favorite mugs."

Foster arched a brow, lifting the hideous orange mug in one hand. It was lumpy and covered in poorly painted flowers in all colors of the rainbow. "This mug is ugly as sin."

The old man glared. "My granddaughter made that for me."

"Still ugly." Foster sniffed, but he brought it to his lips for a sip. The zip of mint danced over his tongue, chased by a floral taste. Lavender?

Chamomile? It wasn't bad, so he took a longer swallow. "Why are you keeping the book from me?"

"For your own good," the elder insisted roughly, but sighed again when Foster gave him a dirty look. "Listen, Foster. As much as I personally disagree with that book, I couldn't give it to you even if I wanted to."

"What the hell does that mean?"

He cleared his throat, fidgeting a bit in his wingback armchair. "That is to say…the Gospel has been…misplaced."

"Misplaced," Foster echoed, his tone droll with disbelief.

"Ah… yes." The old man at least had the decency to look sheepish. "When you first requested access to the book I…well I *did* try to locate it for you and—" He cleared his throat again, deliberately avoiding eye contact with the young demigod.

"Praeceptor," Foster nearly growled, quickly losing the battle with his own patience.

"I must have mislaid it somewhere. You know how vast the archives are, and—"

Foster closed his eyes, tuning out the old man's continued ramblings, and counted very slowly to ten. He repeated this process until the urge to snap the man's neck subsided and then opened his eyes to glare hard at him.

"All this posturing about right and wrong has been to cover up your negligence."

"No!" the elder insisted. "I would even call it a blessing in disguise, Foster, because the book is *wrong*."

"Wrong," he echoed sourly. "Care to elaborate?"

The praeceptor sank into his armchair as all the fight drained out of him. Foster thought he suddenly looked very small and very tired, and ignored the gnawing pang of guilt worming through him.

"There are stories about the Gospel," the man finally spoke, tone low and resigned. "Stories that were intended to discourage anyone from seeking it out, lest they come to pass. We've stopped passing these stories along, in the hopes that the damned book would simply fade from memory." He fixed Foster with a hard look. "How is it you came to know of it?"

"Did you forget that I am not a human, Malik?" Foster leaned in, fixing him with a hard stare. "Did you forget I was raised hearing stories directly from the mouths of deities who were *there* when they took place?"

The older man shrank even further into his chair. His robe pooled around him like an oversized blanket, and he looked every bit the chastised child Foster wanted him to feel like.

"Ah. Right."

"But not all the stories were told to me, and I want to hear yours."

"Yes, well," Malik sighed. "They aren't pretty stories, and frankly they may only hold grains of truth. They're ramblings—rumors, honestly—and could well be exaggerated."

"Tell me anyway."

Several hours later, Foster stepped back onto the sidewalk at the front of the Church, looking back briefly at the praeceptor's small home. There was a long moment of stillness, a twitch of the upstairs curtains, and then the lights went out in the bedroom.

The man had been right. Foster strongly suspected the stories of the Gospel were exaggerated. A fallen angel raising an undead army of damned souls? An archangel stealing the book to bring about Armageddon? The earth crumbling to ash in a cataclysmic disaster? They were laughable ideas. Completely insane. But the one that hit close to home was the one Foster believed may actually be true—at least partially.

"The Divine who chooses to raise a loved one from the dead must be prepared for great loss," Foster murmured to himself as he started the walk back to his apartment building, echoing the words of the old clergyman. *There will be a great cost needed to balance the scales; many souls for the cost of another.*

What Christos had done was considered a miracle, raising Lazarus of Betany from the dead and returning him to his home and family. But the man had gone on to become consumed by his own existence. He spent his life obsessing over what had happened to him, tried to recreate the process more than once as his family members took ill or died of old age around him.

It was a horrific choice, and Lazarus was branded a heretic for meddling in the will of the Divine. Every test he had performed, every ritual and trial he had attempted to use to replicate what had been done to him, failed. They failed, as Gabriel put it, because Lazarus wasn't made of the right 'stuff.'

"Look at it like this, Foster Flake," Gabe's words of reassurance echoed through his mind even now. *"The Lamb is made of the same stuff you are. A little mortality to ground the magic, a little Divinity to give it that push. It worked for him and it will work for you because you both have the same magic. Lazarus was just a guy who got picked to be a spectacle, he never had a chance of making it work for him. It's like asking a house fly to build you a house, or a horse to fly you to the moon. There's a reason it's called Playing God—you need Godblood to make it happen."*

Godblood. The mana that flowed in the veins of all the Divine and marked them as Other. Gods and demigods literally bled gold and even Risen deities bled silver. But Lazarus had been a mortal man and doomed to fail even with the rituals perfected. And they *had* been perfected. Gabe assured him of that fact, and Foster had felt the surge of power when he was kneeling in that pentagram.

You're making a mistake, Foster, Judas's warning drifted back through his mind. *It's forbidden for a reason.*

His mind conjured the image of a small arm, bare and splotchy and spilling crimson from a wound *he* had inflicted. He could still feel the tiny hand he had held while her blood ran into a basin, her slender wrist cold and clammy in his grip. He shoved it down violently.

It was a mercy killing, he pleaded against his conscience, but it was a hollow excuse.

The praeceptor's warning could be referring to the death he had been required to cause, yet Foster suspected it likely meant his own immortal soul which had already become blackened by his actions. He had killed a little girl before her time and would bear that stain for the rest of his immortal life.

Chapter Twelve

The room was warm, vast, and airy as mid-day light spilled over the wooden-paneled floor, a soft breeze drifting in from the wide double doors that opened onto a back patio. Lucifer stepped into the space, feet bare and clad in a gray silk robe that was fastened loosely at his waist, breathing deep to inhale the scent of the incense that wafted from a nearby burner.

He loved his ritual space more than any other in his home, more than the garden or the kitchen. It was his most sacred space, one not even Remiel would dare to breach, and soothed him like little else. He needed to be calm and collected when he wove his enchantments if he wanted the best outcome, and though the sunlight was artificial, he loved basking in it to relax and meditate.

Bookcases lined the walls, all containing his various spell components. From crystals to herbs to candles to vials of liquids from a variety of sources, he had an extensive collection of materials to choose from, and all of it was organized by purpose. He walked now toward the shelf that contained items that would help with truth seeking, honesty, and revelation.

He took a deep blue cloth to lay on his spell board, then carefully chose several crystals from their shelves—aquamarine, selestine, and a vivid blue sapphire, as well as several small pieces of iolite and charoite. Setting these aside, Luce hummed softly to himself while he picked up bottles of herbs, un-stoppering them and inhaling deep as he made his selections. Violet and foxglove, primrose and bluebell, and of course anise to focus all the energy.

"I think I might be ready now," he murmured, laying the bundle of herbs on the board. "I'll just need an empty vial and a pestle and mortar—ah, and a candle."

Finally, he settled cross-legged on a velvet cushion, materials laid before him, and prepared to undergo an ancient truth ritual. The steps were simple: gather the materials, add a bit of Divine blood, and speak the words of the spell. Then tell the truth. It should be child's play at best, though Lucifer had a nagging suspicion it would be more complicated than it seemed to earn another piece of the Armor. It had been the first time, at least.

He pushed back the worry, dropping his flowers and herbs into the heavy mortar and beginning to grind with a practiced hand. It was soothing, in a way. Once he'd reduced the plants to a fine powder, he picked up a crystal athame, lifting his open palm over the bowl and dragging the blade across his skin to let a trickle of gold spill onto the herbs.

The wind picked up outside, the breeze becoming stronger as it wound through the room. Not enough to disturb things, but enough that Luce knew he was on the right track. He began to chant old Enochian words about conjuring truth and dispelling imbalance; words that were heavy on his tongue and rough in his throat.

He felt every minute of his countless eons upon the earth when he used his native tongue, every long day and sleepless night, every joy and sorrow of his life. It pulled him to a secret space at his core, which was exactly where he needed to be to make this ritual a success.

Luce closed his eyes, and when he opened them again, he was in darkness. The breeze still enveloped him, but gone were the shelves, the warm afternoon sunlight, the view from his patio.

Cold black stretched around him, making his skin tense at the change in temperature as he cautiously rose to his feet.

"Hello darkness," he sang softly, a smirk tugging the corners of his lips, "my old friend."

The ground beneath was now cool stone, smooth and slick as he walked slowly toward the only object he could see in the dim gloom—a shimmering, smooth mirror in a golden frame, suspended in midair and level with his line of sight. He circled the mirror, inspecting it curiously. No ropes suspended it; no wall held it aloft. It simply hung, still and delicate, like a wafer-thin slice through space itself.

"Approach," the toneless voice he had come to associate with his inner conscience commanded. "Speak your truths, son of Perdition."

Luce winced at the title. Somehow, the flat delivery made it worse, as if it were a fact and not the opinion he had always considered it to be. "Right, yes."

He returned to the front of the mirror, touching his fingers to the glass and smiling fondly at his own reflection. The image rippled, and his mirror visage suddenly lost all affect, its face falling into a placid, neutral expression.

"Speak your truths," his reflection commanded again, and it was utterly bizarre to see his own face speaking with that toneless voice.

"Okay, truth number one is that I find this experience highly disturbing."

"Irrelevant, and meaningless," his reflection droned. "Do better."

"Rude," Luce huffed, and paused. "Do you have to wear my face?"

"I am you. Confront yourself. Speak your truth."

He shifted uncomfortably, and his reflection did not move with him. "So creepy," he muttered, shuddering. "And about as helpful as an automated call line."

No response this time. Luce sighed. "Okay, okay. Commencing with the truth-telling, got it."

He paused, considering, and then touched his hand to the mirror again. In his other hand, the vial he had prepared appeared, empty and waiting to be filled.

"I neglected my son," he said quietly, and a thin wisp of smoke trickled from his lips, hazy and insubstantial. "I abandoned him in a time of need."

The smoke collected in the vial, barely enough to cover the bottom of the container.

"That is hardly a valuable truth," his reflection observed, raising its mirror image of the vial Luce cupped in his palm. "You must delve deeper."

Luce frowned. "Who decides the weight of these truths?"

Sharp eyes cut to meet his gaze, and Luce was almost cowed by his own intense stare. "You do, Morningstar. I am you, and you judge yourself."

The Devil turned away from his reflection, a chill passing down his spine. This was not a test that could be passed easily, after all. It made sense that it would be difficult, but if there was one thing Lucifer knew he was good at, it was avoiding uncomfortable discussions—not embracing them. With a groan, he turned back around and found himself waiting patiently.

"Continue."

"I still care for Michael," he admitted softly, and another trickle of smoke spilled forth, stronger than the first but still barely there.

"Do better," his reflection commanded again, cool and even.

"If you're me, why don't *you* try, hm?" Luce snapped, defenses coming up in the face of critique, even from his subconscious.

"This test is yours." Detached, impartial, and infuriating.

"I know!" He threw his hands up in exasperation, and only the ritual's magic kept the smoke from spilling out of the vial. He cupped it hastily to his chest and sighed again. "I know."

He turned away from the mirror, unable to face himself while he dug into his wounds and pried out the things that truly hurt. The things he whispered to himself in the dark of night, when he really wanted to suffer, but had never said aloud even in those lonely hours.

"I am...a bad father," he forced the words out slowly, like pieces of glass scraping their way up through his throat and into the air. "A terrible one, actually."

The smoke was pouring freely now, a steady stream from his lips to the glass vial he clutched like a lifeline. "I'm selfish and stubborn and I care more about my own needs than my son's. I left the burden of raising him to his mother, out of fear and out of convenience, and so I hardly know him."

The vial was slowly filling; a viscous purple substance twisted and coiled within the glass as Lucifer choked on his own pride and regrets. He turned, facing his apathetic reflection where it waited for him.

"The world is careening towards destruction because I was more concerned with protecting my peace and my heart than I was with being a father. I should have been there, and I chose myself, and now it might be too late to fix this."

"Yes."

Luce brought his palm to the mirror, and for a moment it flickered. He caught a glimpse of his true face, of the pain that had been dragged up to the surface etched across his expression. He looked ready to cry. But the vial was almost full, he couldn't stop now.

"I'm scared," he confessed, watching the smoke pour thickly from his own lips. "I'm scared that I am not strong enough. That I will sacrifice and try and desperately pray and still *fail*. I'm afraid, more than anything, that my brother was right, and I will never be enough."

The pain of saying those words, of confessing his deepest fear aloud, brought him to his knees. Shame and terror burned in his chest, warring with each other and his pride—or at least the wounded creature he had made of it. He gripped the vial in both hands, curling over it protectively as if it needed to be guarded.

This was the manifestation of his oldest scars, and Luce trembled as he came to terms with how truly terrified he was that they might fail because of him. Because of *his* mistakes, and his inability to correct them.

"Rise, Fallen Star," his reflection urged him, and Lucifer tore his gaze up to meet the mirror. "There is much to be done."

"Am I enough?" Luce rasped, throat tight with restrained emotion. "Can I even do this?"

"Truth is subjective," the mirror Luce evaded his question. "I am the echo of your conscience, and nothing more. Decide your own fate."

Lucifer scoffed. "Helpful, thank you."

"If I could answer you, you would not need to ask me."

"I suppose that's true," he sighed, and got back to his feet again. He eyed the vial dubiously, turning it from side to side to examine the shifting substance. "Now what? Did I pass the test?"

"You will know once you drink."

"Drink?"

His reflection cast its gaze to the vial.

"What, no," Luce said, furrowing his brow. "I just went through a lot to produce this stuff, and you want me to put it back?"

"You were changed by the process, and your perception of truth shall be changed by the drinking, as your 'truths' are only your own."

Luce blinked. "So the ritual...changed my truth?"

"Drink, Morningstar, and answer your own questions."

He tossed back the contents of the vial like a shot.

A wave of power rushed through the space with a boom of noise, before the world tilted sharply on its axis. The nebulous dark shifted wildly around Luce like shadows come alive. His vision blurred, rendering him completely disoriented as the mirror shattered, bursting into a thousand crystalline shards that glittered like falling stars.

Luce felt himself falling, but had no perception of which direction was up, or even the speed at which he fell. Then colors burst behind his eyes as his head smacked a hard surface, and suddenly the world stopped spinning.

He was back in his ritual room, panting and sweating with the cool breeze fanning over him where he lay sprawled on the wooden floor. Luce could feel his pulse racing and began taking deep, calming breaths while he waited for the nausea to pass.

"Well, that sucked." He imagined this was what a hangover might feel like, if he could get one.

He had expended a great deal of power; more than he had used for a single ritual in longer than he could recall. He didn't remember it taking this much of a toll when he had forged the first piece of the armor—though Luce had been a much younger god then. Regardless, he knew he would need at least a few days to replenish the stores of his magic before he could even consider forging another piece.

Even now, he couldn't yet tell if this ritual had been a success. Once he was able to compose himself, Luce pushed himself up and groaned at the deep ache in his muscles. It felt like he had just tried to bench press a semi-truck. He rubbed the back of his neck, stretched his arms up and felt the pop of his joints releasing, and moaned in relief.

Then he caught sight of his reflection on the glass door. Startled, his hands flew to his waist. He was both stunned and gratified to feel cool metal beneath his fingertips. Fastened around his waist was the unmistakable gold and sapphire glint of the Belt of Truth.

"Holy fuck, I've still got it."

* * *

Michael knew things were going to go south very quickly if Mags had stolen the book. He didn't expect it was going to begin during dinner on a Tuesday evening, or that Jehovah was going to overturn a vat of soup in his fury.

The dinner table was a seldom used fixture in their massive dining hall. It was typically only occupied during special occasions and parties, but every so often Queen Mary found herself in the mood for a 'family sit down dinner' and the archangels were obliged to join the royals at the table.

Michael and Christos exchanged wary glances as they entered, both stewing over their poorly concealed worries about the situation. Michael had been making plans with Uriel, his trusted lieutenant and one of his closest companions, to venture into the living world and attempt to contact Mags. He had to speak with her, to convince her to return the Gospel of Peace before Jehovah noticed it was missing and called her a trial for treason. Michael caught the stocky angel's glance as he made his way to his seat, directly across from Jehovah, and Uriel nodded his head slightly.

They were prepared. They would leave under cover of night, to reduce the chances of their absence being noted, and they would be there and back with the book before Jehovah woke for his coffee in the morning. It was a solid plan; a good one.

His plans were derailed during the first course of the evening meal, when the world seemed to tilt sharply on its axis and a ripple of power rolled through the early evening air. It was like being lapped gently by waves in the ocean; a soft cry of power that skittered down his spine, with the familiar weight of a magical signature he still recalled like it had only been a day. *Lucifer…*

A spell of that magnitude, strong enough to echo all the way to Heaven's gates? It had to be something significant; something that would have repercussions for all the realms, mortal or otherwise.

Jehovah lunged up from his seat with a bellow of rage, sweeping his arm across the table in front of him and sending everything in its path scattering. Glasses and decanters of wine, silverware, bowls, and of course the entire tureen of soup went splashing and clattering across the linen tablecloth and over anyone unfortunate enough to be seated within range of the King.

His wife let out a shriek and jumped up, overturning her chair in her haste to remove her expensive velvet gown from the line of fire. "Jeho!"

"Shut *up!* You foolish woman, so caught up in gowns and gossip," he snarled, gripping the edge of the table as if he might topple it, but visibly restraining himself. He took several deep, ragged breaths, and clenched the table hard enough that the wood groaned under his hands. "You have no *idea* what has just happened, the calamity unfolding under our very *noses!*"

Queen Mary recoiled, flushed with embarrassment at her public scolding. "Well! I suppose I shall retire for the evening, if I'm merely to be a burden here."

She gathered her skirts and swished from the room imperiously. Jehovah watched her go, a frown on his lips and a touch of remorse in his deep blue eyes. Then his gaze hardened, and he whirled on Michael.

"I have it on good authority that Mary Magdalene was seen entering the Vault of Relics, and that later the Gospel of Peace was discovered to be missing."

Michael managed to contain his reaction, if only barely. He knew better than to try to speak now and simply clenched his jaw and waited for the rest of the tirade. The King was many things, but concise was not one of them.

"Let me be explicitly clear, so there may be no mistake. Despite her standing and relationship with my son," Christos flinched, but

Jehovah barreled on, "Mary Magdalene is hereby and immediately to be considered persona non grata in this Kingdom, apart from her trial by fire."

Christos shot to his feet, horrified. "Father, please—"

There was no warning. One moment, Christos was upright and pleading, the next he sprawled on his back, a stinging red handprint blooming across his tanned cheek as he looked up at his father. Brown eyes wide with shock, he touched shaking fingers to his rapidly swelling lip. They came away stained golden with blood.

"Do not dare to argue, Christos. You may be my son, but your role in this remains to be determined. There are three keys to that vault, and mine is always accounted for. Anyone who may have aided Mary in her treachery is under equal suspicion and thereby house arrest."

Michael tensed, frowning at the floor. He'd need to delegate to Uriel then, and make sure Jophiel would—

"But not you, Michael."

His head jerked up, confusion furrowing his brow.

"Oh, no." Jehovah narrowed his eyes. "No, I can't lock away my best tracker when I have a fugitive to apprehend."

Michael swallowed hard, and nodded sharply. He wasn't a fool; this was the same as it had been before with Lucifer—a test of his loyalty and resolve. Even as the devoted soldier within him yearned to prove himself still faithful, part of him recoiled in horror at the thought of turning Mary over to that fate.

"You will surrender your key to the Vault, and to the Gates," Jehovah continued sternly. Though his chest tightened at the implication, Michael knew he had no grounds for an argument. "You are not above suspicion, Michael—a position you find yourself courting unfortunately often."

The insinuation stung, but the warrior simply gave another terse nod. Speaking was liable to get him into more trouble, and what would he honestly say? He couldn't in good conscience deny that he seemed to have a habit of mixing with heretics.

"Go, Michael," Jehovah decreed. "Leave immediately and take only as many soldiers as you absolutely require. Find that damned girl and drag her to me at once! Do *not* fail me in this."

With a deep bow and short glance at Christos's troubled expression, Michael hurried from the room as fast as his long legs would carry him, Uriel hot on his heels. The situation felt as ridiculous as it did dire as they went racing down the hall, covered in tomato bisque, with Jehovah's orders hanging over them like an ultimatum.

* * *

Jophiel entered the bath chamber with a swish in his walk and a scowl on his pouting lips.

"You'll get wrinkles frowning like that," a smooth voice echoed from further within the room, where Gabriel disrobed beside a powder blue chaise.

"Don't say things like that," Jophiel gasped, slender fingers flying up to prod gently at his forehead, needlessly smoothing skin that had never seen a wrinkle or a blemish. "I have good reason to frown, thank you very much."

"The soup," Gabe agreed solemnly, gesturing at his own discarded, orange-stained shirt with a grimace.

"The soup!" Jophiel repeated, hands thrown up in a gesture of frustration. "And it's not like I can complain to the Almighty for running up my dry-cleaning bill."

"You could," Gabe mused as Jophiel crossed the room to sink onto the chaise beside him. "Though you might be reduced to a smoldering pile of ash, so probably not worth it."

He bent at the waist and leaned toward Jophiel, stopping within a few inches of the other man's face, smirking. "You're prettier in this form, after all."

Jophiel smiled. "Even wearing soup on my Versace?"

Gabe settled on the lounge beside him, trailing a finger down the blonde's chest to outline the splash of bisque. "I think the soup actually improves the aesthetic. Very Avant Garde."

The blonde laughed, and Gabriel felt a strange twisting sensation in his chest. How odd, to feel genuine affection like this after so long. Jophiel draped an arm over Gabe's shoulders, planting a kiss on his smooth cheek, then sighed.

"Do you think Michael and Uriel will be successful?"

The other man scoffed. "Maybe. I think it's more likely they'll betray us as well."

"You don't mean that."

"I do. They're thorns in the side of Heaven. Nuisances to everything we hold dear."

"*You're* the nuisance." Jophiel smirked, leaning closer so his lips brushed Gabe's ear. Gabe turned, twisting to face him with a look of mild amusement.

"Me? Never." he grinned. "I just like to have a little fun now and then; I'm not trying to wreak havoc."

"Aren't you?" Jophiel teased, and Gabe frowned. "Oh, come on, Gabe. You're the last person I'd expect to see looking so serious."

He slipped from the chaise and turned to face Gabriel, offering his hands to pull the other man from the bench. Gabe arched a brow but slid his hands into Jophiel's and allowed him to drag him up. With a grin, the blond yanked sharply and sent them both toppling into the bathing pool.

The water was warm, but the shock of being abruptly immersed was jarring enough to make Gabe gasp. "Joph what—!"

"You like to have fun!" Jophiel grinned, water dragging his pale fringe into his eyes and making him slick it back. "Sometimes that means being spontaneous, Gabe."

"I was planning on having a bath, but not with my *wool slacks* on!"

Ice blue eyes seemed to darken. "You could take them off. I certainly wouldn't complain."

"No," Gabe laughed. "I'm sure you wouldn't."

Jophiel grinned. "Can't blame a guy for knowing what he wants."

"Touché," Gabe grinned back. He swiftly unbuttoned his fly, sliding the fitted slacks down his long legs before tossing them onto the tile in a sodden heap of black fabric. "Come on then, you next."

He didn't need to prompt him; Jophiel was already wiggling out of his own clothes.

"You're very eager," Gabe laughed, sweeping his own dark fringe out of his eyes.

"It's not often I get you to unwind with me," Jophiel reasoned, pointing an accusatory finger at the other man. "You've been so distracted lately."

"It's Foster," Gabe admitted, sobering slightly. "He's been going through some things, and Lucifer came to visit him a few days ago. It really upset him."

"Really?" Jophiel asked, surprised. "Glory told me Luce banned them all from visiting him and hasn't seen his son in years."

"Fifteen, actually."

"That's awful."

"I know." Gabe sighed and splashed water on his face. He scrubbed gently, trying to loosen the tension in his brow before it could build into another stress headache. "I try to be there for him, but with everything that's going on I can't help but worry."

"You don't need to be his dad, Gabe." Jophiel spoke quietly, as if unsure of himself.

Gabe frowned. "I'm not trying to be. I just want to make sure I'm not... I don't know, Joph. I wonder sometimes if I'm doing the right thing with him, is all. This ritual..."

"It's what he wants, right?"

"Of course it is."

"Then you're right to help him."

"Yeah...I know. I also can't help but wonder how tonight's events will change the game."

"What *were* tonight's events?" Jophiel swam in lazy circles, drifting ever closer to Gabe with each circuit.

"Well," Gabe reached out to snag the blond and drag him in closer. "I suppose we'll hear all about it when Michael and Uriel return from their adventure."

Jophiel smiled, letting himself be caught up against Gabe with little reluctance. "You're right."

"I'm always right," Gabe snorted, and Jophiel grinned, nuzzling into his neck. "You should know this by now."

"Of course, Gabe. Whatever you say."

Chapter Thirteen

Sometimes, Rag had brief flickers of concern over Lucifer's mental health. Typically, Luce was very good at pretending to be sane, but when Rag stood in the Pit watching the Drogar demons dangle prisoners over pits of hot acetone, he couldn't help but wonder what twisted tendencies their dark leader was covering up.

One of the creatures caught sight of him observing the punishment and made a keening sound, unfurling massive wings and launching itself from its perch to bound across the cavern to him. Rag smiled, bracing himself for impact as Catharsis launched into his arms.

"Hey boy," he laughed, scratching the gargoyle beneath his scaly chin while the demon licked his face with a rough tongue. Catharsis was one of the hybrid Drogar—a race descended from the gargoyles that had fallen with their angel masters, who had developed dragon-like adaptations to better suit their new environment. In fact, Catharsis was a direct descendant of Rag's own gargoyle, Custos. "Keep up the good work, okay?"

Catharsis yipped in response, giving him a headbutt under the chin before flying back to his post, and Rag lingered for a moment before he continued deeper into the Pit.

It had a proper name, once, but Rag had forgotten it years ago.

Now it was just called the Punishment Pit, and it was by far his least favorite place to be in Hell. While the sprawling fields and gardens above were home to small communities and villages of spirits, happily living their afterlife atoning for minor sins, the Pit was for those spirits who Lucifer felt had earned eternal torment. Souls that could not be saved. Murderers, rapists, sadists and abusers. Those who died and were guilty of these crimes were relegated to various levels of the Pit, where they would spend their days experiencing agony like they had inflicted while alive.

The Fallen were obliged to patrol the Pit in shifts, to keep an eye on things and ensure that none of the prisoners there were getting out of line. Today wasn't his shift, and Rag wasn't here to oversee them. He was looking for Sachiel, at the request of the other man's wife.

Rag made his way down the winding hall, carved from the natural dark stone of the earth and lit with witchlight sconces, until he reached the elevator. Pressing his palm to the sensor pad, Rag waited patiently for the stone doors to slide apart, revealing a gleaming silver box within. He stepped inside, pressing the button for the lowest floor and watching the numbers flicker down until he reached level thirteen.

"Sachiel?" he called, stepping out of the elevator. His voice reverberated through the circular, tiled hallway. This floor had a more modern feel, closed cell doors tucked neatly within white brick walls curving in a gentle arc in either direction. It was a study in contrast to the rough-hewn cavern on the first floor, but it also limited his range of view.

"Sach, man, we've been looking for you." The only sound was the reverb of his own voice, and Rag sighed. "Why do I always have to come chase you down?"

He started down the hall, steps echoing as he passed the barred doors closed over soundproof glass. Inside each room a figure writhed, strapped to a chair. Their mouths opened in screams he couldn't hear as the small, winged demons hovering over them squeezed cut lemons into mouths that leaked blood from their severed tongues.

"Liar, liar," Rag murmured, and tore his eyes away from the painful sight. He rubbed his own jaw at a phantom twinge.

"Sachi!" he called again, and this time there was an answering sound in the distance. A deep rumble, and a snort shortly after. Rag paused, and after a moment, the sound came again. A long rumble, a snort, a sort of snuffling sound.

He rounded a bend in the hall, and in the distance, he could make out a figure sprawled on the ground. As he approached, it became clear that the figure was broad, blond, and completely unconscious, snoring blissfully away with his legs stretched out to the far wall and his head leaned back against the white brick.

Raguel sighed, coming up short beside his friend and resting his hands on his hips. "Sachi, what the hell, man."

He kicked the other man lightly on the thigh, prodding him with his boot a few times. When he didn't respond except to snore harder, Rag clicked his tongue. The redhead crouched, falling into a squat next to the blonde and gently brushing his hair out of his slack face. "Just remember, I tried to be nice."

Still gently, still carefully, he dug his hand into Sachiel's hair, getting a nice, firm grip on the soft blond waves. Then he pulled hard, using most of his strength to lift the other man from the ground by his scalp.

"Ow ow ow!" Sachiel woke up screaming, hands flying up to scrabble uselessly at Rag's, while he kicked his legs to get his feet under him. "Stop! Ow!"

Rag laughed, letting go of the strands he was clutching and watching Sachiel scramble to his feet. "Sleeping on the job, you deserve worse than that."

Sachiel scowled and rubbed at his newly acquired sore spot. "There hasn't been an attempted jail break since the humans were living in caves."

"And a good thing, with a security team like you to keep an eye out."

"I was having such a good dream, too," Sachiel spoke through a yawn, pouting as he continued to rub his scalp.

"You'll be nothing but a fond memory yourself if you take any longer to get moving. Camiel is pissed."

Sachi paled. "Oh no what time is it?"

"Mhm," Rag nodded. "You're already in trouble."

"Shiiiit," he groaned, dropping his face into his palms.

The ride back up the elevator consisted of Sachiel frantically pacing and chewing harshly on his thumb nail, while Rag leaned against the back wall and watched him with mild amusement. The grin was quickly wiped off his face when the elevator doors slid open, revealing Remi and Camiel waiting with furious expressions.

Sachi whimpered. "Please tell me someone else pissed you off more than I did."

"Actually, yes," Cami hissed. "Those stupid feathered fucks wrote a letter asking Mags to come meet them in the mortal realm! As if she's that stupid!"

"Judas went to deal with them," Remi picked up where she left off, "but you know who has balls bigger than I thought?"

"Michael!" Cami threw her hands wide to emphasize her shout. "He has some nerve, writing to Luce *now!*"

Rag blinked. "I can't tell if you're upset they asked for Mags, or excited to have new gossip after a couple millennia."

"Yes," Remi dodged the question and grabbed her husband by the wrist, hauling him from the elevator and leading him towards the exit. "So now we have to go fill Luce in and figure out which level of 'oh fuck' our defenses need to be on if they're onto our plan for the armor."

* * *

Uriel felt a bone deep sense of dread as he waited on the rooftop. It gnawed at him relentlessly, like an animal instinct warning of danger, but without any seeming cause for the sensation, he was left frustrated and anxious as he waited for his commander to return from his attempt to contact Mary Magdalene.

The soft tread of footsteps alerted him to Michael's approach, so light that most wouldn't have picked up on the sound but one that should have been easily detected by those with superior senses. Uriel turned, cursing himself for his slowed reaction time. It had been a long while since they had needed to scout and stalk, and apparently, he was more out of practice than he had thought.

He smiled ruefully as Michael knelt beside him. "Well, there's no denying it now, old friend. We're caught between a rock and a hard place."

"Indeed." The taller angel was clearly troubled by his task, and Uriel hated that he was about to press on the wound.

"Will you really turn her over to Him?"

"Jehovah demands her brought to him for trial."

"That is not what I asked you," Uriel countered sternly.

"I know."

"So, you haven't decided." They both fell silent, and Uriel peeked back over the edge of the rooftop they crouched on. "I hate this."

"As do I. But you know if we go against these orders, our punishment will be just as awful."

"Maybe we shouldn't be serving such a broken system," Uriel muttered. It wasn't the first time he and Michael had had a conversation like this, though they were always careful to do so far from Heaven's gates. Even now, he felt a tremor of anxiety knowing that Jehovah had eyes and spies everywhere.

"That's heresy," Michael chastened him on instinct, but there was a look of resignation on his face.

"So it is." Uriel laid back on the rooftop, marveling at the absence of his russet wings. It was always such an odd sensation to have his wings glamoured—essentially folded into his being rather than out on display.

Though he had to admit, it was nice to be able to wear mortal clothing without having to have it custom tailored. The humans were constantly innovating with fashion and style, and the latest trend of comfortable, functional clothing was just fine with him. It was a definite improvement over the tights and doublets of the renaissance.

A tap on his thigh had him sitting back upright as Michael murmured, "We need to move."

"What is it?"

"I think we've been—"

He was cut off abruptly as a hand landed on his shoulder and yanked him to his feet. Uriel scrambled to bring himself upright, only for two hands to clamp down on his own arms from behind.

"Judas?" Uriel cried out in surprise when he recognized the man who held a blade to Michael's throat.

"Hello Uriel. Sorry to meet again under these circumstances, but when I intercepted your message for Mags, well." The Fallen Angel smiled tautly. "You understand why I couldn't let her come and be dragged off to a cell."

"We only asked her to come speak with us," Uriel protested, straining against the grip of whoever held his arms.

"Right, right, because Jehovah would be especially cool with you letting her return to Hell afterwards?"

There was a tense moment of silence, and then Uriel sighed.

"Can we at least speak without being restrained?"

Judas hesitated, then lowered his blade from Michael's neck. He kept it at the ready as he moved a half step apart from the angel, frowning. "Alright. For old time's sake, I'll trust you won't try anything stupid."

The hold on his arms disappeared, and Uriel blinked in disbelief when he saw that the one who had been restraining him was a monkey skeleton with flaming hair and bat wings. He wore a three-piece suit of burgundy velvet and a surprisingly clear expression of distaste despite his lack of skin and tissue.

"Sorry...what *are* you?"

"Rude," the demon huffed in a strangely accented voice. "I'm a Dirge, if you must know."

"Shapeshifting skeletal demons," Judas clarified. "Great for recon missions like this one, especially because they have natural glamours. Mortals see him with skin and particularly posh hair, like a little businessman."

"Stop talking about me like I'm some charming pet," the Dirge scowled, the flames of his hair dancing higher with annoyance.

"Do you have a name?" Uriel asked.

"What kind of question—of *course* I do! My name is Zaj."

"What kind of name is *Zaj?*" Uriel furrowed his brow.

"The kind that's short for Zajezjahval," the response was blunt, thrown out with the air of someone tired of repeatedly answering the same question.

Uriel recoiled. "Did your mother not love you?"

"I'm not even dignifying that with a response." Zaj turned away with haughty sniff.

"Zaj is one of the highest ranked demons in Hell," Judas deadpanned, and Uriel winced.

"I didn't mean to offend."

"Can we call a truce and resume our discussion?" Michael cut in, exasperation clear in his strained tone.

"Oh, sure." Judas smiled. "Here's the discussion. I say 'go back to Heaven' and you say 'okay' and that's it."

"You know we cannot do that." Michael frowned.

"Well, you also *cannot* take Mags to Jehovah."

"She's given a valuable artifact to Lucifer," Uriel argued. "She *stole* it."

"Technically, Jehovah never had sole dominion over the book," Judas shrugged. "It's meant to be public property for the Divine."

"Semantics are irrelevant." Uriel frowned. "It was in a secured vault and she violated Jehovah's hospitality. He's calling for a trial."

"Yeah, and those are always so fair," Judas snorted. "No go, dude. She stays in Hell."

"Then allow us to speak with her there."

Judas jabbed a finger towards Michael. "That is *also* not happening. After what you did to Luce, you think we'd let you anywhere near him?"

Michael tried to conceal his recoil, but Uriel saw it, and he bristled. "You don't have to be a dick, Judas."

"It's kind of my thing," the young man retorted. "Just ask my brother."

"So you're saying that Lucifer makes a habit of surrounding himself with slimy traitors."

Judas's eyes went stormy, and he grabbed Uriel tightly by the bicep.

"Say what you want about me," Judas growled, "but do not *ever* speak poorly of Mags in my presence."

There was a snapping sound that echoed in Uriel's ears before his body processed what had happened. A second passed in blissful confusion, and then white-hot pain lanced through his left arm. Uriel bellowed, sagging hard against Judas for a moment as his body registered the clean break in his humerus. The Fallen pulled him close before shoving him away, and the pain increased tenfold at the rough handling and the inevitable collision with Michael's chest.

"Bastard," Uriel growled, unable to conjure a more devastating insult as the pain lanced his senses and Michael did his best to keep him upright.

The demon made a noise curiously similar to a boiling tea kettle and dug at his own eye sockets with clawed finger bones.

"Judas!" he groaned. "Why do you always do this? Now we need to fix that one!"

"We don't *have* to do anything," Judas huffed.

"If we send him back damaged, it's an act of war."

Uriel whimpered. He wasn't looking to give Jehovah more fuel for his fire, but he wasn't as keen as Michael on going to Hell. Unfortunately, it didn't seem like they were going to be given very much choice.

* * *

Michael was out of his depth. The strange little demon had insisted on blindfolding them to protect the location of the Gates to Hell. He had no idea where they had been taken, which was a tactician's nightmare. He tried to time their travel by counting his footsteps but gave up somewhere around twenty minutes. Not knowing the direction of travel would render his calculations essentially useless anyway.

At some point they stopped moving, and he heard Judas speaking in a low tone, followed by an affirmative noise from Zaj, and then footsteps rapidly departing. Soon after, their demonic guide yanked the blindfolds off, looking as apologetic as a skull could manage, and shrugged.

"Can't take chances, you understand."

Michael did. They would have done the same thing, if required to invite demons into their sanctum. Realistically, though, he knew Jehovah would let an enemy rot sooner than heal a servant of the damned. What he was most displeased about were their current surroundings.

It was a dark room hewn from rough stone that was cool and slightly slick with moisture where he touched it. Unsuitable for climbing, even if there weren't a low ceiling of the same stone hemming them in. The only light came from scattered torches set in iron sconces securely bolted to the stone. A chill wound through the air, and Michael frowned.

"This is hardly an appropriate place to treat an injured man."

The demon stared blankly then gave a snort of derision. "This is just the foyer. You'll follow me to the welcome center, then we'll sort out your visitor passes and head to the estate."

"*Visitor passes?*" Uriel echoed as they followed the monkey demon into the dim corridor. "What in hell?"

The demon looked at him with disdain. "Yes, *Hell*. I assume in Heaven you just let them wander in willy-nilly, unaccounted for and undocumented? Do you even keep records?"

"Peter keeps the ledger," Uriel said defensively. "He confirms inbound souls are listed, and then they can enter the Gates."

"Terrible." The demon clicked his skeleton jaw, the sharp incisors snapping. "So casual, so unorganized."

"And I guess your system is flawless?" Uriel was aiming for condescension, but the pain from his broken humerus had him speaking in a strained tone instead. His arm gave an itchy throb as the muscle tried to knit back together around his bone fragments, and he cringed. This was going to be a messy healing.

"Watch your step," Zaj ignored Uriel's weak comeback and paused as a glimmer of light appeared around a curve in the hallway, turning to give them a grin. "There's a few steps down coming up when we cross the threshold."

They rounded the corner and the light grew, making Michael blink after the darkness of the passage. When his vision cleared, he kept right on blinking in stunned surprise at the sight that unfolded before them.

"Wow," Uriel murmured, speaking for both of them. "Whatever I expected, it wasn't this."

Michael nodded. Hell was an entirely different beast than he had anticipated.

For starters, it was much brighter than assumptions and the dreary entrance hallway would lead one to believe. Instead of a doom and gloom realm of mist and shadows, they'd paused on a cliffside at least two hundred feet up, with a clear view across sprawling fields of crops dotted with small clusters of buildings.

A pale winter sun beamed down over the land, giving everything a cool glow, and Michael could tell the brisk wind that tugged at them at this elevation would be a gentle breeze closer to the ground. It was a peaceful setting, and even the massive palace in the distance was more colorful and livelier than he had expected.

A sprawling estate of cream-colored stone was enclosed by a low wall of dark shale, and the spires and rooftops were crowned with umber shingles. Burgundy wood framed the windows and doors, and even from this distance Michael's sharp eyesight could pick out several balconies, what looked like an observatory, and a wide court-yard garden. It was downright pastoral, and he felt a bit hypocritical for his initial surprise. This was exactly the kind of setting Luce thrived in, this relaxed and homey elegance.

Yet some part of him had pushed aside the things he *knew* to make room for biased expectation. It made sense on some level that his banishment would change Lucifer, but he should've known better than to think it would be extreme. A new layer of shame settled onto the familiar pile.

"Yes, it's lovely," Zaj interrupted his musing, flapping around to hover in front of him. "But we have places to be and an arm to repair, so maybe save the sightseeing for your next visit? We have a wonderful tour on Thursdays."

"You... do?"

"I don't have time to educate you on how sorely lacking Heaven must be compared to Hell. Just follow me, and try not to slip under the guardrail, alright? One injured angel is bad enough; we don't need it happening on our turf the second time."

Michael glanced to the side and noticed the roughly carved stone steps winding along the face of the cliff, with only a thin metal railing between them and a drop hundreds of feet. Uriel followed his gaze and groaned.

"What a time not to have the wings…"

Michael nodded. They had expected to be in the mortal realm much longer than they had been. The glamour that kept their wings tucked away wouldn't wear off for at least another few hours.

"Less yapping, more stepping." Zaj clapped his bony hands impatiently. "We have to get a move on if you want to beat the rush."

"The rush?" Uriel felt more exhausted than he had in centuries, and they hadn't even begun the descent yet. It didn't help that every word out of Zaj's mouth was more confusing than the last.

"Oh, you'll see."

As they wound carefully down the steep incline from the cliff's peak to its base, a large brick building emerged from the gentle mist and tall pines. It was easily three stories, nestled into the side of a hill, with large windows that allowed them to glimpse a long line of people stretching from the top floor to the first-floor entrance. The line snaked out even beyond the doorway along a cobblestone path to a massive pair of wrought-iron gates that gleamed imposingly in the pale light.

Uriel was so busy looking at the crowd, he skipped a stair and stumbled the last few steps to the ground. Michael gripped his good arm firmly, pulling the other man upright and giving him a moment to catch his breath.

"Thanks," he said, giving Michael a grateful smile.

Zaj groaned. "This is exactly what I wanted to avoid, the new souls take forever to process. And today looks like a longer line than normal. We'll have to pull rank to skip ahead."

They closed the gap from the cliffside path to pass between the massive gates and crossed the lawn to the building's front door, bypassing the line completely. They received several disgruntled looks for their behavior, and Michael kept his gaze averted.

The freshly deceased tended to be a bit...well, *unkempt,* to put it politely. But Uriel stared openly through eyes half-lidded from pain as he stumbled along, allowing Michael to essentially drag him forward.

"They look mad, Zaj," he murmured distractedly.

"Because we are!" One of the spirits in line snapped back, a furious look in his dark eyes. "Been waiting hours, and you're just skipping right ahead!"

"Official court business," Zaj sniffed haughtily, fishing a pendant out of his suit jacket and dangling it in front of him like a barrier. A symbol of angel wings in black overlaid with golden stars was embossed on the front of the medallion. As it spun, the back was revealed to bear a second set of wings, this time rendered in gold, pierced with a dark sword. "Important emissaries from Upstairs."

"Is this going to add to our wait?" Another spirit piped up, peering curiously at the angels. Michael winced at the knife protruding from her sternum. Hopefully someone would help her alter her essence soon.

"Not in the slightest! In fact, I'll make sure to have a word at Processing and get this line moving double time."

"Yeah, sure," the first speaker snorted, but the others in line looked grateful.

"How long *does* this normally take?" Uriel asked curiously.

"Oh, several hours at least. Usually five, give or take." Zaj led them up a winding staircase, impatiently bumping spirits to the side so they could pass. "It can take all day if we're particularly busy. We need to check the inbound ledger, then document their date and cause of death as well as what they've done to earn a ticket down here. Finally, after we file that away, they proceed to the aptitude test."

"Aptitude test?" Michael raised a brow in confusion.

Zaj glowered briefly in Michael's general direction, focused on moving them along. "It's how we decide where the spirits will go. The worst of them go to the Pit. It's basically Hell Jail."

"And the others?" Uriel asked.

"Well, some of them don't belong here, in our humble opinion. But you guys have some pretty strict policies, so we take the stragglers. Murder's a sin, but killing in self-defense? Hardly." He sniffed again.

"But we take who you reject and they're free to wander. Everyone outside the Pit gets a shot at reincarnation if they want, but they have to work for it. There's basically three groups; The Second-Chancers, The Happy Haunters, and the Rotten Eggs."

"Those names have Mags written all over them." Uriel smiled, but it faded when his bad arm brushed the banister and he cried out. Zaj looked over his shoulder, frowning.

"Okay, we're going to have to hurry this along." His wings flapped harder as he led them up the stairwell to the top floor, where a trio of bored looking old women were seated behind a wide mahogany desk.

At first glance, they looked relatively normal; a bit like grand-mothers as they snapped photos and noted down names and filled out Cause of Death forms. But then a veil seemed to shimmer out of exis-tence, revealing violently purple skin and twisting horns. Michael blinked, and the matronly disguises were back in place.

Zaj caught his stunned expression and grinned. "Yeah, we try not to freak them out too bad when they first arrive. You won't notice because you're in the loop, but when they see me, I look like a human with that little people thing—dwarfism?"

"But you're floating," Uriel stated bluntly. "Humans don't float."

"That's not precisely true in the afterlife, is it? Anyway, they over-look a lot as long as you're not visibly terrifying. Humans see what they want to see, most of the time."

He made his way to the desk and settled down on it, his tail stretched out behind him and flicking playfully at a stack of papers. The shortest of the women scowled at him, slamming her palm down to trap the appendage.

"Straeng." Zaj said sweetly, and she swatted him with her other hand.

"No! Stop messing my papers!" Her accent was as heavy as the glare she leveled on Zaj.

"Don't be like that," he crooned, leaning in towards her, and she swatted his face away.

"Stop! No closer!"

"I need two visitor badges, Straeng my love. Can you or one of your lovely sisters help me with that?"

"Ask Geber," she snapped. "That her job, no mine."

"Here." The middle sister thrust her hand at him, long nails scraping against bone as Zaj accepted the bits of hard red plastic. "Viv see you coming, I have prepare."

The third and tallest sister didn't deign to respond verbally, only raising a hand briefly before she resumed clicking away at the camera.

"Well, as much as I love to see you girls, I can also see you're very busy," Zaj hopped off the counter, dipping at first before he righted himself. "Come on boys!"

* * *

Luce had made a terrible mistake letting Mags keep the Gospel. His skin had begun to crawl as soon as Remi had come pushing through the doors to his study, and it only intensified as Camiel relayed the message Judas had intercepted. It had to be a response to his ritual. The wave of magic that had knocked him on his ass must have been strong enough to touch Heaven.

Jehovah knew the Gospel was gone, and he had sent his best soldiers to retrieve it—and surely Mags as well. This was going to go so terribly wrong; he could feel it.

"Will you *sit down?*" Remi snapped, lunging out of her chair to grab him as he paced by in another endless circuit. Rag grabbed the back of her sweater and pulled her back into her seat, shaking his head at her answering glare.

"Let him pace," he rumbled, idly flipping pages in the cookbook Mags had lent him. "It's better than him trying to bake something."

"He's making me dizzy!"

"So go check in with Bal instead of just watching him."

"Fine!" Remi hopped back up, unimpeded this time, and stomped out of the room.

"I'm going with her," Camiel sighed. "Just to make sure she doesn't hurt someone."

With the women gone, only their husbands remained in the study with Luce. Judas was intercepting the emissaries, while Glory and Bal were off doing who knew what. Luce didn't like having everyone scat-

163

tered with everything balanced so precariously on the edge of chaos, but it helped to at least have company.

They shared the silence for another several laps, the only sounds the pad of Lucifer's shoes on the carpet and the turning of Rag's pages. It was enough to settle the king's nerves, slowing his pace and his breathing.

"Thank you," Luce murmured, pulling gently on his beard as he turned back to begin another loop. "I can't help it, I'm just—"

"Terrified." Rag nodded. "It's understandable."

"I'm the King of Hell, Rag, not some lowly demon, I am—" he broke off his insulted tirade when he glanced up and saw Rag's knowing smile. "I am absolutely terrified, yeah."

"About them asking for Mags, or the fact that it's Michael?" Sachiel asked, ignoring the warning look Rag shot him.

Luce went pale and looked like he was torn between vomiting and shouting. "How dare you—"

The sound of rapid footfalls from the corridor startled Luce to a halt and the other Fallen to their feet. They all turned to the doorway as Remi burst back through it, looking as if she'd seen a ghost.

"What is it?" Luce demanded, the frantic nature of her movements sending a spike of adrenaline through him. "Oh, Damned Souls, Remi! What *happened?*"

"Judas is back," she stammered. "And Zaj is... he's back too, and he's with—"

Luce crossed the room and gripped her shoulders firmly, leaning so close they were sharing the same breath. "Tell me!"

"Michael," she finally croaked, eyes wide.

Luce froze, hands falling away from Remi and settling at his side like dead weights. He blinked slowly, once, twice, and tried to calm his breathing. His heart thumped frantic rebellion against his ribcage.

Here, now.

It was so much worse when it was a certainty and not a possibility. He swallowed hard, tongue darting out to wet his suddenly dry lips, and his fingers came back to life to curl and uncurl in fists.

"I can't," he moaned, closing his eyes tightly. "I can't be near him, I can't."

"You have to," Remi said, stepping back into his space and taking his hands in hers. "Uriel is with them, and he's got a bad break."

"Oh no...Oh please..." Luce shuddered. "Can't someone else?"

She hesitated, and Luce groaned.

"Cami is there trying to help," she started, then paused, chewing her lip. "It's splintered badly. I think it's beyond our skill level."

"Fine," Luce said, straightening his spine. He took a steadying breath, then another. "Someone has to set it before it heals all wrong."

"You'll have to re-break it," Remi said softly. "It's already starting to fuse."

"Fantastic," Luce deadpanned. "This day gets better and better."

He took one last moment to collect himself before drawing himself to full height. A snap of his fingers and his favorite cloak appeared on his broad shoulders; rich black velvet lined with crimson satin draping and falling around him like a shield. The ghost of a black iron crown appeared around his temples like a circlet of mist. Squaring his shoulders, the King of Hell swept from the room.

Chapter Fourteen

"This is the fanciest infirmary I have ever been in." Michael wandered around the room in fascination.

He inspected the state-of-the-art equipment, took note of the crisp white curtains and bed linens, and gazed into a tile floor polished to a sheen so fine he could almost see his reflection. Fully stocked glass-front cabinets lined all the walls, bursting with tinctures and salves and countless bottles of potions alongside modern medicines.

"We need to get on this level," Uriel agreed, shifting on his assigned cot to better gaze up at the skylight that cast the room in a gentle afternoon glow. "Just being in this room already makes me feel better."

"I think Camiel's healing had something to do with that."

"Maybe so," Uriel admitted cheerfully, already feeling the sedative effects of the tincture the brunette angel had practically poured down his throat. "She looks good, right?"

"Don't let her husband hear you pining," Michael said diplomatically. He had never had much interest in the appearances of women, but he had to admit Camiel had always been a beauty, even among Seraphim.

"Please, Rebecca would kill me first," Uriel chuckled. "But really, I think Cami was utterly shocked to see us."

"It has been quite a few centuries."

"I wonder why Judas helped us," Uriel mused, bouncing through topics like a toddler on a sugar rush as the medicine loosened his tongue and his grip on the present. He tried to peer around the room, twisting to look under the neighboring cot as if he expected to see Zaj hiding there. "He broke my arm on purpose, you know. To make Zucchini bring us here."

"Zajezjahval," Michael corrected automatically, then realized what Uriel had said. "Wait, what?"

"That's what he whispered to me. Weird, right?" Uriel laughed as Michael filed that information away to address later. Then the black angel's medicated gaze sharpened on Michael. "Are you alright?"

"Maybe." Michael groaned, running his hands anxiously through his wild curls. "No, not really."

"Being here can't be easy for you." Uriel spoke softly, his tone already slipping back into a drug-addled fog.

"He must despise me, and I don't blame him. I don't even know how I feel about seeing him. What can either of us say, after we betrayed each other?"

A soft sound from the hall caught their attention, and Michael strained his hearing until he could discern the steady click of hard soled shoes on the tile. A spike of adrenaline raced up his spine when he realized who must be headed their way, and Uriel gave him a sympathetic look. The door creaked open at his back, and Michael tensed as if waiting for a blow. The footsteps didn't falter, rising in volume as they steadily approached, until they came to a stop at his side.

"Uriel," a rich, smooth voice broke the hush that had fallen over the room, and Saints above, Michael's knees went weak. How long had it been since he had heard that voice outside the confines of his memories? "I was horrified to hear that one of my own manhandled you this way."

Michael swallowed hard, trying to force his body to cooperate, to turn and *say something,* anything, but anxiety and a lingering flare of resentment kept him frozen in place.

"To be fair," Uriel raised his good arm and jabbed an accusatory finger at Lucifer, "I would've been safely up in Heaven if we hadn't been sent to track down Jeho's stolen property."

Luce winced and sighed. "Circumstances are... more dire than you realize. This wasn't a decision we came to lightly."

"I hope not, since now they want Mags tried by fire for *treason*." Uriel frowned.

Luce made a pained sound, and Michael turned at last, terrified and bracing himself but desperate to stop Luce making a sound like that again. His knees gave another traitorous quiver when he finally saw him.

Luce hadn't changed whatsoever in the time they had been apart; he was still as handsome and regal and purely divine as he was in the memories Michael treasured. If anything, time had only sharpened his beauty like a finely crafted blade.

"Lucifer..." He openly stared at him, reaching out as if to touch him, only to draw back his trembling hand at the raw power rolling off the other man. It was like a living shield blocking him from getting too close, and Michael tried not to feel too offended, because he knew he deserved the rebuff.

"Well," Luce cleared his throat, ignoring Michael as if he hadn't spoken, though the King's own voice tight with emotion. "I am deeply sorry for that, but I can't begrudge Mags her free will. Let's look at that arm, shall we?"

Uriel hesitated, then shifted so his injured arm was accessible to Luce. "I'll try not to scream," he muttered bitterly.

"Here." Luce snapped his fingers, and a thick piece of rope dropped into Uriel's lap. "I'm going to sedate you, but you'll likely burn through it before I'm done."

"I always was a quick healer."

"Unfortunately, that's working against us here." Luce frowned as he assessed the damage carefully, prodding and stroking Uriel's bicep and feeling the way things shifted beneath the skin. "I'm going to re-break your humerus, but I'll have to open the flesh to make sure I properly sever and reattach the fused bone and ligaments. I'll need to use a special salve to prevent your wound from resealing while I work, so you'll have a lovely scar when we're finished."

"Rebecca will love it." Uriel grinned.

"Wonderful."

Michael stood frozen, torn between wanting to touch Luce and cursing him inwardly for the audacity to have somehow gotten *more* attractive. Luce refused to even look at him. He gazed directly at Uriel, eyes never even shifting towards Michael, and pretended the blond wasn't even in the room.

"Please, Lucifer," Michael's voice shook as he stepped closer to his former lover and winced when he hit the wall again. It was like a living thing pressing at his shoulders to keep him firmly away from Luce.

Uriel cleared his throat as Luce reached for his arm. "Mike, maybe you could step out?"

They both started at his words, Mike at the dismissal, and Luce at the blatant acknowledgement of his presence.

"I just mean," Uriel pressed on quickly, "that I don't want you to see me crying like a child. I have my reputation to uphold."

As if he hadn't seen Uriel shattered both physically and emotionally before? It was a thinly veiled attempt to spare him this humiliation, and Michael seized it gratefully.

"Yes." He gave a quick nod, setting his hand on Uriel's good shoulder briefly before he turned and fled the infirmary. He remembered seeing a garden as they descended the cliffside. If he followed this hall, surely he'd come across the courtyard at some point.

Uriel watched the door for a long moment after Michael pushed through it, clearly distraught. As much as he understood there were deep, untended wounds between Michael and Luce, he couldn't help but feel protective over his stoic friend. He turned a small frown on the King, that biased part of him angry with Luce for refusing to even acknowledge the other man.

"That was decidedly harsh," he said, voice soft but steady.

Luce flinched, long fingers tightening on the jar he had just summoned from a cabinet across the room.

"You speak out of turn," he said at last, voice taut with an emotion Uriel couldn't name. It was somewhere between anger and anxiety, and it gave him pause.

"You're right." He tried to shrug, and gave a little gasp at the pain that lanced his arm.

"Try not to break yourself more, when I'm about to try and fix you?" Luce asked drily, and Uriel offered a weak grin.

"Apologies," he chuckled. "Camiel gave me a potion that almost had me forgetting it was broken."

"Ah, that would be one of mine." Luce beamed with pride. "I made it for battlefield surgery, when we needed to alleviate the shock to get the wounded to safety quickly. It's essentially a sedative that targets and numbs injuries."

"If only we'd had that one back when I nearly lost my wing at Babel, eh?"

"That was actually what inspired me to start developing it," Luce admitted with a sly grin. "You were crying like a child then, if I recall?"

"I essentially *was* a child," Uriel said, a bitter cast to his tone, and then sighed. "Ah well, that's the past. Sometimes it's best to let go of the past, right Luce?"

"Nice try." Luce frowned, giving him a stern look as he poured a measure of ruby liquid from the jar to a glass and passed it to Uriel. "You know very well that this isn't nearly that cut and dry. Drink this, it's more of what you had earlier."

Uriel accepted the glass and tossed the contents down in a single swallow. "I think you need to talk to each other," he tried again, stubbornly.

"Uriel, I still consider you a friend," when he answered, Luce's tone was hard and cool, "but if you press this subject with me, it will not be a pleasant conversation for either of us."

"He just wants a chance to make amends and try to...understand."

"He has had several millennia in which to try!" A cool wind swept the room, sending the curtains fluttering and the glass cabinets rattling. Luce turned away sharply, swapping the jar of sedative potion for a metal tin of salve to occupy his hands.

Uriel waited, gazing at Luce with something close to sympathy. When the wind settled and the curtains drifted back into place, he reached out with his good hand and touched the King lightly on the arm. "Luce...you hurt him too."

"I did no such thing," Luce snapped, turning away from the bed and pacing across the room to rummage through a cabinet. *"He* is the one who refused my requests to speak then, so why should I entertain his now?"

Uriel said nothing. The slow spread of warmth along his damaged limb was distracting and soothing, and he allowed his mind to wander while the other man burned off his emotions. A gentle tug on his damaged arm pulled him back to attention, and he looked over to see Luce gently slicing around the shoulder of his jacket. He looked conflicted but determined.

"You're going to lose this sleeve, I'm afraid," he murmured, and Uriel nodded distantly.

"'Sokay," he slurred, the stronger dose of tonic lulling him into a dreamlike fog. "I borrowedit from Jophi..."

He dipped into darkness to the sound of Lucifer chuckling, and when he bobbed back into consciousness, his sleeve was gone, and his dark skin split like paper under Luce's steady and careful blade.

"Ow."

Luce froze. "You can feel that?"

"No," Uriel muttered. "Just looks painful."

He slipped back under, and this time he stayed there.

* * *

Michael was lost in more than one sense of the word. He wandered through the halls restlessly, without noting anything specific enough to orient himself, essentially just following his feet wherever they were heading. He would've reprimanded his soldiers for acting this way—blindly wandering around alone in enemy territory? Unacceptable.

But Luce wasn't really his enemy, was he? Even now the King himself tended to Uriel's wounds. It was hard to imagine Jehovah doing the same for one of Lucifer's people.

*What you do for the least of these, you do for me...*Michael thought bitterly.

It was a credo he had done his best to honor for centuries, and yet his King considered himself above such things. The nature of goodness was fickle in Heaven. It came with the added weight of rules and qualifications.

Zaj's words at the welcome center came back to gnaw at him. *You guys have some pretty strict policies...* Wasn't that the truth? He was so distracted by his thoughts that he almost toppled into a fountain.

"Who puts a fountain in a hallway?!" He teetered on the edge of it, bracing himself against the statue that topped the basin to regain his balance. Lifting his head, he blinked in astonishment at the sprawl of plants and greenery unfolding around him. He had stumbled out of the palace into the garden without even noticing.

Michael smiled; he had always felt at home in nature, especially gardens; small pockets of the world's beauty, carefully curated and preserved for admiration. Closing his eyes and breathing deeply in, Michael reveled in the strong smell of warm earth and the various floral scents mingling into something unidentifiably pleasant that made him feel warm and content.

It was a familiar smell, and not just because he enjoyed nature. That specific blend of nightshade and lily, the pop of morning glories with lavender. His eyes flew wide to confirm with his sight what his nose and his heart had already understood, and this time he let his traitorous knees bring him down to that warm dirt.

It was *his* Garden. *The* Garden. *Eden*, painstakingly recreated. He laid his forehead on the cool stone of the fountain's basin, trailing his fingers in the sun-warmed water. In the home that Luce built after banishment to shield and protect himself; in the heart of his palace. Even after everything that had been said and done, Luce built this same garden again.

The swirl of emotion built towards a crescendo. His throat tightened and he lifted his head, only to fall back in shock at the sight of the statue he'd been leaning on. His own face stared back, screwed up in a bellow of rage as he lunged for some unseen enemy, sword aloft and tears streaming freely from his eyes.

He knew this scene. He remembered the way his throat had ached from the force of his rage tearing through it. The way the tears had felt as they dried on his face. The simultaneous weight and reassurance of his sword in his hand. He had never realized how terrifying and heartbroken the whole picture looked when you viewed it at once from the outside; it was like a painful mirror.

Confronted with too much stimulus and memory at once, he let his gaze drop as he hung his head and Michael wept. The soft patter of footsteps hit his ear like pebbles on a window, but he still flinched when a small hand settled between his shoulder blades.

"Mikha'el," Mags whispered, her voice like silk but rubbing his already raw nerves like sandpaper.

"Mary," he rasped, looking up at her with desperation. She cradled his face in her hands like a mother, the scars on her palms rubbing against his skin as she drew him in to lean against her where she perched on the fountain's edge.

"You were not meant to see this," she said, gently rubbing her thumbs over his temples and weaving her fingers through his curls. "This is his grieving place."

"He made it for me." Michael shivered reflexively. "And now *because* of me."

"You have to stop carrying the burden alone, Michael."

"The blame is mine."

"Not *only* yours," she insisted, pulling back to meet his tormented silver gaze. "You were one part of a flawed system, and you need to open yourself to the possibility of forgiveness before you can begin to earn it."

"I will not accept what I don't deserve." He tried to swallow against the roughness of his throat.

"You also won't accept what you *do*, you stubborn fool." She shook him gently by the shoulders. "Look at that statue. Find that passion and use it for good."

"I am no longer that man. He died when Lucifer Fell."

"But you could be something better, if you allow change into your life."

There was a heavy pause between them, and then Michael made a sound like a sigh meeting a laugh. "When did you become so wise?"

"When I started *listening* to Christos instead of arguing with him," she said, giving him a pointed stare.

The mention of the prince had Michael's spirits sinking again. "Mary, there is something you should know.

She went still, reading something in his expression that sent a chill down her spine.

"He knows." Her shoulders slumped, and she closed her eyes tightly. "I knew it was a matter of time."

"He is calling for your arrest…and trial."

"And he sent you." It wasn't a question, so he didn't answer. Mags drew back and rose from their crouched position, wrapping her arms around herself with a look of resignation and pain. "I'm sorry, I…"

"I understand." He rose to his feet and laid a hand on her shoulder. "I'd like some time to reflect on things alone, anyway."

He watched her drift back along the stone walkway, hugging herself tightly as if for warmth, and his heart ached for her. They both knew that a trial by fire was the highest form of judgement Jehovah had at his disposal, and they resulted more often than not in either banishment or… he flinched.

Banishment or death. Jehovah expected him to drag her back to Heaven to face that horror. *Dutiful Michael,* he cursed himself internally, glaring at his own stone face twisted in broken rage. *Always so sure of the right path, but now you have no idea what you should do, do you?*

Luce stood up from his stool at Uriel's bedside and stretched with a groan, pulling off his gloves and tossing them into the trash. He gave the careful sutures a last inspection and, satisfied, sent the blankets to cover the angel with a casual flick of his wrist.

"Rest easy," he said softly, placing his fingers on Uriel's brow to gauge his temperature. No signs of fever, and the herbal poultice he had applied would ward off any infection. The arm that had previously been a tangled mess of tissue and splintered bone was once more intact, and Luce hummed with the sense of pride and self-satisfaction that always accompanied the resolution of a difficult injury.

Stepping away from the bed, he pulled the curtains in and dimmed the lights so it wouldn't be too bright if the other man woke before they expected. He mulled over Uriel's surprising declaration as he set about cleaning and organizing his tools and workspace. Michael claimed Luce had hurt *him*? That was rich.

Though maybe it was true; maybe Luce should have confided his feelings in Michael, instead of protecting his morally rigid lover from complicity. What was the point in regretting that now? There was more than enough of that nonsense going around already, even though the real blame rested with a system that forced people to extremes of morality.

He lifted two vials of medicine, one deep violet and the other a shocking aquamarine.

"Dark and light," Luce muttered, swirling them in their stoppered bottles before popping the tops and mixing a measure of each into a third bottle. The colors swirled and blended into a murky brown, and he scoffed. "Yes, that's closer to the truth, isn't it? We all end up dragged through the mud at some point."

He scribbled a quick note for his slumbering patient—*Don't mind the color, drink this for any lingering pain*—and set both on the bedside table. This job, at least, was done. He rubbed the bridge of his nose to work out the headache forming, giving himself a spark of magic to soothe it when that failed.

"Luce," a soft voice interrupted him as he closed the infirmary door behind him with a soft click. His eyes flicked up to meet Glory's, concern clearly written across her face. "I think something has happened to Mags."

"What?" His heart skipped a beat.

"She just left the Garden. I ran into her as I passed, and it was like she was looking right through me."

He frowned. "I think I know what happened. Try not to worry, sweets, I'm going to handle things."

Her expression relaxed slightly but retained a touch of worry in the tightness of her jaw.

"You'll get wrinkles frowning like that," he teased gently, and she made a sound like a startled cat, hands flying up to prod and pull gently at her flawless skin. Luce laughed. "I'm kidding! You know you're radiant, Gloriana."

"You're a real brat sometimes," Glory pouted, and Luce patted her cheek fondly.

"We're both divas, darling, it takes one to know one."

She rolled her eyes, but he had succeeded in drawing out a smile.

"Oh, I almost forgot," she said, eyes widening. "I was coming to find you because Cwall is back."

His mood instantly sobered, the levity giving way to concern. "Any news?"

Cwall's surveillance had been invaluable to him during Foster's rebellious phase, ensuring that Luce could keep his distance without entirely abandoning his son. It had backfired spectacularly, but it had seemed like the only way at the time.

"Some." She worried her lip between pearly white teeth. Luce waited patiently despite the anxiety urging him to shake the words from her lips. Finally, Glory sighed. "Foster is seeking a second sacrifice."

"*What?*" Luce drew back, eyebrows flying into his hairline as his eyes went wide with alarm. "I know my visit to him went poorly, but I had hoped..."

"You hoped it would at least give him pause," Glory filled in softly.

"Yes," he croaked, heart and throat constricting in tandem. He closed his eyes against the burn that threatened—the King of Hell simply did *not* cry openly in the corridor.

He opened his eyes to Glory's tortured expression, tears flowing freely down her porcelain cheeks. "I'm beginning to fear we're going to fail him."

Luce reached out and took her small hand in his, squeezing it with a reassurance he desperately needed himself. "I'll try to speak with him again. There has to be hope, Gloriana."

"There's always hope," she murmured back, even if she sounded a bit unsure. Luce gave another gentle squeeze before releasing her.

"Try not to worry," Luce said, knowing full well that it was a useless sentiment.

Glory made a non-committal sound at his request, but Luce didn't have the luxury of time to reassure her further. Instead, he angled towards the courtyard, fixing his face into a stern and distant mask. It seemed there was a pest issue in his garden that needed attending to.

Chapter Fifteen

Some things, Lucifer thought to himself grimly, *you simply are never prepared for.* It was a sentiment he often expressed, and he found it to be inherently true. The birth of your first child, the death of a loved one, and of course, seeing your ex after a traumatic breakup.

He loitered in the archway that led out into his Garden, pretending to take in the lush scenery while he fought down the panic that crawled stubbornly up through his torso to strangle him. The bewitched sunlight beamed down into the atrium, lighting on upturned leaves and delicate blooms and the golden curls of Michael's hair where he bowed before the statue of…himself.

"Normally people know better than to intrude on my personal space," he finally forced himself to speak, pleased by the level, slightly sardonic drawl that came out. He had been afraid of sounding like a nervous preteen, the way his pulse was jumping under his skin. "Or at least they ask my permission first."

Michael lunged up with that predatory swiftness that made him so lethal on a battlefield, yet somehow managed to fall back in hesitation. His beautiful face was guarded, anxiety laying across high cheekbones and pulling down the corners of his full lips. Luce's chest constricted with the need to kiss and strangle him simultaneously. He settled for leaning back against the doorframe with his arms folded tightly across his chest.

Michael opened his mouth, then closed it, unsure of how to even begin this conversation.

"Oh no," Luce snapped. "You're on my turf, so you have no excuse not to explain what the fuck you're doing here."

Michael visibly started but quickly schooled his features into mild annoyance. "I didn't come here willingly."

"I know," Luce sneered. "If you'd wanted to be here you would've come years ago."

"That's not fair."

"Life isn't fair."

Michael scoffed. "You were never this cynical before."

"I was a different man before," Luce retorted, tone sharp and laced with warning. "A lot has changed between then and now."

"Yes, now you kidnap people after you brutalize them."

"No, I interrogate spies." His eyes narrowed. "We both know why you were on that rooftop, and we both know who sent you."

"Your brother has cause to be concerned. That book contains knowledge of powerful artifacts, and he does not trust you."

"I'm well aware of that." Luce shifted off the wall, advancing slowly on the other man with gold sparking dangerously in his dark eyes. "I was the one who was cast out, after all. Denied access to my rightful place and all of the artifacts within it."

"Of course I know this," Michael was getting irritated, his pulse jumping in his veins. At least he told himself it was due to annoyance, and not fear or—Saints forbid—*longing* that stirred in him as Luce stalked closer, radiating power and dominance. "I never said that I disagreed with her actions, for the record."

This made Luce pause. He blinked slowly, frowning. "Well, that sounds borderline heretical, Michael."

His name from that mouth after all this time... it sent a tremor through the blond that he hoped didn't show on the surface. This was rocky ground; they needed to tread carefully here.

"Perhaps sometimes... what is right and what is easy are not... congruent."

A wry smile tugged at Luce's lips against his will, one corner quirking up. "You and your damn doubletalk." He shook his head. "Always saying what people want to hear and never what you really want to say."

"It got between us in the end, didn't it?"

Luce abruptly closed off, face slackening into a bland mask of disinterest. "We're not talking about that."

"We should," Michael pressed. "I need to—"

"This is not about what *you need*," Luce hissed. "I don't want to talk about it, and as a guest in my home you will respect my wishes."

"An unwilling 'guest'," Michael threw up air quotes with a sneer, "should not be bound by the laws of courtesy."

"You're right," Luce agreed readily. "And since you've already intruded on my hospitality, you would do well to remember what I do to those who makes themselves my enemies."

"You're threatening me, after I just told you I agree with you." Michael scoffed. "This is why you struggled to lead."

"I do not, nor have I ever, 'struggled to lead'." A tangible feeling of cold swept the room as his tone turned icy. "I rescinded control to my brother because he wanted it more, and my subjects here find me quite an amicable King. You have some nerve to speak of threats when you've done more harm to me than I ever inflicted upon you."

Michael tensed. "We hurt each other."

Luce snorted. "Maybe so, but only one of us still has his *wings*."

He spat the word like it was something foul, and he might as well have struck Michael for the way he recoiled. For a moment Luce looked at the closed off form—the hunched shoulders, the bowed head—and he almost felt guilty. Then he remembered Glory's concerning message, and simmering anger slipped back around him like a shawl.

"I have been sorry for that since the day it happened."

"You say that like it matters," Luce murmured darkly, turning away. "You were brought here for Uriel to be healed, and so I could gauge what my brother plans to do. I don't need an admission from you to know what he plans for Mags."

Michael stared at those broad shoulders, taught with restrained emotion. He felt a flare of anger that Luce would turn his back on him *again*, but it died quickly. What had he expected? A warm reception? A tearful reunion? Apologies and forgiveness?

He was a fool.

"You are not prisoners here," Luce's voice drifted over his shoulder, softer but still carrying a chill. "You're free to leave at any time. But you will not take Mary Magdalene. She comes and goes of her *own* will, and I don't permit manhandling of my family."

Michael wanted to shout but kept his tone controlled through great effort. "I had no plans to *take* Mags anywhere. I am not some mindless drone for your brother."

"Could've fooled me," Luce called as he stalked from the Garden without another word or glance.

* * *

Mags lay on her back, fingers skimming plush carpet as she stared up at the vaulted ceiling of her room. The hand-painted stars glittered back at her, wavering in the film of tears that ran steadily over her cheeks and into her splayed chestnut hair. There was a chance, once Jehovah got his hands on her, that she would never see these stars, this room, this *Kingdom* again. But she had known the risk. She had made the choice. These were the consequences of her actions, and she could live with them.

A quiet, firm knock on her door interrupted her musing, and she lifted a hand to swing the door open. Footsteps approached, and Luce sank into a crouch beside her.

"Hi," he said quietly.

"Hi," she murmured, trying to dredge up a smile for him. He clicked his tongue and pressed a slim finger to the corner of her mouth.

"Stop that," he chastised gently. "No pretenses between us."

The tears redoubled, and he settled down cross-legged, pulling her head into his lap.

"Let it out." He ran his fingers along her brow, then wove them through her hair slowly.

The motion was calming, and his presence made her feel safe. Mags released the tension coiled tightly within. She bawled openly, tears spilling hot and fast as she curled into Luce's embrace, a damp patch spreading along his slacks where she pressed her face to his thigh. He continued murmuring soothingly as he stroked her hair over and over, nonsense ramblings in Enochian just to fill the space between the silence and her sobs.

"I have to go back," she finally whispered what felt like hours later, voice hoarse from a throat stripped and raw. She levered herself out of his arms and into her loveseat. A blanket drifted off the bed and settled around her like a shroud.

"Absolutely not." His rejection was immediate, in a tone that implied no argument. "That's insanity."

"I can't escape this."

"Of course you can, your home is here."

"But Christos is *there*." Mags curled into her chair and leaned her head against the arm, fingers gripping the blanket tightly.

"He could come here," Luce offered.

"He won't leave his mother," she countered.

Her continued rebuttals were going to drive him mad. "My brother could very well have you *killed* for this!"

"I know!" The flash of pain and fury in her eyes took his breath away. "I knew that, and I chose this anyway, because it had to be done. And now *this* has to be done. Actions have consequences, Luce."

"No." He gripped his own knees tightly, as if to prevent himself from grabbing her and either shaking sense into her or spiriting her away to some secured room. "This is the overbearing whim of my idiot brother, not some plan laid down by the cosmos."

"I can't run from this, you know that."

"I refuse to allow it."

"It's not your decision to make."

"Like Hell it isn't!" He sprang up quickly, long limbs unfolding so he could pace impatiently before her. "You did this for *me*, for *my* son. I cannot allow you to take the punishment for actions that are my responsibility."

"It's not," she insisted tiredly, burrowing deeper into her blanket swaddle as the stress settled into her bones like lead and sapped her strength. "For an advocate of free will, you sound unbearably controlling at present."

This stopped him in his tracks. "That's not fair."

"Life isn't fair, it just *is*." Mags sighed. "You faced this choice once. Tell me, why didn't *you* run?"

He stubbornly avoided her measured, probing gaze. "That was different."

"How?"

"Because no one was going to miss *me*."

"We both know that is *not* true, Lucifer Morningstar."

He swallowed harshly. "Mags, please. Don't put me through this. You and the Fallen are all I have left."

"You can still have your son. That's the point of all of this; saving him." She looked away. "And I love you too Luce, but I can't live my life based on what's best for you. I have to do this for myself, and for my conscience."

Luce went very still, and then he nodded. He crossed the room swiftly and dropped a kiss onto her hair, resting his forehead on hers. "Then I'll have to beg your forgiveness."

"What?"

"Sleep, Mags." He blew gently on her brow and her eyes closed abruptly, head lolling as she dropped into unconsciousness. Scooping her into his arms, Luce carried her to the bed and laid her down carefully, drawing the duvet up over her. Settling onto the edge of the mattress, he frowned at how small and fragile she looked, almost swallowed up by the piles of pillows and blankets. She would be furious with him when his spell wore off, but by then he would have a plan—something to appease his brother so he called off her bounty.

"Dream easy, little sister." He stroked her hair softly, before drifting out and sealing her door behind himself with a locking rune. "I promise I will save us all."

Uriel woke feeling like he had just run a marathon with iron weights on his limbs. He blinked in confusion for a moment, taking in the sterile room and the warm sunlight dappling the floor, and then the events that had led him here came back to him.

"Michael." He sat up abruptly, wincing at the dull ache in his left arm. He blinked blearily down at it, at the fresh scar that ran in a pale curve around his bicep and halfway toward his forearm. "Well, shit."

"I think it makes you look dashing," a soft voice spoke from his left, startling him.

"Saints above, Gloriana!" he swore, placing a hand to his racing heart. "I was just healed and you're trying to kill me!"

"Sorry." She smiled, dimples flashing. "I know you're recovering, but I was hoping to ask about…"

Uriel watched her fidget on her little stool beside his bed, the smile faltering as she averted her gaze and chewed on her thumb nail.

"Jophiel," he finished.

"Yes."

Uriel sighed, tossing back the sheet and swinging his legs to the edge of the bed. "I thought you two were speaking again?"

She looked away. "It's… complicated. He's so distracted by his devotion to Gabriel; I hardly hear from him anymore."

"Maybe the distance is good for you," Uriel hedged, but Glory still recoiled.

"How can it be when all I think of is him? Worrying if he's safe, if he's happy, if he thinks of me. Wondering if I'll ever see him again, or if he even *wants* to see me?"

"I'm sure he does," Uriel tried to soothe her, hauling himself from the bed to lay a hand on her shoulder. "You're his sister, his twin."

"But I chose Lucifer," she sighed. "I left him behind. He was furious, Uri, you didn't see his face that day…"

"I didn't, but I'm sure he still loves you. You two were always so close, I can't see him giving up on that."

She pulled her hair over her shoulder, twining and untangling the golden strands to occupy her hands. "Tell me he's okay?"

"He is well," Uriel assured her, pacing in a small circle to wake up his muscles as he worked his arm to test the mend. "As dramatic and vain as always. Spends his free time lounging about, complaining that he's bored."

This drew another small smile. "Ah, so nothing has changed much at all."

The sound of a door slamming interrupted Uriel's reply, and he instinctively drew Glory behind him as they whirled around. Michael blinked in surprise at the door that had been flung against the wall, examining his hands as if they had acted without his consent before stepping inside and gingerly shutting the door behind him.

"Saints above, Mike! Between the two of you, I may as well get back into the bed!"

"Sorry." Michael smiled sheepishly, but it didn't come close to reaching his clouded grey eyes. "I'm a bit distracted, apparently."

Uriel softened. "Are you okay?"

"Maybe." His eyes lit on Glory, still tucked halfway into Uriel's shadow, and his expression brightened. "Gloriana!"

He stepped towards her, lifting his arms to offer a hug, and froze midstep when she flinched away from him. His brow furrowed, and she cleared her throat daintily.

"Sorry, sorry." She apologized and came around to embrace him tightly. "I'm a bit on edge and you startled me, that's all."

Michael relaxed, breathing in the old familiar scent of sweet flowers that always hung on the delicate woman. Her slender arms were deceptively strong, enclosing his waist with a steady pressure that touched a sore spot deep inside him. Some things were still constant.

"You haven't changed at all," Glory pulled back, releasing his waist to fuss with his hair, and trying in vain to tame the unruly curls. "You should consider going bald like Uri if you're not going to bother styling this mess."

"As if he could pull off this look," Uriel grinned, running a hand over his smooth-shaven scalp and tossing her a wink.

"Still a menace, I see," Glory giggled. "I missed you both, and of course, Raphael. How is he?"

"He's well." Michael smiled. "As lost in his books as ever. We should hurry home to make sure he remembers to eat something and take time to see the world beyond his archives."

"Speaking of home," Uriel cut in, "are we free to go, or does Luce—?"

"We aren't prisoners, apparently, though it goes without saying Mags will not be joining us." Michael frowned. "And while you might be well received, I'd wager I've overstayed my welcome."

"How are we supposed to find our way home when we were blind-folded coming in?"

"Oh," Glory clapped her hands together, smiling wide. "I know just the man for the job."

The man for the job turned out to be another demon – a female demon, at that. She was as tall as Zaj was short, with skin of acid green. Her slender, willowy limbs were just a touch overlong, with fingers that stretched and flexed like curling vines towards the floor as she hovered on skeletal wings. A hint of scale patterning ran down her reptilian face from forehead to collarbone and disappeared beneath her gauzy black slip dress. Dark pits of violet smoke smol-dered where her eyes should have been, and a shock of pure white hair poured down her back like pale water.

"Pyzyk," Glory smiled, but she looked puzzled. "I was expecting Porb."

"Yess," the demon confirmed in a low, hoarse whisper with a slight lisp that belied a reptilian ancestry as she shrugged. "He iss otherwisse occupied, helping in the Pit."

"Oh no…"

"It iss fine," Pyzyk dismissed her concern. "I will be returning to put the fear of Pyzyk into them when I am done with you."

"I can't imagine you're especially terrifying," Uriel smirked.

"You have never sseen my other facess, dark one." She grinned, revealing a mouthful of razor-sharp, serrated fangs.

"Dark one," Uriel laughed. "I like that, it makes me feel edgy."

Glory rolled her eyes. "Dramatic boys, all of you. It makes me miss Jophiel even more."

Uriel sobered. "I'm serious Glory, you should call him. He'd be glad to hear from you, I know it."

"Maybe," she deflected, patting him on his unscarred arm. "But you can also give him my regards when you get home."

"We can indeed," Michael nodded seriously. "It is…very good to see you again, Gloriana."

"You too," she croaked out, tearing her gaze away as her eyes went misty and clearing her throat. "You both look so good, it's like nothing has changed."

"The things that matter most are constant," Uriel assured her softly, resting a hand on her shoulder.

Michael brushed a knuckle against her jaw to turn her face back to them. "Distance does not change the love we hold for you, or the other Fallen."

She seemed to shrink under the weight of their declarations. "Sometimes it's hard to comprehend such unwavering love and support."

"Well, you have it," Uriel pulled her into an embrace. "And you may not be able to return to Heaven, but we will always come to you if you call us, here or on Earth."

"Do not think of us with sadness, Gloriana."

"I don't," she promised, but a trace of lingering grief haunted her features.

"Thiss iss very touching," Pyzyk interrupted, "but if you wissh to leave it sshould be ssooner than later. Ssome of uss have ressponssibilitiess to attend to."

Uriel laughed. "I like you, Pyzyk."

"Thankss." Her fangs glinted as she grinned again. "Now let'ss get going."

Glory watched them go, somehow feeling both warmed and broken. Seeing the two of them after all this time… she wondered if she should've heeded her initial instinct to avoid them until they left. It made everything even harder, knowing that they were up there, and she was down here, and that their paths, which were once so aligned, were now so at odds. With a sigh, she dug in her pocket for her projector cube and sank onto one of the infirmary beds, rolling to face the wall as she waited for the dull hum to resolve into a connection.

"Hello?" A smooth voice floated out cautiously, and Glory's heart skipped a beat. Her brother's face appeared in the dull wash of light, and her chest went tight with emotion.

"Hello Jophiel," she murmured, tension and levity warring within her at hearing his voice after so long. "We have a lot to catch up on."

Chapter Sixteen

Foster waited impatiently for Gabe's portal to form, the rift in the air growing wider before the other man's silhouette appeared in the glimmering gap. Gabe slowly came into view, poking first his head through with a roguish grin before the rest of him followed.

"Foster Flake," there was a smile in his words, but Foster was not smiling.

"It's interesting, Gabe," he began speaking without preamble, too frustrated to restrain himself. "I went to the Church yesterday, and I spoke with Praeceptor Sceros, and it's just *so* strange—"

"What are you rambling about, Foster?" Gabe sighed. "Also, your manners are terrible. Hi, how are you? Yes, I would love a drink, thank you."

"No drinks, Gabe, and no more bullshit," Foster snapped. "You told me these rituals were from the Gospel of Lazarus, so I have to assume you've read it. I would *also* love to read it, but the book is missing."

"Ah." Gabe sank into one of the armchairs in Foster's living room, summoning his own glass of wine with a snap of his fingers. "Yes, I took it."

"So I have to wonder—" Foster caught himself mid-sentence, and the anger rushed out of him like a deflating balloon. "Wait, you what?"

"I took it," Gabe repeated, casually sipping his pinot noir. "It doesn't belong in the hands of mortals."

Foster paused for a long moment, processing this information. It seemed the praeceptor had at least a portion of his crazy stories right, after all. He took a seat in the other armchair, steepling his fingers together and pressing until the tips of his skin went white, while counting slowly to ten in his head.

When he spoke, his voice was carefully controlled. "May I please read it?"

"You don't need to, really," Gabe dismissed the request. "I've studied it cover to cover; I have it memorized."

"Yes," Foster continued to speak in his carefully modulated tone, though frustration was straining it. "But *I* haven't, and *I'm* the one performing these rituals, right?"

Gabe beamed. "And you're doing splendidly with my guidance!"

"Gabe!" Foster groaned. "Can you please, just once, see me as an equal and let me read the damned thing myself? I'd rather go into these things feeling prepared, not waiting for you to dole out scraps of information when it suits you!"

The older man sighed, setting down his glass of wine and leaning towards Foster. "You will not like what you read."

"That's for me to decide," Foster rebuffed. "You can't treat me like a child and then hand me such heavy obligations."

"You're right," Gabe sighed, leaning back in the seat. He picked up his glass and lifted it to the light, examining the dark liquid within. "But don't say I didn't warn you."

He extended his free hand, palm up, and a small, hidebound journal with a cover worn from age and years of handling appeared. He tossed the little book to Foster, who snatched it gratefully from the air.

He opened the book carefully and began to read. The pages within were delicate and inked in old Hebrew. His translation was slow and clunky at first, since he rarely used the language, but he began to piece things together. He skimmed through crossed out sections, annotated with frustrated notes on why or how another test had failed, focusing on the parts of the diary that seemed to denote proper rituals.

There was the first ritual, The Sacrifice of the Innocent, and he recognized the runes and sigils Gabe had directed him to paint. He skimmed a few more pages, mostly scribbled over with curses and ranting, and all the while Gabriel watched him carefully, still sipping at his wine.

Foster turned the page and his fingers stilled, his heart squeezing painfully before settling in his gut. He blinked, closed the cover, set the ancient book on his lap, and rubbed his eyes vigorously. He read it wrong, obviously. Or mistranslated it; old Hebrew was tricky. The next ritual couldn't be that, *anything* but that.

Foster took a breath, and then another, and reopened the grimoire to the page he had marked. *The Sacrifice of the Elder.* If he knew Gabe at all, he could guess who the angel had in mind for the ritual. He looked up sharply at Gabriel, who was still watching him intently.

"No," Foster ground out once he was able to find his voice.

"Yes."

"No!" Foster repeated, bolting up from his chair and throwing the book down in his place. "Why didn't you warn me?"

"Because I knew you would balk," the angel sighed.

Foster's gut twisted as he began to pace. "Did you plan this? Hand-pick people from my everyday life? First Piper, and now Señora Delgado?"

"Of course it wasn't planned," Gabe snorted, "but you have to admit the old witch is the perfect candidate. With power of her own, the ritual will be bolstered."

He had agreed to these rituals before he understood the cost, and Foster could feel the world crumbling around him at this revelation. "I can't. You can't ask me to do that."

"I never said this would be *easy*, my boy." Gabe frowned sternly, running a hand through his meticulously styled hair and then immediately flattening it back into place. "There's a reason not just anyone can do this, why it takes someone special."

Foster paced back and forth, clearly distressed, and tried to rationalize his feelings with what he had learned and was hearing.

"This isn't just a ritual; it's a test of will. You can go through all the motions, but it will not *matter* unless you do it with conviction. You need to stay focused, or it's all for nothing."

Foster cringed away. "But does it have to be *her*? It would be easier if it was a stranger."

"Then your ritual would be flawed. The closer the connection, the more power drawn from the sacrifice. Such are the laws since the beginning of time. Think back to Cain and Abel. Would a lamb have been enough? No. It isn't meant to be *easy*. If it were, everyone would bring their loved ones back from the dead."

"I don't want it to be her!" Foster roared, heart aching. "She's the closest thing I have to family, Gabe!"

"First of all, that hurts." He pressed a palm to his chest, and Foster scoffed. Gabe continued, "Secondly, we just had this conversation. It's about what you want more—a woman who lives downstairs and is 'almost like family'? Or your *mother?*"

The younger man turned away, trembling with rage and despair. "I don't think my mother would want me to become a murderer."

"Well, there it is then," Gabe's tone went cool and clinical, his expression glazing over in the way that indicated he had checked out of a conversation. "You found your limit, and we won't cross the line. Fair enough."

Foster relaxed slightly, even though the thought of giving up on his mother...was unfathomable. But he couldn't do this. Piper...that had been mercy. He had spared her from suffering and pain and an inevitable awful demise.

This would be murder, plain and simple.

Señora Delgado had a tricky hip, but she had an unknown number of full years ahead. He couldn't steal that life from her in exchange for his mother's; Angela would be disgusted to return to a son who was so cruel.

And it would change him, he could feel that. If he crossed this line, it would dig deeper into something dark that had been settling around his heart ever since the night of Piper's ritual. Even now, some tender part of him was tempted. He yearned so desperately that for a moment, he wanted to take back his refusal and force himself to follow through. Instead, he steeled himself.

"Thank you, Gabe." He turned back around, looking at the man with a mixture of gratitude and remorse. "I just... regardless of my mother's disapproval, I wouldn't be able to live with *myself.*"

"Of course, Foster." Gabe softened, gaze refocusing as he extended a hand to Foster and pulled him into a tight hug. "I don't know what I was thinking. I suppose so many centuries apart from the world have made me forget how strong the bonds of mortals can be."

Foster stepped out of the embrace. "How do you mean?"

"Well, it may sound callous, but I suppose the longer you live, the more irrelevant mortality seems?" He shrugged. "I haven't cared about a mortal since...well, since your mother. I forget that such a short span of time can be so precious, when you have so little of it in the first place."

Foster mulled the statement over. "I guess that makes sense."

Even if it did make his stomach twist like a live snake. He couldn't imagine having such disregard for life, but maybe it couldn't be helped once you were as old as Gabe.

"Now, let's put all this negativity behind us." The angel smiled, with a tinge of sadness. "Why don't we go grab a drink?"

"Yeah," Foster sighed, "I could use one right about now."

"Come on, then!" Gabe snapped his fingers and the door swung wide, and he led the way out into the hallway. "Ugh, I always forget how tragic your apartment is. You still won't take my offer of putting in a word with that nice realtor woman in the northeast?"

"No." Foster smirked, watching with amusement as Gabe prodded the splotchy wallpaper with one finger, squinting, and gingerly swiped along the dusty, wobbling banister.

"Look at this!" he yelped, holding up his finger, caked in grime. "You're so lucky you don't get sick, no wonder that little girl had lung cancer!"

Foster sobered, grin falling. "Yeah, no wonder..."

Gabe frowned. "Ah. I've put my foot directly into my mouth. Apologies."

"It's fine," Foster shrugged, adopting an air of indifference despite the uncomfortable sensation prickling at the back of his neck. "Let's just get that drink."

There is not enough liquor in this glass, Luce decided, and with a lazy wiggle of his fingers, another bottle of whiskey floated from the cabinet to his outstretched hand. He poured it liberally, sloshing a bit over the side, and cleared the mess away with a muttered curse and a wave of his hand. Lifting the glass, he admired the way the cut crystal and amber liquor caught the light for a moment before he brought the glass to his lips and drained it in two long swallows.

He poured another and reclined in his chair, regarding the glass with resignation and annoyance. "I thought you were supposed to take my pain away," he muttered.

The liquor sat motionless in the cup, defiantly offering no answers.

"Terrible, useless poison," Luce said bitterly, draining it again. "I drink you as punishment."

"Please tell me you aren't talking to your brandy."

"It's whiskey," Luce corrected the blurry shape in his doorway, squinting until the figure resolved into Sachiel.

"That is *so* not the answer I wanted," Sachi said sternly, but the grin stretching his lips betrayed his amusement. "Isn't it almost impossible for you to get drunk?"

"It's not easy," Luce agreed, "but if you have enough liquor, it's possible."

"How long have you been drinking in the dark?"

"Not long enough," the Devil muttered.

"So much muttering," the other man chuckled, blond waves falling in his face in a way that had Luce's feelings in a riot. "You're normally more eloquent."

"I'm depressed and drunk," Luce snapped, taking out the days' worth of frustrations on his subordinate. "Cut me some slack."

Sachiel sank into the armchair across from Luce's desk. "The girls are looking for you."

"Of course they are."

"Rem says you drugged Mags."

"I did not," he protested. "I only put her under for a while with my magic, just long enough to make sure Michael was gone."

"That's kinda fucked up, Luce."

"I didn't ask for your opinion," Luce glowered at the Fallen.

"Yeah, you never do." Sachi leaned forward, looking troubled, and braced his forearms on his knees. "You have a real bad tendency of getting yourself so worked up that you don't have any room in your head for other people's thoughts."

"I wasn't aware I needed to leave room for *other people's thoughts,*" Luce sneered.

"You're a King, Luce. What you do affects the whole Kingdom, so it makes sense that you should keep that in mind."

"I love this Kingdom, and I always protect the souls in it."

"There's a windstorm raging out there right now," Sachi said calmly, "and there's a lightning storm over the Pit."

"Fuck." Luce slammed his glass down and it shattered into crystalline fragments. "Fuck!"

Sachi sighed, snapping his fingers to vanish the spilled liquor and repair the glass. "And I'm not just talking about the weather."

"What else?" Luce pointedly avoided looking at the other man, because he knew—especially in this state—that it was a different blond's face he would see.

"You *know* what else," Sachi countered. "You can't impose your will on your friends, Luce. It's always been kind of your core belief."

"You don't tell me what I can and can't do, Sachiel."

"Wow. You always turn into an ass when you're stressed out, but drunk Luce is even less sorry about it. Great."

"You're right, I'm not apologetic at all." Luce stood abruptly, leaning over his desk to get in Sachi's face. "I don't need to be."

"Yeah? You're in here drinking your feelings, man. Shouldn't you be working on the next piece of the Armor?"

Luce scoffed. "It's not that *easy,* Sachiel. It takes a great deal out of me each time, especially with my powers depleted by—"

Sachi's eyes narrowed. It gave the typically relaxed man a dangerous look as he motioned for Luce to continue. "Finish that sentence, Lucifer."

"There's no need."

"Sure there is. You were about to blame us for your lack of power, right?"

Luce risked a glance at his Bearer of Sloth to find a pale blue gleam creeping into Sachi's eyes. Trails of azure spilled from his eyes like tears and down his throat to wrap around his biceps, exposed by the casual tank top he wore.

"First Remiel, and now you?" Luce hissed, clenching his fist around the freshly repaired glass. "I gave you these powers to fight *for* me, not *with* me."

Sachiel rose, slowly but purposefully, and his eyes were bright with rarely displayed anger. "Then stop giving us reasons to stand against you... my King."

Luce bristled at the way the title was tossed out like an insult. "Stand down, Sachiel."

"No!" Sachiel slammed his palms flat on the desk, sending a rippling shockwave of gleaming blue outwards from the point of impact. "You used your magic so you could *force* Mags to stay in her room. You can't just do whatever you want to us, like we're your toys, Luce."

"That was to protect her, Sachiel. She wants to run off to her death!"

"You don't know that," Sachi protested.

"I know my brother. He doesn't tend to be *forgiving*," Luce sneered.

"It's not your choice to make."

"Wouldn't you do the same?" Luce demanded. "If Camiel was at risk, you would let her run headlong into danger?"

"Yes," Sachi said immediately, "because she's a *person* with opinions and feelings of her own, and she can make her own decisions."

"My brother cast me out, Michael discarded me, my wife is dead, and my son despises me." Luce ranted, his voice lifting in volume with each point he ticked off, eyes blazing. "Mags is *all I have!* I will not lose her!"

"You *will* lose her! You will push her away with this controlling bullshit, because you're going to strip away the trust and make her resent you." His anger spent, the glow of borrowed power leeched out of Sachi's eyes and he sank into his chair with a sigh.

"Fuck you," Luce hissed, whirling around and stalking toward the window. Sure enough, harsh winds whipped across the fields, uprooting crops and rustling trees and sending debris flying. He willed himself to calm, to stop the storm.

Lucifer felt suddenly wearier than he had been in a long time.

"I'm not trying to be an asshole, Luce," Sachi's voice interrupted his concentration, and Luce tensed. "I just don't want to see you tearing yourself and everyone else apart."

"Yes, well," Luce bit out, "you sure are helping make things worse."

"Don't be a dick," Sachi grumbled.

"You know what?" Luce spun back around. "I need some air."

The other man's eyes narrowed. "Now you're running away?"

"I *said* I need some *air*," he ground out, crossing the room and shoving past Sachi. If he didn't leave now, the damage would be far worse than it already was. "I'm going to find somewhere to drink in *peace*."

"Typical," the blond muttered. "As soon as anyone says something you don't want to hear, the conversation is over."

"I'll be back when I can deal with this clusterfuck," Luce continued, as if Sachi hadn't spoken. He stormed out the doorway, leaving the other man glaring furiously after him.

* * *

Maybe it was the four bottles of whiskey, maybe it was the effect of Sachi's uncomfortable visit, or maybe it was just the horrible results of the disastrous meeting with Foster. Whatever the reason, Luce was trying hard not to curl up in bed and ignore the world until it collapsed around him.

Instead, he found himself standing outside a rough-looking bar about ten minutes' walk from his son's apartment. Beside him, a portly Italian man in a leather jacket tugged nervously at his handlebar mustache.

"You sure about this, boss?" Cwall frowned, looking uncomfort-

197

able with his disguise and this plan as he gazed up at Luce with concern.

"Not really," Luce shrugged. "But I'm desperate and drunk enough to give it a shot."

The bar was unassuming at first glance. The worn wooden sign above the door read *Georgia's* in chipping gold cursive. A petite blonde pinup with devil horns and tail was painted lounging across it, lifting a glass at the approaching patrons and winking salaciously. Luce snorted. *Fitting.*

"Yer funeral," Cwall muttered, looking away. "For the record, I didn't tell ya shit if Fostie gets pissed."

"Yes, yes." Luce waved him off. "My son has *my* temper; I know better than to throw anyone in its path."

Cwall made a noise that suggested he wasn't entirely convinced but let the matter drop. "Well," he patted the medallion looped around his neck. "Ya know how to reach me if ya need me."

"Of course."

Cwall reached out, as if to clasp the taller man reassuringly on the shoulder, but his hand stilled halfway and fell back to his side. "Good luck," he murmured as he stepped away, turning down an alley and vanishing into a split in the air.

"Thank you," Luce replied to empty sidewalk, nerves jittering despite the generous portion of alcohol that worked to numb his anxiety.

Then he squared his shoulders and made his way to the heavy oak door. The faint beat of some rock song he didn't recognize pulsed under his feet. His shaking hands curled around the oxidized brass handles and he tugged hard against the sticky joint.

A rush of warm, heady air washed over him, scented with the tang of sweat and an undercurrent of liquor. His lip curled instinctively, but he tugged the outer door shut behind him and opened the smaller one ahead. It was like entering another world.

Instead of the dim lighting and faded vinyl booths he had expected, the room was awash in red neon and blacklights, with sleek metal fixtures surrounding a dance floor that pulsated faintly with white strobe. Waitresses in skintight red leather circled around, some in mini-dresses and others in pants and cropped tops, but all wearing plastic headbands topped with red horns. As he adjusted to the unusual lighting, he started to pick out the posters and signs and neon fixtures in detail.

"Oh no," Luce groaned, eyes darting around frantically as his buzz started to give way under the shock. "Oh *no*."

The entire place was a shrine to *him*—or at least to the face mortals expected to see. The cheeky, grinning devil with a pitchfork and a bottle of beer painted on the menu board that hung behind the bar. A tiny flashing sign with a devil juggling shot glasses. A weird devil statue carved from wood, draped in a string of red fairy lights.

It was like a funhouse mirror that had his head spinning, even before the song switched over to a new track; some synth and pop monstrosity that grated horribly. He needed another drink, and fast.

Pushing through the swarm of bodies on the dancefloor, Luce crossed to the crowded bar at the center of the throng. "Drink," he practically begged, reaching into his pocket for his wallet and slapping a platinum card on the counter.

"Yeah?" the bartender shouted back, looking annoyed. "Kinda need to know what *kind*, man."

"Surprise me."

With a shrug, the young man snapped up the card and swiped it through the till before handing it back. "That's one shot of Fireball coming up, and a Devil's Advocate to chase it."

Luce fought the urge to roll his eyes, casting them around the room instead. A neon standee of a twerking cartoon devil caught his attention and he rested his head on the bar. This was a nightmare. How the hell was he supposed to find his son when he was too busy dying of embarrassment?

His son. Luce sat bolt upright, startling the bartender delivering his drink, and snatched up the shot glass before him. He downed it in one toss and accepted the neon pink cocktail gratefully, spinning around and pushing back through the crowd towards the edge of the room. He was here for a reason, not to get trashed. This was his last chance to get through to Foster, he could feel it. Every day the sense of creeping dread was stronger and more persistent.

He took several calming breaths, prying his attention from the flashing dancefloor to scan the perimeter of the room. His son was ultimately a solitary creature. If he was in a place like this, it wouldn't be at the center of the crowd. After a moment, he spotted him. Halfway down the left wall, between two girls snapping selfies over their enormous margaritas and a couple making out rather aggressively, slouching in his seat like he wanted to become invisible. *Foster.* Luce smiled.

"You really need to come out with me more." Gabe grinned at Foster, leaning over the table and resting his chin on the back of his laced fingers. "Isn't this place so fun?"

"I thought we were going to McHenry's," Foster grumbled, sliding down in his seat and glowering at his beer. It was some fancy craft bullshit called Brimstone Brew, and he only ordered it because everything else was either fruity, loaded with vodka, or absurdly complicated. Or it had a stupid pun for a name. He raked his scathing glare across the room. "This place is a fucking joke, and it's not a funny one."

"Don't be such a grump." Gabe frowned. "I thought it would cheer you up to see them making a mockery of your father. That's why *I* like to come here."

"I'd rather just pretend he doesn't exist, thanks."

"Can't say I blame you," Gabe said sympathetically, leaning back and unfolding his hands to pat Foster gently on the arm. "He hasn't—"

He broke off abruptly and Foster glanced over, only to see Gabe gaping at the doorway like a fool. He followed the stare and felt his blood pressure increase. His father shoved his way through the dance floor to the bar. Foster twisted sharply toward Gabe.

"Is this why you *insisted* on coming here? Is this, what, an intervention?"

"No," Gabe croaked, fixated on Lucifer with a look of intense longing mingled with grief. Foster pulled back, momentarily thrown for a loop, but quickly recovered.

"Then why is he *here?*"

The angel licked his lips and glanced at Foster with a grin, though it didn't reach his still-wide eyes. "I guess the Devil *does* go down to Georgia's?"

"*Gabe*," Foster hissed, too irritated for jokes, and the other man just smiled.

"I guess that's my cue, good luck!"

"What?!"

"Don't kill anyone!" And then he was gone, slipping into a gap between space and vanishing before Foster's enraged eyes.

"Un-fucking-believable."

Foster sank into his seat, praying for invisibility and cursing that it wasn't one of his natural born talents. *Please just let him fucking drink and leave.*

As always, the Universe decided nothing could go his way. He risked a glance back in the direction he'd seen his father, only to start in alarm when he made direct eye contact with the man as he stood mere feet from the table. "Fuck!"

"No," Luce chuckled, "the word is 'father', actually."

"We're not going down that road again," Foster groaned. "Not today, please."

Luce sobered slightly at the weary undertone in his son's words. "Is something wrong?"

"Not that it's any of your business, but yeah, I got some bad news today."

"I'm sorry to hear that."

"Are you?" He glared at his father, every muscle in his face twinging with the force of clenching his jaw. "I'm so sure."

"I am," Luce insisted, inviting himself to settle across from his son in the booth when no invitation seemed forthcoming. "I'm here to try and make amends, Foster."

"Why?" he demanded. "Because of some stupid *vision* that I'm going to cause Armageddon?"

He missed the older man's flinch at the casual statement, too busy rolling his eyes.

"Well...yes," Luce admitted, swallowing against the tightness in his throat. "Mags's vision was the catalyst, but it shouldn't have been. I want to make an effort, Foster. I want to start atoning for my failures."

"I'm going to level with you," Foster sighed, straightening up and folding his hands on the worn shellac tabletop between them. "I do not care how bad you feel. I have been *alone* apart from one sympathetic angel and an infuriating demon for almost two decades. You denied me the *one thing* I ever asked you for, and then you abandoned me."

"Foster, please—"

"I'm not finished," he cut across the interruption, tone like ice. "You don't get to speak right now. You're going to sit there and shut the hell up, and I'm going to explain exactly how badly you fucked up my life until you get it through your *thick skull* that I am not going to forgive you any time soon, if ever."

Luce frowned harshly but kept his silence. He could at least start with listening, since that seemed to be step one in Foster's healing.

"Good, you're learning," the young man sneered, then shook his head. "Sometimes I forget how clueless the fully Divine can be. Between Gabe and now *you*, I'm getting emotional whiplash from how callous you are. Mortals have *feelings*, not just those shallow imitations you have."

"I have—"

"Maybe, but you'll never understand the *intensity* of mortality. Everything means more when you could lose it in an instant. However much you 'hurt' or how 'bad' you feel, it doesn't compare; it just can't.

And half of me is like them. The part of me that came from my mother still remembers her smell, her laugh, the way her hair was like a waterfall of honey... That part of me is *still grieving* like it was yesterday."

Silence descended between them, and Luce's fingers tightened around the stem of his glass. Pain coated his son's words, so visceral it was almost tangible in the air between them.

Foster had a point that Luce tended to dilute his emotions. All Divine beings did, because it was one of the few things that maintained their sanity across the millennia. Even then, not everyone had the same level of success.

It was always harder for the Risen Divine, who had to first teach themselves distance from their human past and the sensations that came with it. It was all too easy to lose yourself in pain, in anger, even in love or joy, when you had an eternity to sink into those spirals.

"Because of *you*, I have to live without her. The part of me that learned distance and moderation *broke* when she died. I can't turn off the anger. I know I can't, because I've tried! I tried for years to separate from the pain and all it did was make me bitter. And it all comes back to one day, and one choice."

"Foster—"

"You could've *saved* her!" Foster shouted, pounding a fist into the table so hard, a spiderweb of cracks spiraled out beneath it. "You knew she was dying, and you knew what she meant to me! She was my *mother!* You loved her once, but you *let her die!*"

There was so much Foster didn't know about that day, or the circumstances that led to it. There were still things even *Luce* wasn't sure of. How could he even begin to explain to his son that it wasn't for lack of wanting to save Angela, but rather that he simply *couldn't?*

"It's not that simple," Luce pleaded. "The ritual wouldn't have worked."

"That's why I'm so furious with you," Foster seethed. "You just make that claim; you didn't care enough to *try*."

"Foster, please—"

"No." He slid abruptly from the booth, turning his back on his father. "No, I said my piece. I don't care whatever stupid defense you have. We both know what happened. The difference here is that you think you're blameless and I can't accept that. So *I'm* doing something about it, like you should have."

"You have no idea what you're doing."

Foster didn't respond, because at that moment a man came rushing at them. He braced for the impact, but it never came. Gabe skidded to a halt mere inches from him, eyes wild and hair disheveled, foreboding wafting off him like a bad smell.

Foster's pulse quickened as he demanded, "What?"

"Your apartment is on fire."

Chapter Seventeen

Foster went very still while his brain took a moment for the words to sink in. The idea was simply too ridiculous. *His* apartment? The apartment no one knew about, that was warded more heavily than the oldest grimoires? Impossible.

Time slowed to a muddy crawl. The noise in the bar dulled to a muffled roar, as if someone had stuffed his ears with cotton. When he felt a touch on his elbow and turned to look at Gabe's panicked expression, it was like moving in slow motion. He felt detached from himself. Then he blinked and took a breath before Gabe shook him roughly by the arm.

"Foster! Did you not hear me!?" the other man implored. His voice had the same muffled quality as the music, and Foster slowly realized it was from the rush of blood, his pulse hammering in his ears, blocking out all the sound. "Your apartment is *on fire!*"

His apartment, in all its disarray and disrepair, was his home. His safe space.

It had everything he needed: food, shelter, a place to work his spells, his gourmet coffees, and the last few connections he had to his mother.

Abruptly, he came back to himself. The world spun with a whoosh that rocked him back as if he'd been punched in the gut, and sounds returned with a bang. His heart dropped into his feet and his chest tightened.

His mother.

The Gospel, the rituals, *her photo.*

Luce could see the devastation slip over Foster's face, and it stirred something in him that he didn't have a name for, some primal urge to grab his son and fold him into his chest and protect him from the horrors of the world. He needed to hold him, to feel him warm and alive in his arms.

He was reaching out unconsciously, just barely grazing his son's sleeve, when Foster yanked his arm free of Gabriel's grip, shoving through the dancefloor with a single-minded focus on getting out and getting home.

He burst through the door, ignoring the disgruntled shouts in his wake, tearing off toward his apartment. *I'm coming, Mom.*

Luce's fingers closed on empty air and his chest constricted.

"Foster…" he murmured, forlorn.

"Aren't you going to come with us?" a snide voice demanded, and Luce glanced up at Gabe's furious expression.

"What?"

"Your son is clearly in the midst of a tragedy, and you're staring into space with a cocktail in hand."

Luce glanced down, almost surprised to see the violently pink drink still in his grip. "Oh."

"You know what?" Gabe sneered. "It's probably better if you stay here. Seeing you is likely to upset him further." He spun on his heel and took off after Foster, leaving Luce alone in a booth, staring at his hands.

Foster ran like he had never run before. His feet skimmed the pavement, each long stride interrupted by barely a pause to tap against the concrete and propel him further on. The wind buoyed him as he used just a touch of his magic to weave between the thinning crowds on the sidewalk.

People shifted aside without knowing why, suddenly drawn to a shop window, a vendor on the corner, or a compulsion to cross the street. Foster tore through the gap that opened, making the five-block trip in record time. The acrid smell of smoke and charred wood tickled his nose from two blocks away. His eyes watered, and it wasn't from the sting of the heat and ash, though that came next as he rounded the corner and saw his building up in flames.

Later, he would kick himself for his reckless stupidity, his blind desperation. As soon as he saw those tendrils of fire climbing quickly up, up, towards the fifth floor, sending columns of billowing black streaming into the early evening sky, all rational thought fled. A choked bellow tore from his throat as he pushed past the frantic tenants huddled on the edge of the street, running headlong into the wall of heat pouring from the gaping hole where the front door once hung.

Immediately, the fire licked at him like a hungry beast. His skin was unharmed, but it caught and sank into his clothing as he raced up the stairs, giving the impression that he himself was made of deadly fire. Foster cursed, shrugging out of his burning jacket and leaving it in a smoldering pile on the third-floor staircase. His t-shirt followed on the fourth, his tank top on the fifth, as the flames continued chasing him up to his landing.

His demigod lungs were powerful, but the creeping smoke still rose, still invaded every crevice and corner it could reach, until even Foster struggled against it. He coughed and swung his arm in an arc, opening a small pocket of air and sealing the bubble around his head like a diver's helmet. Gulping down a semi-clean breath, he raced to his apartment and grabbed unthinkingly for the knob, searing his palm on the scorching metal.

"Saints and whores!" he cursed, shaking out his stinging hand even as the skin knit and sealed before his eyes. Carefully, he placed his palm against the heated wood and muttered a spell of unlocking before kicking the door inward and rushing into his apartment.

More smoke poured through the heating vent, drifting up to pool at the ceiling in ominous clouds. Foster swore again, bolting down the hall to his bedroom and shoving through without hesitation, the heat pressing on him like a snug blanket. The room was already aflame, and he made a beeline for the bedside table, snatching up the picture there and searing his palms and his chest as he cradled it tightly to his bare skin.

"Fuck!" He dropped the photo and the glass cracked and splintered. "Dammit!"

Snatching up a discarded shirt, Foster wrapped the damaged frame in the fabric and tucked it into the waistband of his jeans, warm and secure at the small of his back. A loud crack made his heart skip a beat, only to relax when he saw Cwall in his imp form, hovering frantically in the doorway and coughing.

"Fos," the demon croaked, and Foster quickly conjured a similar air shield around him. "What the fuck are ya doin' ya stupid kid?!"

"My mom," he stated, knowing how stupid and pathetic that made him sound but not having any better answer. "Her photo."

Cwall softened slightly but kept glowering at him. "Yer an *idiot* kid. Let's get the hell out before this place comes down on us."

"One more thing, in the living room." Foster ran back to the apartment's main room, fighting against the waves of heat sweeping in through the door he'd forgotten to close—not like it mattered much. The entire place was going to come down at this rate.

"What's so important it's worth riskin' your *life*?!" Cwall gaped at him.

A soft pulsing light emanated from the seat of the chair he'd abandoned earlier, the protective wards around the Gospel of Lazarus fighting against the encroaching danger.

"The one thing that might save my mom." Foster snatched up the book and rushed after Cwall into the hallway.

"You Morningstars an yer fuckin' *books*," Cwall griped, but there was no real bite to it. He started towards the stairs, only for the ceiling to give a mighty crack as it dropped down in their path.

"Back this way." Foster tugged on his arm, dragging him back into the apartment. "The fire escape."

"That thing is a rusting death trap," Cwall grumbled, but his wings were growing weak from the effort of beating against the thickening air, and he followed Foster's lead to the bedroom.

The sound of popping sparks and wood splintering chased them down the hallway. The floorboards groaned under Foster's weight and the warping heat. The grimy carpet began emitting a smell of burning rot, the fumes making even Cwall's head spin.

Foster laid the book down to claw at the window, cursing the damn thing as it stuck fast under several layers of thick white paint. "Come on," he pleaded.

Oppressive heat poured down the hall, beads of sweat dripping into his eyes as he pulled and pried the window upwards. There was a sudden rush as the window was yanked from his grip, the abrupt displacement of air throwing him off balance and knocking him halfway over the windowsill.

"Gabe," he gasped raggedly, as said angel caught him by the shoulders. How out of place his angelic mentor looked, perched awkwardly between the rickety railing and window, his neatly pressed slacks stained with rust where he had obviously clambered bodily up the ladder.

"Hey kid," he grunted slightly as he heaved Foster further over the windowsill. "When did you get so heavy?"

"When I started lifting weights, probably." Foster grinned, finding his balance and clambering out onto the metal structure.

Cwall shifted forms as he slid over the sill behind them, until he once more resembled a stocky European man and not a denizen of Hell. "Let's blow this pop stand 'afore it blows *up*, yeah boys?"

"Indeed." Gabe clapped sharply, and they found themselves safely on the ground. He looked at his hands with disgust, rubbing his thumbs over his palms to remove the faint orange stains. "I should have thought to do that the *first* time."

"I didn't really need rescuing," Foster pointed out. "Immortal bloodline and all that."

"Well," Gabe sniffed haughtily. "I was a bit distraught, wasn't I? It's not every day your pseudo-son goes running headlong into a *burning building*. What even possessed you to do something so reckless?"

Foster started violently. "Shit!"

"Beg pardon?" Gabe recoiled slightly.

"No, I mean—*fuck*." He spun to face the building. "The Gospel!"

"Ah," Gabe frowned. "It's warded, so it'll be fine. You can go back for it *after* the fire."

"Wheneva that is," Cwall muttered. "Should we do somethin' Fos?"

"No," Gabe said, waving him off. "There are too many mortals around to see. Why do you think I didn't just portal in to get you? I'm sure the fire people are on their way already."

As if on cue, the wail of sirens pierced the night and jolted Foster back to awareness.

"Besides," the angel smiled, "everyone seems to have made it outside, so there's no real danger."

Foster turned, scanning the assembled residents he'd pushed aside in his panic. How careless of him, not to stop and check on their safety. He was immortal; the other tenants were decidedly *not*.

It was controlled chaos, people huddled and terrified as they watched their home go up in smoke, and Foster tried to pick out individual faces.

There was Mr. Fernandez from D2, who made washing his old blue Nova a weekly ritual that put religious zealots to shame. Mr. and Mrs. Hem corralled their five sons, the youngest of whom wailed in his mother's arms despite being almost ten years old. Miss Darcy clutched her spoiled pug, the poor thing's bulging eyes darting frantically in its smushed-in face. With every face he counted, panic built in Foster's chest. He swept the crowd once, twice, a third time.

Where was she?

"No," he murmured, heart sinking. "No no no."

"No what?" Gabe tilted his head to the side, eyeing him quizzically.

The fire crew pulled up and leaped from their truck, quickly assessing the scene. Foster started toward them, at the same time Mr. Fernandez spotted him and came running over.

"Foster!" He grabbed him by the elbow. "I can't find Carmen!"

It was like his worst nightmare come true. After losing his mother, Señora Delgado had become the closest thing he had to a maternal figure. A cold sense of dread settled into his bones as he turned slowly back to face his building. The world blurred around him as the beat in his chest seemed to slow. Around him, life moved in the same sluggish pattern.

Firemen unwound hoses and shouted to each other, moving toward the blaze. Mr. Fernandez tugged on his arm insistently, lips moving in soundless shapes as Foster stared over his head at the horror unfolding. She lived on the fourth floor; she had a bad hip. He had run *right past her* to save a photo of a woman who would be ashamed of his selfishness.

Slowly, *so* slowly, Foster turned back to meet Gabe's eyes. There was a flicker of something like regret, or maybe concern. He knew what Foster was about to do.

"I have to," the younger man croaked.

Cwall jolted towards him from his place beside the angel. "Foster, no!"

But he had already shaken off his neighbor's grip, and pulled the photo of his mother from his jeans. He tossed it to Gabe, who caught it easily. "Hold this for me."

"Be careful," Gabe frowned.

Cwall skidded to a stop and turned to gape at Gabe. "Ya ain't gonna stop 'im?!"

"I couldn't if I tried." he smirked softly, something like wonder in the softness of his gaze. "That's Lucifer's boy if I ever saw it in him. Stubborn as hell and determined to get there."

For once, Foster felt something like pride in the comparison. But he wasn't just Lucifer's son, he was Angela's too, and she always knew right from wrong. And this was right, he knew that. He took off like a shot, racing back toward the apartment.

"Stop!" One of the firemen shouted, a look of alarm clear on his face. "Kid, ya ain't even wearin' a shirt!"

"He's crazy!" Another man shouted back, angling his hose higher to blast at the relentless flames. "Somebody stop 'im!"

One of the emergency responders tried to snatch at his arm as he passed, but Foster blew past. There was no chance of a mortal stopping him. He was divinity, born of the Godblood. He was untouchable.

He was slammed roughly from the side and tackled to the ground, rolling twice before he ended up on his back.

"What the fuck?" he groaned, attempting to rise to his elbows only to be pinned back down. He blinked, and the shadows above him settled into his father's face. For a moment, he would've sworn the expression there was terror. Then he blinked again, and it was gone.

"You reckless, ridiculous child!" Luce bellowed, eyes alight with rage. "You could've died!"

"No, I couldn't!" Foster protested, struggling against the iron bands of his father's grip on his biceps. "I have to go back in, she's still *in there!*"

"Who?!" Luce demanded, shaking his son as if he could force the answers out of him.

"Señora Delgado!" Foster shouted back, fighting to get free. "My downstairs neighbor! She's still inside!"

"These firemen will get to her, that's their job."

"I can get there faster!"

"At what cost?" Luce shook him again, fear creeping back into the edges of his tone. "Tell me, what mortal is worth my *son?*"

Foster stilled, momentarily caught off guard by the question, then renewed his struggle. "Any of them! That's the problem with you Divine pricks! Mortals matter too!"

"I will not risk you!"

"It's not your choice to make!" His throat was raw as the words tore from it. "Who are you? Who are you to show up now and decide my life?!"

"Your *father!*" Luce snapped, hauling Foster to his knees. "Your father, who wants a chance to make amends before I lose you for good!"

"Too little, too late!" Foster staggered upright and shoved his father away. "I have so few people left that matter to me. I won't let you stop me from saving one of them!"

He started to run back towards the doorway, only to freeze in his tracks at the sight before him. The blaze was lower but still burning. The firemen advanced steadily on the building, beating at the flames with jets of water. From the blackened doorway, a team hauled out a black and yellow stretcher with a prone form atop it.

"Carmen!" Mr. Fernandez gasped, and Foster dropped to his knees like a stone.

"No," he murmured, whimpered, pleaded. "Please no."

A hand settled on his shoulder, and for a moment, he leaned away from it. Then Gabe sank to his knees beside him and forced him to meet his gaze.

"She is not dead."

Foster's heart, which had been slowly tightening in his chest, skipped a beat. "What?"

"Look." He tapped under Foster's chin with two fingers, lifting the younger man's gaze to the stretcher again. "She moves."

It was true; her fist clenched and unclenched repeatedly on her rosary as the old woman moaned and muttered prayers in Spanish.

"*¡Abuela!*" Foster shouted, springing back to his feet. "*¡Abuela, todo estará bien!*"

He pulled away from Gabe and rushed to the stretcher. There was a small commotion, but the firemen settled when he declared himself her grandson. Luce watched him climb into the ambulance at her side, riding safely away from the dwindling inferno.

Relieved, he murmured, "Thank my brother that she lives."

"You should thank *me*," Gabe snapped, rocking back to sit heavily on the ground. "She was barely hanging on; it took everything I had stored up to keep her there. And I still cannot be sure it wasn't all for nothing."

Luce gave him a long look, raking him critically from the top of his tousled head to the soles of his designer wingtips. "I'm not so sure I *should* thank you, Gabriel."

The other man flinched slightly at his name on Luce's lips, at the frosty core of his tone. He swallowed hard. "Why?"

"I saw more than you might think." Luce crouched down to be level with the younger angel, dark eyes flaring gold around the pupil. "You were willing to let *my son* run into a burning building."

"He's immortal," Gabe pointed out drily.

"We both know that's not entirely true, is it?" Luce spoke low and soft, his speech sounding pleasant enough to an outsider, but anyone who knew him could hear the threat laced within. And Gabriel knew Lucifer better than most.

"It doesn't count, if he doesn't know," Gabe insisted. "It has to be willing."

"You and your loopholes," Luce sneered. "That boy was ready to rush in, with no regard to himself. That's enough to satisfy the conditions."

Gabe looked stricken. "I—I never knew that."

"Sure you didn't."

"It's true, I swear!" Gabe shook his head violently. "I thought he had to know the risk, that's what happened with Christos! Michael had to tell him, and—"

"That's enough," Luce cut across his ramble, pressing a slim finger to the air between them and forcing Gabriel's lips firmly closed with his power. He still wasn't fully restored after his ritual, but he was close enough—and he would always outrank an Archangel, leaving them at his mercy even when he was weakened.

A long moment stretched between them, deep brown locked on sapphire blue as they silently sized each other up, the weight of the years apart evident in the subtle signs of age they wore. Fine lines pinched the corners of Gabe's eyes, and Luce knew he wore his own across his brow and bracketing his smile. Rogue strands of silver threaded through their dark hair now.

More than anything though, there was an unfamiliar hardness chiseled into Gabriel's visage; a cool detachment that likened him to a finely wrought statue rather than the eager, open warmth the pale angel used to display.

Finally, Luce cleared his throat. "Now, let me be perfectly clear, Gabriel."

Unable to reply, the other angel simply waited, eyes narrowed slightly.

"We both know you are not a fool. You were my closest friend, once, yet you did not speak in my defense when I was wrongfully accused. You watched my nephew walk to his unnecessary death. And tonight, you almost let my son run to his. Those are three strikes."

The silence was deafening between them. Luce could see the desire to speak written plainly on the other man's face, but he ignored it.

"They call me a snake, but I wonder if perhaps they gave that title to the wrong man."

Gabe shook his head sharply, and Luce clicked his tongue.

"That's one of your fatal flaws, Gabe. You're always ready to make permanent decisions, but you can never accept responsibility." He rose to his full height, leaving Gabe sitting mute in the dirt as he glowered down at him. "Whatever friendship we once had is utterly lost, I'm afraid."

Luce turned away and snapped his fingers twice. Cwall came to his side at once, bowing slightly. "Yes, my King?"

"I would like you to ensure that Gabriel no longer sets foot anywhere near my son."

Gabe made a strangled noise, muffled by the spell Luce held over him.

"If you see him near Foster," Luce pressed on firmly, "I want to be contacted *immediately*."

"Yes, my King," Cwall swore, bowing lower.

"Come, Cwall," Luce tapped his shoulder, prompting him to rise to full height. "I think we need to speak with your boss and ensure all of the Eyes are aware of this development."

"Of course, my King."

Gabe glowered at Luce's back, as if trying to burn a hole in his shoulders. The King of Hell turned back around and snapped again, releasing the angel from his bonds.

"Your son is right," Gabe grumbled. "You have some nerve, acting as if you give a damn about him after all this time. I was the one who was there all these years, who helped him find his way and master his powers. *I* am the one who comforted him after Angela—"

Luce made a zipping motion and the words choked off again. It was reckless to be spending so much of his magic when he was meant to be storing it back up for another Armor ritual, but Gabriel always knew exactly which buttons to push to get a rise from his target.

"You don't get to say her name," Luce hissed. "Does my son know *your* role in the death of his mother?"

Gabe went pale.

"Oh, you thought *I* didn't know?" the Devil laughed darkly. "I deluded myself for so long, telling myself it was an accident, but now I wonder. Don't pretend that 'helping' my son with his grief hasn't just been some way for you to appease your conscience."

He took a step forward and Gabe shrank back, trembling at the fury that radiated from Luce. The space seemed to warp around them, leaving them in a tense bubble where Gabe struggled to draw a breath in the thinned air.

"You are self-serving and fickle, *Gabriel*. Foster is not your redemption project, and he is not a bargaining chip. Your role in his life is effectively redundant. If you defy my request and I see your conniving face before me, so help me, I will *not* be lenient again."

Gabe closed his eyes tightly, trying to still his shaking limbs, and nodded. When he opened them again, Luce and Cwall were gone.

* * *

Raguel had learned, over many eons, to pick and choose his battles. In fact, he often chose to avoid them altogether for the sake of sanity. He was married to a veritable pipe bomb, and his 'boss' could oscillate from dignified badass to melodramatic toddler in the span of minutes. It was a trait Lucifer had always possessed, Rag was forced to admit, and one that wasn't lost on others.

Rag's own best friend had denounced him when the Fallen chose to follow Lucifer into exile, warning him that he would come to regret it. Thinking back to the 'conversation' Sachiel had recounted with Lucifer from just hours ago, Rag wondered if Ezekiel had been right.

He brought his cleaver down, chopping through the carrots on the counter as if metaphorically severing that bond of friendship again. Rag had deflated in the face of his closest friend's utter disdain, but—as he had said then—how could he be happy without his wife? It would be like cutting off his own arms.

As wild and 'unladylike' as she had always been, Remi had never had to fight for Zeke's approval. The other man knew Rag well enough to know she suited him. The redhead would never have been happy with a partner as vain as Gloriana, or as placating as Mags. He needed to be challenged, kept on his toes, and knocked down once in a while. Remi might be a handful, but she had never drawn Zeke's ire like Lucifer had.

Even as they'd argued that day, Ezekiel had known Rag would go. If Remiel went, Raguel followed. But Zeke had hated Lucifer for drawing her in. He was a rigid man, fond of rules and structure, and had often scoffed at Lucifer's antics openly. He had been smug, Rag remembered, when Lucifer was cast out.

His knife came down again, this time into a freshly peeled onion. Rag had learned *that* lesson the hard way when Mags had pulled a peel from her mouthful of stir fry and gently informed him that it was, in fact, intended to be removed.

Mags...by far the sweetest of their motley crew, and even more impressive for it after the life she had lived. His knuckles went white on the handle of the cleaver as he wished, not for the first time, that he could punch her disgusting father in the face once more. But the man was no longer in the Pit. Luce had made sure of that as soon as he'd learned the bastard had crossed over.

Cooking was the shared bond between them because of that instance. Rag had seen the shadow looming over the small woman; had seen her listless drifting in the aftermath of her father's reappearance and demise. He knew she loved to cook, so he made himself a willing student. Her gentle smile and quiet manner suited teaching, and soon Rag even found himself enjoying their lessons.

He wasn't a fool; he knew he was terrible, but Mags's constant encouragement and the soothing effect of working in the kitchen kept him at it. Plus it was fun, sometimes, to see the look on someone's face as they struggled to compliment a dish he well knew was rancid.

As if his thoughts had summoned her, his wife appeared in the doorway. "Wow, Rag. That smells...different."

'That' being the pot of stock he had boiling on the stove, bubbling merrily as it waited for the chopped vegetables and emitting a stench most closely defined as old sneakers. Horrendous, but he hoped the sugar would counteract that when he added it later.

"Thank you." He motioned her closer, drawing her in with one arm and kissing her brow. "Why do you look so cranky?"

She groaned. "Why am I always cranky?"

"Because you live to be offended and are always half looking to punch something?"

She struck his ribs and Rag laughed, his point proven.

"It's Lucifer," she grumbled, bumping him with her hip to move him over and grabbing a knife. She followed behind him, mincing the carrots he had already chopped into chunks.

She was ruining the texture, but he suspected she needed the release of violence. And besides, did it *really* matter if the pieces were in chunks or in a finely crushed pulp?

"What has he done now?"

"It's what he *isn't* doing!" she snapped, chucking the carrot bits into the dark brown liquid on the stove. "He came storming back in yelling about forbidding Gabe to see Foster, but now he won't talk to me. He's hiding in that damn firetrap he calls his 'memories room' again."

"I keep telling him to have a Yard Sale," Rag murmured. "Mortals love those."

Remi made a non-committal noise and grabbed the onions, chopping them into miniscule pieces as Rag started on the mushrooms.

"Why are you worried about Luce, anyway? He's always moody, he'll come out of it."

"We don't have the luxury of time, Rag!" She brandished her knife at him accusingly, as if he had *told* Lucifer to hide in his rooms. "The fucking Apocalypse seems hell bent on coming, and for some reason I feel like I'm the only one taking it seriously!"

"Well," he shrugged, "We can't really proceed until Lucifer manifests the other pieces of the Armor."

She made a noise like a cat that had just been stepped on and stabbed him in the bicep. Rag yelped, then pulled out the knife and tossed it in the sink.

"You're gonna get blood on the food, and then I can't use it," he chastised, carefully angling his injured arm away from the counter as he waited for the cut to seal itself.

"Sorry," she said, not sounding the slightest bit apologetic. "I just can't believe you would say something so incredibly stupid."

"How do you mean?"

"He's being useless!" Remi stomped her boot-clad foot on the tile hard enough to crack it. "That's exactly the point! He should be doing more rituals, but instead he's being a baby!"

Rag hummed thoughtfully for a moment and then shrugged. "That's Luce, isn't it? We both know he comes through when he has to."

Remi scoffed. "He's sulking like a fucking teenager right now. His son *rightfully* rejects him, so he just gives up?! This is the man we're meant to follow into battle?!"

"Yes," Rag said simply.

For all his faults, Lucifer had never steered them wrong in battle, and Rag was confident every time he followed him into a fight. When the time came, he would strap on his armor, lay aside his grievances, and put all his strength and magic onto the field at Luce's disposal. He would fight hard and true, and he would either claim victory, or go down fighting.

It was the way of the warrior; the way of the angels. It was the only way Rag truly knew in his soul how to be. He could spend hours in this kitchen, or in the mortal realm, or curled up with his wife. He could be kind and soft and jovial, but he had the heart and soul of a man born for war.

Remi went very quiet and very still, watching Rag's eyes mist over, and knew he was in his faraway place again, reliving some long-forgotten battle. She had married a savage man who let her run rampant. He had become relaxed in these times of peace, but he was still her perfect match. A fond smile touched her lips, and she laid a hand on his sturdy jaw.

"Hey," she brought him back gently, fingers tracing his cheekbone and sliding down to his chin. "Let's go do something fun, blow off some steam."

Rag grinned back, sharp with the promise of violence. "Wanna go torment the Pit demons?"

"Raguel, you know exactly the way to my heart."

Chapter Eighteen

"Come on, old man. Keep up!"

Michael grumbled, pacing in a steady circle with his eyes fixed on Uriel's fist, the line of his shoulders, the slight shift of his feet that hinted at his movements.

"I know you can do better than this," the other man taunted, attempting a punch that Michael deflected easily. "I need to break in these new muscles, you gonna help me or just keep dancing around?"

Michael grunted and dodged, ducking a blow aimed at his shoulder, but staggered as a second heavy blow landed on his exposed left side. He grumbled as a dull ache shot through his ribs.

"I'm surprised I even landed a hit." Uriel panted lightly, lifting the hem of his loose tank top to wipe the sweat from his face. "Something is weighing on you."

Michael cast his eyes aside, adjusting his wrist wraps to avoid having to respond.

"I'll take that as a yes."

The taller angel sank down on a bench, wiping at his sweating brow with a hand towel. "You wouldn't have been hurt if we weren't caught up in this mess."

"I'm sure I would've found a way to get hurt without help," Uriel snorted, dropping down beside him on the mat and rubbing at the

219

back of his neck. "But I know you, after all these centuries. Something else is wearing you down."

Michael shook his head, and Uriel frowned. "Don't insult me with a lie, Michael."

He avoided answering right away by sweeping the gym for potential threats. Their glamours were refreshed, but a soldier was a soldier, and Michael was never really able to let his guard down. Uriel waited patiently, sipping from a bottle of water and laying back on the mat to stretch his muscles.

Finally, unable to avoid the topic further, the warrior raked a broad hand through sweat-dampened curls, then dragged it over his weary face. "All these years…and he still hates me. I can't say I blame him."

"Don't take this the wrong way, but…have you ever, you know, apologized?"

"And when would that have been?"

"You don't have to be sarcastic, jackass."

"Sorry. The point stands."

"It is a fair point," Uriel paused for a long sip of his water. "We still have no idea where Hell is. The others don't seem to leave very often."

"Mags is the only one with the ability to come and go from both Heaven and Hell. Or at least…she *was*."

"I can feel the self-loathing from over here, Mike." Uriel chided, then sighed. "You're not at fault for this."

"If I hadn't dismissed her ideas—"

"Then you would have taken her to Jeho, and she would have been arrested for heresy instead of treason. And potentially you too, for 'collaborating' with a heretic." Uriel set his water bottle aside, starting to stretch as a warm up to return to sparring.

"But I—"

Uriel looked up from his position bent in half to grip his ankle and stretch his hamstring. "You can feel helpless and upset on her behalf without taking on the responsibility and blame."

Michael grunted, scanning again around the near-empty gymnasium to avoid looking at his friend. They couldn't return to Heaven without Mags, and they couldn't find their way back to Hell—Pyzzyk had made sure of that when she deposited them back on the same rooftop they had come from.

It was frustrating, but they were soldiers who knew the best way to deal with frustration was to fight it out. So, they found a gym to spar, and yet nothing had helped Michael quell the turmoil in his heart and mind.

"Come on then." Uriel rose from the mat, extending a hand to his superior. "If you're going to brood, I want another chance to get a hit in!"

Michael made an affronted sound, and Uriel laughed.

"Pardon me, sirs," a small voice interrupted, and they turned in unison to see a boy around the age of twelve or so. He was slight and pale, with sandy brown hair falling around his ears and the subtle shimmer to his skin that marked him as a young seraph, still new to glamouring.

God, he was so young.

He wore a determined expression as he thrust a small parcel wrapped in twine towards them. "I have a message from the King."

Michael bolted to his feet and took the proffered package. "Thank you."

The boy nodded curtly and went back out the way he came, leaving the angels to wonder exactly how they were about to be reprimanded.

"You kept me waiting, Michael," Jehovah rumbled from his throne, glaring fiercely at the blond once they had unwrapped and powered up the projector cube.

"Apologies." Michael straightened from a full bow to genuflect on one knee, the rough concrete digging into his skin and grounding him as his anxious pulse jumped. "We had to find a suitably private space."

They had slipped through the back halls of the gym and up onto the roof, the best they could manage on short notice. Uriel was walking the perimeter while Michael crouched behind some duct work to keep the image from the cube shielded, and the general tried not to think about how ridiculous he must look in this position.

"It wouldn't have been an issue if you had simply completed your mission and returned." Jehovah plucked a candied fig from the bowl at his elbow and popped it into his mouth. He leaned back, looking completely at ease as he brought one leg up to cross it over his knee. "I demand an explanation for your failure."

"Uriel and I managed to gain access to Hell, but we were kept ignorant of the location. When I was able to strike out on my own, I traveled a majority of the stronghold and its surroundings. Unfortunately, I could not gain custody of Mary Magdalene."

"Why." Not a question, but a demand.

"Lucifer has hidden her from us. I went so far as to confront him, but I was rebuked and cast out. The girl is beyond our reach."

"No." Jehovah skimmed the bowl of figs, picking pieces out at random and inspecting them before tossing them back. He finally selected one and held it aloft. "You see, Michael, I have this bowl of candied figs. They're delicious—my favorites, in fact. Unfortunately, there is always the chance that even the best fruits will spoil. Fortunately, I am quite skilled at determining which fruits are the sweetest, and which have begun to turn."

A tremor of fear began in Michael's legs. With a massive effort, he willed them to still, for his face to maintain its mask of stoicism. Just out of the cube's range, Uriel's expression was blatantly alarmed.

"You see," Jehovah continued, his tone measured and cheerful as he tilted the fig so the sugar crystals caught the light. "All the sugar coating in the world is never going to hide that persistent, slow, creeping rot that ruins a perfect fruit. And I only keep the fruits I'll enjoy. Anything with a spoiled core, well..."

He popped the fig into his mouth, chewing slowly and making direct eye contact with Michael, whose pulse steadily climbed as he waited for the axe to fall. Uriel looked like he was about to be sick, all pretense of keeping watch abandoned as his dark eyes bored into Michael's face with concern.

"I simply have no desire to abide those things. Why should I? I'm *God*. I'm the Father of the Heavens, the Maker of Worlds, and King of all Creation. I made this palace. I made everything around it and the entire world that sprawls out for the mortals. I made *you*. And

Michael?" He uncrossed his leg and leaned forward, bracing both hands on the arms of his throne. "I can *unmake* you just as easily."

Michael kept his head bowed, lips and palms pressed firmly together as he waited for permission to rise.

"Get up, soldier, and return to your mission."

Straightening slowly, Michael lifted his head and rose to his feet. "But sir... my King. How do you expect me to surpass your brother in skill?"

"I don't," Jehovah snapped, ocean eyes narrowing to slits. "I expect you to stop *lying* to me, because I can discern your half-truths. You failed to gain custody of her? That doesn't mean you didn't find her; it only means you left without her."

"Because Lucifer—"

"Because of your bleeding heart, you mean." The King sighed, sitting back and pinching the bridge of his nose. "I know you care for her. We all do. She's the consort of my own son; you think I care nothing for the girl?"

"I never meant to imply—"

"The boy lives for millennia, and he never even looks at another woman. I know he loves her, so a part of me does as well. But we have *laws*, Michael, and you know this better than most. I, more than anyone, am bound by those laws.

It is a heavier burden than I would wish on you, and I bear it best I can. There are times I fail, and it is because of this that I rely on you— my soldiers, my sentinels—to help enforce these laws. You swore that oath to me, Michael."

Michael swallowed hard around the lump in his throat.

"I understand you have reservations, my son. But everything must be kept in line. She broke a law; she must be punished. I couldn't bend these rules for my own flesh and blood, so I certainly can't for anyone else. Even *I* am bound by the laws."

"Yes...I understand."

"Then go. Find the girl and return her to Heaven."

Michael nodded slowly and reached to close the connection.

"Oh, and Michael?" He paused, and Jehovah smiled warmly at him.

"If you aren't coming back with Mary Magdalene... Don't come back at all. Or it will be *your* trial."

Michael gritted his teeth but kept his expression blank and his tone measured. "I understand."

"Then go in peace, my child. Have faith and do well."

The connection closed, and in the silence, Uriel pocketed the cube. "What are we supposed to do now, Mike?"

Michael had always considered himself above such 'cowardly' actions, and yet he could feel the temptation to run away from it all simmering under his skin as he avoided looking at his lieutenant. Because what was he supposed to say? *Sorry Uriel, you've been my right hand for centuries, but you may lose another friend, because Jehovah will kill me if he finds out I have no plans to obey him?*

Instead, he turned his focus on the only thing he could: desperately trying to piece together a plan, *any* plan. Anything that would save Mags and hopefully prevent the horrific future looming over them all.

* * *

The first thing Mags noticed was a soft pressure over her eyes, and an accompanying darkness tinged in red light. A moment of panic threatened, but her sharp inhale brought with it the scent of burning jasmine and bergamot. So, she was still in her room. Mags calmed slightly, settling into the plush surface she laid on, recognizing it as her bed. A few more deep, steadying breaths, and she felt ready to figure out what in hell was going on—literally.

Slowly, she brought her shaking fingers to her face and relaxed when she felt smooth silk under her fingertips.

"A sleep mask." She breathed out, giggling slightly at the crazy possibilities she had been cycling through. She had slipped back, albeit briefly, into a past that lingered at the back of her memories like a bad smell. That was no longer her reality, and her frantic pulse started to settle.

"Mags?"

She startled slightly and lifted the strip of padded silk from her face, blinking in the dim lighting.

"Remi," she croaked, and raised a hand to her throat to massage the sore muscles there.

"Here," Remi handed her a glass of water and Mags accepted it gratefully, each cool swallow soothing and refreshing.

"What happened?" she asked when she found her voice again. "I remember Michael was here, and Luce came to my rooms to... check on me?"

Remi huffed, sinking onto the edge of the bed and resting the back of her hand against Mags's forehead. "Oh, is that how you remember it?"

"Yes?" Mags pulled her hand away and held it between her own. "What am I missing, Rem?"

"The truth," Remi sighed, squeezing her hand gently. "I didn't think he would stoop as low as removing your memory of it, too."

"Removing my memory..." the brunette trailed off, brow furrowing as she racked her memory of the encounter. A few fuzzy recollections surfaced from the fog that lingered, and she sat up slowly, expression twisting. "He wouldn't... he didn't..."

"He did," Remi corrected her gently, a hint of anger coloring the words. "The son of a bitch swore to never use his powers against us, and then he goes back on it when it suits him."

A soft knock interrupted, and Camiel slipped into the room ahead of Gloriana, who carried a tray with sandwiches.

"Mags!" She smiled broadly. "I didn't realize you were awake yet."

"Oh, I'm awake," she said, kicking off her blankets. "I'm awake and I'm furious and I'm about to go murder a god."

"You just woke up," Glory looked taken aback, brow furrowed. "You should rest for a minute or at least have a sandwich."

"No," she swung her legs over the side and rose. Remi caught her by the elbow when she swayed slightly. "I've done *enough* resting—against my own will—which is what I'm about to go discuss with *dear* Lucifer."

"Don't be so hasty," Glory set the tray down and hurried to her side. "You shouldn't overwork yourself."

"Do not *coddle* me, Gloriana," Mags snapped, and the blonde reeled back in surprise. Mags collected herself for a moment, then grabbed her favorite shawl and wrapped herself in the pink silk for comfort. "I may be gentle, but I do not take well to being forced into submission."

"There's the Mags with fire." Remi grinned. "I missed this side of you."

"I didn't," Mags sighed. "I never like becoming this person, but damned if Lucifer doesn't *push* people."

"Go get 'im!" Remi cackled. "Raise some Cain, hell, take Cain *with* you!"

"I hardly think I'll need such heavy artillery." Mags raised a brow. "You seem almost too excited by this, Remi."

"Oh, I am." She grinned. "Luci's about to get his ass whooped and he is *well* overdue."

Mags mustered a small smile of her own. "Well, have a little faith then. Who needs a man to fight their battles for them?"

"Honestly? Go let some stress out properly," said Cami, smirking. "It's not like you can actually kill him."

Mags smiled wider this time, and a dangerous glint lit her eyes. "Well then, there's no harm in *trying*."

Glory watched nervously as Mags stormed from her rooms, Remi tracking her path with delight.

"Why are you encouraging this?" the blonde asked, frowning and worrying a napkin between her slim fingers. "She's going to get hurt."

"Are you joking?" Cami snorted. "She's the one person who won't be in any danger. Luce, stupid as it was, did this because he loves her. Her life is worth more to him than his honor, or his word. That's no small thing."

They let this sit for a moment, and Glory sank onto a pouf with a sigh. "I still don't like it."

"You don't need to like it." Remi shrugged. "This is for her."

"I guess so…"

"She's a tough one, Glory," Camiel reassured the other woman with a smile. "She may be a little newer than us, but she's formidable in her own right."

"I still think she could use some backup."

Remi laughed sharply and began to pick through the sandwiches Glory had assembled. "Yeah, no thanks. *I* have no such immunity, and I'm still licking my proverbial wounds from my last attempt at reasoning with Lord Fucker."

"You're so crass. Here, I made pastrami for you."

"Yes!" Remi snatched the sandwich and took a huge bite. "Actually though, I think you're right."

"Chew first, ew."

After a hard swallow, Remi said, "No seriously though, we should go after her."

"Thank you," Glory sighed with relief. "I knew you could see reason."

"Yeah no," Remi interrupted, jumping up with a malicious grin. "I just don't wanna miss out on seeing Luci get beat up by a little girl."

Glory groaned in disbelief, pressing her building migraine with her fingertips. "You're impossible, truly."

"Thank you." Remi chomped happily at her sandwich. "I do my best."

* * *

The sound of the heavy ebony door slamming wide was enough to startle anyone, the way it hit the wall with the force of a small truck. A fitfully resting King was an even easier target.

Lucifer bolted upright with a gasp, flinging himself out of bed and halfway across the room before his mind caught up with his instincts. As he took in the scene, his nerves spun on a tangential path from alarmed to anxious, and he gulped.

"Lucifer," Mags said, smiling sweetly, but her eyes flashed with something dark and dangerous as she stood backlit in his doorway. The shadows of his unlit room concealed most of her expression, but a chill still ran down Luce's spine.

"Mags," he attempted to soothe her. "How are you feeling?"

"Betrayed," she said shortly, tone clipped and cold. "I find myself feeling utterly *betrayed*, Lucifer. And yourself?"

"Uneasy," he admitted, deciding that honesty was the best course of action here.

"Yes, I should hope so." She lifted a hand to inspect her nails, enjoying the way he flinched at the motion before he understood it. "Why don't you come out of the bedroom, Lucifer? Let's speak out in the light, shall we?"

"I'm not quite sure I like that idea."

"This is no longer about what *you* like, I'm afraid." She stepped back, revealing her distinctly displeased expression. "Come out of the bedroom, now please."

He bit his tongue and followed her into his sitting room, suppressing a shiver. "Mags, before you say anything, I need to explain myself."

"No." She closed her eyes, as if unable to bear looking at him. "No, I understand, Lucifer."

"Oh good." He relaxed slightly and attempted a smile. "If you understand—"

"I *understand*," she continued firmly, eyes flashing as she glared, "that you took it upon yourself to decide what I would be doing. I understand that you consider your thoughts and desires tantamount to infallible. I *understand* that you must have absolutely no faith in my decisions, or respect for my desires."

"Mags, no."

"Then tell me," she demanded, advancing on him until she had backed him up into his coffee table and he fell backwards onto it. "Tell me how else I should interpret your actions."

"I was protecting you!" His claims were somewhat diminished by his current position sprawled across lacquered mahogany, and he scrambled back to his feet.

"From *myself?!*" She let out an incredulous laugh. "That's absurd."

"From making a mistake," he insisted, reaching to grip her shoulders. Mags swatted his hands away and slapped her palms flat on his chest.

"No!" She shoved hard, knocking him away. "It's my *right* to make my own mistakes! You can't treat me like some porcelain doll waiting to smash on the floor!"

Luce recovered from his slight stumble, brows raised as if to challenge her assumptions of his feelings. "Obviously you aren't fragile," he snorted, attempting to enfold her hands in his own. "It's not your strength I question, but the motives of others."

"You can't seal me away from the world." She yanked her hands away as if burned, curling into herself for a moment. "I have a life, and it is *my own*. I swore when I underwent the Rising that I would use my power how *I* chose, that I would live the life *I* wanted, and that I would never be caged or chained again. You will *not* undermine my oaths to myself, *Lucifer*."

"I had no intention—"

"Bullshit! Your only thoughts were of what you wanted, and damn whatever anyone else might think or feel!"

"Stop acting hysterical and *listen to me!*" He bellowed, and her entire body went still.

"Go fuck yourself," she hissed, then slapped him hard across the mouth. "Always about you, Lucifer! Listen to *you*, do what *you* think is best. You can't even keep your own life in order, and you have the audacity to dictate other people's!"

"Mags..." He slowly brought his hand to his stinging cheek, blinking in surprise at the gold smudge that came away from his throbbing lower lip. "You just *slapped* me."

"And I'll do it again!" She paced away a few steps before turning back and repeating the motion. "If it gets through to you, I'll slap you a thousand times or more."

"You will *not*," he frowned harshly. "Mags, you know I adore you, but I have to draw a line, even for you."

She laughed, a bitter, hollow thing. "Lines? Luce, you skipped a line and threw me right in a *cage!*"

"That's an exaggeration."

"No, it isn't!" She groaned. "And the real issue is that you don't *see* it!"

He scoffed. "Maybe that's because you're seeing something where there's nothing to see."

She threw up her hands. "That's rich! You're so arrogant, it's absolutely astounding! You don't want to face your mistakes, so *I* must be overreacting? It's a miracle Michael ever put up with you, let alone Angela!"

His eyes darkened to black pits, the whites all but gone. "That's enough, Mary."

"Oh, it's my proper name now?" She stomped across the gap between them and shoved his shoulder roughly. "All fake platitudes until I touch a nerve, and then it's suddenly an issue."

He knew when he had done it that it was a mistake but keeping her out of harm's way had taken precedence. It was her turn now to prioritize her feelings, but his own temper was flaring in response. "You're crossing the line."

"And it sucks, right? To have your boundaries disrespected by someone you care about, who's supposed to care about you?"

She shoved him again, and Luce tensed. He was keeping his footing now that he was expecting her blows, but his irritation could only be kept at bay so long.

"I do care about you! That's what this is all about!"

"No!" Another shove, harder. "This is about *you!*"

"I was protecting you!"

"You are *smothering* me!" She beat her clenched fists against his chest, furious.

"Stop this nonsense, Mary!" He gripped her wrists tightly, drawing her close in a crushing grip, and she flailed like a wild creature. "Stop fighting!"

"Let me go!" Her cries rose, frantic, as she fought to get free of his grip. "Lucifer stop, please! Let go, let go, let *go!*"

"Oh," the realization dawned, and he released her as if her skin burned him. "Mags, I'm sorry, I didn't mean—"

"Stop!" Tears were flowing freely now and her eyes were wild, like a terrified animal. "Just leave me alone, please," she begged.

"No, I—"

He stepped towards her and she panicked, stepping back so quickly that she fell to the floor. Still, she kept going, scuttling back without pause until she bumped up against the sofa.

"Stay away from me, I mean it." Her quavering tone broke his heart, and Luce fell back.

"I'm so sorry."

"You're never sorry." Mags shrank into herself, curling against the sofa and resting her head on the cushion. "And when you are, it's only once you've gone too far. *That* is your problem, Luce."

The truth in her words impaled him. Luce turned away, ashamed, and struggled to find the words to convey his regret. Before he could, a sharp pang settled at the base of his spine and drew his focus.

"No..." he murmured, brow creasing. His newest wards had been triggered, the ones keyed into a specific magical signature that definitively did *not* belong in Hell.

"Yes," Mags snapped back, assuming he spoke to her.

"Not you," Luce said, shaking his head. "I have to go."

"I'll show myself out." She rose stiffly, ignoring his offered hand and refusing to even meet his eyes. "Don't look for me for a while, please."

"Mags... I never meant..."

"I know," she sighed. "I know, okay? Just...leave me be."

Luce watched her go, something like grief twining around his heart and squeezing. He wanted to chase after her, to fall to his knees and beg forgiveness, but she needed space, not pressure.

She was right. He needed to look hard at his motivations and behavior. In the meantime, he had something else to investigate, and it was the source of the disturbance sending alarm bells through his nervous system.

* * *

The Eyes of Lucifer, while expected to perform a variety of duties, were best described as the Advance Guard. They did reconnaissance for the King, kept the peace among the newly deceased, and formed the first line of defense in the event of a siege. To join the ranks was an honor among demonkind, and the Captain Overseer was notoriously particular about who met his strict criteria.

The crown jewel in this formidable order of demons was an elite class of warriors known as the Aogyn Fun Toyt—the Eyes of Death. This was an honor reserved for demons who had gone above and beyond, demonstrating advanced skill and innate prowess, who set the standard for all the Eyes to aspire to. Only ten demons had ever earned this designation, and only six of those still served.

Zajezjahval was one of them, and he took extreme pride in this achievement. It was a position of dignity and power that marked him as one of the best and entitled him to certain privileges and special missions. It also made him responsible for submitting status reports directly to their boss, Balthazar, on in this case, his second in command.

"Master Judas," Zaj swept into a bow, which was somewhat diminished by the fact that he was hovering several feet off the ground.

"Ew, no," Judas screwed up his face in distaste, leaning back in Bal's chair and kicking his boots up on the desk. "Does Bal make you call him that? Prick. Just call me Judas."

"Of course," Zaj straightened with a disapproving sniff. "I've just been to receive the updates from the Eyes, would you prefer I start with the status of the Pit, or the mortal realm?"

"Whichever is less boring," Judas waved his hand with a sigh, angling the chair even further back so he was looking up at the high ceilings. "I hate the mindless shit, where the hell is Bal anyway?"

"Master Balthazar is in the mortal realm, attending to matters of—"

"I don't actually care," Judas interrupted, dropping his chin to fix Zaj with a bored look. "Cut to the chase, please."

A hard knock at the doorway interrupted them, and Lucifer poked his head into the room.

"Oh," he blinked. "I was looking for Bal."

"Mortal realm," Judas explained, his tone conveying his disinterest.

"That could work in our favor, actually. Zajezjahval—"

"Please, your highness, call me Zaj."

"Zaj," Luce amended. "I have need of your boss, and I was hoping you might pass a message along to him."

"Consider it done," Zaj bowed. "You should hear from him within the hour."

"Perfect," Luce smiled, but a tinge of anxiety crept into the edges, and soon wiped the grin from his face. Hopefully an hour wouldn't be too late.

Chapter Nineteen

"Hi, yeah, get me a venti smoked butterscotch latte, *no* foam, *with* almond milk, 2 pumps butterscotch, 2 pumps toffee nut, *extra* butterscotch topping and whipped cream, okay?"

Michael blinked rapidly at the highly teased platinum blonde hair standing in front of him in line. This was a *coffee* shop, right? What in the name of Jehovah did this woman just order?

"Ma'am," the cashier said flatly, smiling, the look in her tired hazel eyes screaming that she'd rather be anywhere else. "This isn't a Starbucks."

"So?"

The barista blinked slowly. Michael could feel a barely contained anger emanating from her, but the customer ahead of him seemed none the wiser.

"*So,*" the cashier said cheerfully, "we don't have a size venti. Your options are regular or large, and we don't do smoked butterscotch here."

"So just smoke the normal butterscotch," the woman snapped, as if it was common sense and she was wasting her breath explaining it. Michael frowned, brow furrowing. He was pretty sure it didn't work that way.

"Ma'am, that's not an option. Would you like a regular butterscotch latte?"

"*No*, I want a *grande smoked* butterscotch latte!"

Wasn't she listening to the barista at all?

"I'm afraid that's impossible, ma'am." The barista maintained her forced smile. "You're welcome to place your order at Starbucks if it absolutely *must* be a grande smoked butterscotch latte, or you can order something else."

"Well, now I'm 'ordering' a conversation with your manager!" The middle-aged woman actually *stomped her foot* and slapped her hand on the counter. "What's your name, you little bitch? I'm getting you *fired*."

The barista arched a brow, pointing at her nametag, which read "Kim" in blocky chalk letters.

"Manager!" The woman fumed, slapping the counter again. "Now!"

"Okay." Kim shrugged, and turned to the back office. "Hey Mom! Some rude lady wants you to fire me!"

The customer's face dropped as a petite blonde woman came out from the office, looking tired but stern. "Is that so?"

Michael watched in astonishment as the irate, screeching woman did a complete one-eighty in personality.

"This is a misunderstanding," she demurred. "Your daughter was explaining the difference in your sizes, and I was a bit short with her, because I'm in a rush. I was hoping she'd be able to make a modified version of my Starbucks order."

"Ma'am, this isn't a Starbucks, the sign clearly says 'Java di Jody' above the door."

"Right, but I was in a rush..."

Kim tossed her long blonde ponytail. "If you're in such a rush, wouldn't it have been easier to just order the modified drink I suggested instead of throwing a fit?"

"Kimberley," her mother chided.

"She called me a bitch!" Kim defended herself, and Jody's head snapped toward the customer so fast the woman shrank back, alarmed.

"Out." Jody said simply. The woman seemed frozen in place. "I said, out. Out of my café, immediately."

"B-but, I didn't—"

"My daughter may be blunt, but she isn't a liar."

"I—I didn't—"

The mother turned to Michael, as if noticing him for the first time. "Did this woman call my daughter a bitch, sir?"

All eyes swiveled to Michael, and he flushed at the attention but cleared his throat and nodded firmly. It felt good to pass a deserved judgement again.

"Well, that settles it." Jody smiled, a hint of something dangerous in her almost sharp expression. "Get the hell out of my café before I have you removed."

The woman huffed out a disgruntled breath but quickly snatched up her purse and stormed out on her tottering heels. The three remaining at the counter watched her go, until Kim broke the spell with a rap of her knuckles against the counter.

"Thanks for clearing that up, sir," she grinned. "Your drink is on us today."

Jody nodded her consent. "But you, young lady, have *got* to work on your customer service skills. I can't afford to keep pissing off every Karen that comes to the counter."

"Sorry, Mom."

Jody kissed her brow and waved it off. "Do better next time, Kimi-Pops."

"Mooooom, we're at work!"

Michael smiled at the clear love between the two, despite the way Kim stuck her tongue at her mother's retreating back. Then she turned to him and smiled.

"So. Watcha drinkin'?"

Michael opened his mouth to speak, then hesitated. "I...don't know."

She eyed him shrewdly, lifting one perfectly arched brow. "Haven't been on Earth in a while, huh?"

It was like a bucket of ice water had been dumped over his head. "I—what?"

She laughed, a little chuckle with an edge to it that did nothing to help his nerves. "We can tell, you know? Even with the glamour on."

She made a flapping motion with her hands, giving him a pointed look.

Michael swallowed hard. "Right..."

"So," she picked up her little order pad from the desk and pulled a pen from behind her ear. "If you have no idea, then we can do this the fun way. I ask a question, you only have to say yes or no. Got it?"

"I think I can handle that."

"Perfect!"

She began rattling off questions about his coffee preferences. Did he like sweet drinks? Strong ones? Hot, cold? Any flavored syrups? Almond milk, soy milk, milk milk—here she broke off with a laugh. "I mean, y'know, milk from a cow."

"Of course," he smiled.

"The last question is the most essential," she informed him gravely, placing both palms flat on the counter and leaning in. "You need something to eat with your drink. So. Muffin, or donut?"

"Donut, of course," Michael responded just as gravely, though inside something was loosening around his chest. It was nice, a bit of levity amidst all the chaos.

"A man of common sense, and good taste. The answer is always, *always* donuts." She gestured to the pastry case. "There's so many, just pick whatever you like."

Michael hemmed and hawed over the options laid out and finally made a selection. It was simple but interestingly shaped, and he pointed it out. Kim peered over.

"Cruller! Nice choice."

Important beverage and pastry concerns addressed, Michael was bustled off to a small table in the corner. The café was on the emptier side, which was to be expected on a weekday afternoon, but he could tell this would be considered one of the 'best' tables either way. Placed a bit removed from the other tables with a small succulent garden in a fishbowl set on the tabletop, soaking up the warmth and light pouring in through the front window.

Kim made a show of setting the plate with his donut onto the table with a flourish and a mock bow, giggling softly. "Enjoy!"

Michael smiled as she slid back behind the counter, then turned his gaze to the small clusters of people passing by outside the glass. He lifted his coffee, sniffing curiously at the plastic lid and frowning when he couldn't discern the scent. He glanced curiously back at the counter, and Kim mimed a drinking motion with a wink before returning to her book. Michael shrugged and took a tentative sip.

Something rich and earthy burst on his tongue, immediately chased by a subtle sweetness. Was that…hazelnut? And caramel? It was delicious, and he took a longer, eager sip. Mortals were always innovating and inventing such wonderful things. The last time he had coffee in the mortal realm, it had been a bitter, dark thing the Italians were quite fond of and subsequently named espresso.

This was far and above an improvement. He turned to commend the young barista, only to freeze mid-twist. A flicker of movement in the corner of his eye drew his attention back out through the front window.

Could it be the guest he was waiting for? Or was it Uriel keeping a watchful eye on the meeting? He closed his eyes, as if to block out some unwanted sight, and for all the world seemed to be soaking in the warm sunlight. In reality, he was utilizing an ancient practice known as *sentientia privation*, also known as Deprivation Sensing.

By methodically shutting out sight, smell, touch and sound through focused concentration inward, he essentially led his awareness to a blank slate. In the void behind, there was space to unleash his power, only slightly. Just enough to spread outward and search for traces of other Divine.

It unfurled from him like a tendril, soft warm air pushed out under the guise of an exhaled breath and spreading out like a wave on the shore. His power brushed through the room, at first relaying nothing, and then there was a sudden answering push from behind the counter.

Michael started slightly, eyes blinking open at the unexpected rebuff, and watched Kim closely as she washed a few mugs in the sink. She had carefully marked her spot in her book with a clean coffee filter. She was humming something that sounded like a boy band song from last decade. And she was giving off a gentle, steady pulse of contained magic.

The way she moved, the fact that she didn't react to his probing—she was either completely unaware of her power or much practiced at maintaining a separation from it. But for a mortal to have so much raw magic... He understood why this place was known as a haven for the Divine, and how she had known what he was.

Michael reigned his power back in before she could potentially sense him. This was too small a space to unravel more of it, anyway; he had seen the effects of angelic power on mortals before, and it was never pretty.

When he turned back, the chair before him was no longer empty.

"So you see now why I suggested this place," Sachiel grinned, settling back in the chair and running his hand through his long blonde waves.

"These humans have magic," Michael raised a brow. "Witches?"

"They're witches," Sachiel confirmed. "And this is a Waypoint."

Waypoints were considered to be completely neutral spaces. Located over natural ley lines and protected by powerful enchantments, they were meant to be a haven for any Divine being regardless of affiliation, and for mortals who possessed power. Typically, they were operated by a Coven and blended into normal society in the guise of businesses and other inconspicuous buildings.

"That explains a lot."

"So, Michael," Sachiel leaned forward, resting his elbows on the table and steepling his fingers. "Bold of you to send another message after Judas got the last one."

"What choice do I have? I must return to Hell, and I don't know the way."

Sachiel fixed him with a look. "If you were wanted there, you would know."

Michael said nothing, looking out the window instead of meeting the Fallen's emerald gaze, trying to pretend his hopes weren't sinking into his gut.

"That being said," Sachiel sighed, sitting back with a mischievous gleam in his eyes, "I am a sucker for a star-crossed love story."

Michael's head whipped back around, eyes wide as his cheeks reddened. "This is not—"

Sachiel lifted his hand to stop him. "Don't bother, I can tell."

The angel rolled his eyes. "But you'll take me? To appeal to…him?"

"On two conditions." The other man held up his fingers to demonstrate. "One, only you. Tell Uriel he's gotta keep loitering in that alley. And two, if anyone catches you, I will deny my involvement until I'm blue in the face."

"I can respect those terms," Michael agreed, making a mental note to lecture Uriel about the *stealth* factor of a stakeout.

"Perfect," Sachi flashed an easy grin, lounging in his seat and draping an arm over the back of the chair. "Hey, how are the pastries here?"

* * *

Click. Click. Click. Click.

Foster was going to go mad watching the clock, but counting the steady tick of each passing second was all he felt capable of right now. Well, that and worrying himself sick, but *that* was becoming as second nature as breathing. Every second the damn doctors didn't come give him an update was another second that he spiraled deeper into guilt and grief and fear.

Click. Click. Click.

The rhythm blurred with his pulse. He nearly shook with barely contained energy, his leg bouncing a frantic beat against the floor tiles that pulled an occasional squeak from his sneaker in complement to the clock.

Click. Click. Squeak. Click. Squeak. Click. Click.

A low growl built in his throat and Foster raked his hands through his hair, tugging hard. He wanted to scream, to rip that damned clock off the wall, to start throwing chairs around the room until someone came to stop him. At least then there would be another living being in this tiny, impersonal waiting room. The half dead ficus in the corner did *not* count—he wasn't even a hundred percent sure it wasn't made of plastic.

Click. Squeak. Click. Click. Click. Squeak squeak.

With a frustrated groan, he pushed up from the uncomfortable plastic chair. He wasn't sure if he was planning to track down the doctor or maybe just a vending machine. Anything to occupy his mind and body for even a few moments was going to be a welcome diversion, at this point.

Then there was a firm knock against the doorframe, and a middle-aged man with silver hair stepped around it to enter the room. He was stocky and stern-looking, life worn hard into the lines on his face, but there was a kindness in his weary eyes. "Mister... Morningstar?"

"Yes!" His frazzled nerves tensed, and he cleared his throat. "That's me."

"My name is Doctor Kontogeorgos. I'm the primary physician that's been attending to your grandmother." He paused, and the hesitation ramped Foster's anxiety up another level. "Why don't you have a seat, young man?"

"All due respect," Foster swallowed hard, "I've been sitting too long. Just tell me, how—how bad—"

The doctor adjusted his glasses as he watched him struggle. It felt like he was sizing him up and seeing how much Foster could handle. He laid a consoling hand on his shoulder. "She's alive, but it's touch and go at the moment. I won't sugarcoat this for you, son. Are you sure you won't sit?"

"No," he croaked, throat tightening until he thought he would choke. "Please."

"Alright," the older man sighed. "She's in bad shape. I have no idea how she's holding on, but for the grace of God."

If it wasn't such a tense situation, Foster might have laughed at that. The doctor had no idea just how close to the truth he was.

"Of course," Dr. Kontogeorgos was saying, "we're doing everything we can to keep her comfortable, but with third degree burns over thirty percent of her body, that's no easy feat. We're lucky to be maintaining stability, let alone comfort."

"And... third degree burns are really bad?"

"It doesn't get much worse. First degree involves blisters and pain. A really bad sunburn can get to that point. Third degree is one step shy of melting down to bone."

His knees wavered, and Foster locked them. He would not fall apart here, when she needed him to be strong. "Fuck."

"I'm so sorry," the doctor squeezed his shoulder gently. "I'm afraid to say there's… not much we can do for her, son. She's heavily sedated, but… well, I recommend that you see her while you can."

The words rocked through him so hard that it took a moment for his brain to process them. "What—what are you trying to say, Doc?"

A long pause. The doctor swept his gaze around the room, taking in the utter stillness, the empty chairs. "I'm saying it's very good of you to be here with her, especially since it won't be easy to see her in this state. But I suggest you take this time before it's too late."

He didn't remember following Dr. Kontogeorgos down the long, sterile corridors, but he must have. He must have, because he was standing before a closed wooden door in a busy hallway, raising and lowering his hand in an endless cycle of *almost* turning the handle.

The doctor had deposited him here and vanished again, off to save other lives, and left Foster standing alone to face down his demons. Actually, demons would have been preferable to the horror that was mounting within him.

"I can't," he murmured, a nervous shiver rolling down his spine. "I can't bear it."

A familiar presence appeared behind him, and warm hands settled on his shoulders.

"But you must," Gabe spoke gently, punctuating his words with a light squeeze. "If not you, then who?"

"You're right."

"I often am."

Foster huffed. "Prick."

"I am also this," Gabe agreed easily, releasing him to saunter around and lean into the doorframe. "But you love me for it, Foster Flake."

"What I *don't* love is that stupid nickname. I'm not five anymore."

"You'll always be a baby to me," Gabe's eyes twinkled, and Foster rolled his.

"Ridiculous." He lifted his hand back to the doorknob; gripped it tight. "*Ridiculous.*"

Gabe softened. "It is not an exclusively mortal concept, you know. Anxiety...fear."

Foster said nothing, just turned the knob and swung the door inward. Gabe touched his shoulder again before drifting ahead of him into the room, drawing him along like a boat caught in a wake. He stepped slowly in Gabe's footsteps, keeping his eyes firmly fixed on the floor ahead of him.

The sound of slow, steady beeping reassured him, but it was drowned out by the mechanical hiss of the machine breathing for his neighbor. He reached the side of the bed, staying tucked behind Gabe like maybe he *was* still five. Part of him was ashamed of the way he cowered, but dignity be damned, his heart was breaking at the simple thought of how Sra. Delgado must look. The actual sight was liable to kill him.

"Fossie," Gabe said solemnly, stepping aside and resting his hand on Foster's back. "I'm so sorry."

"Me too." He finally jerked his gaze up from the crisp white bedsheet, like ripping off a bandage. There was a moment of disconnect, where his eyes hadn't yet told his brain what he was seeing. This wasn't Sra. Delgado. This was a pile of old rags someone had left on the bed while cleaning up. He was in the wrong room. His mind supplied any explanation but the truth.

Slowly, horribly, it sunk in. Those were bandages, not rags. That was blood starting to seep and stain them. The greyish bits peeking through, the spots that looked like paper with charred edges... that was *skin*.

"*¡Abuela!*" His chest tightened, his stomach twisted, his heart tried to hammer out of his chest through his ribs.

The last vestiges of beer and bar nachos rolled in his gut and he retched, dry heaving for a moment to fight the urge to vomit. Slender hands gripped his upper arms with surprising strength, hauling him up against a warm chest. Gabe folded him into a tight embrace, pulling him into the chair by the bedside so he could sit.

"Shh," he crooned, stroking long fingers through dark waves, soothing and shushing him just like he had fifteen years ago. "The first step is to breathe. In and out."

He tried and failed, shuddering on each breath as hot tears poured down his cheeks.

"Again, Foster."

He took another shaky breath, focusing on Gabe and the steady, grounded cadence of his voice. Once again, a woman he loved lay dying and Gabe was his only lifeline. Once again, his father was nowhere to be found. The irony was like salt in the wound.

A few long moments of stilted breathing in response to gentle murmuring, and Foster had calmed enough to regain his composure. He scrubbed at his damp eyes with frustration, hating the display of weakness but hating the situation more.

"Foster," Gabriel said, and the subtle trace of steel in his voice had Foster bracing himself before the other man could even continue. "The time has come to do what needs to be done. I'm sorry to be so direct, but you must stop being stubborn."

Foster could almost feel his eyes bugging out as he opened his mouth to protest, but Gabriel kept on. "You are the closest thing I've ever had to a son. You may feel weak right now, but I know your true strength. And you are strong enough to give this woman the release she needs."

Silence stretched. Foster refused to speak, turning over those words that were like so many knives in his heart and whatever was left of his soul. How could Gabe be suggesting *that*, of all things, right now?

"Look at her, Foster. She's in unfathomable pain. Nearly half of her body has been melted off. Her wounds are oozing blood and Jehovah knows what else. The agony must be excruciating." He paused, studying the young demigod. "Surely you can't be cruel enough to let her endure for the sake of your selfish desires. You're not your *father*, after all."

Foster fought back another heave at the sucker punch statement.

"Fuck you," he finally managed to croak, but there was no heat behind it. Gabe was right, and it fucking sucked. "I don't want to kill her, Gabe."

"Foster," the response was sad. "She's beyond saving."

No. She couldn't be, she wasn't *allowed* to die. He would fight all of Heaven himself to prevent it.

"What would she want, Foster? To suffer in pain for hours until she's eventually called home in the end? Or to go peacefully through your mercy right now, and give you something back in exchange?"

His frantically beating heart stilled at this, stuttered, skipped a beat, and kicked back in harder. To trade one life for another…it made him feel dirty to consider it. He flashed back in his memories, to a tiny body laid ever so gently on a ritual pentagram, to the sticky, wet slide of her blood against his fingertips.

He could feel the echo of those tears in the trails of damp salt on his cheeks now. *Mercy…* it was a concept dependent on perspective. Sra. Delgado's ventilator whirred and clicked, breathing for her while she lay unconscious.

It sent him back to another bedside he had cried beside, fifteen years ago. The woman in that bed had been pale, not charred, covered in a sheen of feverish sweat instead of bandages. But once again, he was about to lose a woman he cared deeply for.

Carmen was old, and she lived alone. She always tried to take care of him despite her bad hip and dwindling health. Is this what she would want? To be… set free? To help him one last time?

Gabe's hand closed on his shoulder again. "You know what you should do, son."

Foster hung his head, tears redoubling. He had no idea what he *should* do, but he knew, deep down, the choice he had already made.

Chapter Twenty

The path Sachiel had marked out wound languorously through the city, and Michael cursed the other man for his laissez-faire demeanor. He was ninety percent certain there was a more direct path, and he would've accused Sachiel of leading him on a wild goose chase if he didn't know the Fallen had always been meandering and relaxed, even when he needed to be serious.

Eventually the trail led him into an alley between a deli and a barber shop. Michael scanned the grime-streaked brick walls of the alley. Pops of color peeked through in broad swirls and what might be letters, but unless the graffiti contained some secret code, it wasn't going to make this any less of a dead end. There were no doors, no archways. He quickly swept the ground and affirmed that no, there were no trap doors or manholes hidden under the piles and bags of garbage, either.

"Dammit Sachiel," he groaned. First he leads him on a ridiculous path, wasting his time and energy, and now he's expected to what? Walk through solid brick?

No. He had to stop, center himself. He was the best tracker Heaven could claim, and he was better than this. If he could focus…he could find the entrance. The golden angel steeled himself for what he needed to do. Drawing a dagger from its sheath strapped to his thigh, he weighed it carefully, then slashed it quickly over his forearm.

A twinge of pain, a spray of golden blood, but nothing he couldn't bear. Already the pain dulled, and the flesh began to knit over the shallow wound. That was fine; he only needed a small amount of blood. Dipping his index finger into the shimmering gold, he went down on one knee and began to carefully trace symbols onto the slimy pavement, trying to ignore the potential sources of years of layered residue.

Getting a general sense of direction or following a trail was one thing. That was like echolocation, telling him which way to move. But when the trail died out, the only option left was to dig deeper and peel back the layers of interference, until he could expose the living memories embedded in the fabric of reality.

The simple sigil relied mostly on the blood of the caster to determine its strength, and he finished it quickly. Almost instantly, trickles of magic echoed back to him, a testament to his skills as well as the recency of the trail. A small smile danced over his lips. *Still got it.*

Closing his eyes, Michael did not sink back down into the void of his senses but instead pulled at the edges of the magic spreading through the alley. Unlike tracing someone's steps by the feel of the magic alone, his fingers trailed lightly through the air, reaching along invisible threads as if there was a rope there, guiding him deeper into the alley. Flickers of images teased the corners of his vision, a scene like a movie clip forming in his mind.

A hidden door, here in the back wall. And to open it… Suddenly, there was a flare in the connection. The difference was as drastic as overpowering a candle by turning on a lamp. The image shattered before he could make out the method of entry, and Michael cringed.

A man stood before him. A man he knew well, which was unfortunate. Despite his long hair, pulled into a low tail at his nape, and the layers of jewelry and black leather he wore, this was no common punk. This was a fellow immortal, one who was every bit as deadly and nearly as powerful as Michael, if more inclined to work in the shadows than on the front lines. When Balthazar chose to show himself to you, it was already too late to run.

"Come on, Mikey," his voice was like smoke over stone, smooth with a touch of roughness, and he looked distinctly displeased despite the pleasant tone he attempted. His false smile was betrayed by the hard anger in his gaze. "You should know better, really. My Eyes see everything, and we're very careful about monitoring our borders."

Michael said nothing, his hands hanging still at his sides but within reach of the dagger he had re-sheathed. The other man clicked his tongue and wagged a finger at him.

"Well, that's just bad manners, Mike. Breaking and entering, and now you're thinking about trying to, what, *stab* me?"

A long, tense moment hung between them. Michael's narrowed silver gaze locked on that cold, ebony glare. Then, "I need to see Lucifer."

Bal smirked and dropped his hand, laden with numerous, mismatched rings, heavily onto Michael's shoulder. "Don't worry, friend," he smiled brightly. "That's exactly where I was planning to take you."

"I'll bet." Michael cursed himself for his carelessness.

If anyone should have been prepared for this, it was him. He had been Bal's commander for eons, utilizing the man's penchant for slipping into pockets between space to their advantage more than once during battles and reconnaissance missions. Yet he had walked into this trap like an errant fly, never pausing to look for the signs. He was either becoming careless or reckless, and neither option appealed to him.

"Hey, cheer up, Mikey," Bal maintained his cheery facade, throwing an arm around Michael's shoulders, which were unencumbered by his glamoured wings. A tendril of unease uncurled in his stomach at the vulnerability his exposed back presented, and he found himself casually inspecting Bal's layered belts for a knife sheath. Finding none, he relaxed a fraction.

"You're getting what you want, alright? Unfortunately, I will have to...well, *put you under*, for lack of a better term."

Bal's hand slid up quickly, over Michael's shoulder, to grip him by the nape of his neck. Michael tensed, but he knew it was already too late as a spark of magic zipped under his skin and the world began to tilt.

"Sorry, old friend," Bal's grin was genuine now, because he was most certainly *not* sorry in the slightest. He had always had a penchant for mischief. "I didn't make the rules, I just enforce 'em."

The last thing Michael heard before he passed out was a low, dark chuckle that sent chills rolling down his spine.

Darkness, a touch of cool breeze, and the scent of burning herbs roused him from his stupor. Michael shifted, restless, and winced at the kiss of something hard and surprisingly cold against his skin. He groaned, shifted again, and felt a flare of concern at the restricted movement of his limbs.

With a concerted effort, he forced his eyes open, blinking in the low light from a crackling fire in the grate beside him. He was seated in a sturdy wooden chair; shimmering cords of white magic bound him securely in place. Thinking quickly despite the lingering fog, Michael tried to rock the chair to either side in an effort to tip it over and get onto his feet.

It was a wasted effort; it had been carved from a dense wood that gave it considerable weight. This was not good. Instinctually, he began looking for a fire poker, or some other tool that could be repurposed as a weapon.

"Don't mind the fire," a low, sensuous voice taunted him from the darkness, and Michael jerked in surprise. *Lucifer.* The man himself came into view, sliding out from the shadows at the room's edge with deadly grace and the threat of violence glimmering in his eyes. "It does get a bit drafty in here."

Michael stared blandly back. The only betrayal of his indifferent mask was the stubborn set of his jaw; the quick calculations running behind his eyes.

"You can give up on plotting your escape, Michael." Luce settled against the edge of the desk placed opposite the chair, arms folded, with his long legs stretched out before him, crossed at the ankle.

"Even if you somehow managed to free yourself, you'd have to get past *me*. If by some miracle you managed that, there's a veritable army of my most loyal, highly trained soldiers between you and the Rift. You are well and truly fucked, angel boy."

He was. *Damn*. Even Michael could admit that—skilled tactician he may be—there were some odds even he couldn't beat. And this deck had been stacked well in advance. They had known, somehow, that he was coming, and that he would be alone. He pictured Sachi's easy smile and wanted to curse. It had been a carefully laid trap, and like a wobbling newborn, Michael had practically tripped over himself to fall into it.

Luce eyed him steadily, refusing to even blink as he circled slowly around. When he stood directly behind the chair, he paused, and Michael tried not to panic. Lucifer had never been needlessly vicious in the past, but he had no way of knowing if that still held true. Time could change a person in endless ways, and though he hated to admit it, Michael could no longer claim to know this man.

No angel would be comfortable with an unassessed threat standing at his back, and Michael silently cursed himself again for his foolishness. He had been stronger, once. Balthazar would never have been able to incapacitate Michael in his glory. This was disgraceful.

As if reading his mind, Lucifer reached out to rub his fingertips along Michael's bare shoulder blades, at the exact spot where tawny wings normally sprouted from sun kissed skin. Michael did his best to suppress the shiver that ran down his spine as he was stroked and prodded.

"Your glamour should be nearly depleted," Luce mused thoughtfully, and a shard of fear embedded itself in Michael's gut. It would be only fair, he knew. An angel's wings were their greatest treasure, and he had been the one to destroy Lucifer's own. "I'll get to see those *glorious* wings again, *angel*."

It wasn't an endearment any longer. The slight edge, the almost imperceptible mockery of what they had once shared… it wasn't lost on him. Swallowing around the tightness of his throat, Michael made another futile attempt at escape, refusing to simply sit and be taunted until Luce decided on who knew what form of revenge.

Tugging stubbornly at his bonds, he wasn't prepared for them to abruptly vanish. Only dedicated centuries of training kept him from toppling forward and face planting into cold stone. Instead, he caught himself, straightened, and spun to face Luce with an expression of either shock or suspicion—he wasn't entirely sure what his own face was doing.

"Don't give me...whatever that face is," Luce said, waving his hand in a broad sweep. "You can agree there's no honor in besting a downed opponent."

"I wasn't sure we still saw eye to eye on matters of honor. I thought you had left such inconvenient ideals to me."

Luce scoffed. "Ah, yes, because your betrayal was so honorable."

"*My* betrayal?!" Michael's eyebrows flew upwards. "Do not speak to *me* of betrayal!"

"Personally, I wouldn't speak to you at all, but you seem to keep finding your way to my doorstep uninvited." His eyes flashed. "I'm sure you understand why I can't allow this?"

"I know I'm not wanted here, but you've put us in a position beyond our control, Lucifer."

The King scoffed. "Perhaps beyond *your* control. Some of us are made of stronger stuff."

"This is not a contest of strength," Michael seethed, struggling to contain his irritation for the sake of a civil conversation. "At this point, it's about undoing the damage you've caused and keeping the world intact!"

"We live in two very different worlds," Luce rebuffed. "What makes you so certain I care about maintaining *your* status quo?"

"Because Mary Magdalene is precious to both of us, and to people we care for."

Luce kept silent, but the rigidity of his spine and shoulders telegraphed his barely contained rage. Michael had turned this conversation into dangerous waters, and now he dove headfirst.

"Jehovah sent me with instructions to collect her, or to not bother returning."

Luce was so still, he seemed to not even be breathing. For a long moment, nothing happened. Then his hand twitched, fingers clutching the empty air at his side, and Michael was flying backwards through the air before he had time to brace.

He impacted the far wall at the exact moment his glamour faded, wings unfurling just in time to be slammed and pinned to the wall. White hot pain raced along their arch, telling him there were fractures in the hollow bones there, and he knew Luce had timed this strike intentionally to ground him and even the stakes for the fight he was about to pick.

The gale force winds that had flung him back continued to rage, holding him captive and simultaneously ransacking the room they were in. Books, papers, bottles of ink and various knickknacks, even a second, smaller chair—nothing was safe.

Several of the newly weightless items would abruptly change course midair to fly at Michael, striking him hard on the shoulders, the broad plane of his chest, even his face, which brought white sparks popping in his vision.

"I thought I had made myself clear, Michael, that Mags makes her own decisions?" Was that a flicker of... guilt? The storm raged harder. "I thought you realized you are *not welcome here*."

He couldn't catch his breath to speak, and he knew it was rhetorical, but he managed to force a nod. The pressure of the winds relaxed, then halted completely.

"Then *why?*" Luce practically screamed as Michael dropped to the stone flooring, jarring his knees and catching himself on his palms in a stinging slap. He noted with some astonishment that at close range, you could see a pattern of *feathers* embossed on the tiles.

"Why are you here? Why do you keep invading my *home?* As if I haven't suffered; haven't been dealt enough hardship by your hands? You come to rip apart my sanctuary and take the few things I have left away from me?"

His foot came down hard on Michael's back, pinning him to the floor and re-breaking the slowly mending fractures in his wings. The angel half-whimpered, half growled as sparks popped under his skin like hot kernels. And yet, he had endured much worse. He could take his hits and bear this pain, because he could hear the naked grief in

Lucifer's voice. This was a man on the verge of a breakdown, and the last thing he wanted was to push him over that edge.

Slowly, excruciatingly, stubbornly, Michael shifted his weight. He dug deep inside himself, braced for the rush of hot agony he was about to receive, and shoved backwards with his full weight. His breath caught at the pain that seemed to wrap his chest in a bear hug and squeeze, as expected, but it also worked. Luce was knocked enough off balance that Michael was able to get to his knees and get his bearings.

He scrambled to his feet, trying to cobble together some kind of plan. He wasn't enough of a fool to think he could take Lucifer in a fight. They were equally matched in swordplay, even if his weapons hadn't been taken while he was knocked out, and on top of that, Michael's powers were definitively non-offensive. All the skills that made him a superior tracker did little to assist him in battle, but if there was one thing he could do, it was strategize.

Luce eyed him coldly, circling in slow, fluid steps that kept him squarely facing the angel. "You never knew when to quit."

"One of my redeeming qualities."

"Debatable."

A smile tugged at Michael's lips. This was almost like old times, bantering and sparring with Lucifer. It was more fulfilling than sparring with Uriel or Jophiel, even if it had always earned him more bruises. As if reading his mind, Luce scowled.

"Don't you fucking smile at me, like we're friends. This isn't fun for me; this is about you violating my sanctum and putting my people at risk. It's not a *joke!*"

He lashed out on the last word, jerking his hand upwards as if tossing a drink in Michael's face, and a hard slash of wind came rushing. Michael dodged, falling back and twisting to the side, but Luce was ready, sliding up beside him and striking out with another slice. This one caught his drooping wing, the fractures interfering with his attempt to draw them in. The smile vanished, replaced with grim focus. This was *not* a joke or a game, and if he forgot that, he could very possibly die.

He continued to evade, outpacing the King of Hell by barely half a step, keeping his eyes peeled for anything that could possibly be a weapon. But Lucifer, of course, knew all his strengths and would have prepared this room to keep any potential advantage from Michael. *Think*, he chastised himself. *What's here that I can use?*

He was in what must be Lucifer's study. There were no weapons, he had never been able to generate portals at will, and his wings were too damaged for flight. *That's it!* He might not have use of his wings, but he was faster than Lucifer, more agile. If he could just gain the high ground...

He leapt backwards without warning, breaking their cyclical dance and landing atop the heavy wooden desk, quickly stepping backwards to put distance between them.

"Really? What is it with you people and climbing on my desk?" Luce grumbled.

He stepped forward and Michael seized his moment, lunging forward and flinging himself through the space between them. He folded his wings in as best he could, leaned back, and brought both feet up into a tuck position, slamming them squarely into Luce's gut.

The King grunted and went down hard on his tailbone, cursing and shoving at him even as Michael spread his knees to cage Lucifer between them. The angel didn't hesitate to rear his fist back and slam Luce across the face, his jaw making a harsh clacking sound.

He managed to get one more hit in before a deceptively strong hand shot up between them and gripped his wrist hard enough that his bones ground within. Black lacquered fingernails elongated into sharp claws as Luce glared up, bleeding profusely from his lower lip.

"This is my second split lip this week, and I find I don't enjoy it any more the second time around. That was a mistake you just made, *Michael*," he snarled the name and tightened his grip, bones snapping like popsicle sticks.

Michael made a guttural sound and wrenched his arm free, scrambling up and away. He eyed Luce warily, bracing for a strike. His former lover didn't disappoint, lashing out with another whip of air that kissed his skin with the threat of frost. Michael shivered, diving out of the way so the desk was back between them.

He scanned the floor again, and this time his eyes landed on a heavy paperweight that had been tossed in the windstorm. He gripped it with his good hand, gauged the weight, and flung it in Lucifer's general direction. There was a hard *thunk* and an ugly squelch, followed by an affronted gurgle.

Michael peered over the lip of the desk to see a sizeable dent in Luce's throat. The King looked up with eyes burning gold and made a violent ripping motion with both hands. A miniature tornado spun out towards the angel, splitting the desk in half.

Tucking and rolling to the side, Michael ended up sitting a safe distance away, leaning on one palm and tensed to evade another attack. Luce made no such moves, only watched him with an inscrutable look.

"Give up, Michael," the King demanded. "You can't best me, and I would prefer not to expend more of my power on this nonsense. I have greater priorities to attend to."

Michael took several panting breaths and slowly lifted both palms, facing outward in a gesture of placation. Fighting was never going to work; Luce was too strong. His only hope was to try and reason his way out of this. His broken wrist itched and throbbed as the bones tried to mend themselves, and Michael winced.

"I'm not here to 'take' anything—or anyone. People are not things to possess. Isn't that what you believed, even... in Eden?"

It was the wrong thing to say.

The room—no, *Michael* suddenly flipped upside down. His head swam, a pulse of heat and pain spiraling out from where he had knocked it against the floor. The air above him became dense and pressed him flat on his back, damaged wings splayed awkwardly, with his chest going slightly concave under the weight.

At the edge of his vision, feet approached. Confident, heavy strides that brought designer loafers to a stop inches from his trapped form.

"Fuck you," Luce hissed, stroking the air roughly, and the force on his body increased.

A mortal would have either blacked out or died from a lack of air by this point, and Michael shuddered. Luce was willing to kill him. Something cracked within him, and he wasn't sure if it was the fragile shell of his heart, or one of his ribs. The radiating ache suggested the latter.

The fight flickered and faded in him. Michael nearly resolved himself to die on this floor. Maybe he welcomed it. Let someone else deal with the mess they'd all stumbled into. No more pressure to conform or betray his ideals. No more grief or regret over what used to be or could've been.

But something stubborn and angry pushed back, and he saw Mags's broken spirit in the Garden, Christos bleeding on his father's dining room floor, Uriel's arm dangling shattered and useless. He couldn't betray them by giving up now.

The weight abruptly vanished, and Luce crouched down beside him.

"No, I won't kill you, Michael," he murmured softly, stroking his fingers from the blond's temple to his jaw. "I can't say I find you worthy of being put to death by my hands."

There was something glassy and alien in his eyes, and Michael would have recoiled if he'd had anywhere to move.

"I swear," he forced the words out with considerable effort, his entire body aching and reluctant, "I am not here to kidnap Mary. I came...to beg for your help."

Luce blinked down at him, expression unreadable. Michael would have called it longing, if not for the haunted, sharp gleam in his eyes.

"For my help," he repeated quietly.

The breeze stirred again, papers rustling as they were pushed and swept across the stone floor. The curtains fluttered, letting shards of sunset pierce the room. The light played unusual shadows across Luce's face, obscured his eyes behind a reflected gleam.

"We always made a good team," Michael continued cautiously. "You are the only one who could dream of rivaling your brother."

"Rivaling... my brother." Luce continued to repeat the words, as if he needed to hear them aloud to make sense of them. Slowly, a look of comprehension dawned in his eyes, but it was quickly chased away by dark suspicion. "No. I've been down this road before, and I won't play the fool again."

Michael's brow furrowed. "What do you mean?"

"Every time you've suggested we work against my brother, I end up taking the fall—quite literally, in fact."

He was utterly lost now. "Forgive me, as I know this isn't going to gain me much favor, but I have only wavered in my loyalty to your brother one time before now."

The words hung unspoken between them, but they both recalled a cold throne room, a moment's hesitation, and a cry of broken-hearted pain.

Unconsciously, Luce's fingers skimmed a familiar path along Michael's smooth jaw to ghost over soft lips. There was a foreign intimacy in the touch, an echo of something old and primal that neither of them had ever been able to replicate in other partners. Luce's expression twisted, and he gripped Michael's face firmly, carefully manicured nails cutting crescent moons into his jaw.

"You *lie*," he hissed, tightening his grip. "I should cut that lying tongue from your poisonous mouth, but then I suppose you'd just lie with your hands."

A phantom memory bloomed of sturdy palms that curved over sharp hipbones and tangled in long hair; the slide of hot skin and fervent whispers, both of them so *young* and drunk on each other.

"My silence may have been complacence, but I never lied to you and I won't start now," Michael countered, summoning the strength—and courage—to pull himself up to a sitting position. His aching wings drooped, falling around him like a makeshift shawl. "I should have spoken for you that day, but I was too blinded by your betrayal. I impugned my honor by allowing it to color my judgement."

Luce scowled. "I never betrayed *you*. What are you talking about?"

"You really don't consider seducing Eve to be a betrayal of...what we were?"

"*What?!*" Luce recoiled, annoyance transforming to horror. "I looked upon Eve and Adam as one might a child. A *child*, Michael! I would never."

"I saw you!" He beat his balled fist against his palm, brows furrowed and mouth set in a snarl. "I saw you, in the Garden, with Eve in your arms. As much as I've tried, I've never been able to erase that scene from my mind. I know what I saw."

The look of horror mingled with disgust. "I don't know what you saw that day, but I can assure you, it was not me."

"How so?"

"Because I wasn't with Eve in the Garden that day, Michael. I took your advice and went to the Garden, yes, but I was planning for the rebellion with *Adam*."

Chapter Twenty-One

Humans were so unbelievably fragile. Gabe could admit that he was fairly detached, even for an immortal. Trying to cultivate relationships was difficult for him—it was part of the reason Foster was so precious to him. It was inconceivable for him to imagine expending that much effort to connect with a mortal when their existence would be a blink of his own.

The woman on the bed before him was a prime example. At the tail end of her lifespan, only a few revolutions from slipping the mortal coil, they considered her an "elder". He scoffed. At her age, an angel was barely an infant. He had *sweaters* older than this woman.

And yet, she was beyond important because Foster loved her. Gabe bent over the woman's still form, assessing her wounds and probing with his magic to ensure her life force still flickered within. After all he had suffered, Gabe would not allow Foster to lose this woman and gain nothing in return.

The sound of the doorknob turning caught his ear, and Gabe glanced up to see Foster returning with a brown paper bag cradled in one arm. He snapped his fingers and the bag rose from the boy's grip, bobbing slightly as it drifted across the room and overturned itself. The contents spilled across the bedside table for Gabe's appraisal.

Neatly tied bundles of herbs, expertly cut spheres of amethyst and selenite, a small vial of oil stoppered and sealed with black wax. He moved aside the purple and black taper candles and lifted a jar full of neatly sifted yellowed white powder.

"You're *positive* this is bone powder from an Arcanum Praeceptor?"

"The Praeceptor Dominus, in fact. Would you like a copy of the death certificate?"

"Forgive my dubious nature." Gabe marked the boy's agitated tone, and reminded himself to be patient. Foster still wavered over this decision. The angel smiled in a way he hoped was reassuring. "The remains of the highest devotees are sacred, and a rare prize to come by. I'll take your word."

"I would hope so," Foster muttered, crossing to the window and staring out over the small courtyard to avoid looking at the hospital bed. A long moment passed as Gabe arranged the spell components, and then he said, "This feels wrong, Gabe."

"Wrong in what way?" A swell of irritation bloomed in his chest, and Gabe squashed it. The boy was half mortal with an unbearably human heart; his struggles with loss were a natural consequence of feeling so deeply.

"I don't feel qualified to make this call."

"You *aren't* making it." Gabe rolled the amethyst sphere between his fingers. "The universe works in mysterious ways."

"And my uncle." Foster turned, frowning, and his attention skipped over the bed to land on the small vase of flowers one of the apartment neighbors had sent. "He can do nothing?"

Gabe sobered as a bitter recollection tickled the edges of his memory. "No, Jehovah doesn't interfere in the designs of fate. Not for mortals."

"No, just for my *dear* cousin Christos." There was a bitterness there that made Gabe's frown deepen.

"Saving Mary Magdalene was a…different case," he hedged.

"As if God himself doesn't have the power?"

"The laws are the laws," Gabe sighed. "Which is why we're here."

Finally, Foster looked to the bed. His expression immediately darkened, eyes going flat and distant. "I wish there was any other way."

"There is not."

"I know!" Foster raked his hands through his hair. The vial of peppermint and lilac oil rolled to the edge of the nightstand that trembled in the wake of his overflowing emotion, and Gabe snatched it from the air as it fell.

"Calm yourself," he commanded the younger man.

Foster glowered at him with tear-filled eyes. "How?!" He wailed softly, and Gabe felt a twinge of sympathy. How confusing and over-whelming, to have a mortal heart paired with the curse of immortal-ity. But there was work to be done.

"I say this with love, Foster." he came to his side and gripped the boy's shaking shoulders. "But you—"

A soft, shuddering cough interrupted the moment. Foster whirled to face the bed.

Gabe turned slower, brows lifting in astonishment. "She wakes."

The boy was by her side in an instant, scrutinizing her face as Sra. Delgado gave another soft cough. Her eyes flickered open, closed, opened again, and fixed on his.

"*M-mijo*," she croaked, wincing at the strain, her words muffled by the mask strapped over her nose and mouth.

Foster whimpered. "*Abuela*."

Gabe cringed and averted his gaze from the…touching scene. *Speak your piece and go, old woman.*

"Foster… *mi amor*…" Her breathing was labored and pained. Foster leaned in close to listen to the whispery words she managed to force out. "*Ayúdame*."

"Help you how, *abuela*?" The boy was on the verge of tears, and his obvious affection for the woman brought a lump to even Gabe's throat. He turned to the window to allow them some privacy.

"Let…me go…" The old woman rattled and wheezed. "Set…me free, *angelito*."

Her eyes slipped shut again and stayed closed. A long silence stretched over the room, broken only by the steady beeping of the monitors and the soft whirr of the breathing machine. Gabe ran his fingers over the curtain, picking at a loose thread on the bottom. This was a hideous plaid pattern and an awful color.

Then Foster began to cry. He couldn't even begin to comfort the boy; what was he supposed to say? It was terrible, but this was the way it was. They might as well get something back in exchange, it only made sense.

"Gabe."

He gripped the curtain tight, wincing at the pure desperation in Foster's voice. The fabric tore in his grasp. "You should respect her wishes."

More ugly silence. Gabe turned, but Foster wasn't looking at him. He knelt beside the bed with his forehead pressed to the crisp white sheet, both hands folded around one of the old lady's as if he was praying with her.

Gabe folded his own hands before him and bowed his head. Ironically, he wasn't much of a believer in the power of prayer. He had seen too many prayers go unanswered, including his own. He had lain prostrate before his King and pleaded once before, to no avail.

But if it brought Foster some comfort, Gabe could pretend.

* * *

"The rebellion with Adam." Michael kept returning to the same comment, his mind whirling with the implications.

"However many times you say them, the words are the same."

"Technically I'm just repeating *your* words." A sharp tug on his wounded wing had him grunting.

"Semantics annoy me, and you know that." Luce returned the wing to a proper position for splinting, folded neatly against Michael's back. "Hold still, you fidgety child."

Michael made an affronted noise. "I'm not—"

"Oh, shut up, it's the truth." Luce scoffed. "You were always so sensitive about injuries, but only after you ignored them and got yourself nearly killed."

"I suppose I do tend to get... hyper-focused."

"Hyper-focused? Michael, a *bomb* could go off beside you, and you wouldn't notice if you were tracking." He pinched the bridge of his nose, massaging to loosen the tension, and picked up a roll of cloth bandage. "All nonsense aside, you better sit still for me to bind these wings, or they won't set properly."

"I'm not a child, I can keep still without a binding."

"I have absolutely no faith in your ability to control yourself. You can't even follow the simple direction to stay away from me."

"You're still so arrogant."

"And you're ignorant."

They fell into silence as Luce unwound and stretched the bandage, slapping the end against Michael's chest.

"Hold this." He began to wrap around muscled torso and tawny feathers, assuming Michael would follow the command. The angel didn't disappoint, waiting for Luce to overlap the fabric before he let his hand drop.

"You do know you have to *explain* that Adam comment, don't you?"

"I have to do nothing." The Devil tugged the bandages neatly into place, conjuring a pin and stabbing precariously deep to secure the wrap. Michael gave him an accusatory look and Luce glared back. "I *will* tell you, if only to prove to you why you're an utter imbecile, but I do it of my own will. No one commands me."

Michael bit his tongue to avoid pointing out the contradiction there, not wanting to disrupt the tense truce they had entered. Instead, he rolled his eyes and waited for the explanation. Luce busied himself with righting his desk—or rather, the halves of it. He shot Michael a dirty look, and the angel glowered right back. He hadn't told Luce to try and cut him in half!

The King continued avoiding his gaze, wandering the room and collecting pieces of his office by hand, as if the manual labor was helping him compose himself. Michael's wings itched as the torn tendons knit back together, but he suspected the shiver down his spine had more to do with anticipation. This had to be one hell of a story, if it had led to such a monumental misunderstanding.

When Luce finally ran out of books and knickknacks to collect, he turned and locked their gazes for a long moment, as if he was trying to read something behind Michael's eyes. "I just can't understand it."

Michael folded his hands in his lap, pointedly waiting for him to go on. Luce narrowed his eyes, but continued, "I can't wrap my mind around the fact that you've thought the worst of me, all this time."

He resumed pacing, no longer bothering to mask his agitation in the guise of cleaning. "That I could actually betray you that way…that I could destroy Heaven!"

While he wasn't quick to anger, Michael still had a temper—and now it stirred itself inside him like a stung bear. "What was I supposed to think? I came to the Garden at Jophiel's urging. I saw you—and I think I of all people would know your face! I saw that face pressed against Eve's, kissing her the way you would kiss *me*."

Luce opened his mouth to interrupt, but Michael barreled on, finally able to get the weight that had festered and tormented him for centuries off his chest, "As if that wasn't enough, Gabriel told me of your plots and machinations. He told me how you spoke of using me, how I was to be your excuse and alibi, how you never loved me."

"All lies! Eve, of all people?!" Luce threw his arms wide, then buried them in his hair and pulled. "I cannot believe you actually thought—The way you came accusing me, it makes so much more sense now."

His eyes burned golden, and he leveled the full force of that glare on Michael. "I was with *Adam*, Michael! And before your ever-flexible imagination begins its cartwheels, it wasn't for adulterous purposes."

"Yes, I remember you were with Adam!" Michael was shouting now, but he didn't care. "*After* I saw you with Eve! You say I never gave you a chance to explain what you were doing that day. Clarify it for me now if I'm so *misinformed*."

"With pleasure!" Lucifer spun on his heel and stalked across the room. "I have just the thing to settle this once and for all."

Michael scrambled to his feet and followed, coming up short as Luce stopped abruptly in front of a simple wooden door. He shot Michael a glare before yanking the handle and throwing the door dramatically inward. The angel blinked, looked towards the doorway, and arched a brow at Luce.

"Yes, yes, go in!" He shoved impatiently at Michael's shoulder, making the angel wince. "I didn't open the door for you to look at it!"

Michael rolled his eyes, then peered cautiously around the doorframe. He almost expected some sort of trick or trap to assail him as soon as he stepped inside, but Luce's impatient huff and his own pride made him shove aside his worry to cross the threshold.

It was a simple space, but a cluttered one. In fact, so many seemingly unrelated objects littered the room that there was barely a path winding through it. Towers of boxes spilled over with yellowing papers and scrolls, and wooden crates of rolled canvases and maps and assorted weaponry formed barricades and obstacles to traverse.

The dark-paneled walls were visible only in slivers, hung heavily with frames housing priceless artwork. Bags of jewelry and gemstones were plopped unceremoniously on the floor. Shelves lined the walls bearing a bizarre variety of pottery and figurines. He shifted some electric guitars aside with his foot and had to lunge to grab a rack hung with fur coats before it toppled into an ornate Chinese vase on a pedestal.

Lucifer glared and swatted his arm. "Be careful you bull! These are my *things*. Many are fragile, and all of them are old and treasured."

Michael rolled his eyes but moved with more care as they advanced into the space. Lucifer hung close behind him, casting his gaze about and making sure Michael didn't crush any priceless artifacts underfoot.

"What is this?" He paused, something shiny catching his eye. Bending down, he shimmied an unusual looking weapon out from under a finely woven carpet.

"*That* is a blunderbuss."

"Is it… a gun?" He turned it every which way, looking at the brass mechanisms and the unusually large barrel, hefting it in his hands to feel the weight.

"Of sorts, though it doesn't fire bullets." Michael arched a brow and Luce answered with a wickedly tinged smirk. "It will fire anything you put into the end. Nails, broken glass, small rocks, et cetera."

"Interesting…"

He carefully replaced it on one of several large pieces of furniture that had been shoved into the room. Other bulky pieces were buried under piles of books, or old clothing. Some were draped in sheets and paint-splattered tarps. Michael spied an old fiddle with chipping gold paint, half-hidden beneath a cluster of medieval weapons, and what he strongly suspected might be *the* Holy Grail balanced on a mannequin's shoulder pad. A sad, half-finished dress drooped from the form to the floor.

It was a fascinating look at Lucifer's taste in hobbies—and his haphazard organizational system—but Michael wasn't sure what he was supposed to be seeing that would explain this eons-old wound.

"So you're proving your innocence with...a storage room?"

"Oh, for Hell's sake," Lucifer groaned, shoving past him to grasp a tall, dark cloth hanging on the far wall. "No! This!"

He gave a hard yank, pulling the curtain aside to reveal an ornate door set into the wall. Its strange material shimmered softly in the dim light of the storage room, swirling symbols and sigils carved into the frame that Michael couldn't recognize. It was curious and unusual, but...

"A door," Michael observed flatly, and the other man hissed in frustration.

"*The* door!" Luce slapped the wall beside the doorway. "Are you seriously telling me you don't know it? The Portus Praeteritum!"

Well, that changed things. Michael reached out tentatively, fingers brushing the delicate details bordering the door. "It was thought to be destroyed. I had never even seen it."

"Well, it was never for public use." He sniffed haughtily. "This power is not for the faint of heart or those with delicate minds. It takes a powerful will to withstand the temptation to meddle in the past."

"Is that even possible?"

"It could be. We are forbidden to try."

"Forbidden by whom?" Michael's brow furrowed. "You...*and* Jehovah? Who outranks you?"

Luce softened, arching a brow. "You truly believe there is no higher power? In all the world, in all the boundless universe, you think that my brother and I are the most powerful creatures?"

Michael blinked slowly, processing this. It wasn't as if he had never considered it, but... "I suppose that would be quite incredible."

"Trust me, if we were the top of the food chain, my brother would be much less intolerable." He rolled his eyes. "Insecurity issues abound with that one. Constantly afraid of being overthrown."

"And you've always followed the rule? That doesn't sound like you."

"Shut up," he swatted Michael's shoulder. "In all honesty, no. I tested the water, once. It... didn't go well."

"What happened?"

"That's a story for another time." He shook his head. "Right now we have a record to correct."

"And how exactly does one do that?" Michael stroked his fingers over the door and noticed with wonder that they came away shimmering faintly. "There's no handle."

"That's where you come in, my *feathered* accomplice." Luce flashed a grin that teased a hint of fang. "This door opens only at the touch of a special key."

He reached out and traced his finger over the arch of a tawny wing.

Michael tensed. "An angel's feather."

Luce made a noise of agreement. "Only one that's willingly offered. That bit is meant to dissuade would-be meddlers from 'acquiring' some through illicit means."

Michael considered this. A single feather was nothing. He molted them often enough that he hardly noticed when one came loose. But knowing Lucifer, he would need to carefully specify that, or he'd soon find himself stripped of *all* his feathers. "You may take *one* feather at this time *only*."

That fanged grin split wide and took on a sour cast. "You've learned to be careful with your promises I see. You don't trust me?"

"Should I?" He glared. "You did try to slice me in half not even an hour ago."

"Touché." He wiggled his eyebrows. "Alright, pluck it yourself then. Just so you can be sure I'm not trying anything *untoward*."

Michael grunted but carefully felt through the edges of his wings to find a loose feather, presenting it to Luce with an overly dramatic flourish. The Devil smiled, taking it from his hand with a gentleness that caught him off guard.

"Come along then." Luce pressed the feather flat to the center of the doorway. "Let's settle this once and for all, so you can admit that I'm right and begin properly groveling at my feet."

"I know what I saw, Lucifer."

"Your inferior eyes clearly deceived you."

Michael rolled his 'inferior' eyes. "Okay, but how do you—"

A sound split the air, stunning Michael into stillness. It was like a sudden burst from a cannon, followed by a slurping, sucking sound akin to walking through mud.

"Sorry, it's been a while," Luce stroked the doorframe. "Hard to open it once I used all my stragglers. Normally it's much quieter."

"What did you use them for? Was that when you tried to change the past? To undo your banishment?"

* * *

The door began to shimmer and spread, the strange substance becoming almost liquid as it shifted in the frame. A dull outline of white light spread rapidly from the doorway across the surface towards the center.

"Among other things," Luce said, averting his gaze. "It was much easier to relay our stories to the devout by showing them. And it allowed them to fully commit to their beliefs."

"You… *you* created the first of the Praeceptors. That's how Lucio-Arcanism grew alongside Judo-Christolicism."

"Well, I knew I couldn't rely on my brother to tell the truth of us, and I'm sure you've read his 'Bible'. If I'd left it to him, I'd be cast as an even darker villain than I am now. No, it was much better to show them everything and allow free will to decide their interpretation."

"So you've revisited this scene before."

"No. I…" Luce trailed off as he continued to stroke the doorframe absently, as if seeking comfort. "I couldn't bear it. I kept most of our failings to myself…which could be why they seem to have an inflated idea of us, in retrospect."

The light winked out suddenly, a black void filling the space and leaving grey specks dancing in his vision. Michael blinked. "Is it supposed to do that?"

"Uh…" Luce frowned. "Well, no. Actually-"

As if they had triggered it, the door began to wail. Michael leaned back in alarm as the sound rose towards earsplitting levels. "Is it supposed to do *that*?!"

"Definitely not!" He waved his hands quickly through the air, and the sound cut out. Ears ringing, Michael cut his eyes to Luce, who sighed. "This is embarrassing, I am woefully out of practice."

"Performance issues?"

Luce flushed, whirling on him. "You shut your whore mouth!"

"Oh, certainly. At once, your highness."

"I feel like this sarcasm is the reason we had issues communicating." Luce narrowed his eyes at the angel.

Michael arched a sardonic eyebrow. "I personally think it was your need for secrecy and inability to compromise, but to each his own."

"Alright, alright! Enough!" Luce swatted the air as if batting away the criticism. "Come through this door and you'll see for yourself."

"Is it even safe? It just blacked out and then screamed at us."

"I'm…sure it's fine."

Michael gave him a droll look and shook his head but said nothing. As if refuting his criticism, the doorway began to glow once again, a softer, warmer light than before.

"Ah! You see!" Luce grinned. "Perfectly fine!"

Michael narrowed his eyes. "I have no faith in your judgement."

"…I'll go first?" Luce offered, and Michael nodded firmly. "Right. I'll just…give it a bit of a test."

He stepped forward and pressed both hands to the space that should have housed the door, but instead of hitting any surface, they passed through and vanished in the wash of amber light.

"Ooh," he chuckled. "Bit of a tingle; I forgot to mention. Refreshing, in a way."

Luce took another measured step, immersing himself up to the elbows. Nothing horrible happened, and he drew his hands back, examining them carefully. Eventually, he turned to smile reassuringly at Michael. "Alright. Everything seems to be in order, so just...step in after me."

Then he walked backwards into the portal, disappearing into the wash of golden light with a cheeky wave. Michael couldn't help the smile that tugged his own lips, and he shook his head in exasperation. Some things never changed. Then his smile fell away.

For a long moment, Michael debated turning and leaving. He had been kidnapped, tied to a chair, his wings were broken, and he had very nearly been smothered and cut in half. Any sane person would be running for the door, and this was the perfect opportunity to do so. He could be halfway through the estate before Lucifer realized what was happening.

But while Michael was certainly sane, he was also extremely curious. If he walked away now, when the answers were literally a few steps away, could he ever forgive himself? A part of him had been aching for centuries, blaming himself but then wondering if he was truly in the wrong. This could lay all that doubt to rest, once and for all.

As if sensing his doubt, Lucifer's head suddenly popped back through the portal. "What in Hell is taking you so long? I thought maybe you got lost."

"I expect that happens more often in this room than I would hope," Michael said dryly.

"Oh hush, we haven't lost anyone in here since the 1600s...I think."

"Comforting. I suppose, statistically, it's safer to go through the doorway then."

"Even if it isn't safer, you can't say it's not more thrilling."

There it was. The murky heart of their relationship. The duality that drew him ever towards this dark king, even while Michael knew Lucifer was nothing but trouble he didn't need. And just as he always had, Michael threw aside his sense and stepped towards Lucifer, ready to follow him into the unknown.

Chapter Twenty-Two

The portal was different than others Michael had passed through before. Normally, using a Rift was akin to stepping through a lighted archway. Quick and easy, a brief flash of light before you stepped out into your new location.

This was like walking under a waterfall of color. It pressed on him like a curtain, shifting around him in shimmering waves of light and pressure. Wary but intrigued, Michael lifted his hands and tried to press against the flowing mass. It was warm, malleable, and utterly bizarre, bending away from his touch like wet clay.

Then the colors vanished, leaving him standing in a void of pure white, expanding as far as he could see. A shadow appeared before him, and then it solidified and darkened, resolving into the shape of Lucifer. "There you are."

"Here I am."

"We both need to focus on what we're trying to see. Since there's two of us, it should be easier, but technically there's also a greater chance that we could mess it up."

"Oh, that's very reassuring."

Luce narrowed his eyes. "The sass isn't necessary. Just think back to…that day. Remember it, embrace it, and try to picture it in your mind's eye as clearly as you can."

Thinking about that day was always painful, and one of Michael's least favorite things to do. At first, he had tormented himself intentionally, dwelling and obsessing over every hint or sign he could have missed. He had lost the taste for it with time and gentle support from Raphael and Uriel. But it meant he didn't have to focus very hard to draw up the memory in vivid detail.

A soft wind stirred up around them, and Michael closed his eyes. He thought about the way the Garden had always smelled, wild and warm and faintly sweet. He imagined the lilies and ferns bending gently beneath his fingertips as he walked along the dirt path, hands trailing into the foliage. He recalled the sun, warm and soothing where it kissed and reddened his tanned skin. The call of birds in the distance, the soft bubble of water in the creek that wound through the orchards... It felt like he was back in that place, truly.

He opened his eyes and found Eden laid out before him. Unlike the slightly muted and biased recollections he had been left with over the years, this was a riot of vivid color and light. He turned and flinched backwards at the sight of...himself. Younger, clad in armor they hadn't used for several millennia, and facing away from where they had appeared at the edge of the garden's gate.

Michael practically dove behind a tree to avoid being seen, peeking around the edge of the trunk just in time to see Jophiel approaching his past self. Lucifer eyed him with a smirk, remaining boldly in the center of the path.

"What are you doing?"

Michael's eyes bulged as he shushed him, frantically gesturing toward the two angels exchanging greetings only a few yards away.

"They can't hear or see us," Luce laughed. "I would have warned you if being seen was going to be an issue."

"Oh..." Feeling sheepish, Michael rose from his crouch in the bushes and rubbed the back of his burning neck. He could feel an identical flush tainting his cheeks and averted his gaze so he wouldn't have to see Luce laughing at him.

"Come on, you big idiot," Luce tugged at his elbow, then dropped it like a hot stone. He coughed, a flush dusting his own cheeks as he led the way forward. What the hell was he doing, behaving so casually with the other man? "We're just in time. Let's settle this debate once and for all."

Michael turned his gaze back to his younger self. He remembered this, of course, but he hadn't expected to see himself looking... *like that*. So *young*, so bold and sure of himself. How would it feel, to be that confident and steadfast again? How would it feel to know, without a doubt, that he was on the right path?

He shifted his gaze to the man beside him and realized that feeling of certainty and security had been lost when Luce had. He closed his eyes tight. Another brief tug at his elbow and he opened them, waving Luce off.

"I'm fine. Just...surprised to see myself from the outside, I suppose."

"It can be an adjustment." Luce leaned in, eyes narrowing as he watched Jophiel drop a hand heavily onto Michael's shoulder. He snapped his fingers and everything froze, as if on pause. "Let's get closer, I can't hear shit."

"He's telling me—"

"Don't take offense, but I'd rather hear for myself. Your word is thin with me at the moment."

Well, that stung, and it was highly ironic, but it wasn't unwarranted. They approached the scene, stopping a mere few feet from the angels. Luce wiggled his hands and the world blurred a bit before sliding back into motion.

Jophiel squeezed Michael's shoulder where he gripped it, in the space between his neck and shoulder plate. "I know that it must be hard for you...to come braced for war and find betrayal."

"I have found nothing as yet, Jo'theel."

Michael started at the sound of his own voice, deep and resonant with confidence he hadn't felt in millennia. Was that really how he sounded to others? Luce's hand landed on his shoulder in a subconscious mirror of the scene before them.

"I know you want to believe the good in everyone, Mikha'el," Jophiel sighed. "But...I have seen treason that cannot be denied, and you will see it as well."

"Take me then. Show me what was so urgent that you dragged me from

bed in the dead of night."

"*As you wish, but be warned...*" *Jophiel paused, letting his hand drop away.* "*It involves your Morningstar.*"

Michael gripped the pommel of his sword where it hung from his hip. "*So you claim. We shall see.*"

Luce shifted his gaze to the present Michael. "You doubted."

The revelation had waves of conflicted pleasure racing through him, chased by shame. Was he so easily swayed that centuries of pain and heartache could be erased by a moment of hesitation? What did it say about him that Lucifer almost hoped he would be proven wrong for the first time in his long life?

Michael made an indignant sound. "Of course I did! Until I saw with my own eyes, my trust in you never wavered."

"An impressive loyalty. Unfortunate that it never extended to hearing my side of things."

"What else was there to say? After what I saw?"

"I have yet to see what you claim," Luce sniffed. He had to cling to his belief that he had been right all this time, because he wasn't sure what it would mean for his sense of self if he had been wrong. "I think we'll find that you had a skewed perspective of things, angel."

They walked alongside the specters of the past, Jophiel and other-Michael seeming both corporeal and intangible at once. Michael lifted a hand, as if to brush his own shoulder, only for Luce to swat it away.

"That counts as interference."

"They can't see or hear us, but we can touch them?"

"I don't make the rules, I'm only bound by them."

They walked through the garden, as silent as the night around them. The air felt thick, heavy with tension and foreboding.

Michael could still feel the phantom drop in his stomach, mirroring the way his heart had plummeted through his guts that night. He hadn't been sure what to expect, but he wasn't prepared for what they had found.

Lucifer knelt with his back facing them as they stopped and peered through the curtain of foliage. He wore loose, dark pants and a finely tailored tunic of deep burgundy silk, his wings flared out in golden waves of feathers. Partially concealed in the curve of his wing was Eve, leaning back against the oak of the massive tree that sheltered them, wearing nothing but a look of affection and amusement as she gazed sweetly up at Lucifer.

Even now, hot fury swelled in Michael at her brazenness. She hadn't known better, but the nudity of Adam and Eve had always been a point of awkward contention for the angels. Beside him, Luce made a small noise of alarm. Michael cast his gaze to the side and caught a glimpse of astonished confusion on the other man's face.

"That...that isn't *me*." Luce stepped closer, bewildered, and Michael had to reach out and grab his arm to keep him from colliding with the specter of Jophiel.

"Eve, my sweet Eve," Lucifer purred, leaning down to brush a feather light kiss onto her temple. "All you need do is take one bite, one small taste of these figs."

Michael began to creep forward, masking his steps for the element of surprise, only to be brought up short by Jophiel's grip on his shoulder.

"We must wait for proof, Mikha'el."

Michael grumbled but sank back.

"Luci," Eve giggled, looking up through dark lashes. "You know our father has forbidden us from eating of this tree."

"Jehovah fears your mind, sweet girl. He fears what you could be capable of if you unbound yourself from his control."

"His control?"

"There is power inside you, Eve." Lucifer leaned in, voice dropping so low that Jophiel and Michael had to lean in as well. "It is called magic. When Jehovah created you, he left part of his power behind."

"Magic?" Her emerald eyes widened, shining with wonder.

"Mortals were never meant to hold magic, Eve. It was intended to be kept selfishly by the seraphim. When Jehovah realized what he had done, he bound the power within you. But the fruits of this tree have the power to loosen your bonds."

"Really?" Her voice was full of cautious curiosity.

"One taste, and you would have power beyond your wildest dreams. The power to create worlds, Eve, to reshape things in whatever grand and glorious fashion we choose."

"We?"

"You and I, my darling sweet." He kissed her temple again.

"But what of Adam?"

"What of him? A blind sheep, devoted to my brother." He paused. "But perhaps we could help free his mind, once he sees the power you will possess."

"The power..." She raised a small hand, reaching out with delicate fingers to take the fig Lucifer proffered. "I could possess?"

"Enough," Michael gripped Jophiel by the bicep. "We have our proof, we must intervene."

"Lus'ior Morningstar," Jophiel called out, tone laced with authority.

But they could see his knees wobbling from where they stood watching.

"You stand accused of treason and will resign yourself to our custody."

"Will I?" Lucifer laughed darkly. "You seem awfully sure of your ability, Jophiel."

"And you seem awfully calm for someone caught plotting treason, Lus'ior."

The vehicle of that treason was ignorant of their interaction, fixated instead on the small fruit in her fingers, lifting it to her nose to sniff it. She looked up briefly, glancing between them briefly before returning to her inspection of the fig.

Lucifer turned his golden gaze on Michael, a kind of heat simmering in the gaze. "Is it the treason that upsets you, Mikha'el? Or is it jealousy that drives your anger?"

"My duties are to uphold the law, regardless of who defies it."

But of course, Lucifer had been right. He was always able to see right through Michael's flimsy walls. The betrayal of witnessing Lucifer wound so intimately with Eve had burned Michael in such a way that the law was merely a convenient scapegoat. The phantom pain licked his soul even now, and he absently pressed a palm to his sternum as if to soothe the wound.

Luce eyed him warily. "Michael, that...isn't me."

Michael snorted. "It sure looks like you."

"But it isn't!" He groaned. "I had no idea this even happened, though it sure makes a lot of things make more sense."

"Always so morally...rigid," Lucifer clicked his tongue, grinning in a way that showed off slightly pointed incisors. "I think that's why I've been growing tired of you, dear Mikha'el."

"How charming," Michael ground out sharply, his hand going to the pommel of his sword and gripping it hard. Jophiel cast a wary look at his captain, before shifting his focus to Lucifer. Michael tried to ignore that his subordinate was witnessing his humiliation. "This is how you end relationships?"

"Relationships?" Lucifer trailed a long finger down the side of Eve's face. "Is that what you thought we had? A relationship?"

Jophiel's wince added to Michael's embarrassment.

"Forgive my assumption," Michael hissed. "I thought that was the term when you share the romantic and personal company of another."

Lucifer smirked. "When it's more than just a passing amusement, of course. But I've found a much more intriguing pet now, and I'm done with you."

Luce let out a strangled sound. "How repulsive!"

Michael huffed. "And it wasn't even directed at you."

"You can't tell me you really believed I would say these things to you?"

"They're coming from *your* lips." Michael frowned. "I was already struggling with feelings of inadequacy. You were the Morningstar, and I was..."

"You were everything to me."

Michael felt his throat tighten and cast his gaze back to the scene.

"Besides," Lucifer turned back to Eve, who assessed the fig with rapt interest, and cupped her chin. "Look at her. She's marvelous. Do you truly think you compare?"

Before Michael could respond, Lucifer kissed her. He gripped her hip and pulled her to him, claiming her lips in a hot crush of flesh. The fig dropped to the grass with a muffled thump. Michael heard a scream, and realized the enraged cry came from his own lips.

"Enough!" he bellowed. "Submit yourself to the custody of the Law, Lus'ior Morningstar, or be taken by force!"

Lucifer laughed. "Catch me if you can, then!"

He released Eve and tore off into the Garden, whooping and cackling. Eve blinked, stunned where she sprawled in the dirt.

"Does he think this a game?!" Jophiel sneered. "Too much time spent with Gavri'el, perhaps."

Eve said amicably, "Today does seem to be a bit unusual."

But Michael was already rushing after his lover, drawing his sword from its scabbard and trampling the greenery in his path, disappearing into the brush.

"Is that so?" Jophiel sighed, giving the young woman a last lingering look before he jogged after his Captain.

The scene froze.

Luce stood with his hands lifted and his expression horrified. "What...*the fuck?*"

Michael's eyes narrowed. "You really have no knowledge of this. No memory of this encounter."

"That's what I've been trying to tell you!" Luce snapped. "I saw Eve as a *daughter*, and I loved you more than my own life. You were the one person in the world I could be truly myself with."

He folded his arms around himself, hugging his ribs tightly. It gave him the look of a small, lost child.

Michael closed his eyes tightly and took a deep breath. "Show me the rest. I need to understand how we can have such conflicting accounts."

Lucifer nodded, too emotional for words. The scene began to play again.

Jophiel disappeared into the Garden, and Eve was left sitting alone. She picked up the fig that had fallen beside her, rolling it between her fingers curiously. She blew off the dust and brought it to her nose, sniffing it cautiously, and then pressed it to her lips, biting down.

"Lead the way," Luce murmured. Michael followed his past self into the brush. Sounds echoed back—footfalls, the crashing and ripping of branches and plants, the faint peals of laughter. Michael could feel the tension rising, not only internally, but between himself and Luce. He wanted, against all odds, to be wrong, and of course Luce wanted to prove his claimed innocence.

Michael would be a liar if he said he hadn't always found Luce's actions very much out of character that day. But to be wrong would mean he had made a mistake with unbearable and irreparable consequences. He wasn't sure he would be able to survive the guilt.

Before he could come to grips with the moment, light dawned

close ahead. The laughter died, murmuring tones slipped into its place. His past self surged ahead, so Michael and Luce quickened their steps in response. Slowly, the unintelligible words became distinct.

"...and then we enter in tandem, you from the front and I'll come from behind."

The serious voice was interrupted by a burst of familiar laughter. "Careful darling, it's a mutiny, not an orgy."

Michel cut his eyes to Luce, who had the ghost of a fond smile tugging at his lips. He looked abruptly away.

Flustered sputtering transitioned into a quiet, embarrassed retort. "I didn't mean to imply—"

"Stop, I know," Lucifer spoke with an audible smile. "You are adorable, I keep forgetting how new you both are."

They entered the scene a moment behind the Michael of the past, who broke the edge of the tree line fast and furious.

"One is not enough? You need them both?" He nearly roared, bearing down on the two men where they hunched together over rolls of parchment. Adam swiftly rolled the papers and tossed them beneath a nearby bush.

"Sorry, what?" Lucifer's brow furrowed in confusion.

"You know, I always did wonder what the hell you meant by that." The Devil murmured under his breath.

"Don't feign innocence with me!" Michael snapped. "Look at the two of you, cozy here in your secret space. Is Eve not enough?!"

The scene was, admittedly, rather compromising. The gazebo was shrouded by the gentle ivy that had been climbing its walls for centuries. A pale cloth, laden with platters of fresh fruit and sliced bits of cheese, laid over the table. A carafe of wine sat in a bowl of slowly melting ice. And in the center of it all, the two men bent with heads close together, laughing about orgies.

"Mikha'el, you're rambling like a madman," Lucifer protested. "What are you talking about?"

"You think me a fool," Michael spat, advancing on them slowly.

"I think you are acting foolish, at the least."

Adam rose slowly from the bench he sat on, and all eyes turned to him—or at least to the odd cluster of leaves that he wore as some sort of belt.

"Mikha'el, great warrior," he began to plead, and Michael thrust a hand between them, palm flat in a universal gesture.

"Stop."

Adam stilled so quickly he almost fell backwards, his eyes wide with alarm.

"That name is not for the masses."

"I beg your forgiveness."

"You do not receive it."

Adam recoiled completely this time, shrinking in on himself with a stricken look on his face at the rebuke. Michael wondered if this was the first time someone had treated the newly minted being with anything other than deference and wonder.

The air hung taut. Lucifer cleared his throat. "Are you going to explain yourself?"

"Are you?" Michael retorted. "Such sweet settings, and a mention of mutiny. I find myself for want of some elaboration."

A weighty pause. Even the world around them seemed to still, hanging on their every word. And then Lucifer made a choice that would have repercussions echoing across centuries.

"No."

"So be it."

And Michael drew his blazing sword.

*** *** ***

The lights had been dimmed as far as Gabe could get them, and taper candles flickered at either side of the bed. Foster watched him lay out various pieces of their impromptu spell kit, relentless doubt gnawing at the edges of his gut. Doing the right thing wasn't supposed to feel this terrible, was it?

Gabe hummed a vaguely familiar tune as he worked, settling the spheres of selenite and amethyst against the pillow on either side of Sra. Delgado's throat. Foster realized he was humming "If You're Happy and you Know It" and recoiled slightly.

"Really? Of all songs?"

"I'm trying to stay positive. Maybe she can sense the mood."

"It's poor fucking taste."

"Sure." Gabe stopped humming. "Pass me the bone powder, and the Gospel."

Foster sighed but did as he asked. Gabe flipped carefully through the loosely bound sheets of papyrus. He continued arranging the scene, sprinkling the bone powder over the old woman's frail, sleeping form. Next, he tossed the oil in sweeping arcs and arranged dried herbs in meticulous shapes—all the while consulted the ancient grimoire dutifully. A sense of unease crawled over Foster's skin, and with a sudden dawning he identified the source.

"Gabriel," he spoke low, and the quiet calm in his voice had the angel pausing in his work. "How do you have the Gospel?"

"What?" He blinked owlishly. "I went back for it, just like I said."

"How did you get inside?"

"Through the window, of course."

"My apartment is warded."

A long pause. "Against... me?"

"Against anyone that isn't me or Cwall."

Gabe raised his brows. "I'm very impressed by your forethought, but perhaps next time you should use a ward that's not tied to physical structure. The fire must have worn it away."

Foster frowned but let the matter drop for now. "Are you almost ready? I need to do this before I change my mind again."

"There can be no indecision, Foster," Gabe chided. "Make your mind up now and keep it decided. Otherwise, this is all for nothing."

He turned his back on the angel, pressing his palm to the window. The glass was cool against his skin, which always burned just noticeably warmer than a mortal would, and his reflection gazed back, silently weighing him. A line from one of his favorite movies haunted him. *You have been weighed, you have been measured, and you have been found wanting.* He heard the words in his mother's voice, and a shiver rolled down his spine.

Gabriel cleared his throat. "Resolve yourself, Foster Morningstar. We're beginning."

A last flare of panic surged and fluttered in his chest. This was wrong, it was so wrong. He couldn't do this. Once was bad enough, and now—

Gabe laid a hand on his shoulder, squeezing reassuringly. "I have already prepared a place for her, Foster. She will be comfortable and content, happy and untouched by the horror of the world. Horrors like this."

Foster watched the slow rise and fall of Sra. Delgado's chest, guided through the motions by a machine, and closed his eyes. Who was he if he did this?

Who was he if he didn't?

"Begin." Gabe squeezed him once more, bordering on painful, before he turned back to the hospital bed.

* * *

Michael bowed over the bush and continued retching, his stomach heaving and rolling but with nothing left to expel. Lucifer stood awkwardly by, gently patting his shoulder with an absent hand while he looked intently at anything else.

"I'm sorry, it...affects everyone differently," Luce finally broke the silence, withdrawing his hand as Michael rocked back on his heels and fell to a sitting position. Michael grunted in response, scrubbing his mouth with the back of his palm. But it wasn't the timewalking that had his stomach churning, it was his own grief.

As soon as his past self had charged in, as soon as he saw Lucifer's *face*, his stomach lurched at the memory, and he'd shuddered. Lucifer of the past had looked at him as if looking through him, an expression that shifted rapidly from bemusement to alarm to horror. There might have been a flash of fear, but only Michael would have known his lover well enough to detect it.

If he had looked this closely that day...but that was the fallacy of hindsight. He remembered the hot tears blurring and streaking his vision, the hurt and rage that propelled his arm to swing. There was no room for observation on that day, only pain and anger.

He had turned and run. Not his past self; he would never have fled any battle in his younger years. Apparently, age brought with it

282

enough sense for cowardice. This was a regret he could no longer bear to face.

"You think me a coward, I'm sure. A hypocrite," said Michael.

"Occasionally I have thought of you this way, yes, but I wouldn't say that I feel that way at present."

"Oh, sure. Spare me the polite lies, Lucifer."

"Do I strike you as a man who bites his tongue? Running from that scene doesn't make you a coward, it makes you a man that feels deeply." He paused. "It shows me that you've grown considerably from that young, angry man into someone who can weigh his own sins."

The silence was a tangible creature between them. Michael's heart squeezed with something he could only call affection, and he beat that sensation down hard. He had no right to feel anything but apologetic towards Lucifer. Even at surface level, he could see that things didn't add up.

When would Lucifer have had time to run from him, find Adam, and set up an entire picnic? It was an established fact that even the most powerful angels couldn't be in two places at once. While Lucifer could create portals, that still didn't explain Adam's presence or the clear and present surprise at seeing Michael appear.

His anger had clouded his rational thought, and once Gabriel confided Lucifer's comments about using and manipulating him... Michael had chalked it up to a carefully planned alibi. But something tickled in the back of his mind, and a new horror emerged. He hadn't slowed down to see it before, but it was as glaring to him now as a large sign reading "YOU ARE STUPID".

If something was clearly wrong, that meant there must be a clear answer. And if that was true, there was evidence to be found somewhere.

"Do you...want to leave?"

"No." He closed his eyes, steadied himself, and rose to his feet, dusting himself off. "There's an answer here, and if anyone can find it, it's me."

"We don't have to do this today," Luce hedged. "We've probably wasted too much time on this diversion as it is. There are problems back at home we should be resolving."

It wasn't lost on Michael that Lucifer spoke of them as a unit. He said 'we' and not 'I', and for a moment the angel wanted to embrace it. To run from this place and find somewhere dark and quiet to process these revelations, while he let Luce handle things like he used to in the past. But he couldn't.

"Lucifer...please." Michael clenched and unclenched his fists, not making eye contact with the other man. "I'm not sure I could force myself to return to this place. And I can be swift about it. Let's not squander this opportunity."

"Fair enough." Luce cocked his head with a small smile. "Lead the way, tracker."

Michael relaxed and tried to think back. Even as they had chased after the flickering image of his past self, Michael of the present had been subconsciously noticing everything around them. It was part of who he was now, a sense he had developed over time and honing his tracking abilities. All he had to do was tap into that power, dig a little deeper into his core... And there it was.

His echo had swerved left, following the sound of taunting laughter, but there was second path trampled through the undergrowth, curving away from the noise.

"I know where we need to go."

"After you."

He retraced their path to the spot he remembered and knelt to examine a flower that had been snapped at the stem by careless, hurried footfalls.

"Two paths," Luce murmured, pausing the world again and crouching beside him, using Michael's shoulder to steady himself. "I assume this is new information for you?"

"I was so angry," Michael said softly, but it was laced with frustration. "I was so blinded by my rage, I overlooked it."

"I expect someone was counting on that." They rose in unison, and Luce's hand lingered for a shadow longer than maybe necessary. "So, I suppose we must decide if we wish to know the truth."

"How do you mean?"

"'I sat alone with my conscience, in a place where time had ceased'," Luce recited the words as if quoting another. At Michael's confused look, he elaborated, "I said something like that to a poet, once. How badly do you seek your answers, Mikha'el?"

"Why would I turn away from the truth? After everything that's happened?"

Luce gave him a pointed look. "Exactly. After all the havoc it wrought on our lives, how badly will it hurt you now if our betrayer wears the face of a friend?"

It was a fair question. Michael tried to imagine how he would feel if it was revealed to be Raphael or Uriel who had done this to them. The idea alone sent a pang through his gut. But deeper was the sense that he already knew who was behind this.

In the countless decades since he had been here in this moment, Michael had developed a fairly reliable intuition. There was only one person who could craft such compelling illusions, let alone know Luce well enough to impersonate him so thoroughly and convincingly.

But he had to make sure. He had to know.

"It will eat us alive if we don't face this," he said, fixing Luce with a determined look, and the Devil inclined his head in a nod.

"Lead the way then."

* * *

Foster stared resolutely out the window as Gabe recited the ceremonial chants from the Gospel of Lazarus in an archaic language that seemed more hybrid than any one thing. Foster picked up on some Aramaic, a little bit of Hebrew, a phrase in old Enochian that roughly translated to "release the spirit of this body".

The already dim lights flickered, one of the old fluorescent strips dying completely after a brief surge. A soft tremor ran through the floor, and Foster subconsciously shifted away from it. Gabe continued chanting, but extended one hand silently toward Foster, who eyed it with concern. The angel crooked a finger, beckoning, and Foster reached out tentatively to take his hand. Gabe squeezed twice and drew him closer to the bed.

Still he chanted, though this seemed to be a repetition of an earlier passage. Foster caught the words "divine sacrifice" and "blood oath", but not much else. A breeze swept the room, brushing Foster's hair so it tickled at his collar. Gabe's coat fluttered, and he closed his eyes.

Foster watched him, quietly, as the chanting became more rapid and Gabe's lips moved in frantic shapes. A crack like thunder had Foster looking out the window, only to be met with a clear afternoon. The wind kicked up, rushing around their feet and winding up his body like a living entity. The candles flickered but remained lit, and the sacred bone powder was swept up in the coils of air.

Gabe inhaled sharply, eyes flying open and wild as he gripped Foster's hand so hard bones shifted. "Get ready," he said, voice hoarse from chanting.

"For what?" Foster was surprised to find his own voice was taut and ragged.

"It must be you, Foster, I've done all I can. Prepare the final strike."

* * *

They walked casually along the second path, pausing every so often for Michael to observe a crushed flower, a snapped twig, or a trampled patch of weeds that would guide them on. Lucifer hummed a lilting tune, and Michael fought the urge to ask him to stop, even as it grated on his frazzled nerves. This was the most casual interaction they'd had in centuries; he didn't want to ruin it by being petty.

As if reading his mind, Luce stopped humming abruptly. Michael looked to the side and saw him staring straight ahead, eyes round with surprise.

"How sharp the tack that pricks the unprotected side," he mumbled, sounding stricken.

Michael followed his gaze, between two ancient oaks to a small clearing, and felt his stomach twist.

Standing mere feet from them was the imposter.

He was shucking his clothes, tossing them haphazardly into the bushes, and doing a sort of strange shimmy. With growing horror, Michael realized the unusual movement served a perverse purpose.

Lucifer was blessed with perfect skin; a fact he happily lorded over

286

everyone as he tanned beautifully and never suffered a blemish. That deep tan was now splitting, wrinkling, and folding as it was shed and discarded like an old, worn garment.

Skin pale as moonlight was revealed in its wake, and the head of tousled chocolate waves fell like forgotten petals to be replaced with curls of deepest black. The impostor stretched and groaned, shaking out his wings as they molted from purest gold to ebony.

Standing naked as a babe in the early twilight, Gabriel laughed.

* * *

Foster swallowed against the threat of bile and found his throat scratching like sandpaper. His hand ached where he held the athame in an iron grip, his knuckles blanched white by the tension. The jeweled inlay on its hilt cut into his palm, drawing the silvery ichor of demigods from shallow, crescent wounds. His free hand reached to stroke Sra. Delgado's bandaged face with trembling fingers. *I can't do this.*

He drew a breath to say what his heart was screaming, and Gabriel gripped his shoulder hard. "Now, Foster!"

Closing his eyes against the flood of hot tears, Foster plunged the dagger deep into her heart with both hands and a guttural, broken shout.

Chapter Twenty-Three

Luce whimpered. Michael turned to him in shock. For what was simultaneously seconds and days, they stared at each other, equally speechless.

"I should have seen it," Luce finally broke the silence, casting his eyes down at his hands as if his upturned palms would have answers for him. He lifted his haunted gaze to Michael's. "How did I not see his machinations?"

"Because we never want to believe the ones we love could betray us."

"You believed I had betrayed *you*," Luce argued. "And I never considered Gabriel had set me up. I only thought he had abandoned me during my trial."

"He was too busy weaseling into your place to speak in your defense."

"Of course he was," the Devil sighed. "He always was the most ambitious of us. That's why I said you were better off asking him to join the rebellion."

Michael's brow furrowed. "What?"

"What do you mean, 'what'?" Luce mirrored his expression. "The only reason I was in the Garden that day was because *you* encouraged me to hear Adam out."

"I have no idea what you're talking about."

"Yes, you do!" Luce huffed in frustration. "A few nights before, we were in bed. I was telling you how Adam had begun asking questions about his purpose, about the restrictions my brother had imposed. I was considering challenging Jehovah's edict, and you encouraged me to speak with Adam about it."

"I was away, Lucifer." Michael's stomach twisted violently and he slowly shook his head. "I was on a scouting mission with Uriel for almost a week, and Jophiel accosted me the night I returned."

The other man paled. "Oh, no."

"I'm...so sorry. You weren't in bed with me that night."

Luce flinched back with pain in his eyes. "I'm going to be ill."

Michael was lifting his hands to comfort him when a violent shudder raced along the earth and threw him off balance. His hands sought purchase instinctively, landing on Lucifer's shoulders and holding tight.

"Shit," Luce groaned, and answered the unspoken question in Michael's eyes. "We're being kicked back."

Another quake rocked the forest, and the image appeared to waver and flicker. Instead of pushing off the angel's hands, Luce wound an arm firmly around his waist. Michael started to pull away, and that bracing arm became an iron band holding him tight against the other man.

"You won't want to do that, angel. This has only happened to me once before, and I'd hate to leave you stranded in the aether."

Michael grumbled but stopped fighting the unexpected embrace as the very air flexed and warped around them, whipping their hair and clothes. Amid all of this, he was surprised and strangely pleased to note that in this close proximity, Luce still smelled of burning cedar and cinnamon. A traitorous flush kissed Michael's cheeks as the scent wound its way through his blood and sent his heart hammering.

Lucifer chuckled. "No need to be afraid."

"I'm not," Michael protested with a glower.

"Ah, yes, of course. Simply overwhelmed by my sensuality and good looks, right?"

The sarcasm hit uncomfortably close to the truth, and Michael made an affronted sound to Luce's increased amusement.

The lighthearted moment was broken by a rumbling that started in the distance and swelled around them, growing louder as it swept inward, accompanied by the most violent shaking yet experienced. The image went pale and shivered like television static, then drew itself taut and literally shattered around them. Luce tightened his grip on Michael's waist.

"Brace yourself, Michael. We're going back home."

All sound died out, and the world erupted into an expanse of white so blinding, they were forced to close their eyes against it. A violent rush of wind slammed into the pair, tugging at hair and wings and clothing as if searching for anything to catch on and yank them apart. Luce's fingers were a hot brand on his hip, and Michael was sure he was leaving bruises on those broad shoulders. And then, as suddenly as it began, everything stopped.

The shaking, the windstorm, the light—everything fell away, replaced by the familiar scent of dust and a brush of cool air. They opened their eyes, both tensing as they found themselves mere inches apart. Lucifer's sharp inhalation sent a rush of cool air over Michael's chin.

If he bent down just *slightly*, he could brush his lips across those princely cheekbones as he had so many times before. The swell of desire was overwhelming, and he found himself shocked by how badly he wanted to kiss him.

"Don't." Luce's plea was a whisper, a strained shadow of his normally confident declarations, though his eyes burned with a powerful, unreadable emotion. "Please."

Michael recoiled. "No, I—sorry, I, I wasn't—"

"Right." Luce released him first, drawing back his arm and pulling it to his chest. "We need to figure out what pulled us back here."

As if in answer, a violent wave of energy rocked the room, sending items toppling from shelves or the tops of piles or the backs of chairs. A painting of a farmhouse fell from the far wall, followed by a rack of renaissance doublets. Michael lost his balance and wavered, but Luce reached for him and steadied him at the last moment. Then another wave of energy swept through, and Luce lost his own footing.

They fell in opposite directions, Michael landing in an oversized laundry basket stuffed with scarves and silks and discarded fabric scraps. Lucifer went pinwheeling into a steamer trunk packed to overflowing with Victorian dresses and hats. A tea set on a nearby bookcase landed with a clatter in his lap.

Michael huffed a breath and gave Luce a *look*.

"Okay, okay! I'll have a damn yard sale! Can it wait until *after* this calamity?"

"There you fucking are!" a new voice burst into the room, and they both looked to the doorway to see Remiel backlit against the semi-trashed office. "Cwall and I have been looking everywhere for you, you asshole, and you're in here playing dress up?"

"No!" Luce protested.

"Looks like it!"

"Well, we're not!"

Michael tried to push himself to his feet and found the laundry basket firmly wedged to his hips like some children's cartoon. "Oh, for fuck's sake."

Remi blinked slowly, then closed her eyes and placed her hands over them. "I'm not seeing this right now. I did *not* spend the better part of an hour running around the fucking estate looking for you, bothering the Eyes and Zaj and even fucking *Bal,* only to find you wearing a dress and Michael with a fucking *bucket* on his ass."

Another wave of raw power swept the room and interrupted whatever snappy retort Luce was working up. He heaved a sigh and settled for civility. "We were in the damn portal, Remi, and then we got yanked out. Would you care to clue us in, since you obviously know what's going on and we don't?"

Michael gave a good shove and the laundry fell to the floor. He extended a hand to Luce, who waved him off and stood.

"I'm not sure what Cwall needs, but something is wrong with Mags."

"Way to bury the lead, Rem!" Luce gave her a nasty glare and shoved past her to run out the door.

Michael frowned at the smirking woman. "Why do you torment him?"

"Got him moving, didn't it?"

Michael sighed. "I've always wondered about you."

"Oh please, Mikey. If I wanted to wreak havoc, I would. Giving Luce a hard time is just fun."

* * *

The infirmary was a chaotic rush after the silence and isolation of the portal. Demons scurried along the perimeter with worried or purposeful expressions, collecting items such as herbs or damp towels and depositing them on the table in the center of the room. In the center, a cluster of bodies obscured their view: Raguel with arms crossed like a guard and his back to the occupied bed. Camiel applying a fresh towel to Mags's brow. Zaj hovered like a frantic pixie and barked directions to the other demons.

Remi hurried back to her husband's side, but Luce hesitated at the door. He might have stood there all night, frozen in place by worry and guilt, but another blast of powerful magic rocked the room. Bottles rattled in their cases, one of the cabinets tipping wildly before an electric blue demon with two forked tails steadied it.

You have to do this. Luce crossed the room with purposeful strides. "What's going on, dammit?"

Rag gave him a measured look and nodded at the bed they all clustered around. "Mags had an episode. She went into one of her trances, but this one was…really bad. We couldn't bring her out of it, and she just—" He broke off, looking pained.

Cami leaned in close to Luce, grabbing his sleeve. "I have not heard screams like hers since the Plague."

Luce pushed into the cluster of bodies until he could take Mags's small hand in his own. "Who put her under?"

Sachiel looked haunted. "I didn't want to."

"He had to." Glory's eyes sparkled with tears. "She just kept *screaming* Lucifer, I thought her lungs would burst."

Luce extended his free hand to rest on Sachi's arm. "You had no choice, it seems. But now I need her to wake. Bring her back, please."

Sachi stepped in close, kneeling beside the bed so that his mouth was level with Mags's head, and pursed his lips as if to whistle. Instead, he blew out a stream of blue-tinted breath that wafted in lazy coils over her slack, sleeping face. It drifted downward as he rose to his feet, settling onto her skin and sinking beneath the surface. A tense moment brought the room to an unnatural stillness, save for the demons clearing away in anticipation of what was to come.

Slowly, her lashes fluttered. Her lip twitched, and her eyes blinked open. Mags cast her gaze around wildly, breath coming in rapid gasps as she sat bolt upright so abruptly that Luce had to catch her against his chest.

"Breathe, Mags! You're fine, you're safe."

She continued to thrash for a moment, too frantic and disoriented to process what was happening, until she slowly came to her senses. Her breathing slowly regulated as she pressed her forehead to Luce's throat, taking in the steady pulse under his jaw as if to reassure herself he was still living and breathing. Her hands came up to twist in the fabric of his shirt, and she lifted wide, tear-filled eyes to his.

"Tell me what you saw," he murmured.

"He...Foster," she broke off in a whimper.

"Is he alright?" Luce felt his pulse quicken, some primal combination of fear and concern.

Mags chewed her lip. "He completed another sacrifice."

A violent wave of power rocked the room, and Mags clung to Luce like a small child.

"Is that what these power surges are?"

She nodded. "We're too late. He's crossing the threshold, Lucifer. I don't know if we have any other choice now."

Remi picked at the frayed cuff of her sweater, picking at loose threads and widening the hole her thumb poked through. "I know we wanted to try and save him, but this..."

The room trembled under the onslaught of power.

"It's too wild," Rag frowned. "He's coming unglued because he doesn't know how to handle the power. No one was meant to control this much alone."

Lucifer turned, inexplicably, to Michael. The blond cleared his throat to address the room. "He did not choose this path spontaneously."

"He's right," Luce pulled back from Mags's grip to meet her eyes. "Are you well enough to conduit?"

She paused, mentally assessing herself, then nodded. "I can, if it's brief."

"What do you mean?" Glory cocked her head to the side quizzically, considering Michael.

"Foster was always good," Michael said slowly. "Has anyone stopped to ask how he even knew about the Gospel of Lazarus? He was almost certainly pushed down this path."

"And I think we have proof of who's responsible," Luce muttered darkly

"Someone who has been orchestrating a puppet show all this time," Michael grumbled.

"Someone playing a long enough game that he had the foresight to have my wings stripped."

Mags looked between the two men, a smile flickering at the edges of her lips. "I see you found a common enemy."

"More than you might realize, my dear." Luce shook his head. "Are you ready?"

"I'll need a basin." She released him and sat up straighter, smoothing the blankets over her lap. "Fill it with cool water and set it in my lap, please."

Glory was closest to the table and dutifully followed her instructions. Luce could feel the tension rolling off everyone as they clustered around, trying not to appear as stressed and anxious as they all were.

Mags brought him back to reality with a soft touch on his wrist. "One hand in the water, please."

He dipped his fingers in the bowl, letting them splay over Mags's own submerged hand.

"Ready?"

He nodded and reached for the recent memories of his trip into the past. Digging deep, he focused on the last few moments before they had been ejected. The water began to warm, and he glanced down. Mags's skin emitted a soft glow beneath the surface. Her eyelids were shut as she prepared to receive the vision, and for a moment he felt a stab of guilt over asking her to do this right now. But it had to be done.

He closed his own eyes as the water grew warmer still, bordering on uncomfortable. He pictured the clearing, glimpsed between the trunks of the trees, with early evening light filtering into the space. Pale skin, dark hair, the stolen guise discarded on the grass.

The water began to boil around their hands, somehow without causing pain. Then it started to steam, and as the steam rose it condensed together and became opaque. Luce opened his eyes to watch the scene from his memories play out—and, if he was being honest, he wanted to see the reactions.

Oh, there were *reactions*.

Remi was the first to comprehend the revelation, and she turned a most fascinating shade of burgundy. If it had been a cartoon, steam would be pouring out of her ears. She began to tremble as her face settled into a furious snarl, and when she opened her mouth, a noise like a teakettle poured out in place of words. Rag blinked slowly in astonishment and then looked around the room. He nodded decisively, then stalked to the window and smashed it with his fist.

Gloriana fainted, but Cami caught her before she fell off the edge of the infirmary bed and fanned her rapidly. Sachi seemed stunned into silence, gaping at the scene.

Mags herself opened her eyes and turned to Lucifer, expression somewhere between astonishment and vindication. She had never trusted Gabriel but had often wondered if she was just being petty. Now she realized it had been her intuition seeing past his sleek and charming facade.

Michael raised a single golden brow, as if to ask Luce 'was this really the best way to tell them?' and Luce shrugged slightly as if to answer, 'no, but didn't it work?'

Mags removed her hand from the basin, and the steam dissipated. "So, you think this is another plot?"

"No, I believe it's the same plot." Luce frowned. "I think this has all been one long con on the part of my backbiting snake of a 'friend'."

There was a scuttling commotion at the doors to the infirmary, drawing every eye to Cwall as he burst inside. "There ya are!"

He flew inside, Balthazar and Judas hot on his trail, and Lucifer jerked to his feet, nearly toppling the bowl of water as he hurried to meet them.

"We've been looking everywhere for you," Judas panted, bending to rest his hands on his knees. "Gabriel has violated your edict."

"*What?*" Lucifer's expression darkened. As if he didn't have enough reasons to wring Gabriel's slimy neck.

"I was watchin', like ya wanted," Cwall was hovering in place, wings working frantically to expend his obvious nerves. "I swear I came right ta find ya."

"We were in a portal," Luce said, trying to reassure the imp so he would get to the point.

"Fos was at the hospital, an' Gabe convinced 'im ta kill the old lady."

"No," Luce shrank back, horrified. "Foster adores her."

"I know," Cwall said, uncharacteristically serious.

Taking a life was hard enough. Luce had hated himself every time he had needed to do so, and that was with veritable strangers. This act would take a heavy toll on his son. His fury for Gabriel mounted impossibly higher in that moment, burning through him in a blistering torrent.

He turned to Michael. The angel took in his expression, nodding without a word. Luce turned back to his Fallen. "Wait for word from me, but prepare for a fight. I can't predict how Gabriel will respond to this confrontation."

Remi stepped forward, slamming her closed fist to her chest in a salute. "We'll be ready, my King."

Luce laid a hand on her shoulder, then swept his gaze over the others. "Thank you...my friends."

Then he turned and swept from the room, Michael slipping back into his familiar position at the King's side.

* * *

Gabe stood in the middle of a wrecked hospital room, watching a young man fall to pieces. Foster wasn't simply having an emotional breakdown; he was quite literally falling to *pieces*. Long strips of flesh tore from any areas of exposed skin only to be quickly regrown.

Still, the violent wind whipping the hospital room continued to rip at his clothing and body. His t-shirt hung in tatters; his previously distressed jeans were now completely shredded. Gabe remained untouched in a small pocket of space he had shaped around himself in the nick of time.

"Foster," he called out, trying to amplify his voice over the chaos, but the boy didn't seem to hear him.

The fluorescent lights flashed wildly, one of them burned completely out with its pieces shattered on the ground. The candles were long since snuffed out. Violent waves of power sputtered out from Foster in inconsistent intervals as his body hit its limit, tried to burn off the excess, and then repeated the process.

Foster dropped to his knees on the floor, the center of the room cleared as the furniture had been flung to the walls. The hospital bed lay empty; the old woman's body had disintegrated in a blinding flash at the moment of Foster's strike.

The boy wailed, "What's *happening?*"

Gabe moved towards him, the wind and power lashing at the fragile bubble he'd created. A particularly strong blast buffeted him hard enough to make him stumble, falling a few steps to the side.

"I didn't anticipate her life force to be this strong!" Gabe called back to him, fighting against the windstorm to reach Foster's side. He knelt beside him, pressing his palm to the wall between them. Foster lifted his head, but his arms felt too heavy to do the same. Gabe let his hand fall back to his side.

"Gabe," Foster pulled air through battered lungs in deep, slow, rasping gasps, "what...is happening?"

297

"These rituals." Gabe wrung his hands as he tried to find words that would not only explain, but hopefully comfort Foster as well. "They're meant to make you stronger. Strong enough to bend the laws of reality and bring a soul back from the void."

Cracks appeared in the plaster as waves of spiraling power demolished the room. Only the layers of wards to isolate their hospital room kept the power from spilling beyond this space. If not for the precautions Gabe had taken, the entire floor of the hospital would have been at risk of destruction.

"I didn't—I mean, I knew a stronger connection and a stronger host were ideal." Gabe raked his hands through his hair. "No one has done this before, Foster, you have to understand. I couldn't know."

"Gabe," Foster pleaded, forcing his hand up to press it against the force field surrounding the angel.

The angel closed his eyes and lifted his hand to press back. "I knew your Divine blood was the key to surviving these trials, but the sacrifice was stronger than I anticipated. The energy she provided might be too much for your mortal lineage."

"I'm...dying?" His voice was weak, laced with fear, and something in it gripped Gabe's immortal heart with an icy fist.

"Not if you fight." Blue eyes flashed open, as deep and fathomless as midnight tides. "*Fight*, Foster. Think of your mother. Draw on your power. Control this energy like you would your own."

There was something wary and so very young in the way Foster met and held his gaze. Then he closed his eyes as he dropped his hand and curled his arms around his abdomen. Bending at the waist, so low his forehead almost touched the floor, the younger man began to scream, so raw and full of pain that Gabe winced to hear it.

He continued screaming as the wind reached a tumultuous peak, buffeting the window hard enough to shatter the safety glass. The storm blew outwards, and in the sudden silence, Foster's agonized wails sounded twice as grotesque.

Gabe slowly approached the boy kneeling before him. The power surges coming from the young demigod were slowing; weakening. That was either a very good or very bad sign. Gabe dissolved his protective bubble and dug deep into his own reserves of power, resting both hands on Foster's shoulders. He gave a concentrated push, sending tendrils of his own life energy out to bolster the younger man.

He cannot die, Gabe thought determinedly, and redoubled his push. *I need you, Foster. Stay with me.*

The screaming stopped. Or rather, it petered out into a mix of whimpers and gasps as Foster collapsed to the floor and began to convulse.

"No," Gabe yanked him up, cradling him to his chest tightly. "You are going to *live*, dammit!"

He gave a final, desperate jolt of his own energy to the other man. The world went a bit gray at the edges, and he worried for a moment that he had expended a bit too much. But then things stopped wavering on the fringes of his vision, Foster stopped trembling in his arms, and the world went very, very quiet.

Foster slumped against him where they knelt on the tile, and Gabe relaxed only when he felt the boy resume consistent, steady breathing.

"Am I…alive?" Foster's voice came out as a croak, and Gabe leaned him back to smile down at him.

"I'm not sure. You're looking at an angel, after all. That's usually a bad sign."

The boy laughed weakly, and it turned into a cough. Gabe softened and smoothed the dark curls back from Foster's sweaty brow.

"Foster," he murmured. "You did so good, son."

"Speaking of," a new voice sounded at the shattered window, and Gabe startled. They were on the third floor of the hospital. "I thought I told you to *stay away from my son.*"

Chapter Twenty-Four

"I was wondering when you'd show your face, Lucifer. You missed the main event, but make the after party? Classic."

"Gabriel," Lucifer stepped through the shattered window, brushing aside the tattered remains of the hideous curtains. His focus was solely on his son, cradled loosely in Gabe's arms and slowly regaining his strength. "I need you to shut up *immediately*. Because I will kill you, and my brother will be cranky about it."

The angel snorted. "As if you care what he thinks."

"Not usually, but unfortunately, I'll need him on my side as much as possible when I present you for treason."

"Me? Treason?" Gabe laughed. "A little too pot-kettle there, isn't it?"

Lucifer's eyes glittered dangerously as he moved slowly into the room. "I know what you did, Gavri'el."

Gabe went very still. "A very long time...has passed since you called me that."

"A very long time has passed since I knew you well enough to do so."

"What has changed?" His voice was hoarse, with an almost desperate undertone.

"I told you." Luce went down to one knee beside the pair, and gripped Gabe firmly by the chin. *"I know what you did."*

There was a tense moment where they were both profoundly aware of how badly Lucifer wanted to snap his neck. His fingers tightened enough to bruise, and they spent a moment wondering if he would do it. Then Foster's hand came up, weakly, to grip his father's wrist.

"Don't…hurt him." His cold tone sent a shiver down Luce's spine. That was not the voice of the son he knew.

"Foster, I know that for whatever reason you care about this man. But you have no idea what he's done."

"Saved…my life."

"Now, son, I know I haven't been there for you, but I think that's an overstatement."

"Not a… metaphor… asshole," Foster groaned. His voice was getting stronger, his breathing evening out and relaxing. "Literally….just now."

Luce hesitated, glancing from his son to his former friend. "Is that true?"

Gabe blinked. "Well, yes."

Luce released his jaw. "Well, that earns you another five minutes of consciousness. However, since I'm entirely certain it's your fault he needed saving—*again*—I expect I'll be threatening your life again shortly."

"Such a prick," Foster grumbled, shifting out of Gabe's hold and into a sitting position. "You're such a *prick*."

"You have no idea." Luce rose from his crouch. "This man is dangerous, Foster. Possibly the greatest liar I have ever known, and clearly willing to risk your life for his goals."

"At least he shows up when I need him," Foster carefully shifted his weight, getting his bearings as he rose to his feet slowly. Gabe was quick to get back up as well, reaching for the young man's elbow to steady him. Foster shot Luce a look that said 'see?' and Luce rolled his eyes.

"Oh yes, he can put on a good show." He turned back to Gabe and stepped closer, gripping him firmly by the upper arm. "He performs like few others could, even when he has to play *other roles*."

Gabe tensed but said nothing.

"I went back, Gavri'el." His eyes flashed, the gold deepening and lighting up like disks of molten metal. "I *saw* you. We both did, and now everyone knows."

"Both?"

Michael stepped in through the shattered window, and Gabe blinked, glancing between them incredulously. "Dramatic entrances Mike? Are you taking drama lessons from his royal heinous?"

"If I never heard you speak again, it would be too soon," Michael said, his voice low and laced with threat.

"He certainly seems to be taking *asshole* lessons," Foster muttered.

"No, that was a few millennia ago," Gabe laughed. And then suddenly he was on his back. The insanity of the situation finally sank in, and he continued giggling despite the heavy weight on his chest.

"You have some fucking *nerve*," Michael had his throat in both hands, slowly and painfully tightening his grip until Gabe could no longer pull in a breath, let alone laugh. "Was it worth it, Gabriel? To steal my face to feed your unrequited desires?"

"Michael!" Luce grabbed him by the shoulders but couldn't budge the bulk of muscle hell-bent on choking the life from the smaller angel. "Mikha'el, you need to let go!"

Foster was stunned. He had met Michael on few occasions, and he knew there was a past between his father and the other man. Although he couldn't say he knew Michael *well*, he had certainly heard stories of his feats. This was completely out of character for the stoic, noble man he'd heard about. It was enough to make him hesitate, but not to render him useless.

Instinctively, Foster brought his hands up, as if he was going to grab the warrior by the arm. Instead, he felt something stirring within, guiding his movements. He closed his fists, and Michael reared back as if he'd been struck, grabbing at his chest with both hands. Foster blinked. Was that because of him? Interesting. He threw his hand to the side as if shoving open a curtain, and Michael flew backwards across the room, knocking into Lucifer and bringing them both to the floor of the trashed hospital room.

"Very interesting," Foster murmured, looking at his palms curiously. It would seem Gabriel was right; he was much stronger now. A sense of cool detachment settled over him as he looked at the three men sprawled on the floor. There was too much drama happening here. He needed to get away and find somewhere that he could think.

"Son," Luce tried once more, seeing the intent to flee clearly written on his son's face. "Please, you need to see what we have seen. It will make everything clear to you."

"I think things are clear enough, actually." Foster arched a brow. "You claim Gabe has done something horrible and is using me for some nefarious purpose. I think it's interesting that you only show your face in my life once I start growing stronger, and suddenly you want to be father of the year."

"It has nothing to do with—" Luce started, but Foster spoke over him.

"In the same vein," the demigod said, turning to where Gabe sat looking back at him curiously. "It is true that I've almost died twice in as many days under Gabriel's guidance."

"Son, I can explain everything."

"Don't call me son." Foster turned sharply back to Luce. "I still don't consider you my father."

He walked toward the open window, gripping the empty frame and peering over the edge. In the courtyard below, he could see the chaos of their ceremony had drawn the attention of what seemed to be the entirety of the local police department.

Drawing on his new reserves of power, Foster carefully cloaked himself in glamour that would render him sightless to mortals. Even to those of Divine blood, he appeared as a simple shadowy outline of himself.

"Don't follow me," he demanded, and stepped out the same way Luce and Michael had come in, vanishing from their sight entirely.

* * *

Foster was in turmoil. It would likely have been worse if he could actively feel it. It was like there was a glass wall between his conscious mind and his emotions now. He knew he had done something horrible, and a part of him regretted it. The rest of him was drowning in the wash of power flooding his system, unable to truly feel the grief and pain. It was horrifying, in a strangely detached way.

He needed to ground himself and work out the full capabilities of his new power. There was one place he could think of that would fulfill both of those needs, and he made a beeline for his apartment building.

The charred exterior was even more depressing in daylight. Despair and a pang of longing rolled beneath the barrier that separated him from his emotions, and he strained towards them, desperate to feel something, *anything*.

Foster ducked under the yellow ribbon and crossed the grass, sodden with runoff from the fire hoses. Everyone who made it out had abandoned the foreclosed property, and they were probably busy looking for new places to live. The gaping hole in the building's façade that had once housed the front door beckoned, and he stepped inside as if answering a siren call—dazed and a little uncertain, but unable to stop moving forward.

His feet, guided by muscle memory, stilled outside A2 as he had done every time he passed for the last week. Familiar guilt beat at the glass divide, and the waking Foster felt relief that it couldn't reach him for once. He turned, dull-eyed, and started up the stairs. They creaked and strained but held even as his feet brought up little clouds of ash.

He paused on the landing of D floor. A shard of agony broke through the glass barrier, and he found himself looking at the soot-blackened door of D3 for a very long time, clutching his chest and gasping for breath. When he was able to fight back the threatening swell of panic, he nearly ran up the last flight of stairs.

E floor was always a bit shoddy. Being the fifth floor meant that when the landlord *did* splurge and schedule a yearly cleaning—coincidentally when the city would be scheduling inspections—the cleaners would always be worn out by the time they reached his landing. They'd show their faces, do a quick sweep and wipe the walls with an already well-used rag, then hurry back down to disappear for another 364 days. He often wondered how the building's condition might have been improved had there been an elevator.

Regardless, he was used to the run-down state of his building. The flame-licked edges of the wallpaper peeling from the drywall were new, and unfortunately the threadbare carpet was no longer just filthy, but also alternately soaked and singed. Foster sighed and smoothed back a piece of hideous, flaking paper. An electric jolt went through his gut, and he tensed so hard that his hand punched through the weakened drywall.

"No..." He snatched his hand back, pieces of broken plaster raining down on the ruined carpet. A dark blue mark like an ink stain spread across his palm, though it was vanishing before his eyes. *No, no, no, no.*

A mark like this was a glaring indicator that someone had been casting destructive magic recently, leaving a physical stain only visible to those with Divine power. Foster knew it hadn't been him—all magic he worked was within the walls of his heavily warded apartment, to prevent any interference in his process.

A thought brushed the back of his mind, a fleeting glimpse of a memory, and he shoved it down under the glass with his emotions. *No, nope, not going to happen.* He refused to even consider that possibility.

Foster stomped as furiously as he dared to reach the familiar ground of his apartment. The fire had been ruthless with his building, but his own apartment had been relatively spared by his protective warding. Though that wasn't to say it had been untouched. His furniture was heavily damaged, and soot singed the walls. The carpet was a squishy, sodden mess.

The wards on his closets had mostly held, though the bookshelves were barely upright. He entered the kitchen and opened a charred cabinet, smiling faintly as he plucked out the fresh bag of coffee beans Cwall had tried to pilfer just days ago.

He tossed a handful in his mouth and crunched down, curious, only to gag and spit them into the sink. How the hell did the little demon just eat *raw beans* like that? Disgusting. He brushed off the coffee pot as best he could, giving the hot plate a little zap of energy to account for the lack of power and setting a pot to brew as he walked down the hall to his room.

Foster looked into his mirror, cracked from the heat, and frowned at the shredded remnants of his clothing and the blood splatter that dominated his chest. A kernel of regret burned in his gut. This was his favorite shirt. Tugging off his ruined top and throwing it over the mirror, he dug into his closet for something clean to wear.

Redressed and refreshed, Foster made his way back to the living room. He dug his favorite mug out of the cabinet, poured himself a cup of freshly brewed coffee, and smiled when he saw his favorite chair was relatively unharmed. Settling in, he crossed one leg over his knee and took a sip from the mug, waiting.

The knock was both ridiculous and unnecessary. True to form, his father had no respect for his wishes, and Foster sensed him hovering out in the hallway for a good two minutes before he announced his arrival. He waved a hand lazily and the door swung inward with a creak. Lucifer swept inside, casting his gaze around the room as he crossed to stand in front of his son.

"Your manners are terrible."

Foster looked up through his lashes. "Blame my upbringing."

"Don't insult your mother like that."

He gripped his mug so hard the handle snapped off. "Don't speak about my mother."

"You're not in a position to tell me what I can or cannot speak about, Foster."

"Aren't I?" He scoffed and drained his cup. "Who knows the limits of my new power?"

Luce leaned in and gripped the arms of the chair, eyes glinting with fury. "I can say with certainty that your limits are irrelevant. You have not surpassed me."

Foster tried to lunge out of his seat but found he was unable to move. "You have got to be fucking kidding me."

"You need to *listen*, Foster!"

"It may be destroyed, but this is *my* fucking house." He strained against his gleaming white bonds, writhing with furious determination. "You come into my home and bind me to my own fucking chair and expect me to *hear you out?!*"

"In fact, I do!" Lucifer snapped, stalking forward and leaning into Foster's face. "Because I love you enough to want to save your life, even as you're happily throwing it away!"

"What the fuck does that even mean?"

Luce sneered. "I'll gladly explain if you *settle down.*"

"And you had to restrain me?"

"Would you listen if I hadn't?"

"I won't even listen now." He scoffed and focused on harnessing his new power to direct it towards unravelling his binds. Trying to grasp the power was like trying to grab a live snake with soapy hands, but he concentrated on reaching deep and pulling it up.

"Of course you won't," Luce grumbled. Stubborn, arrogant—he was his father's son after all. "But I'm going to speak because you need to hear it. You are aware, of course, that I was exiled from Heaven for treason."

"Not surprising, given how unreliable you are."

"Enough!" Lucifer shouted, his power cracking like a whip between them.

Foster bit back a retort as he tried to focus, and Luce tried a different tactic.

"Foster," he tried to speak as gently as he could, but frustration and the sense of urgency colored his tone with impatience. "Gabriel is a conniving, manipulative traitor. You have no idea the crimes he is guilty of, or the sins he has committed."

Foster rolled his eyes. His father's magic *was* stronger than his, loathe as he was to admit it. But if he could distract him, then maybe the lapse of focus would be enough to even the odds.

"That's why you're lucky to have me as a father," Luce was saying as he paced the floor before the chair. If he rolled his eyes any harder, Foster might be at risk of permanent vision loss.

"This *angel* you're so fond of is a fraud, a charlatan. A *liar.*" Luce spat the word as if it was poison. "He framed me, Foster!"

"I mean, I would frame you for something right now if it would get you out of my face, so I can't say I disagree with the choice."

"So cavalier with your venomous retorts, ha-ha yes, so witty." Luce narrowed his eyes and leaned in, his breath hot against Foster's face and making him flinch involuntarily back. "But if he was willing to betray me, who he followed so devoutly and loved so dearly, what will he do to you when you outlive your usefulness?"

"He loves me like a *son*," Foster spat, relishing his father's own recoil, "which is more than you ever did."

"I adored you, always," Luce snapped. "You are *my* son, not Gabriel's, and I have borne burdens for you that would crush him."

"Not from my perspective," the younger man snorted. "What burdens you've had to carry! Oh, it must be *so* difficult lounging around a castle while your son grieves and struggles alone!"

"My distance was my sacrifice!" Lucifer roared, gripping the arms of the chair so hard they splintered. Foster fell silent, shocked that he had coaxed such a reaction from his flippant father. "I was so afraid, so convinced I would ruin you, that I alienated you. I see now that I fed the very beast I meant to starve, and for that I curse myself a thousand times over. But that's why I need you to *understand*."

"Understand what?"

"This is what he *wanted*, Foster! This wedge between us, this animosity! It makes you easier to control."

"Liar!" Foster surged up from the chair again, severing the bonds that had contained him. He flew at his father, caught off guard, and wrapped strong fingers around his throat. "Gabe has always taken care of me! He would never use me!"

"He was willing to risk your *life* in pursuit of power!" Luce pried at his hands, forcing them off his neck and tossing his son into the nearby wall. The apartment shook from the force, small chunks of charred plaster raining down on them. "What if you hadn't been able to handle the surge?"

"Gabe knew that I could! He taught me to use my powers; he knows my limits!"

"He doesn't care if you live or die!"

"You're just jealous!" Foster came right back at his father, eyes glowing red with fury. "He's a better father to me than you, just by showing up. And you can't stand it."

"I am a better man than Gabriel on my *worst* day," Luce said coolly. "He corrupted two innocent souls in my name, lied under oath about it, made my lover complicit in my destruction, *and* had a hand in the death of your mother."

"Shut up!" The fury boiling in Foster's veins rose to uncontrollable levels. At the callous mention of his mother, Foster lost himself. "Shut up, shut the fuck up!"

Something surged in his blood like an electric shock, and without thinking, he raised his hands and released a brilliant white blast of energy. The force of it rattled the cabinets and shook the floor. It sent the very walls groaning as the building strained to hold itself together. Foster himself was thrown backwards from the recoil, crashing through the remnants of his coffee table and sliding back into the exterior wall. His head rocked back into the plaster with a *thunk*.

Across the room, Luce still stood—with Michael down on one knee before him. The angel panted hard, winded from his sprint up through the building and from bearing the brunt of Foster's attack. His gorgeous tawny wings were badly singed, steaming from the impact, and his shoulders twitched from the strain of holding them aloft as a makeshift shield.

"Michael!" Luce dropped to his knees, grabbing the larger man by the jaw with both hands. "You absolute *moron*, what were you *thinking!*"

"You restrain yourself with him," he said, his voice wavering slightly, and Luce cupped Michael's hands flat between his own palms.

"An astute observation," his tone was equal parts fond and chastising. "Please refrain from getting yourself killed on my behalf."

"Yeah," Foster groaned, pushing himself to his feet. "He sure doesn't deserve it."

Michael turned to him, wings drooping as he let them fall back to rest. "I owe your father much more than this. If you had seen what we have seen..."

"Blah blah, 'we saw some shit, and you should change your mind' yeah," Foster scoffed. "I prefer to base my feelings off my own experiences and not what you *claim* to have seen."

"I'm willing to show you, but you're being ridiculous," Luce snapped. "The measure of your character is admitting when you're wrong, Foster, not clinging to your bias to feel comfortable."

"Do you even *realize* how hypocritical you sound?"

Luce arched a brow. "I thought you were trying *not* to be like me?"

Foster snarled, then blinked in confusion at his own reaction. He looked up at Luce, and for a moment he was young, vulnerable, and confused. "What is happening to me?"

Luce softened and rose back to his feet to approach his son. "I'm not sure. But I'm willing to help you work it out."

His son's expression darkened. "I don't need or want *your* help. I know where to find Gabe when I want someone's opinion."

"That's not happening."

"Excuse me?"

"He's too dangerous, Foster, how are you not understanding this?"

Foster scowled. "I understand perfectly fine; I just don't agree with you."

"It's not a matter of opinion! Gabriel impersonated me so I would be exiled and has almost gotten you killed in pursuit of who knows what ends!"

"That's the kicker for me," Foster jabbed a finger towards Luce. "All I'm hearing so far is that he did something to screw you over, which I don't personally blame him for, and you can't even tell me what his supposed evil goal is in all of this. You sound like a bitter old man."

Luce was at the end of his patience and grabbed Foster by the upper arm. "Bitter? Possibly. Old? Yes, ancient. I am the first of the Seraphim Eterna. I am Lucifer of the Morning Star, and I am your *father*. Honor thy father, Foster. You will do as you're told and let me save your ungrateful life."

The tension between them was tangible, and Foster leaned toward Luce for a heated, electric moment. "No. I'm officially done listening to you."

He yanked his arm away, and Lucifer lost his cool.

"That's it. I tried to be compassionate and patient. I tried to reason with you." Luce clapped his hands together firmly, then slowly spread them apart, a warm golden light emanating from his palms. "Apparently, I must employ the age-old tradition of putting my foot down. You're grounded."

It was so unbelievable, Foster laughed. "I'm a grown man!"

"A grown man who will be forcibly confined to his room until I deal with the matter of Gabriel."

Foster threw his arms wide. "What, here in my ruined apartment?"

Luce sniffed disdainfully. "Absolutely not. Even if it wasn't an absolute wreck, I clearly can't trust you to make your own choices. You'll be returning to Hell where I can keep a closer eye on you."

"You're about twenty years too late to be giving a shit." Foster rubbed his own palms together as if scrubbing off a stain, then mimicked his father's actions and pulled the space apart. His own hands gave off the bright white light he had created before, and he marveled at it for a moment. "You can let me walk out of here, or we can have this fight. Personally, I'm happy to have a chance to beat your face in."

"Insolence is unbecoming," Luce sneered. "Your mother would be ashamed."

Foster could hear himself yelling, but his world narrowed to a furious blur centered on his father's face. He rushed forward, throwing his hands ahead of him in an attempt to maim or at least to wound with his power.

Luce swiveled to the side and returned the volley, golden light arcing out in a sweep toward his son. Foster ducked, and Michael made a guttural sound of alarm as he rolled his battered body out of the way.

"Sorry!" Luce yelped.

"Look out!" Michael pointed frantically behind him.

Luce whirled around, only to catch Foster's glowing fist across his cheek. "Damned Souls, Foster, this is madness!"

"What's madness is that you're so desperate to control my life!"

"To *save* it!"

Another bolt of gold swept past Foster's head and blasted a hole clean through the wall. Foster peered over his shoulder at the smoldering drywall and rickety stairwell.

"Oh yes, it definitely looks like you're saving me!"

"You're a demigod," Luce said dryly. "You'll heal."

Foster gave a guttural shout and rushed at Luce, catching him around the waist and sending them tumbling into the kitchen. He reached up on impulse, grabbed his freshly brewed coffee from the warmer, and sloshed it into his father's face. Luce bellowed in pain, covering his face with his hands, but when he pulled them away the blistered red wounds were already healing.

"This is my favorite jacket," he declared indignantly. Foster only grunted before bringing his fist down hard on Luce's nose. It gave a sickening crunch, and the Devil yowled.

Foster continued raining down blow after blow, driven by deep seated resentment and centuries of repressed anger, hot tears pouring almost unnoticed down his cheeks. Lucifer barely resisted, bearing the onslaught with the occasional weak attempt to push his son away. It was so uncharacteristic that it was almost obscene.

Michael averted his gaze and groaned, shifting himself to all fours. He'd taken a stronger beating than he had expected, but it was downright humiliating to be laid low by a novice as if he were completely untrained. But what was he supposed to do? Sit aside and let Luce be brutalized by his own son?

No. He had to summon the will—and then a thought crept in. *Summon.* He might be too injured to help, but he knew someone that rivaled his own abilities. Someone who would gladly risk his life to serve Luce. Michael pushed himself up, using a splintered chair leg as a makeshift cane, and fell heavily against the wall.

With a quick movement, he dashed his palm across a jagged remnant of the shattered window and dipped his fingers into the ichor that came spilling out. Carefully but quickly, he sketched out the summoning spell best suited to the situation. It had never been his forte, but he was good enough for an emergency.

Luce hissed on the kitchen floor, finally flinging his son away and scrambling back to his feet. His face was a horrifying sight. His proud nose was sharply askew, one eye socket broken and rapidly swelling, a lip so badly split that he couldn't fully close his mouth, and every inch of flesh a different mottled shade of purple and black.

Michael winced in sympathy, even as Foster got back to his feet and readied himself to charge again. Enough was enough. The angel slammed his still bleeding palm to the center of the summoning sigil and it flared to life with golden light.

"Balthazar! By divine blood and angelic power, I beseech you come to the aid of your commander, Lucifer, at the plea of Saint Michael the Archangel!"

A fierce wind stirred in the apartment, sweeping from the blown-out window and whipping through the room, before abruptly dying. The light of the sigil died, and Michael's stomach sank. Either his magic wasn't strong enough or he had done the sigil wrong, he wasn't sure. But it hadn't worked, and he wasn't strong enough to try again.

His wings were ruined for at least a few days, his healing all but slowed to a crawl trying to repair his damaged internals. He couldn't teleport, or open portals. There was nothing he could do to help. Michael hung his head in bitter defeat.

"What in the seven circles is goin' on in this dump?" A curious but disdainful voice came from the window, and Michael glanced sharply up. Cwall lounged in the empty windowsill in his skeleton form, inspecting the trashed apartment with mild curiosity.

Michael blinked, then lifted a hand slowly and pointed into the kitchen, where Foster and Luce were currently flinging knives and ceramics at each other with their powers in between bolts of clashing gold and white light.

"Oh shit, they finally workin' out their issues?"

Michael rolled his eyes skyward, seriously considering invoking Jehovah. He was bad at summoning, sure, but to ask for Bal and get Cwall? This was a joke; it had to be.

Foster snagged a knife as it flew past his head, spinning it in his palm and preparing to plunge it into Luce's throat. Immediately, Cwall's demeanor changed. He snarled harshly, lunging off the windowsill, ready to leap in between the two men. But Luce deflected the blade with a dinner plate and knocked his son backwards with a concentrated ball of energy.

"Hey, kid!" the demon called out, but Foster ignored him, lost to his anger again.

"It's no use," Michael cautioned weakly. "He's in a bloodlust."

Cwall frowned. "Wait...wait, I got an idea!"

The Dirge brought his palms together, the skeletal fingers letting out little sparks where they rubbed. Slowly, ropes of muscle and tendon began to spread over the white bone. Color flooded the tissues as the demon carefully formed a body of flesh and blood to cloak his true form, golden skin the shade of Michael's tawny feathers spreading over the framework of a body.

His form stretched and distorted, changing from short and portly to tall, willowy, and graceful. A long blue dress cascaded over his newly formed feminine breasts and hips, while honey blonde hair sprouted from his head. Michael inhaled sharply as warm amber eyes opened, and he found himself gaping at a perfect recreation of Angela Morningstar.

Cwall winked, an odd gesture on the woman's serene face, and strode confidently into the kitchen. "Foster, that's enough."

Even the voice was exactly right. Soft but steady, it was a tone that flowed like water over smooth stones and commanded attention without demanding it.

Foster reared back from his father as if he'd been electrocuted, whirling to face the demon wearing his mother's face. "Mom?"

Luce scanned her from head to toe, squinting, and then went deathly pale as he realized what was happening. He looked sharply from 'Angela' to Foster, slowly inching backwards as if to put as much distance between them as possible.

"No," the woman shook her head, form melting away as quickly as it had come on to reveal Cwall standing in the kitchen. "But I knew ya'd see reason if she was the one who told ya to knock it off."

Foster's expression was heartbreaking to witness; a look of blind, desperate hope shifting to utter betrayal and despair. The air stilled, then seemed to rush out of the room with a swiftness that reminded

Michael of the rip current in an outbound tide. He found himself straining to breathe in a room suddenly devoid of oxygen.

When Foster spoke, his voice was like ice, "How dare you."

Cwall cocked his head. "Huh?"

"I said," Foster hissed softly, "how *dare* you? How dare you impersonate her!? Use her face for a cheap trick!?"

"I wasn't—"

"How dare you insult her memory!" The boy advanced on the demon, eyes glowing like hot coals. Michael glanced down and saw Foster's hands once more ringed in white light—but this time tinged with a core of smoldering black. Lucifer slowly edged around behind his son, crossing towards Michael, eying the boy warily like he was a ticking bomb.

"Fossie," Cwall tried to placate him, lifting both hands and reaching for the young man's shoulders.

He never made contact. The light swelled outward, cloaking Foster in a ball of painfully bright white before it unfurled and washed the room in his furious power.

The impact before had winded Michael, left him with ruined wings and internal bleeding and stung like a nasty sunburn. This was like being inside the sun. Michael's skin stretched taught against his bones as his body was rocked with a wave of hot air strong enough to knock his head back. His damaged wings fluttered like old paper in the torrent. The temperature in the apartment built to a blistering peak.

Something touched his hand, and Michael glanced down at Luce's fingers encircling his wrist as a cooling sensation spread along his stinging skin. Michael leaned his shoulder into Luce's, trying to convey his gratitude without words.

Even if he'd had the energy to speak, the force rippling over them would have whisked the sentiments away. The wrecked foundations of the building shifted; the walls warped and cracked against the strain. The floor rolled under their feet like a wave, and Michael fell hard against Luce. The other man pulled him close to his chest, as if trying to tuck him away and shield him.

But the chaos was all around them; there was no escape. In the center of the ruined apartment, Foster began to scream, a furious bellow of raw fury. With a loud crack, a chunk of the ceiling came down and punched a hole clean through the ratty carpet and into the apartment below.

The last straw had finally broken. The building shuddered violently, and then the floor was yanked out from beneath them, crumbling away to little more than open air and fragments of rotten wood.

Chapter Twenty-Five

Mags was going to pace a hole into Lucifer's favorite rug, partly out of worry and partly just to spite him a little bit. She was still furious for what he had done to her, but time to process his intentions had cooled her fury into something smaller and easier to tuck away for an appropriate moment. Now her main concerns were the revelations they had uncovered, and his attempt to bring Foster back from the brink.

"Can you just sit still for maybe thirty seconds?" Remi snapped. Her leg bounced an erratic pattern against the edge of the desk she perched on, subconsciously jostling faster with each revolution Mags made into the carpet.

"He should be back by now," Mags insisted, cutting an irritated glance at the other woman. "He said an hour, and it's been two."

"And wearing a hole in the floor is going to make it better?"

"Leave her alone." Rag prodded Remi's side, making her jump away.

"We're all anxious." Cami smiled as Remi swatted at her husband, and Rag stepped out of her range. "No reason to ruin the carpets."

They were more than nervous, but they loitered in Lucifer's sitting room, waiting for him to return with his son, content to let Mags do the pacing for all of them.

Suddenly, Glory rose from her seat near the doors to the sitting room. "Someone's coming."

Rapid footsteps echoed into the room. Multiple people, *running*.

"Oh shit..." Remi muttered, leaping off the desk. "That doesn't bode well."

Bal burst into the room first, his normally carefully tied hair flying loose around his face as he shouldered the door heavily aside. "The King requires our aid."

Mags jerked out of her cyclical path. "I fucking knew it!"

Sachi whipped around to stare at her in shock. "Since when do you curse!?"

"That is so not the issue right now," Cami chastised her husband.

Judas was hot on Bal's heels, almost crashing into his boss as he raced into the room behind the spymaster. "We need to go, now."

Remi spun on her heel and came storming at Balthazar like a woman possessed. "Bal, I swear on every soul in the Pit, you have one minute to give me more details before I summon the rustiest blade in this realm and start removing parts."

"You really are a vicious little thing." Bal gave her an alarmed look, then turned to Rag. "Blink twice if you need help."

Rag winked salaciously and kissed his fuming wife on the top of the head. "Willing victim, bro."

Bal shuddered, and Remi snapped, "The point, Balthazar!"

"A call for help came from Michael," the spymaster said gravely, all levity gone. "The sign Luce said to wait for, I think. I sent Cwall ahead while I came to tell you. I was hoping that maybe..."

He broke off, and then all eyes followed his glance to Gloriana. She tensed, shrinking back into the cushions of the couch.

"What?" she asked defensively, clasping her hands over her chest. "Don't look at me!"

"You're the one that makes portals." Remi started towards her, but was cut off by Mags. She crossed the room in three strides, an impressive pace for someone of her stature, and stopped before the blonde, taking Glory's hands in hers as she sat beside her.

"Please, Glory. It's the only way we'll get to Lucifer in time," Mags said, her voice barely above a whisper, giving her a beseeching glance.

Glory yanked her hands away as if scalded. "It's not about *wanting* to do it!" She jumped to her feet, pacing away and then turning back. "I can't without Jophiel."

"Have you even tried?" Remi asked. Rag squeezed her arm, a silent scolding.

"Of course I have!" Glory shouted. "You don't think I've tried to get to Jophiel? To talk to him and convince him to join us here? He's my *twin*, Remiel. I've tried a million times and each time I *fail*." She broke off with a strangled sob.

Remi started to weasel out of Rag's grip, but Rag stepped in front of his wife and asked, "Would our energies boost yours enough to open one?"

"No, it needs to be Jophiel." Glory shook her head. "I'm sorry," she said to no one in particular, as she scrubbed her eyes with the heels of her palms, then sniffed hard.

Mags laid a gentle hand on her shoulder. "We understand. We don't want to upset you; we only want to help Lucifer."

"I think there is another way, right?" Glory's gaze flicked toward Judas, her shoulders squaring as hope perked up in her voice.

Judas looked puzzled. "Do you mean...?"

"I've heard the demons speak of... tunnels?"

"Tunnels?!" Remi exclaimed. Rag reached for her arm, but she wrenched it away. "What, you think we have time to *dig* our way to Luci?"

"I didn't say we had to dig them, did I?" Glory snapped.

"You aren't even supposed to know about the tunnels," Bal pointed out. "But she's right. I hoped a direct portal would be faster, but I have an alternate route, and it seems like we have no choice."

* * *

Mags was going to hyperventilate before they ever got to the mortal plane. Bal had explained on the way that, due to the static nature of the Rifts, the Eyes of Lucifer had established several smaller portals in addition to the one at the main Gate. They led to a variety of locations around the mortal plane to reduce the amount of time spent traveling from one place to another, all accessible through a network of tunnels that spanned out from Balthazar's office.

Fortunately, when Lucifer had asked Cwall to keep a close eye on his son, they had established one which Cwall used to come directly to and from Foster's apartment. As soon as Bal had opened the door to reveal the passage, a fresh type of panic superseded the worry for her friend. When Glory had said 'tunnels' Mags had thought of small but neat corridors, something like an unfinished hallway. She realized now that they were much less established.

The rough-hewn walls seemed to close in on even her petite frame. Bal and Judas led the way, far ahead, with Glory following close at their heels and Cami and Sachiel strolling hand in hand behind them. Even Rag was making decent progress as the tallest among them. Mags barely progressed even with the aid of Remi's ironclad grip on her bicep, practically having to be dragged along.

"Breathe, Mags." Remi clicked her tongue in a way that was both soothing and chastising. "Passing out won't get you out of here faster."

"I didn't think...so small?" She panted, squeezing her eyes shut as a familiar fear raced along her already frazzled nerves. "Too small."

"If Rag fits, you have room," Remi reminded her. "Look, he's twice your size."

Mags peered cautiously up through her lashes. He paused his progress through the cramped tunnel to straighten as much as he could, trying to demonstrate how much space he had. Unfortunately, it had the adverse effect of showing Mags how hunched and uncomfortable he was. Trickles of dirt rained down wherever Rag's ginger head brushed the ceiling.

She shook her head frantically, digging in her heels. "I'll go back; I'll go the other way."

"There's no time," Remi reminded her, gripping the smaller woman by both shoulders as they came to a halt at the rear of the group. "Lucifer is waiting, in who knows what kind of trouble, and he's going to be so relieved to see you not wanting to string him up by his balls."

Despite her terror, Mags choked on a laugh at the thought. "I could never *really* hurt him."

"Yeah." Remi smiled tightly. "*We* know that, but *he* doesn't need to."

"Remi," Camiel called back to them, and they blinked in surprise at how far behind they had fallen. "Bal says we're almost there."

"Hear that? Light at the end of the tunnel, babe."

Mags smiled faintly and realized her frantically pounding heartbeat had slowed to a slightly elevated thrum. "That's usually not a good thing."

"Semantics," Remi grinned. "Now come on, we have a Devil to save."

Minutes later they reached the end, where a gleaming Rift stretched across the path. One by one they stepped into it, slightly dusty but otherwise intact, and stepped out into a scene from a horror movie. They arrived in an alley across from a lot where a heavily charred building sat in the relative center, blackened and damaged and listing slightly to one side in the marshy soup of waterlogged grass.

"What happened here?" Mags frowned, brows knitting together in concern.

"This can't be Foster's apartment?" Rag wondered, and Judas made a strangled sound.

"It was," he sighed. "I've been here once or twice to hang out."

Sachiel whistled, long and low. "Something real bad happened here, I can feel it."

His wife nodded, wrapping her arms around herself. "There's malicious energy here."

"We were called for a reason," Bal said, a grim look etched on his handsome face. "I didn't really think we'd be coming to a welcoming sight."

"But if he needs us, where is Luce?" Remi demanded. A crackle of energy swept over them as though Remi had spoken it into existence. Like birds drawn to a homing beacon, seven heads snapped upwards in unison—just as a vibrant wash of white light came blasting out of an upper floor window like a bomb, until it crashed into a barrier of power that contained and dissipated it.

"He was prepared for the worst," Bal murmured, crossing the street with the rest following like lemmings. They all hesitated at the edge of the property, as if they weren't sure they could cross the barrier.

"Luce," Mags breathed out quietly, and Bal took another step forward. Another violent shock rocked the earth, knocking him on his rear, and Glory hurried to help him up as a strange sound began emanating from the ruined structure.

One moment it was a subtle patter, like a few stray stones had been kicked down a flight of stairs. And then with a loud groan and a sudden shake, the walls crashed down.

Drywall and plaster crumbled and snapped under the weight of the upper floors; brick and concrete broke off in chunks from the exterior. It seemed to happen in slow motion and hyper speed all at once, the sodden ground slowing their progress as they pushed past the wall of power and hurried forward.

Where Foster's apartment had once stood now lay a collapsed pile of waterlogged and charred debris. In the aftermath, the silence felt entirely too loud. And then a sound like a groan came from beneath the rubble.

"Lucifer!" Remi shrieked. Without hesitation, she bolted straight toward the center of the pile.

"Remi, wait!" Rag chased his wife, terror cooling his own blood as the love of his life ran towards something that had been powerful enough to bury *Lucifer* under a building.

Another wave of energy swept out in a blinding white blast. Remi slammed up short against it and was thrown backwards like a ragdoll. She collided with Rag's broad chest, and he instantly wrapped his arms around her, falling to his knees to hunker against the pressure that bore down on them. He shifted to tuck Remi slightly under him, regaining his bearings, but found himself unable to return to full height under the onslaught of power washing over them.

There was a strangled sound from behind them, and a keening wail. Rag lifted his head to look back and saw Mags on her knees, eyes wide with terror. Bal supported Glory, who had apparently fainted. The other man barely kept his footing and lifted a hand to point shakily at the wreckage that had once been an apartment. Rag turned back. His heart sank like a stone into his gut. In the center of the demolished plot, Foster Morningstar was glowing like a small, furious sun.

"Foster," Rag murmured. Remi stirred in his grip, winding her arms around his neck and using his sturdy form to support herself as she struggled to her feet. Rag placed his wide hands on her slender waist, guiding and bracing her as she fought to stand against the crushing onslaught of power.

"Foster!" she shouted, the oppressive wind snatching her words away. She cleared her throat, squared her shoulders, and bellowed, "FOSTER!"

The glowing figure turned to face her, and the light pouring off him dimmed slightly. The wind died down, the pressure lessened, and the world went very still. He was listening.

"No one is here to hurt you," Remi began, but was cut off by an eerie sound like a high, reedy whistle. Rag realized it was laughter and felt his foreboding feeling deepen into fear.

Foster took a step towards them, and when he spoke it was in a detached, slightly muddled voice. "I doubt you could hurt me if you tried."

"We don't want to!" Camiel shouted back, a wounded expression on her face. "How could you think we want to hurt you?"

"Everyone else has tried," Foster scoffed. "I'm tired of being toyed with."

"I'm tired of no one taking you seriously as a threat," Remi said, rising to full height. Her eyes glowed red as her war paint spread over her pale skin. "We've been trying to save you, but maybe we just need to beat your spoiled ass."

"Remi, no!" Rag tried to pull her back, and she shook him off, advancing toward Foster.

"You are a Fallen Angel, who followed my idiot father into exile. You taught me basic sparring moves and how to stab through armor," Foster said, sounding amused at the idea. "But I am not afraid of you."

"I'm so much more than that, little boy," Remi snarled, fists clenched tightly at her sides.

"You're a tired old woman," Foster laughed. "If my father stands no chance, how could you?"

"The only reason your father isn't strong enough to shut you down himself is because he gave each of us a portion of his power. I am the purest rage of Lucifer Morningstar made flesh. I'm not afraid to use that power against you." She advanced on Foster with deadly focus, never wavering, never blinking. "I am fury incarnate. I'm not afraid of the temper tantrum of a *child*."

Foster's eyes narrowed, and the pure white light flared hot once again. "You will remember that I am the Prince of Hell."

"You will remember I was born to wage wars and to win them."

"Remiel," a weary voice called out, and relief surged through Mags. Lucifer staggered to his feet from beneath the rubble, supporting a badly battered Michael by the waist. "Do not attempt to injure my son."

That awful, reedy cackle came again from Foster. "You still try to pretend to be a good father?! Even now?"

Luce squared his shoulders, but his eyes softened. "I can't change the past, only learn from it."

"You cannot change the past," Foster grinned, slow and sharp, "but *I* can change the future. And now I have the power to make things right. To make them as they should be."

"Don't do this," Luce pleaded. "I've seen what happens when people meddle with things that should not be—"

"It is not for you to decide!" Foster thrust his hand toward Luce, a blinding arc of light whipping from his palm. Faster than Luce could move aside, Bal was there between them, lifting his own hands as if to catch the bolt like a ball.

"Balthazar," Luce gasped, and the other man winked at him, letting the energy funnel down his arms from his palms to his chest. The light seemed to wrap his form like a second skin, before dissolving into his body.

"I can still withstand a good hit or two," he said with a smile, but it was taut with effort. "I'm not so out of practice."

"What about three? Or four?" Foster sneered, already amassing energy for another assault. He lifted his arm, but a broad hand gripped him by the forearm and twisted his arm behind his back.

"You think you can defeat all of us?" Rag's tone dripped with contempt, and he fisted his free hand in Foster's disheveled waves. "We tried to be kind, Foster, and now you're forcing our hand."

He refused to break eye contact with Foster, who—to his credit—simply glowered in the larger man's hold.

"Are you quite finished?" the demigod drawled, arching a brow. "If so, I would ask you to remove your hand before I remove it from your arm."

He was slipping further into a cold shell, detached and distant. After centuries of dancing on Lucifer's every nerve, Remi knew exactly the best way to draw the younger man's ire and bring back some of his spark.

"You sound like your father."

The effect was instantaneous and exactly as expected. The wave of pressure weighing down on the property grew heavier, even drawing a small gasp from Mags as she was pressed flat to the Earth. Cami struggled to stay on her feet, eventually caving and falling to her knees beside her husband, who was struggling to reach Rag's side and help restrain Foster.

A spark lit in the storm clouds that had been building behind dark eyes, and Foster's face twisted in a snarl of rage. "I am nothing of my father!"

He wrenched his head free of Rag's grip, ignoring the sting and the slide of golden blood down his tanned neck as a clump of hair tore away. Lightning fast, he spun and dashed his knuckles across Rag's face. There was a crack, a loud pop, and a spray of black that looked like tar.

Foster looked curiously at the substance coating his cracked and swollen knuckles, and then back to Rag. The other man's head had snapped back upon impact, but now he straightened, laughing, and wiped the thick black blood from his broken nose with the back of his palm.

"That's right, little boy." Rag's grin was savage. "Fallen Angels bleed black."

"Fitting that I enjoy the color then, as I plan to coat myself in it."

"A warrior's soul," Remi sounded almost impressed. A short pause, and then with a grin, she taunted, "just like your father."

Foster roared, lunging forward. "Stop saying that! I am nothing like him!"

He gripped her by the neck and yanked, angling to try and bring Remi's face down to meet his other fist. She twisted free, apparently untouched by the power crippling the others if she stayed within a certain distance of Foster.

"This is your best effort?" She drew back her fist, and an angry red aura seeped from her pores, wrapping around to coalesce into the spiked brass knuckles she favored.

"You do not want my best effort," Foster warned, rubbing his palms together quickly and building a ball of white energy between them. The shape warped as he twisted and spread his hands, elongating into a disk and then what appeared to be a glimmering broadsword.

Remi laughed. "Delusions of grandeur can only take you so far."

"Then allow me to prove myself!" Foster charged in, sweeping his blade upwards, only to catch against the handle of Rag's mace. The redhead glowered down at him, heavy streaks of dark orange marring his face like the swipe of claws.

"You telegraph your movements." Rag shoved, knocking the younger man back, and spun quickly to the side to bring his mace down on Foster's shoulder. Foster howled, ducking to avoid a second strike, only to be caught in the chest by a surprise blow.

"Stop!" Luce cried out, seizing the momentary lapse in pressure to stagger a few steps toward his son. "Raguel, *please*, stop."

"We can't!" Remi protested, "Foster is determined to be the death of us all."

"Only you," Foster said, eyes glinting with fury, "and perhaps my father."

Without warning, his legs were swept from under him, and Foster found himself staring up at an overcast sky, the air knocked from his lungs. Remi sauntered forward, placing a heavy boot on his chest and leaning down to grin viciously at him.

Foster gripped Remi just above the ankle, his hand glowing white as he wrenched her leg to the side and rolled in the opposite direction. Remi hit the ground, catching herself on her forearms and pushing back up, murderous intent clear on her face. Cami dashed forward, a curved blade glowing a vibrant green in her fist, Sachi close on her heels with a barbed whip in his hands.

"Relent, you idiotic child," Cami demanded, launching herself up and angling her blade towards Foster's throat. He rolled further, out of her way, and she landed in a crouch where he had lain moments before.

"I heard legends about you all," Foster sneered, springing back up and jumping out of range of Sachi's whip. "I find myself disappointed by the reality."

Rag dispelled his mace and summoned his preferred weapon, a large war-hammer, gripping the haft with two hands and swinging it downward to rattle the earth. "You seem better suited to insulting us than fighting."

Foster laughed. "From what I have seen so far, you seem best suited at inflating your egos."

"We earned our accolades in *true* battles," Camiel hissed, summoning another blade and gripping the pair of scimitars tightly as if to avoid throttling the demigod. "We were ancient before you were a thought, boy."

"Well, that explains why your ideas and methods are so outdated," Foster said, extending his hand and manifesting his sword in his palm. "But I am happy to provide physical proof that I now surpass you, since you seem to need it."

Bal rose from his crouch beside Lucifer, summoning his spear and using it as a staff to steady himself. "You're the one with the over-inflated ego, kid."

Foster smirked. "Then please, attempt to make me eat my words."

They were on him in an instant. Luce struggled to follow the movements as his Fallen began the deadly dance of war with his son, partly because he was too afraid of the outcome to watch. He had expected they would need to face *Gabriel*, not Foster.

Where Remi struck and was parried away, Cami ducked low to

follow her attack. When Foster leapt back to avoid Rag's hammer, there was Sachi attempting to snare him with his whip. As Foster struck out at Judas in a clash of swords, Bal jabbed from behind with his spear.

They were a well-oiled and fluid machine, working in tandem as they had long trained to do. Souls built for war and justice, who had chosen to follow him into oblivion... and now they were tasked with putting a stop to his own son's reign of chaos. It was a bitter irony.

Across the clearing, abandoned by the others as they ran to fight, Mags watched with a look of desperation on her face. Luce averted his gaze. He couldn't simply sit here and watch, not when he could already see the Fallen were waning in the face of his son's unnaturally enhanced strength.

Closing his eyes, Luce reached down into his reserves of power, preparing to rejoin this fight. He had used too much power already, fighting Michael and then Foster in such quick succession, but he had to do something. A horrified shout from Mags had his eyes flying open, and Luce saw what she had seen, moments too late to stop what was coming.

Foster raised his broadsword over his head, preparing to strike Cami where she had been knocked to the ground before him—and then an arrow pierced his exposed chest. Foster gasped, staggering backwards, bringing his hand to the shaft of the arrow protruding from his sternum. With wide, alarmed eyes, he looked past his fallen target to find Glory, kneeling on the ground with her face and chest decorated in swirls of pink and her gleaming bow still held in its firing position.

"I'm sorry," she said quietly, bowing her head. "You have to stop."

Foster gripped the arrow firmly, expression shuttering as he quickly locked the shock and pain behind his glass wall. He breathed in, paused, then ripped the arrow from his own chest with little more than a wince. Silver blood spurted from the wound, pulsing down his chest with each rapid beat of his heart. It slowed to a trickle, then stopped.

"That was a mistake," he said, eyes gleaming with fury. "You will live just long enough to regret what you have done."

Foster lifted both hands high above his head, the pressure increasing tenfold and bringing the Fallen to their knees. A sound like shrieking wind ripped the air, bringing with it a biting chill, and Lucifer's chest tightened when he realized it was his son screaming.

"*Meyn zun*," he croaked, and fell to his own knees.

"Lus'ior," Michael croaked out the name as he crawled to his side, reaching for Luce's outstretched hand and clasping it as tightly as his shattered bones would allow.

Luce gripped his hand back tightly, closing his eyes as hot trails spilled over his cheeks. "My son is gone somewhere I cannot reach, Mikha'el."

"I am done!" Foster bellowed, the wind whipping harder and colder, leaving them shivering from more than just fear. Glowing light obscured his form in a sort of armor. The effect was a blinding halo of white that was like trying to peer through a frosted window. "The time for games has ended! If you stand in my path, I will cut you down like bugs to be squashed beneath my heel!"

The wind swelled, raging around the clearing. Foster brought his hands down slowly, cradling them to his chest as a massive ball of energy built between them. Remi cursed her waning strength, not sure if it was due to Foster's influence, or if her borrowed magic had somehow grown weaker through lack of use. But she struggled up from the ground, determined to bring the boy down before he unleashed the power.

Her prayer was answered.

As if someone had hit a pause button on the world, all the wind died out and an eerie, unnatural stillness settled. There was the briefest of pauses, and then a thunderous boom rocked the clearing, knocking Foster backwards under the deluge of power that accompanied it. Lucifer cringed away, and Michael gripped his hand tighter. He knew what was coming.

Even if he hadn't been able to identify the traces of that unearthly power, every nerve in his body was standing on high alert. He knew only two people with the magic ability and flair for the dramatic to make such a grand entrance, and one of them was crouching at his side.

Jehovah was finally showing himself.

Chapter Twenty-Six

So many poems have written about the angels of lore, Luce thought bitterly, as the heavenly host approached. *So many ballads composed likening them to glorious golden beings of light and warmth, and they are all wrong.*

There was nothing warm or soothing about the light that poured from the overcast clouds, parting them like a knife through butter. Choral singing rang through the clouds, and a contingent of the host of heaven appeared in the sky, astride gleaming horses fashioned from pure sunbeams.

Like a clap of thunder, a booming voice cried out above the choir, echoing over the clearing at near-painful levels. "And so, the heavenly host rode forth, to cleanse the earth of wickedness and restore peace."

Jehovah flew in the lead, resplendent in golden armor as he descending from the heavens with his snow-white wings spread wide to slow the fall, each feather capped in deadly serrated gold.

Michael knew that those wing blades took a full half hour to apply properly. Few situations could justify the wasted time for the showmanship and slight combat advantage they provided, especially for a warrior like Jehovah who so rarely saw direct combat. It was a frankly disgusting show of vanity with everything at stake.

Uriel and Jophiel flanked him, a small group of perhaps four other angels rode behind, and Ezekiel and an angel Michael believed to be called Ithiel brought up the rear. It was almost an insult, to appear with so few of his guards—a slap in the face that Luce knew his brother had taken great pains to orchestrate.

"I do grow so weary of cleaning up your messes, brother," he spoke in grand overtones, projecting an aura of regal calm as he led his cavalry down through the barrier and into the clearing, but Lucifer knew his brother well enough to detect the steel and fire beneath Jehovah's honeyed words.

"Your interference is not wanted or needed, Jehovah." Lucifer struggled to his feet, assisted as best he could manage by Michael. "This is a matter of *my* son, not yours."

"No." Jehovah touched down at last, his warriors settling in formation behind him. Jophiel sneered at Lucifer, carefully ignoring Glory's wounded stare, while Uriel bowed his head in shame at Michael's lingering glance. "*My* son knew his place and his purpose. Only the son of a traitor could prove such a malignant disappointment."

"He is *not* a disappointment," Mags protested, leaning heavily on one arm as she struggled to rise. She got to one knee, then paused to collect herself. "Any one of the children of Heaven could be led astray as he was. You judge his actions without knowing their cause."

"Led astray," Jehovah scoffed. "And what is the *'cause'* for your own treason, Mary Magdalene?"

Remi blinked slowly, becoming more alarmed as she processed the severity of the situation. "Mags, you need to shut up."

The other woman ignored her, eyes gleaming bright with defiance as she found her footing and straightened with aching slowness to her meager five foot two. Luce was reminded of David and Goliath as he watched her, unwavering in the face of Jehovah's towering height.

"Some of us understand that what is right is not always what is easy," she said. "I make my choices for the betterment of all who live, not in effort to maintain my own standing."

Uriel went visibly tense as she spoke, knowing exactly how well those words were going to go over. Ezekiel raised a delicate brow but masked his emotions better.

Jehovah scowled. "We shall see how free you are with those blasphemous remarks when we return you to Heaven for your trial."

"She is going nowhere!" Lucifer snapped. "My son, my court...you have no dominion over my people, brother. I invoke my right as her King to Sanctuary."

"You dare to challenge me? I think you shall find I have a greater dominion than you believe, *Lus'ior*." Jehovah clicked his tongue and slammed his staff down roughly, sending a ripple through the earth. "This is why I hate when you attempt to playact as a King. Always dreaming and making up your own rules as you go."

Lighting fast, a thin strand of golden light flitted across his throat, and suddenly Jehovah was choking as golden ichor spilled down the front of him, staining the robes beneath his armor and dripping in rivulets to the grass. The wound was ugly, but nothing close to fatal for a Seraphim Eterna. It was healing before the first drops of ichor hit the dirt, and Jehovah whirled angrily on his brother.

Luce still had his arm extended, fingers splayed in an arc and pointing straight at the other man. "Choose your words more carefully, Jehovah, or I shall do more than deliver a flesh wound."

Jehovah's laugh was mocking and cold. "You're almost tapped out, Lus'ior, don't try to bluff me. Why any of these fools left my paradise to be exiled with you is a wonder, when you've become so pathetic."

From the center of the clearing came a drawn-out groan as Foster slowly returned to consciousness in the rubble that now shifted around him. Remi took the momentary reprieve to drag herself to her feet, radiating a determination unique to those with nothing left to lose.

Eyes glowing crimson, she turned from Foster to face Jehovah directly, moving Mags aside to safety. "There's more than one reason we chose to follow Lucifer, you golden fallacy."

Bal pushed himself up and crossed to Remi's side, placing a hand on her shoulder. "You're an arrogant prick, for starters."

"And a hypocrite for holding others to standards you reject," Camiel added, taking Remi's hand and gripping it tightly.

Judas staggered to his feet, stepping up beside Bal. "You're a real selfish bastard."

"You use your affection as a tool for manipulation," Glory rose unsteadily to her feet, leaning on Sachiel for support as they joined the other Fallen in forming a wall between Jehovah and their King. Jophiel made a wounded sound but refused to meet his sister's searching gaze.

"You let others fight your battles for you," Sachi said, wrapping an arm around Cami's waist as he reached her, Glory standing at his side.

"You thrive on praise you've done little to earn," Rag walked with heavy steps to stand behind his wife, expression grim but resolved.

Remi's lip curled in a derisive sneer. "You lash out like a child with a temper and then claim your actions to be justice."

Their auras flared powerfully to life as they tapped into the reserves of power Lucifer had granted them, colorful light dancing through the clearing brightly enough to rival Jehovah's golden glow. Lucifer felt a swell of pride and adoration for them blooming in his chest. These were his people; *this* was his family. And they were risking everything to protect him.

"We chose our side long ago," Rag said firmly. "We choose it again every single day."

"We followed Lucifer because we believe in him, and we're willing to die standing up for what we know is right," Cami added.

Jehovah watched impassively during their speech, looking almost bored. It was only the slightest tick of his gaze up over Camiel's shoulder that made her tense up and start to turn. The blade sunk deep into her back before she could complete the movement, sliding through muscle and sinew like so much wet paper to emerge from the front of her chest.

Uriel flinched, reflexively reaching for his own sword at the same time Jophiel gripped the pommel of his. Jehovah stilled them with a gesture, waiting to see what would come next.

"So die," Foster said quietly, the cold whisper clearly audible in the stunned silence of the clearing. Cami hissed, trying to twist away from Foster's ironclad grip on her shoulder, but it quickly died into a guttural cough as the blade lodged in her sternum prevented her from healing. Thick black blood spilled freely down her torso.

"Cami!" Sachiel wailed, trying to pry Foster off of his wife, but it was like wrestling with a statue. "Foster please!"

"Camiel," Luce choked, stumbling forward while gripping his own chest. "No!"

"Yes," Foster smiled, a slick and lifeless facsimile of joy, and gave a heavy shove that sent Cami's impaled form sprawling to the dead grass. Her aura surged one last time, brilliant emerald against the pale gray sky, before flickering out like a dead bulb.

Remiel let out a bellow of rage, rushing toward the boy, only to slam up short against an unseen barrier. Rag beat his fists against the walls of their invisible prison, while the other Fallen seemed too stunned by Cami's demise to even react. Sachiel knelt brokenly at her side, hand hovering over his wife's lifeless body as if he could somehow turn back time.

"What is this?!" Rag punctuated each word with a bang of his fist.

"A precaution." Foster wagged his finger at the two still fighting as if chastising naughty animals. "It is not yet your turn to perish."

The King of Angels laughed. "Clearly it was a mistake to loan your power to those who cannot wield it."

"Only you would twist the knife over such a loss," Lucifer's voice was hollowed out by anger and grief. Even as the power he had gifted to Camiel trickled back into him, replenishing his dwindling stores, he would have given anything to have her back instead.

"And only you are a blind enough dreamer, head full of heretical nonsense, that you would risk your own survival by loaning your power to anyone who asks for it."

"The cost of my survival cannot be measured against the weight of the shame it would incur," Lucifer said, with shocking calm, "if I were ever to cavort myself as you do. Neither of us is the center of this Universe, as you well know, and yet only one of us insists upon clinging desperately to a false crown."

Jehovah nearly snarled but quickly smoothed his expression back into a patronizing mask. "You have always spoken like a man with his back to a wall, Lucifer. All grand overtures and empty threats. Anything to deflect from your own failures."

"For the love of all unholiness, can either of you ever stop?" Foster stepped over Cami's corpse and strode confidently between his father and uncle. "This is why you accomplish nothing and ruin everything. This eternal contest of wills, desperate to prove yourselves on some moral high ground, when you are both idiotic, over-inflated, laissez-faire monarchs."

Jehovah cut a glance to Luce, as if to say, 'I told you so'. Lucifer did not return his look, focused only on the cold mask covering his son's face, rendering him a foreign and dangerous creature. The boy he knew had become a man he had no desire to recognize.

"Foster," Luce finally forced himself to make one last effort. "We can still fix this. I can forgive you for this. I can…help you. With your mother."

Foster turned to him, a dead quality in his eyes as they slid over Luce that had the older man shivering. "I wish you would not lie to me anymore."

He turned back to Jehovah, dismissing his father. "You, pompous show horse that you are, have more power than my pitiful father at present. I will make you an offer, and you will consider it."

Jehovah's own mask slipped, a flare of indignation at Foster's audacity peeking through before he slid the genteel, benevolent expression back into place. "Of course, child. Even the most lost shall have the opportunity to repent their sins and be purified in the Lord's name."

"I do not wish to repent." Foster tucked his arms behind his back and glanced over Jehovah's shoulder at the tensely watching cavalry. "I wish to negotiate."

"Negotiate."

"Indeed." He met Jehovah's gaze steadily. "I desire my mother returned to the world of the living. I have my own means by which to achieve this goal, but I cannot deny that your assistance would expedite the process. In return, I offer you something you desire."

"What could I possibly desire, child, which is in your power to attain and not my own?"

That slimy grin slipped onto Foster's lips, an ugly thing that gave Luce chills to see. "Mary Magdalene."

Remi tried to launch herself towards him, reaching into her boot for her concealed blade, only to slam uselessly into the barrier. "You can't!"

"I can," Foster said, simply. "Or would you prefer I continue killing you all, to keep you from getting in my way?"

He stalked to where Sachiel still knelt, a trembling hand brushing the hair from Cami's slack face. His palms were coated with her blood, his eyes wide and haunted. Foster grabbed him roughly by the hair, pulling Sachiel to his feet with surprisingly weak resistance.

He didn't struggle or shout—he simply waited for death with those wide, unblinking eyes fixed on the corpse of his wife.

"Sachiel!" Bal yelled and lunged against the barrier that held him. Foster simply laughed and dashed a blade across Sachi's throat. The man's severed head dropped beside his feet with a sickening thud, and though Lucifer closed his eyes, he knew the sight would burn in his memory for eternity.

Luce pressed his hands to the dirt, using the returning energy from Sachiel to sendi quiet waves of energy through the earth and place his own protective barriers around the other Fallen. In the chaos, it went unnoticed by all but Jehovah, who looked at him with disdain.

"You would expend your meager remaining power to protect them?"

"Always," Luce said quietly. Jehovah turned away from the earnest resolve there.

A sharp yank on Luce's arm drew his gaze to Michael, whose expression was both horrified and sad. "We have to do something."

"We cannot do much more than this in our state."

Jophiel twitched every time Foster moved, long fingers fluttering over the pommel of his sword as if aching to join the in the debauched violence. Ezekiel looked bored, in a way that made the expression seem almost calculated. Ithiel looked like he might be ill, and Uriel closed his eyes so as not to see what was happening.

But Luce could see. He forced himself to watch instead of looking at Michael's expression, heartbroken and dismayed. He watched while his son advanced on Judas, praying his magic was strong enough to prevent more unnecessary death.

"Judas," he sneered, giving the man a once-over. "All this time you posed as my friend, and yet you were my father's spy."

"I was never a spy," Judas protested. "I truly was your friend, Foster."

"As if I could believe you."

"Frankly, I don't care what you believe," Judas sighed, and dropped his gaze. "You're no longer the man I called a friend."

He sat cross-legged on the dirt, running his fingers through the remnants of charred grass, and met Foster's gaze directly when he crouched in front of him.

"No fight left in you?" Foster hesitated for the first time, tilting his head curiously.

"No point in fighting," Judas murmured, eyes half-lidded and expression bland. "Your mind is made up."

"Indeed," Foster echoed his tone, but there was something else layered in it. An edge of sadness or maybe regret. "I think I might be sorry, for you. I almost wish I could spare you."

"Enough boy," Jehovah called out, and Lucifer wondered if he intervened for his wife's benefit. "You have proven your point."

Foster rose to his feet, leaving Judas watching him warily as he crossed to where Mags knelt, watching in a state of shock. Without a word, he reached down and gripped her by the arm, hauling her to her feet. Mags found herself stumbling along beside him, unable to process what was happening until Foster deposited her in a heap at Jehovah's feet.

"Now you will uphold your end," he spoke almost robotically, meeting the older man's gaze evenly.

"I do not recall accepting your terms," Jehovah rebuffed. "Indeed, I find myself bound to no agreements of any sort regarding you."

Foster stilled, hands dropping limp at his sides. He turned, eyes burning with hatred in an otherwise placid face. "I should have known better than to have any faith in such a being as you—cut from the same cloth as my deceitful father."

"I came here for two reasons, *boy*, and they were to retrieve Mary Magdalene for her trial and put a stop to your wildly unstable tantrum. You have done both things for me willingly." Jehovah stepped away from his small contingent of soldiers, advancing slowly on Foster. "You have noted yourself that I am quite powerful, but I am also merciful. For this favor you have done me, I am willing to spare your life this day. I suggest you accept my generosity."

Foster hissed, his expression darkening, and he spit on the ground at Jehovah's feet.

"You insolent whelp!" Jophiel lurched forward, sword halfway drawn from its scabbard as if he'd been waiting for any reason to fight. Jehovah held out an arm to block his path and the younger angel stilled on command.

"I am a forgiving man, Jophiel. We cannot fault the boy for his slipshod upbringing. Not everyone can be raised properly."

A flash of anger across that dark countenance, and Foster clenched his fist around the hilt of his broadsword. "My mother did an exceptional job with my upbringing."

"If she had, would she not be disgusted with your poor manners?" Jehovah lifted a brow.

"She would be more forgiving than you have ever been. She was an example of pure goodness. My mother should be classed as a Saint."

"Saints do not reside in the void, child."

"Which is why I beseech you to help me retrieve her."

"Souls are consigned to the void for specific reasons of which you know nothing—to the benefit of all present, as you should not be meddling in the affairs of your betters."

"My betters," Foster said slowly as he locked furious eyes with Jehovah, hot fury meeting cold indifference, "can die slowly under my heel."

He pushed off his rear foot, using the additional boost of momentum to propel himself toward an astonished God. Foster whipped his sword up and around, bringing it above his head with both hands wrapped around the hilt and driving it down in a cleaving arc.

Chapter Twenty-Seven

It was obvious his strike would never land—his movements were too telegraphed, his target too heavily guarded. But Luce had to admire something in the no-holds-barred attempt. Jophiel lunged forward again, unimpeded this time, and pulled his sabre from the belt at his waist to block with the flat edge. He knew Gabriel might be furious with him later, but his loyalty to Jehovah compelled him to act, and frankly, he doubted Gabe would approve of the young demigod's actions.

He was shoved back, heels grinding in the dirt as Foster's momentum carried them both towards Jehovah. With a grunt of effort and a hard push against the younger man, Jophiel was able to deflect the blow aside, but not without a long slice from shoulder to wrist.

Jophiel cried out but stood his ground. Across the clearing, Glory shrieked and tried to run towards him, only to be blocked by Lucifer's barrier.

"Glory, stop!" Bal said, gripping the blonde by the forearms. "Would he want you in danger?"

"I don't care!"

"I am *fine*, Gloriana," Jophiel grunted, keeping his eyes on Foster, who seemed torn between attempting a second strike and surprise that he had wounded someone. As with Camiel, Jophiel's wound lingered as a result of Foster's strange blade.

The tension simmered long enough for Jehovah to lift his hand, to do what no one could be sure. Then Foster bolted across the clearing as if freed from some spell keeping him in place.

"After him, if you would," Jehovah said, waving his raised hand lazily. Jophiel nodded and tore off after the young demigod, disregarding his still healing wound despite his sister's shouted protests. Two other angels from the contingent followed their lieutenant; enough to offer him support while keeping the King properly protected.

They disappeared around the ruins of the building, and Jehovah turned to Lucifer with a cold glare. "There has been enough chaos this day."

"For once, brother, I can agree with you," Luce said, albeit bitterly.

"I will take my fugitive and go, before the barrier around this place wanes thin enough for mortals to traverse."

Luce frowned. "You will be taking no prisoners."

Jehovah laughed. "Do you forget, Lucifer? Your son promised her to me. He is also of royal blood, is he not?"

"You can't be serious that you think his word voids my claims."

"What authority have you to claim sanctuary when *my* kingdom was violated? The girl will face her trial." His gaze hardened. "My laws are clearly defined, and she willfully defied them. It is a slight against my intelligence and my hospitality."

"I did not intend offense, Your Highness," Mags said quietly where she knelt in the grass. "I was seeking to avert the very calamity we see unfolding today."

"You have chosen a very reckless and ill-advised path in your haste to decide." He softened, but only slightly. "Actions have consequences, Mary."

Mag's decision dawned on Luce, before she even made a single movement. Like an ache in the throat, slow, paralyzing terror crept down through his torso to settle in his gut like a stone. It was written in the cast of her features; the firm set of her delicate jaw, the square of her tiny shoulders, the way her gaze was cut with steel. This was not a woman who would run or debase herself with tears or pleading.

"Mags, no." Lucifer struggled to his feet, relying on the surge of panic-fueled adrenaline to carry his utterly drained body through the motions. "Please."

"You speak as though there are choices to make, Luce," she spoke softly, but her voice was steady.

"Indeed, there are not." Jehovah inclined his head briefly. "But to be certain, Ezekiel, if you would?"

The angel at Jehovah's left shoulder stepped out and hesitated, silver wings fluttering awkwardly. He was tall and slender, with a shock of pure white hair pulled back in a neat ponytail to highlight a stern countenance. Dark, angular eyes flicked across the field to Raguel, who met his gaze with a mingled look of reproach and pleading.

Ezekiel looked away first, something akin to anger in the action. He crossed the grass with long strides, hand resting threateningly on the hilt of his rapier.

"Zeke." Mags lifted her chin, and the angel gripped it firmly. She immediately tried to shrink back, but he gripped her forearm with his free hand to still her.

"Do not speak." His normally smooth voice was rough with repressed emotion, the mellifluous tones cut with gravel. "Do not make this more difficult than it needs be."

Mags went small and rigid in the angel's grip.

"Release her!" Luce roared and attempted to surge to his feet. Between maintaining the barriers in place and the damage his body had taken, his magic was almost fully depleted, even with the bolstering waves from Cami and Sachi. Lucifer crashed to his knees halfway to Mags's side. "Please, Ezekiel, release her."

"He will not," Jehovah dismissed his brother with a lazy wave, but Ezekiel hesitated, gripping Mags tightly but not moving to return to Jehovah. "You disgrace yourself with these pitiful displays, Lucifer, honestly."

"I do not care," Luce said, bracing his palms in the dirt. He shoved himself up, struggling to get one foot planted and wavering from the strain. "I will debase myself a thousand times over for the ones I love."

"Not for your son, however?"

"Some of us draw the line at murdering our children."

A darkness stole over Jehovah's face like a cloud across the sun, something ugly flickering there. With a swift and violent slash of his hand, a tendril of light came down like a whip across Luce's straining back, bringing him to the ground again.

"How dare you," Jehovah hissed, bringing his whip down again, and again. It tore through Luce's shirt and bit into his back like a fiery brand, singing the flesh even as it was split. "You know nothing of why Christos was asked for his sacrifice, or what it cost me to even consider it."

"And yet," Luce hissed, voice low and taut with strain from the assault, "you allowed your son to die. Encouraged it, even."

Another swing and crack of the whip. Glory began to cry, while Remiel unleashed a string of curses in several dead languages.

Fury cast Jehovah's face in hard lines, rendering him a vengeful sculpture. "Unlike you and yours, my son understands the balance of the universe, and his place within it."

"So you claim." Luce looked up from the ground, disdain clearly etched in the lines of his mouth, the furrow of his brow. "Or is he simply afraid of your reaction should he refuse your wishes?"

The golden light reared back again, angling to strike Luce across the face this time. Instead, the whip cracked down across a broad, tanned chest, leaving a nasty split in the skin like a flayed fish, its edges smoldering. Michael grunted, falling back and landing on his back in the dirt before Lucifer.

"Not me, you beautiful idiot," Luce murmured, running his fingers over Michael's forehead to brush loose curls out of his eyes. "I can take it. If you must defend someone, go to Mags."

Michael's healing factor had been almost completely depleted when he took Foster's blow for Luce, and the building collapse had left him severely injured. Luce dug deep, pushing himself past his long-reached limits, to send the last dregs of his power into the angel, offering him as much healing as he could muster in the hopes one of them could save the girl.

Michael stared up, the pale blue of the sky haloing Lucifer's dark, disheveled head, and thought the Devil might be more beautiful now than he had ever been in their youth. Sparks of healing magic raced across his temples and down his neck, shoulders, and torso.

Bones snapped back into solid form; torn muscles knit back together. Then the magic fizzled out, only able to address the most urgent of medical concerns. Michael grunted, rolled to the side, pushed up from the ground on trembling arms, and got unsteadily to his feet. His still shattered wings drooped and dragged along the grass.

"You are entirely out of line, Michael," Jehovah warned him, voice taut with fury. "To lie to me, defy me, and now to interfere with my justice?"

"This is vengeance, not justice," he spoke slowly, knowing to speak his mind was to invite his own punishment. He turned to Ezekiel, delivering his best disappointed glower. "You were trained to be better than this, Ezekiel."

"I was trained to follow orders," the younger angel rebuked him. "A lesson you seem to have forgotten since teaching it to me."

"You will learn much with age that cannot be taught, youngling." He extended a hand. "Please allow Mary to come to me. I do not wish to fight you."

"You know I can't do that," Ezekiel gripped Mags more tightly, pulling her rigid form to his side. Mags whimpered, and Michael couldn't hold himself back anymore.

"So be it." Michael lunged forward, only for Ezekiel to spin nimbly aside, dragging Mags with him. Michael pulled up short, wheeling around and making a second attempt at tackling the younger angel.

Ezekiel dodged again, stumbling slightly over Mags's feet and yanking her behind him as Michael reached for her again. With a growl of irritation, he pulled a thin cord from his belt, looping the golden strands over Mags's thin wrists and letting it pull taut. She winced, recoiling, and Ezekiel pushed her to her knees.

"Stay out of my way," he hissed, ducking another swipe from

Michael and elbowing the taller man in the gut, pushing him away from Mags. Michael tried to draw his sword from the sheath down his back, but Ezekiel wasn't foolish enough to allow his former mentor a weapon. He beat him back mercilessly, blocking every strike and countering with another immediately after.

Jehovah merely watched the show, an expression of amusement on his face. Uriel cleared his throat softly, then louder, until God turned to look at him. "Yes, Uriel, what is it?"

"Sir," he swallowed, cleared his throat at the sharp look he received, and tried again. "Your Majesty, should you not...interfere?"

Jehovah hummed. "I think not. Michael is treading on the thinnest ice, and I think he deserves the shame of losing to a former protégé."

Uriel swallowed again, his throat like sandpaper with a golf ball lodged in it. This fight, this scene... All of it was wrong. His commander in chief was content to gloat over a broken man taking a beating—and for what? What had Michael done, but protest injustice?

Ezekiel spun and twisted, dancing around Michael with inhuman grace and speed, unimpeded by injuries or fatigue. In contrast, Michael clearly operated at about ten percent, broken and bruised yet *still* matching Ezekiel strike for strike. A swell of pride in his best friend burst in Uriel's chest, chased by a deep-rooted shame. What was *wrong* with him, standing here watching Mike struggle and strain?

His dark eyes flicked to Lucifer, slumped over on all fours and still struggling to push himself up. But the King of Hell had given all that he had available and was clearly in agony. He looked across the field to the Fallen still locked inside Lucifer's bubbles even after Foster's had dissipated.

Remiel shrieked and slammed her fists on the barrier, Raguel right beside her. The redhead looked traumatized and hurt, hands pressed flat to the barrier as he watched Ezekiel with an expression of clear, pained betrayal. Gloriana sat dazed on the ground, looking away from the fight in the direction her brother had run, anxiety and fear written all over her delicate features.

Balthazar hunkered down in a crouch at her side, eyes fixed determinedly on the ground as if he couldn't bear to watch. Judas had his face buried in his hands, hunched over.

Uriel turned slightly, watching Jehovah as he watched the fight. Watching the way his eyes gleamed with delight as Ezekiel landed a hit that sent Michael sprawling to the ground, his already damaged wing bending awkwardly beneath him. The blond screamed, a primal sound that broke the ever-thinning resolve that kept Uriel where he stood. Before he realized it, he was moving.

He sprinted across the grass, ignoring Jehovah's enraged and indignant shout, ignoring Ezekiel's look of shock and dismay, ignoring his own subconscious screaming at him that this was a mistake, a reckless decision, a terrible idea. He dropped and slid the last few feet of his sprint to wrap his arms around Ezekiel's knees and bring him down hard.

"Uriel you fool!" Ezekiel hissed, but there was no stopping now.

"Which of us is the fool, Zeke?" Uriel brought up his knee, planting it firmly on Ezekiel's chest and pressing his forearm to the other man's throat. "The one who acts against the grain, or who knowingly betrays his conscience?"

A grunt, eyes blazing furiously, as Ezekiel kicked his legs and thrashed in Uriel's hold.

"Uriel!" Jehovah snapped, voice rising and deepening as he spoke. "What in the name of Heaven are you *doing*?!"

"What is right, Jehovah," he replied, voice unwavering despite his inability to look at the fury he could feel bearing down on him.

"You my believe that to be so." Jehovah stalked towards him and caught the back of Uriel's armor in his grip, yanking back hard to force the angel to look up into his eyes. Behind him, Ithiel balked at the sight, seemingly torn between scampering after the King or bolting in the opposite direction. "But you are fallible, which explains how you have become *confused*. However, I am only willing to forgive you so far."

Uriel swallowed, his throat flexing as Jehovah's grip pulled taut and the edge of Uriel's breastplate bit into his neck. This was the God of the Old Testament—the God who flooded the earth when he decided humans were not to his liking, who commanded a young man to murder his brother as a test of faith. The God that smote the Tower of Babel for daring to encroach on the Heavens.

Uriel's scarred wing gave an unconscious twitch at the memory of the stray bolt that had clipped him, of falling from the sky with his wing nearly torn free, and of how Jehovah had not even spared a glance to watch him plummet toward his death.

He strained against Jehovah's grip to catch Michael in the corner of his vision. Michael had been the one to save him that day, to dive for him through a storm of arrows from below and sweep him into an alcove of the nearby mountain. Dark brown locked on stormy silver as their gazes met, and for a moment Uriel was a fledgling again, sweating and cursing on a rocky cavern floor while his wing was reattached through a hasty combination of magic and battlefield medicine.

Michael blinked slowly, scanning his face, and found something there that made him wince. Uriel looked across at the Fallen and met Remi's fiercely burning gaze, with Rag at her side looking somber and resolved. Judas's eyes were open now and watching ravenously to see what would happen. Gloriana stared brokenly off, but Balthazar nodded with something like approval. He had seen exactly what Michael had. So it was decided, before Uriel even realized he had come to a decision.

"Then it is a very good thing," he croaked, "that I do not seek your forgiveness. I no longer require your good will."

Jehovah went very still. "This is not a jesting matter, Uriel."

"Indeed, it is not."

A breeze swept the clearing, the only sound the whisper of wind against charred weeds.

"So, this is the end of you as my faithful warrior." His tone was now almost wistful, and Jehovah relaxed his hand and released the other man. "Allow Ezekiel to rise, please."

"I don't trust him to leave Mags alone."

"Ezekiel will not lay another hand on her."

Uriel paused, then relaxed his hold on the other angel, rising and allowing him to stand. Mags watched Ezekiel warily from her position on the grass, like a wounded animal tracking a predator. He ducked his pale head to avoid her judging eyes.

"You understand the choice you're making?" Jehovah's voice was surprisingly gentle, and he watched Uriel's face carefully as he spoke. "You are forfeiting your right to enter my kingdom henceforth. You are electing to strip your privileges and wings, forever to be known as one of the Fallen."

"Unless you're one of us, you don't get to use that name!" Remi sneered. "It's ours!"

Jehovah shot her a withering glance and Rag clapped a broad hand over her mouth, wincing.

"I understand, Jehovah, but I cannot continue to serve you in good conscience. Our ideals are no longer aligned."

For once, Jehovah seemed to wear his age plainly. The lines around his eyes seemed to deepen, forehead and laugh lines creasing as he frowned. He suddenly seemed every bit as ancient as he was. "I appreciate your honesty. As you have done me no personal wrong, I cannot find reason to deny your free will."

A commotion came from behind them as Glory unleashed a shriek that could have woken the dead. Following her horrified gaze, Luce could see Jophiel emerge from a copse of trees, coming back around the edge of the demolished property with his armor dismantled and his hand fisted tightly to his side. Golden ichor spilled between his fingers as he stumbled toward Jehovah.

"My King," he gasped, falling to his knees before the other man. "I have failed you. The child evaded me."

Without a word, Jehovah pressed the palm of his hand to Jophiel's forehead, a warm golden light washing over the angel. The flow of ichor halted and Jophiel relaxed, hands falling to either side as the healing magic washed over him. When he deemed him sufficiently restored, Jehovah took back his hand and gestured for Jophiel to rise.

"And the others?"

Jophiel swallowed hard. "Slain by the boy."

"I see." Jehovah's eyes narrowed, but he offered the angel a slight smile. "You may yet prove your worth, Jophiel."

"Anything, my King."

"Uriel has chosen to defect from our ranks." He paused, the momentary vulnerability quickly squashed and replaced with his usual calm veneer. "You may do me the service of stripping his wings."

Chapter Twenty-Eight

Jophiel flinched, alarm flashing over his face. Luce thought, for a moment, the young man might refuse. His hand wavered over the hilt of his sword, fingers twitching slightly. But then Jophiel closed his lips, pinching them tightly shut, and drew his weapon. He turned to Uriel, expression carefully smoothed into a neutral mask, and Uriel sighed.

"One stroke, please, Joph."

"Do you question my ability?" He stiffened, offended.

"No, my apologies." Uriel looked at him for a long moment, searching that blank expression for... *something*, and then finally turned his back on the blond. Lucifer wanted to look away, but something kept him fixed on the scene. His back itched in the exact spot where he bore his own ragged, silver scars. Ezekiel averted his gaze, and Ithiel turned completely away, looking like he might be violently ill.

Poor kid, Luce thought, with just a smidge of pity. *Never even seen combat before, I'd bet.*

Jophiel, to his credit, took both wings in one fell swoop. He made no spectacle of it, but neither did he offer any warning. There was simply one moment where Uriel stood, stiff-backed and tense, waiting for the strike, and then in the next breath, two gorgeous russet wings lay severed on the grass.

Luce—and his Fallen, of course—knew what was yet to come. Michael had watched, stubbornly and perhaps with a touch of masochism, as the wings had been severed. He closed his eyes now, as Uriel dropped to his knees, a scream of agony ripping from his clenched lips.

Across the field, Remi flinched, coiling in on herself. Rag shuddered, and Balthazar dropped to a crouch, ducking his head into his knees. Luce felt the phantom pain slice through his own back and rolled his shoulders to assuage it. It was a specific agony that you never quite forgot.

Jehovah looked away, refusing to acknowledge his former soldier any further. "Ithiel," he murmured. "Please help Mary Magdalene from the ground."

The young angel scampered to do as he was bid, nearly tripping over his own feet in his haste to help Mags up. She accepted his hand hesitantly, and a bit awkwardly with her own still bound.

"Oh!" Ithiel pulled out a small dagger. "Allow me to remove this."

"No."

The angel froze, dark hair falling in his eyes as he hesitantly turned to look at Jehovah. "No, my King?"

"Did I stutter?" Jehovah spoke coldly, giving Ithiel a heavy glare beneath his arched brow. "I do not see the purpose of unbinding her before she is placed in her cell."

Judas cursed. "You swore to Uriel that she would go free! Is your word so worthless now that you could dishonor his last request as your servant?"

"I swore that Ezekiel would not touch her again. Is that not being honored?"

Uriel groaned, shivering on the ground as he wrapped his arms tighter over his chest. Golden blood trailed slowly down his back, dripping onto the dirt. "You and…your damn loopholes…"

"Bastard!" Remi wailed, banging her fist on the barrier Luce still struggled to maintain. "You insufferable, awful *bastard!*"

"Rem, please!" Rag tugged at her shoulders, but she shook him off with an agitated snarl.

"Shut up!" She shoved at his chest, fury boiling over to its limit. "Where is the man I bound myself to? Where is the man who sliced off *his own wings* to throw them at Jehovah's feet? Stop shushing and restraining me and dig your balls out of whatever hole you've buried them in!"

Rag reared back as if she had struck him. "Remi..."

"I told you she was a bitch." Ezekiel frowned intensely. "I told you it was foolish to follow her into oblivion; that you would come to regret choosing her over everything Heaven could offer."

"Heaven is fickle." Bal spat on the ground, then placed his hands on the barrier, leaning as close to it as he could. "Says something that Jeho is content to let Uriel bleed out, while Luce is giving more than he even *has* to protect us. I would choose this side a thousand times over."

"Then you would be a fool a thousand times," Jophiel sneered, marching up to stand toe to toe at the barrier with Bal. "As opposed to just twice."

"Twice?"

"To defect," Joph said, ticking off the offenses on his fingers, "and then to run your mouth as if Lucifer's protection doesn't wane with each minute passing."

"Your lack of comprehension is astounding," Luce grunted. Slowly, achingly, he leveraged himself from his knees to his feet. He was utterly drained—between the barriers around the property and his Fallen, and healing Michael, he had nothing left to give.

But he did not waver. Carefully watching each step, Luce picked his way through the debris until he reached Uriel's side.

"Hurts," Uriel muttered, shivering against the pain that wracked his back; the searing heat of his wing stumps where the nerves were flayed and exposed.

"I know," Luce said gently, and placed a hand on the other man's arm. "But I have something for you."

He snapped his fingers and a little bottle appeared in his palm. Uriel laughed when he saw the familiar liquid within.

"Drink up," Luce poured the sedative into Uriel's trembling mouth, and the other man sighed in relief.

"That is the good stuff," Uriel murmured weakly, and Luce pressed a soft kiss to his sweating brow.

Then without warning, he sent a quick blast of healing energy into the throbbing flesh of Urie's back, making him gasp and flinch. The stumps of his wings crumbled to ashes, the dark flesh knitting roughly together where they had been.

"Those might scar," Luce said. "I can try to do more once my magic isn't so depleted."

"That's... okay." Uriel tried to smile, giving more of a bared teeth grimace. "Makes me look more badass."

Lucifer gave him a gentle pat and smiled kindly, but it vanished as he turned back to face his brother. "Would it have killed you to heal him?"

"He is your responsibility now." Jehovah lifted his nose haughtily. "He should see the extent of your ability."

"This is not my limit," Lucifer laughed. "Not truly."

"Is it not? Go on then. Lick your wounds, put on a show." Jehovah scoffed. "It changes nothing. I am leaving here with my prisoners."

Luce stilled. "Prisoners... plural?"

"Oh yes," it was Jehovah's turn to smile, a smarmy, nasty thing. This was the time to play his final ace. "Surely you didn't think I would allow Michael's crimes to go unpunished?"

A chill rolled down Luce's spine, and he shifted his stance. "And if he defects as well?"

"That is not an option. He flouted my laws, not to mention my direct orders, and he will be held accountable. Jophiel?"

"My King."

"Seize the traitor, if you would."

There was no hesitation this time. Jophiel marched to where Michael sprawled in the grass, halfway between where he had fallen during his fight and where Uriel hunched on the ground. Even with his wounds lingering, with his damaged wing dragging awkwardly in the dirt, he had been trying to crawl to his best friend.

"Give up, Michael," Jophiel crouched beside him, digging his fingers into Michael's golden curls as if trying to soothe him, in a strange way. "Aren't you tired of fighting? Broken, beaten… and for what? Let it be over."

The angel was tempted. Luce could see it in the exhaustion that settled over Michael like a weighted blanket. Hell, he felt it himself. The angel's shoulders slumped, his chest falling into the grass when his arms gave out from the weight. Jophiel gripped his shoulder and pulled him up.

"Sometimes you need to quit, Mikey. Rest."

Michael tensed, pulling away from Jophiel slightly, and looked to Lucifer.

Luce weighed the situation. He looked at Uriel, still kneeling hunched over, but no longer shaking. He looked at the Fallen and found Remi looking back at him with tangible intensity. He looked at his brother, smug and cold, and he looked at Mags, small and shrinking in his shadow. Then he looked back at Michael.

The few days he had spent with Michael—had it really only been two days?—had gone a long way toward helping them feel at ease around each other. Where things had gone wrong, the root of their falling out… Luce could say he understood things much better now, but it didn't completely erase the pain.

A wounded part of him wanted Jehovah to take Michael, to punish him so that he could feel how Luce had felt. The sensible part of him knew that was vengeful and misguided. Similar feelings warred behind Michael's eyes.

His angel had always been prone to self-sacrifice, especially for what he considered the 'greater good'. Michael had sacrificed love for honor. He had sacrificed his morals for loyalty. Lucifer could see it right there on his face: he would sacrifice his freedom for peace.

"You have to," Luce murmured sadly. "I cannot protect you from this."

Michael shook his head. "I don't expect you to. I knew I would need to atone, and I made my own choices."

"I wish we had more time." Luce swallowed harshly. "For what it's worth… and considering what we've learned… I think I can forgive what happened in our past."

"You... have no idea how much that means to me. I'm not certain I can even say I deserve your forgiveness."

"Well, you have it regardless."

"Yes, this is very touching," Jehovah said, clearly at the end of his patience. "Can we get on with things?"

"Oh, I'm sorry, do you have better things to do?" Luce snapped, whirling on his brother in cold fury. "You are taking two of the people I care for most, to do who knows what to them, with the possibility that I never see them again. Forgive me for not moving at a pace that suits *you*, brother."

Jehovah arched a brow, unmoved. "Are you quite finished?"

"You are *unbelievable.*"

"I have been called worse." Jehovah shrugged, then extended a hand to Jophiel. "Come, son. Michael knows better than to fight his punishment."

The sheer arrogance almost made Michael want to fight, but Luce gave a sharp shake of the head. In his battered state and with Luce powerless to back him, they stood no chance against Jehovah. Michael tensed but ultimately followed Jophiel back to Jehovah's side.

Ithiel hesitated, then quickly followed, pulling Mags by her bound wrists. To her credit, Mags did not panic. She held her head high and dug in her heels, not truly resisting but making Ithiel work for every inch he marched her toward confinement.

Jehovah gave them both a sweeping glance and shook his head in disappointment. "You were both held in such high regard in my realm. My favored soldier, and my own son's consort. And now I bring you back in shackles."

"This is *your* choice," Michael said softly. "These are *your* laws."

Darkness clouded Jehovah's expression again, and he gripped Michael roughly by the jaw. "That's enough, Mikha'el. You're treading a dangerous line."

"You've already made me a prisoner," Michael frowned. "I see no reason to stay my tongue any longer."

"Is that so?" Jehovah's voice took on a deadly cast, and his eyes narrowed to slits.

"I'm tired of keeping quiet when I disagree with your methods and decisions, Jehovah."

The King's grip tightened, squeezing until his fingers were digging into the angel's flesh hard enough to bruise. "You have one more chance to shut your mouth, Mikha'el, or I will do it for you."

Michael met his glare head on. "I've been silent for you long enough."

"On that, we disagree," Jehovah purred, and yanked Michael's mouth open. Before any of them could react, before they could even register what was happening, Jehovah pulled a gleaming knife from a sheath on his belt.

"Hold still," he said sternly, and drove his blade into the angel's mouth. In one swift movement, he sliced out Michael's tongue, casting the lump of flesh to the dirt as the other man began to choke on the golden blood pouring from the wound.

"Michael!" Lucifer screamed, stumbling towards them, but Jehovah flung him back with a flick of his wrist.

"The mouth of the righteous brings forth wisdom," Jehovah purred darkly, as he healed the gaping wound to prevent it from growing back. "But a perverse tongue will be cut out."

The clearing was silent as they all dealt with the shock of what they had just witnessed. Michael's pained whimper cut Luce to the bone. He tried to rise, but he was too worn down, completely depleted and unable to fight.

"I trust I've made myself understood," Jehovah said coldly. "Now, I think it's time we left this decrepit plane."

He clapped once and the horses paraded forward. He clapped again, and a golden cage wove itself from sunbeams, affixed to the harnesses of two horses like a morbid gilded carriage. Jophiel was quick to usher Michael into the cage, while Ithiel struggled to wrangle Mags, ultimately shoving the petite woman into the golden prison with the angel.

Michael took her small hands in his own, carefully unwinding the cord that bound her. She lifted a freed hand and touched his cheek lightly, though she had to fully extend her arm to reach. Michael smiled fondly despite being in clear pain and rested a comforting hand lightly on her shoulder. Luce's heart broke to see it.

There was so much he wanted to say, so many things to apologize for and promises he wanted to make. The weight of Jehovah's power lifted, and he staggered upright. "Michael... Mags..."

"Luce!" The small woman reached for the bars of the cage but recoiled as her fingers met the shimmering metal with a stinging hiss.

Lucifer tried to go to her, but Jophiel quickly stepped into his path, brandishing Michael's sword. "I can't allow you to interfere."

"And I can't allow *you* to keep that blade."

"You have no claim to it."

"I have more claim to it than *you*," Luce sneered, "as I'm the one who originally gifted it to Michael."

"Oh, let him keep it, Jophiel," Jehovah threw his hands up, impatient. "It's just a sword. Frankly, it has a negative history that I'd rather not have around."

"I'm surprised you even want it." Jophiel still hesitated, sounding like a sullen child.

"Call me a masochist," Luce shrugged. "Maybe I just want it to remind me of him."

Jophiel huffed but sheathed the sword and practically threw it into Luce's hands. "Fine, torment yourself."

Luce rolled his eyes. "So glad to have your permission, Lord Jophiel."

The blond sneered but climbed astride his horse without additional comment.

"It's going to be okay, Mags." Luce swallowed. "Christos won't let anything happen to you."

She nodded, not trusting herself to speak. Michael squeezed her shoulder reassuringly.

"You are bold, to speak for my son. Be prepared to deal with me again once I settle these affairs," Jehovah cautioned Lucifer as he climbed onto his horse, and Ezekiel actually took pains to fluff and settle the King's cape before he mounted his own steed.

Rag balked at the action, averting his gaze with an expression of mingled disgust and disbelief. Ezekiel refused to look at any of them, staring off into the distance with a practiced disinterest.

"I would expect nothing else," Lucifer muttered. "You always did insist on dictating the lives of others."

"And you insist on testing my patience." Jehovah frowned deeply. "You tread dangerous ground, Lucifer. If I were you, I would get that wayward son under control before I am forced to address that situation for you."

"I could say the same of Gabriel for you," Lucifer hissed. "It is his fault we're even in this situation, after all."

"Liar!" Jophiel spat. "Always with your lies!"

"Settle down, Jophiel." Jehovah waved a hand, annoyance in the furrow of his brow. "You honestly expect I would take you at your word, Lucifer? That might be your greatest delusion yet. Gabriel is one of my most loyal servants."

"So was Michael," Luce said, flippant. "So was *I*."

Jehovah looked at him for a long time, and then simply shook his head. "Goodbye, Lucifer. This is not the end of this."

They were gone before Lucifer could shield his eyes, enveloped in a brilliant glare of sunlight that quickly faded out. The world seemed duller in the wake of such bright light. Colors were faded, the clearing vaster and more desolate. He waited one beat, then another. After a tense moment, Luce allowed himself to breathe again.

He dropped his barriers, then fell immediately to his knees. Uriel tried to turn and help despite his own pain, only to be cut off as Remi rushed to Luce's side, Rag and Bal at her heels. Glory remained in place, staring vacantly at the space her brother had occupied moments before, arms wrapped around her knees in a defensive hug. Judas sat beside her, watching her cautiously.

"You idiot!" Remi shouted, falling to her knees and flinging her arms around Luce. She hugged him tightly, tears streaming down her pale cheeks, and rocked him like a child. "You could have died!"

Bal sank into a crouch. "You can siphon power from me, if you need to."

"I'll be fine," Luce insisted, absently patting Remi's back as she clutched him tighter.

"Stop putting on a show," Rag said sternly, and gripped Luce's wrist in one hand, Balthazar's in the other. "And take what we're offering."

Rag closed his eyes and focused on drawing enough energy from Bal and transferring it into their King to bolster his shockingly depleted reserves. When he finished, Bal sank back on his heels.

"Damn, Luce." He whistled. "You haven't gone that low since...well, I'd probably say Sodom and Gomorrah."

"Still don't forgive ol' Jeho for that bullshit," Rag said.

"I don't forgive him for existing," Remi hissed, finally loosening her borderline chokehold on Lucifer. Her expression quickly shifted from murderous to depressed. "He took Maggie."

"You know she hates when you call her that," Luce reminded her.

Remi glared at him. "As if it matters now. We're never going to see her again."

"All of this," Bal muttered. "All of this chaos and for what?"

Luce sighed. "It seems like it was foolishness, I know. But it really is the best chance we have to contain my son."

"You mean it *was* the best chance," Rag said, frowning. "Because not to be blunt, but we just got our asses handed to us by a kid. The book didn't help at all."

"And now I've lost two of my Fallen," Luce muttered. "Seven was such a perfect number."

Remi slapped his arm. "How can you joke about this?"

"If I don't laugh, I will cry," Luce said simply, closing his eyes. Remi shrank back slightly, unaccustomed to Luce being genuinely vulnerable. Dramatic tantrums were one thing, but this was too raw.

"Cami and Sachi are gone," Remi swallowed thickly, "And Mags is going to be imprisoned forever at best, but more likely he'll—" She cut herself off, bringing a hand to her mouth to stifle the sob.

Rag placed his hands on her shoulders, not trying to comfort her with words but simply offering his presence. What could even be said?

"All for nothing."

They all jumped slightly at Glory's abrupt appearance, no one having noticed her approach from across the field, Judas trailing behind her with his hands jammed in his pockets.

"You alright, love?" Bal knocked her shoulder gently with his, and Glory shook her head.

"My brother is…not the man I remember," she whispered, hugging herself tightly.

Bal threw his arm around her shoulders and gave a reassuring squeeze. "I can be your new brother, Glor."

"It's not the same," she muttered, but her lips quirked up in the subtle ghost of a smile.

"Not all for nothing," Luce smiled tightly. "Thanks to your slimy worm of a brother and his obviously limp backbone, Glory, we now have the next piece of the Armor of the Gods."

He raised Michael's sword, sunlight glinting off the golden blade as he pointed it to the sky.

"The Sword of the Spirit," Rag said, realization bringing a smile to his face.

"Indeed," Luce smiled, and sheathed the blade once more. "With this to bolster my powers, I can begin to work on restoring the bits of me that I gave to you all."

"Restoring?" Remi frowned.

"You must have noticed, over the eons," Luce arched a brow. "The abilities that came with your standing as my Deadly Sins have been dwindling ever since I bestowed them."

"Is that why I have to use twice as much power and end up with a headache after?" Remi demanded. "I thought I was just stressed or out of practice."

"Yes," Lucifer nodded somberly. "And if we're going to restore your full powers, free Michael and Mags, and stop my son… I'm going to need you all to cooperate with me. We have one chance to get this right."

Remi sobered up instantly, resting her hand on Lucifer's knee. "You know that we're loyal to you until the very end, Luci. Whatever it takes, you only need to ask it."

"I may have to ask a great deal from all of you, before we're through." Luce leveraged himself up from the ground, with Remi following suit. Rag helped Uriel to his feet and looped the other man's arm over his broad shoulders for support.

Glory smiled. "We'll do whatever is needed."

Luce took in his Fallen's solemn and determined expressions. He looked back at the charred remnants of Foster's former apartment, a sense of overwhelming loss mingling with the concern and regret that always warred when he thought of his son. Lucifer closed his eyes as the last rays of sunset kissed the landscape, sliding down past the horizon. When he opened them again, his eyes glowed brilliant gold in the darkness.

"Then we'd better get to work."

Acknowledgments

This book was a long time coming! The earliest zero draft sat abandoned in a Google doc for literal years, just a loose concept I wasn't sure what to do with but really wanted to make work someday.

After seven long years, I met my best friend Kim - the same Kim this work is dedicated to. We bonded over the book she was about to publish and writing in general, and it was her motivation that got me to reopen the doc, which was then loosely titled "7 v 7".

I stumbled through some edits and eventually expanded that into a proper draft that was renamed to "Prince of Darkness". We worked hard on it, cutting some characters and adjusting some concepts, and I truly believe that without her help, this book would not exist. It would be an unfinished zero draft, languishing on a Google drive forever.

I also need to acknowledge everyone who helped me revise and polish this work. I had unknowingly been given an AI cover for the book, and I was fortunate to meet my cover artist Juniper to work together on the gorgeous new cover you currently have! She was so great to work with and the turnaround time was incredible. I'm legitimately obsessed with this cover.

The gorgeous front would be nothing without content to suit it, and that credit goes to two other amazing women who worked on the edits and formatting.

Sarah was instrumental in correcting the content of the book, respecting my voice while refining the words themselves into their best form. Her insights were thoughtful and thorough, and we just meshed perfectly. She respected my intentions and brought her talent and education to the table, and it was a beautiful collaboration that's also become a great friendship.

Sage helped me turn a boring, plain document into a beautiful, carefully formatted work. It was such a relief and a weight off my shoulders, and she was so professional and efficient. She was a delight to work with.

Of course I need to acknowledge my parents, without whom I quite literally would not exist and neither would this work. So Nichole and Jay, thanks for liking each other enough that I exist! I get my obnoxious determination from my mother and my love of reading and writing from my father, two things that were essential to me decision to commit years of my life to bringing new books into the world.

Thank you also to my family, who have had to listen to me ramble endlessly about books and writing since I was old enough to hold a pencil, and somehow didn't smother me in my sleep. Special credit to my cousin Kelly and my sister Morgan who share my love of reading and are always ready and willing to talk about words.

More than anyone, I can't close my acknowledgments without mentioning my boyfriend, Matt. Not only does he tolerate my general nonsense and somehow love me despite my chaos, he has been so supportive of this journey I'm on.

He gifted me Sarah's editing services. He lets me chatter constantly about not only this book, but the many others I have planned to write. He's so patient and kind and supportive, and my world would be so empty without him.

Matt is the love of my life, and I'm overjoyed to have found my person - someone who really cares about my passions and is by my side through the hard bits. I love you, Matthew.

And reader, I love you too! Your support is arguably the most important part of the entire process of writing and releasing a book. Thank you so much for giving my first book a chance, for being here and reading it and helping my dreams come to life in a way that honestly still surprises me.

I hope you enjoyed Prince of Darkness, and I hope you'll be back for the conclusion of the duet when it releases as well!

All that being said, I've rambled enough. Just know that I am beyond appreciative of everyone who helped this book come to life, in even the smallest ways. It means a lot to me.

I'll see you in the next one.

About the Author

 C.H. Rowand is a 30-something chaos gremlin currently living in southern New Jersey with her incredibly patient and supportive boyfriend and their three cat children. When she's not slaving away over her manuscripts, she works as a real estate agent and spends her meager free time reading or creating new merch designs.

She writes primarily fantasy and closed door romance under this pen name, with spicier books written under the pseudonym Caity Rowe so readers know what to expect! Please be mindful of potential triggers (always noted in her books) and always prioritize your mental health and wellbeing.